BEAST OF BURDEN

A Dark Romance

SEBBY RANDALL

For all the girls
who like them just a little bad

CONTENT NOTES

Beast of Burden includes graphic content that may be uncomfortable for some readers, including: underage drinking, drug use, drug overdose, physical abuse, emotional abuse, sexual assault, gun violence, death, torture, mentions of suicide, cheating, sexism.

It includes explicit sexual scenes that include a threesome, public sex, and voyeurism.

Please be gentle with your mental health and only proceed if you feel safe to do so.

PLAYLIST

Beautiful, Dirty, Rich - Lady Gaga
Wild Heart - SPELLES
Numb - Tommee Profitt, Skylar Grey
The High - Bryce Savage
When You Say My Name - Chandler Leighton
Crush Culture - Conan Gray
FU In My Head - Cloudy June
Make Me Feel - Elvis Drew
Figure You Out - VOILÁ
Little Girl Gone - CHINCHILLA
Cute Girl - Diggy Graves
Love and War - Fleurie
Gangsta - Kehlani
stalker - Stevie Howie
Siren Sounds - Tate McRae
Lose Control - Teddy Swims
High - Stephen Sanchez
Fuck You - Silent Child
Bad Drugs - King Kavalier, ChrisLee
The Hunted - The Rigs

I'm a Slave 4 U - Britney Spears
THE DEATH OF PEACE OF MIND - Bad Omens
Warriors - Imagine Dragons
Glory and Gore - Lorde
Freedom - Beyoncé, Kendrick Lamar
Hayloft - Mother Mother
Lavender and Velvet - Alina Baraz
Can't Help Falling in Love - Tommee Profitt, brooke

Listen on Spotify:

BEAST OF BURDEN

1

SLOANE

No one tells you how much it hurts to hit someone. You forget that your own skin and bones take as much damage as theirs. So when I slap my boyfriend as hard as I can, I'm shocked when pain reverberates all the way up my arm. But I grit my teeth, because if there's one thing I'm not going to do in front of Tyler Price, it's show weakness.

"I am not some fucking scrap of metal that you can pass from person to person," I growl, balling my hand into a fist and watching with satisfaction as a red handprint starts to form on Tyler's pale cheek. I hope it hurts. I hope it bruises. Maybe then he'll feel a fraction of the pain I just felt when he told me he put me up as a fucking bet in his stupid car race against Julian Shaw. Julian Shaw, who everyone knows is dangerous. A man so notorious even the Dartmouth folks know about him. The boogeyman himself, whispered about like folklore, tales of beatings, guns, blood, and disappearances.

He's standing beside his car, a long stretch of hot road

between us, sizzling in the summer sun. He looks like an undertaker, a stripe of ink against the New Hampshire landscape in his all-black outfit and dark hair. He's watching us like a vulture ready to pick at our scraps. He's the complete opposite of San Francisco Tyler, all sandy hair and peachy skin in khakis and a polo.

"Babe," Tyler says, face turning slowly back toward me. "This is important. It's what needs to be done."

People are watching, all of Tyler's admirers, his entourage that follows him around like a pack of puppies. Their cars are all parked down the road, sports cars and supercars, all of them humming with still-running engines. I find the people who participate in these races insufferable. Just a bunch of men with too much of Daddy's money and nothing to do with it. Tyler has been bleeding money at these things every week, and watching him has been like watching a child break his own toys and then cry about it.

And now, it would appear he's done tossing his money into the wind; he's just going to bet me instead, like I'm currency.

"Would it make you feel better to know that he's betting his car against you? It's worth like 200 grand. So he thinks you're worth that much, apparently."

I reach up to slap him again, but he sees it coming and grabs my wrist to stop me.

"Calm down, for fuck's sake," he grits out. "He's not going to win. And even if he does, he swore not to lay a finger on you."

I snort and try to yank my arm away, but he holds fast, fingers turning to steel. "Right, because men can often be trusted to keep their word where self-control around pretty women is concerned."

He finally lets me go, crosses his arms and smirks, cocky

and handsome. "You think pretty highly of yourself there, kitten."

I grit my teeth. I hate it when he calls me that. A pet. A possession. That's all he sees when he looks at me. And there was a time when I enjoyed that, when it was thrilling to be claimed by someone like Tyler.

I step closer to him and lower my voice. "He's scary, Tyler. You've heard the stories. You can't honestly be thinking about sending me off with him. Who knows what he'll do to me. You're just... okay with this?" I'm mad at myself for letting my voice quaver. Whatever is going to happen to me if I'm forced to leave here with him tonight, I'm almost certain I've been through worse, but once upon a time, my mother tried to protect me from the bad in the world, and then Tyler did, but right now, I'm floating all alone through the universe, and it terrifies me.

He rolls his eyes. "Don't be so dramatic. He's not an ax murderer."

I narrow my eyes at him. "You have no way of knowing that. Remember Joel? He swears that Julian Shaw is the reason his brother ended up in the hospital with internal bleeding, not a car accident." I duck my head. "I'm not doing it. You can't make me."

Tyler moves so fast that I gasp. Next thing I know, he has my chin in his hand, holding my face still as he leans in close. Over his shoulder, I can see Julian watching us, bent against his car. "Sloane, I'm not asking you if you want to do this. I can't lose any more money to that asshole. I'll make this really simple: you do what I tell you or you pack your shit and take your ass back to California. The choice is yours." He lets me go, giving me a shove so that I stumble back a little. "I trust you'll make the right one."

I can feel myself fading. My hands start to tremble and my legs start to get that feeling they do when I'm anxious, like they're too long, like I'll shoot right up into the sky and everyone will be looking at me.

I take a deep breath and steady myself. My vision starts to blur, but I ball my fists and fight to stay here, stay present, stay focused. I look across the road, take in Julian Shaw's souped-up Aston Martin DBS. I can't pinpoint an exact year, but if I had to guess, I would say 1970, painted midnight blue. It slowly gets easier to breathe as I look at it, as I take in the specs that I can see from this far away, as I separate the purr of its engine from the other engines on the road.

My eyes shoot back to Tyler, and I do what I always do with him: I lock my emotions far away and focus on just surviving this moment, focus on everything Tyler has done for me, on everything he's still doing for me, on how in love we were...once. "How confident are you that you can beat him?"

Tyler drives an Audi. I've seen him race that thing. I've been in it with him more times than I can count. But I happen to know the top speed is only 130 miles per hour. The Aston can probably hit 215. Tyler is banking on Julian being too scared to open it up.

"You just let me handle it," Tyler says, and without my agreement, he turns and walks toward Julian Shaw. The two of them talk for a moment, and I feel so exposed, like I'm standing naked in the middle of a packed airport. I glance over at the crowd watching from down the road. All their eyes are on me, and I turn my face away quick. Julian doesn't have an entourage. It's just him and the man standing beside him. Julian looks to be in his mid-twenties, younger than I would have thought, but the man with him—also all in black —is at least thirty.

Tyler and Julian shake hands, and my chest pulls tight. I can't believe this is real life. I can't believe he just bet me like a fucking pink slip.

I can't believe I'm going to go through with it if he loses. What the hell am I doing? Is this what my life has become?

I watch as they get in their cars. At the last minute, before he shuts his door, Tyler looks at me and beckons me over with a curl of his fingers. I want to refuse. I want to tell him he can't just treat me like a dog willing to perform tricks for him.

Instead, I slowly walk over to where the two men are parked. They sit beside each other on the road, their headlights pointed out at the concrete, getting brighter as the sun gets lower in the sky. Far down the road, after a few winding curves, is another car, waiting to meet them at the makeshift finish line.

I step up to Tyler's window and bend down, knowing full well that I'm giving the men in the other car a perfect view of my ass. I can feel the bottom edge of my skirt riding up.

Tyler leans out through the window. He pulls me toward him, and, in what I'm sure to him is a very serious display of masculinity, kisses me hard. Normally, Tyler is a great kisser. But this isn't a kiss. He's marking his territory, and I want to be sick. When he tries to get me to open my mouth, tries to give me his tongue, I pull away, looking him in the eye and trying to communicate my rage before I straighten and turn, finding myself directly in the sights of Julian Shaw and his right-hand man. They both watch me with dark eyes until I walk away, moving to stand between their cars.

I hate this part. I don't want to be some pretty trophy waving the flags for them. When I'm not here, I'm sure Tyler asks some other beautiful woman to do it because what else are women for, right? These men won't let a woman participate, but they certainly all like to own women, let them be hood ornaments.

I put my hands out, like I've been nailed to a cross, and let them drop.

JULIAN

I throw the car into gear and take off. Beside me, I hear the grunt that Bram always gives in the first stretch. That dick-face is right beside me as we pick up speed, but I know once I hit top speed, I'll smoke him. He thinks that piece of shit he's driving is faster, that he has more confidence behind the wheel than I do. I'm going to leave him in the dust, and then I'm going to take *her*.

Just thinking about it makes my hands tighten on the wheel. She's so close, I can taste her. She's the key to everything. She'll be mine. All I have to do is keep that bastard at bay.

My gas pedal hits the floorboard, and I watch until I know I've cleared his front bumper, and then I swerve right, putting him firmly behind me. He yanks his wheel to the left, and I meet his eye in my side mirror. He flips me off, and I smile. I want to watch this guy burn.

"Don't get him killed!" Bram barks as we come up on the curve in the road. "We can't afford a police raid right now."

I shoot him a look, keeping my wheel steady. "If he didn't want to risk his balls, he shouldn't have shown up."

"You really want to let this fucker sink you over a pissing contest?"

I grit my teeth. I know he's right. We do a good job staying under the radar, but if this shitstick's body turns up in his demolished supercar after his so-called friends have fled the scene, I'll be the first person the cops come sniffing around. That's what happens when you have a record and a dead criminal of a father, who everyone in a two-hundred-mile radius knew.

I take my foot off the gas. The asshat behind me jackknifes around me. He's going to try to take the curve going over a hundred. He thinks he can control that thing, but his back tires are already losing grip and he hasn't even hit the bend yet.

I downshift, knowing this is it. There's no way he pulls that turn. The race is already won.

"Look at the idiot go," Bram whispers under the roar of the Beast's engine.

And like a jet falling out of the sky, Tyler Price loses traction. His back wheels skid first, dragging the rest of him right off the road and into the grass.

I slam past him while his tires are still spinning.

$$2$$

SLOANE

I pull my hair back off my face and stare down into my open suitcase, not really seeing it. I can't believe this is really happening. The panic starts to grip me, my vision going black around the edges. I grab onto the sides of my suitcase to keep myself upright.

Breathe, Sloane. Just breathe.

Beside me, the door to my dorm room flies open and my roommate, Krista, flies in, her arms full of mail. She drops it all onto her bed and then takes me in. I straighten, able to breathe again now that I'm distracted. Krista comes over to my side of the room and drops down on the bed beside my stacks of clothing. My tower of skirts starts to topple but she rights it with her hand.

"What's all this?" she asks, running her manicured fingertips along my pile of bras. "Is Tyler taking you on a trip? I'm not saying you don't deserve it, but it's almost midterms. I don't know that your profs would respond well to you skipping a week of lectures for a trip to Aruba or whatever."

I sigh. It's been an hour since the race Tyler inevitably lost. And it wasn't even because his car wasn't fast enough. It was because he was too stupid to slow down around the turn —too busy trying to prove he was man enough—and skidded off the road and into a tree. I offered to take him the hospital to make sure he didn't have a concussion, but he just got mad and shoved me away.

And then Julian's right-hand man told me I had until 9:00 to get my shit sorted and to get to the house. Julian Shaw's house. Where I'll be living for the foreseeable future. Bile crawls up my throat again.

"Not exactly," I tell Krista. I can't tell her the truth. She wouldn't understand. Krista, just like Tyler, came from money. She wouldn't sympathize with my need to stay with Tyler to secure my future.

She scowls at me, smokey eyes narrowed, waiting for an explanation.

"I sort of told Tyler I would move in with him," I lie.

Krista gives me a disgusted look. "What, you're going to go live in that nasty frat house? Are you kidding? Why? For the rest of the semester?"

One month. That's what was agreed on. One whole month with that man.

I shrug, lifting a stack of neatly folded dresses and placing it in my suitcase. "Just for a while. Tyler just wants me close." I try to say this last part as if he's so sweet and loving, wanting me with him all the time, but instead, all I can think about is him shoving me away from him. I can already feel the bruises forming on my wrists.

Krista makes a face, pursing her lips and glancing into my full-length mirror to fluff up her dark hair. "Okay, well, I won't pretend I won't enjoy having my own room, but for what it's worth, I think it's a terrible idea."

Yeah, that's because it *is* a terrible idea and the reality is a million times worse. I would much rather be living with Tyler in his frat house than in that mansion in the middle of nowhere with a group of men I've never met.

Nerves start to rattle in my stomach again. I'm still waiting to wake up from this nightmare. Tyler swore they wouldn't lay a hand on me, but there's no way he can believe what those strangers told him. What's going to happen to me within those walls?

"Do you know anything about Julian Shaw?" I don't want to ask, but I feel like I don't have a choice. I want to know what I'm walking into, and I only know so much, all of it rumor.

She stops fixing her hair and looks over at me. "Julian Shaw? That car guy that everyone is always talking about?"

I nod.

She shrugs. "Liam is obsessed with him. I swear, all the boys at this school have such hard-ons for that guy and he's basically just an urban legend. All I've heard is that he sells super expensive vintage cars, lives in some kind of mansion with a bunch of other men, and is, like, hot as fuck. One of the girls in my Poli Sci class swears he has a massive dick, but I'm not convinced she's actually seen it. I also heard he killed a guy last year, some drug addict." She raises an eyebrow at me. "Why do you want to know?"

I can't meet her eye. I focus on packing up my makeup bag. "Tyler's just been talking about him a lot," I say, figuring since she mentioned her boyfriend, Liam, being obsessed with Julian that she'll believe it if Tyler is, too. "I think he might, I don't know, want to get to know him."

Krista snorts. "Get to know him? What does that even mean? From what I hear, this Julian guy isn't exactly the buddy type. What does he think is going to happen? They're going to go out for beers and talk shop and jerk each other off?"

I bite back a smile. Even though I know Tyler says he hates Julian, I don't believe for one second that he would turn the guy down if he decided he wanted Tyler to be one of his men. It wouldn't last though. Tyler is a leader, not a follower, and Julian seems like a leader, too. Can't have two kings in a pride or whatever.

She makes a clicking sound with her tongue. "Well, I know he has some kind of fancy car. That's probably why Tyler is into him. They call it the Beast."

"The Beast?" I think about the Aston Martin. Maybe if Tyler had known before the race that people were calling it the Beast, he would have been less likely to put me on the chopping block. Then again, maybe it wouldn't have changed a thing.

"Yeah. It's some classic car. People are always trying to get pictures of him driving around town in it like he's a UFO or something. I don't really get it."

Krista stands and moves to her bed, sorting through the mail she brought in while I start setting the rest of my clothes inside my suitcase. It seems preposterous to be packing my mini dresses and pink tank tops when I'm about to go through who knows what. But this is what I have. I'm a bright colors kind of girl, pinks and yellows and lavenders. I'm sure I'll fit right in with those men and their cars and their all-black wardrobes.

"You have a package," Krista says, tossing a square object onto my bed, wrapped in brown paper. I stare down at it, ignoring the flutter in my chest.

Another package.

They've been coming periodically since the semester started. My hands shake as I reach for it. My fingers brush the wrapping that's become so familiar. It looks like some parcel from an old World War II movie.

The door flies open and Krista and I both jump as Tyler rushes into the room and slams the door behind him.

"Excuse you," Krista barks. "Knock much?" Tyler shoots her a look, and Krista's eyes go wide when she sees the bandage around his wrist. "Holy shit," she says. "What happened?"

Tyler ignores her, coming straight to me. He takes my upper arms in his hands, much too tightly. "I need to talk to you," he says, his voice low. I feel a rush of relief. Tyler has clearly changed his mind. He's here to tell me he'll deal with Julian and that I don't have to go, that he never actually expected me to.

He reaches down for my hand. He drags me out into the hallway, shutting the door behind us. People mill through the hallway but no one is paying attention to us.

"I need you to do something for me," Tyler says. He's shifting back and forth on his heels. I've never seen Tyler nervous before, but there's an anxious energy coming off of him now. It feeds my own.

This is not what I expected him to say, not what I *wanted* him to say.

"What do you mean? What is it?"

He sighs, drumming his fingertips on his thigh, and I can tell I'm not going to like what's coming. "Listen, these guys, they're not just selling cars."

"What else are they selling?" It's bizarre to be having this conversation in the middle of a university dorm hall. No matter what these guys are into, it's far out of the realm of anything I thought I would ever be involved with in my life.

"That's what I need you to find out."

"What?" I hiss. "Are you kidding me? It's bad enough that this is happening at all, and now you want me to, what, spy for you? This is insane. I'm not doing this."

I start to turn away, but he smacks his hand against the wall, his arm blocking my way.

"You don't have a choice, Sloane. I'm finally in a position to make this happen. You can't fuck it up."

A startling suspicion starts to rise like a wave inside me. "Did you...did you lose the race on purpose so that I could spy on them?"

I can tell he wants to lie and say no but he doesn't. I start to shake. Any minute now, I'm going to pop like a firecracker. "I needed a way in."

"I can't believe you," I whisper, unsure if I want to scream or cry. Or both. "What does this man even want from me, Tyler? What is this weird thing you're doing with him? Did you really risk my safety just to prove he's a criminal? I want an explanation."

"Look..." His voice is so gentle, so calm. The complete opposite of how I feel. He takes my face in his big hands, warm and soft. I hate that he's touching me like this, trying to calm me with affection, like a baby. I hate it even more that it's working. "I did this so we can take them down. Those men, they're not good men. I know they're involved in something bad. I just don't know what it is. We could put them away."

I pull away from him. "Why the hell do you care about putting them away?"

His eyes move back and forth between mine. "They're bad guys. They've hurt friends of mine."

"What friends?"

He ignores my question. "Don't you want to do something important? Don't you want to make your mark?"

"No," I say honestly. I can't even begin to understand where all of this is coming from. I feel like I'm talking to a complete stranger, not a man I've been dating for three years. "I want to go to class and live to see graduation."

His lips tighten into a line. "I need you to see the bigger picture here, Sloane. What if...what if I made it worth your while?"

I hate that he knows how easy I am, that he knows this is the way to get me. All he has to do is offer me money. Tyler knows I grew up dirt poor, that I spent most of my life before we met hungry and alone and helpless. He knows that when freedom of any kind is dangled in front of me, I can't resist, and money is freedom.

He nods, like he knows he's got me. "Do this for me, and I'll give you $100,000."

I make sure not to show what his words do to me, the way they strike me like lightning. He doesn't even realize what he's said. Money is so simple to him, so easy to acquire, and his hunger for whatever this is fills up so much of his brain, that he doesn't realize what this number means. $100,000 is enough to pay for Dartmouth. I wouldn't need him or his father anymore.

He watches me, hazel eyes calculating, waiting for me to make a decision.

Or maybe he does realize it. I'm his little performing monkey, so easy to manipulate, so easy to control. Maybe he thinks the future he has to offer me is still enough to keep me here, even if I had the money. But if I had that money, if I had an Ivy League degree, I could make my own future.

"What do you need me to do?"

He crosses his arms. Now that he knows he has me where he wants me, he's not being gentle anymore. Now it's just a business transaction. "I need you to snoop."

"What am I looking for?"

"I honestly don't know. Something fishy. Something they're trying to hide. Evidence that that place is dangerous."

"You mean the place you're sending me to live?"

He cuts his eyes at me. He hates it when I give him attitude, always finds a way to get me to back down. That's what makes Tyler who he is, how easily he charms people into following him. It's something biological.

I'm my own person. I could say no. I could walk away from Tyler, go back to California, just like he said. But without Tyler and his father's money, I don't have a future. Without them, I slip back into my old life, never to be heard from again. Maybe I follow in my mother's footsteps, letting anyone in who offers to pay her. Maybe I already have.

Tyler's right. I *do* want to do something important. I want to do anything that will keep me from going back to the hellhole I was raised in ever again.

So...I'm going to do what Tyler tells me to. Because at the moment, it's my best option.

"You gotta trust me," he says. "I'll get you back as soon as I can. This won't take long, but I need you to help me."

Tyler and I are still staring at each other in silence when two men come around the corner. At first, we pay them no attention. There are people walking up and down these halls all the time.

But then they both stop beside us. When I look, I see that they're decked out in head-to-toe black. Black pants, shirts, jackets, like it's their uniform. They look like Julian Shaw clones. One of them is well over six feet and blonde, clean shaven with ages-old acne scars. The other is much shorter, with a full beard and tattoos inching up his white skin.

"Miss Moretti?" the tall one says.

I look back and forth between them. "Yes?"

"We're here to escort you to the compound," the other replies.

The compound? Jesus, these guys certainly are self-important, aren't they?

"Okay, well, I was supposed to be allowed to drive myself there. No one said anything about an escort."

The tall one smirks, one side of his mouth raising slowly. "You're late, and Mr. Shaw doesn't like being kept waiting."

I resist the urge to protest. I know that arguing won't do me any good and will probably just get me in trouble with Daddy Dearest, so I clamp my lips shut and nod. "Just let me grab my stuff."

"Make it quick," the tall one barks.

I hurry back into my room and start throwing everything on my bed into my suitcase. I can feel Krista watching me, can practically feel the confusion coming off her in waves.

"You're going right now?" she asks.

I don't turn around when I say, "Yeah. I gotta go. But I'll see you in class tomorrow." I sincerely hope I'm not lying. If Julian doesn't let me go to class, this whole thing is pointless. I have to be in class, have to stay focused in order to graduate.

I pick up the package beside my suitcase, feel the rough paper wrapping against my fingers. Without thinking, I toss it into my suitcase and slam the lid shut.

③

JULIAN

"Are you sure this is a good idea?"

Bram and I stand in the foyer and watch the front door. I'm trying to stay calm, but I can't stop the fidgeting of my fingers behind my back. I use the other hand to clasp my wrist to stop the nervous movement.

"We need her."

Out of the corner of my eye, I see Bram's face swing toward me. "Not anymore, we don't. She was supposed to be a bargaining chip. But he just passed her over like junk he was trying to get rid of. If he doesn't want her, what good is she to us?"

I've been asking myself the same question. None of us expected him to offer her up the way he did. But she can still be useful. I've considered every way that this might be the worst idea I've ever had. The problem is, I don't care. This is the only way I'm going to get what I want, what I *deserve*. If I have to make her bleed in front of his eyes to get the satisfaction I want, I'll do it.

"Tyler could be sending her in here to spy on us. He could be sending her in here to hurt us. And now you're not even going to put her in the basement?" He glances sideways at me. "She's going to have free reign? She's going to try and fucking kill you in your sleep."

"No one said anything about her having free reign, okay?" Headlights swing across the front windows, and my blood quivers. "I need you to stay focused on what she can offer us. If I stick her in a cage, she's going to fight. I need her soft. I need her to give up his secrets. As much as I'd like to torture it out of her, we need to keep a low profile. Don't worry, we're going to keep a very close eye on her."

"And what happens when she has information to take back to him?"

I take a deep breath, watch the shapes of Magnus and Hugo as they get out of the car. I feel like I can smell her already. I'm like a coyote scenting a lamb in a pasture. "I don't think he sent her in here to spy on us. I'm not sure what he wants with her."

He makes a disbelieving noise in the back of his throat. "What makes you so confident that this wasn't all just a ploy?"

I shrug one shoulder, keep my eyes trained on the front windows, trying to find her silhouette in the dark. "Well, if it is a ploy, then we're prepared. Maybe he doesn't want us to know he's sending his prize lamb into the lion's den."

"Maybe she's more lion than lamb," Bram says.

"Or maybe he's *trying* to send his lamb to slaughter. And if that's the case, then it will only be a matter of time before she'll turn on him. Maybe he's hoping we'll abuse her and she'll try to retaliate."

Before he can respond, the doorknob on the front door twists, and I tip my chin back, making myself as big as I possibly can. The big bad wolf. I want to have this girl shaking in her boots.

They send her in first, being gentlemen, and she walks into the compound slowly, wheeling a bright pink suitcase behind her like she's about to get on a flight to Paris. I wait for her to notice me and Bram, but she's too busy looking around, taking everything in.

The compound is impressive. I know that. It's why Dad bought it. You get used to these kinds of things when they've been your reality your whole life. But Miss Sloane Moretti? This isn't her reality. At least, it wasn't before she met that used tampon of a boyfriend of hers. No, Sloane Moretti came from dirt. Grew up in a poor suburb of Fresno before she lucked into a scholarship that put her in the same prep school as Tyler Price when she was fifteen. It's all in the paperwork.

When she finally sees me, her feet stutter to a halt and she jumps like she's stumbled on a ghost. Her pink suitcase comes to a stop.

I don't move. I wait for her to come closer, which she does, without my having to tell her to. I figured out pretty early on that if you hold someone's gaze long enough, they'll figure out what you want from them.

As she closes the last of the distance between us, I see her shore up her defenses. She pulls back her bare shoulders, lifts her chin. Her hesitant steps become more confident, until she's practically stomping toward me. I can see why Tyler wants her. She's almost offensively beautiful. Short, fit, with big blue eyes and cheekbones that could cut glass. Her long blonde hair and those puffy pink lips make her any man's wet dream. Oh, yes, she's Tyler's prize, but he clearly thinks he has her locked in, and maybe he does, but the anger in her eyes tells me she isn't the type to be taken in by someone like Tyler.

Interesting.

"I'm fairly certain that the agreement was that I would be allowed to come here of my own volition. You didn't need to send your men in to drag me out."

"Didn't I?"

The crease between her eyebrows disappears, her mouth falling open.

"Miss Moretti, this arrangement is built on trust. You trust me not to hurt you. I trust you to be where you say you're going to be. I'm aware I can't keep you from your life. That's fine. But when you say you're going to be here at a certain time, I expect you to be here. And if I need to have men follow you everywhere you go, I will do that. And if you're even a minute late, I will track you down and I will retrieve what belongs to me."

"I do *not* belong to you," she says between her teeth. I'm surprised by her ire. This isn't the same woman who cowered before her boyfriend. She's not afraid of me, or at least, she won't show it.

I resist the urge to smile at her. I don't want her to think I have any kind of sympathy for her. I close the distance between us, until I'm close enough that I can feel the angry puff of her breath on my neck. "In a legal sense, that may be true. But make no mistake, that absolute twat you're dating gave you to me. It wasn't even my idea. He offered you up. He told me I could do whatever I want to you."

Her eyes blow wide, like I knew they would, clear blue framed by thick mascara and sparkling pink eyeshadow. I don't even have to lie about what that stupid cunt did. I guess she didn't know about the part where he basically offered to let me rape her so he didn't lose an exorbitant amount of money. She's lucky one of us has a conscience.

"He did not," she says, and I can see she's trying to sound confident, but she can't tell if I'm lying or not. If fucking only.

She tips her sharp jaw up. She's at least a foot shorter than me.

"You don't have to believe me, princess, but you're here, aren't you?" I don't wait for her to respond to that one. I motion to the stairs beside us that lead up to the second floor. "Bram will take you to your room."

This seems to startle her. Everything down to the roots of her pretty blond hair jumps. "I have a room?"

"Did you think I was going to make you sleep on the lawn?"

She shrugs. "Maybe. Or maybe in a drafty corner of the attic or something."

Behind me, Bram chuckles. Wasn't he the one arguing against this a moment ago? Her eyes shift to him, clearly taking him in, and I have the urge to stand between them but I'm not sure why.

"Dinner is at 9:00. You are allowed in any of the common areas on the grounds. Someone will take you to your classes in the morning. If you need anything, there's always someone wandering around at all hours. I'm sure they'll be able to help you." I motion to Bram, who steps forward and makes a sweeping motion for Sloane to head up the stairs ahead of him.

She eyes him, gaze stretching down his body and back up again before addressing me. "What's to keep me from leaving?"

I take a steadying breath. I knew this wasn't going to be easy, but she's clearly going to be a pain in my ass. I'm not interested in wasting manpower to chase her down if she decides to take off. "I'm not going to chain you to the furniture. Go out the back and you'll probably get mauled in the woods by a wild animal. You're quite the easy target in that get-up."

She's still wearing her outfit from before—a hot pink tank

top and a white skirt that looks like it was painted onto her skin.

"Go out the front and Frankie will likely shoot you before you hit the road."

4

SLOANE

Go out the front and Frankie will likely shoot you before you hit the road.

Julian turns away from me, most likely knowing that his words have sent me into a spiral, but I refuse to show it, even with his back to me. The other guy, Bram, is still watching me, and deeper into the house, shadows are lingering, watching from a distance.

"Oh, and you should know," Julian says as he walks away, "there are cameras on every inch of the compound, with the exception of your bathroom. Should you need some privacy, that's where I'd suggest you find it."

I clench my jaw, keep my head down as I follow Bram up the stairs. I can't show them that my face is flushed, that I'm on the verge of tears. He just *threatened to kill me* and I'm supposed to just go sit in his guest room like I'm on vacation?

How will I survive this?

Upstairs, down a long stretch of hallway, Bram leads me to a door that's partially tucked behind a wall and opens it for me. I didn't even see him grab my suitcase for me when we were downstairs. He rolls it into the room and parks it against a door that must go to the bathroom.

With one hand on the doorknob, he pauses. "Listen," he says, voice soft, "you're safe here. Just do what he tells you." And then he closes the door.

As if his words make anything better. They just make my stomach churn. *Just do what he tells you.* And what will that be, exactly? I turn my back to the door, press my hands to my stomach, and focus on breathing. *Inhale. Exhale.* Don't cry. Don't throw up. Just breathe.

To distract myself, I finally look around. My room at the compound is bigger than the trailer home I lived in with my mom back in California, with a king-sized bed and a desk, a window that spans the length of one wall. I don't bother turning on the light. The bathroom door is open, the light from it flooding into the room so that I can see the bed, the nightstand, the dresser. It's nice for a prison cell. I stand in the center and suck in breaths. I can't get myself to move. My feet are cemented to the floor. I just want to go home. California, my dorm room, Tyler's frat house, anywhere that's not here.

My chin wobbles and then I remember what Julian said: that there are cameras everywhere. Who's watching me right now? Is some man behind a desk going to report back to Julian everything I do in here? Is he going to tell Julian that his pathetic prisoner cried?

Subtly, I turn in a circle, searching for any place where there might be a small camera tucked into a corner. Back home, my mother invested in a camera early on, when she decided the only way she was going to make us enough money to eat was by putting herself on the market. She'd tucked the camera under one of the shelves in the kitchen that held our chipped thrift store dishes, where it could only be seen once you were lying on the bed, and by that time, the men were preoccupied enough not to notice it. I always wondered where she got it, if she stole it from some electronics store.

"For protection," she said to me as I watched her run the wire through a hole in the wall when I was thirteen. It never protected either of us.

Julian's camera isn't nearly as inconspicuous. I guess it doesn't have to be. Up in the corner of the room, right over the door, is a round security camera with a solid red light staring back at me. I stare up into it, giving up on being subtle. I want to smash it to pieces.

I sit on the edge of the bed and let my head fall into my hands. I can't bring myself to believe what Julian said about Tyler. Sure, Tyler can be an asshole, but there's no way he offered me up to Julian and his men like that. He's an asshole, but he's not evil.

I sigh. It's not as if sitting around wishing things were different is going to do me any good. With no idea what else to do, I decide to study. I have to stay focused on school. I can't let this derail me. I'm stronger than that.

I toss my suitcase onto the bed and unzip it. As soon as I push the lid back, I see the wrapped package sitting on top of my clothes. I don't know if I should even open it. I shouldn't be rewarding creepy behavior, but I'm also a helpless to resist. Because I know what I'll find when I unwrap it.

Books. Always books. Sometimes they're beautiful editions of classics, sometimes they're collections of poetry, sometimes they're books I've never heard of before. And always, they're from someone who refuses to identify themself. Having it in my hand now—something so familiar— grounds me, tethers me back to reality, a strange comfort.

I carefully unwrap the package, still intact even after the irate guy at the gate put his hands on everything in my suitcase, most likely checking for weapons. Why couldn't my pen pal have slipped me a gun?

The card slips out first. There's always a card, a Post-it-sized piece of card stock.

This one is an old favorite. Enjoy.

The book is heavy, hardback and dense but still new. I run my finger over the cover. I've read every single book my mystery person has left me. I don't even know why. Because I can't resist books, I guess, especially not pretty ones. And because the thought of mentioning it to the campus police—which is what I *should* do—makes me hyperventilate. Being one-on-one with the cops? No, thank you. Is it idiotic of me? Maybe. But standing here now, I don't regret it.

I press the book to my face and inhale. Sometimes I imagine that I smell the mystery person on the books' pages, a faint smell of skin in the binding, the familiarity of the scent of someone faceless, even though I know it's all in my head.

A knock on the door startles me, and I drop the book onto the bed. I walk over to the door and open it a crack, finding Bram in the hallway. He has his hands behind his back, the same way both he and Julian were standing when I got here, like perfect gentlemen.

Yeah, right.

"Dinner is set," he says. "We're just waiting on you."

I glance behind me to the clock on the wall. 9:00 on the dot. I turn back to Bram. Something about him makes him seem less scary than the other men I've met so far, especially Julian. Maybe it's because he seems to be a bit older than most of the others. His eyes are a bit softer too, I guess, like he's always on the verge of smiling. Which just seems...out of place.

"I'm not hungry," I tell him, "but thank you."

That almost smile of his vanishes, his eyes going blank just as I close the door and press my back to it. I have no intention of going downstairs and pretending this is somehow normal. What kind of group of dangerous men living in a compound all have dinner together like some kind of after-school special? I intend to hide. I reach down to lock the door and realize there is no lock. I guess I should have expected that.

Someone pounds on the door at my back, and I let out a scream as it rattles, seemingly reverberating down to my bones. I clamp a hand over my mouth, my pulse going haywire, and open the door.

"What the hell?" I growl, fully expecting to find Bram again.

Instead, it's Julian. His jaw is clenched tight, along with his fists. "What part of 'dinner is at 9:00' did you not understand?"

I'm frozen, afraid to open my mouth for fear that a whimper will escape. I'd rather let that Frankie guy shoot me than show Julian my fear. If he's going to hurt me, he's going to do it whether I obey his ridiculous commands or not.

He doesn't seem to appreciate my silence. He bends so that our eyes are on the same level. This close, I can't avoid looking at him the way I did downstairs. I'm confronted by his dark brown eyes, the sharp jut of his jaw, his pale skin, a contrast against his dark, short hair, and the diamond studs in his ears that sparkle just enough to catch my attention when he clenches his jaw. "I suggest you get your ass downstairs to the dinner table. This is non-negotiable."

Julian and I stare at each other for another moment,

locked in a battle of wills, before he turns and storms down the hall, not waiting to see if I'll follow him. He knows I will.

My eyes meet Bram's without a word, silently waiting for me in the hallway, and then he gestures toward the stairs as if to say, *well, get a move on.* Couldn't he have told Julian I wasn't feeling well or something? Did he have to full-on tattle on me to his boss?

I cross my arms as we walk through the foyer and then take several turns before ending up in a dining room. A long, dark wood dining table stretches from one end of the room to the other, and it's full of people. They all stare at me as I follow Bram and Julian in. I avoid their gazes, ignoring the prickle it leaves on my skin. Julian stomps to the head of the table like a petulant child and takes a seat while I find an empty one on the other end from him. There are two others that are empty, and Bram takes one of them, sitting at Julian's right hand.

My eyes scan the faces that I can see from where I'm sitting, all men, all dressed in black. Julian reaches for a bowl of something in the center of the table, serving himself, and everyone else follows suit. I've never eaten dinner like this, at a table full of people like it's some kind of Thanksgiving feast.

"What's the word on the Montreal shipment?" Julian asks seemingly the entire table, but it's one of the men who came to drag me from my dorm who glances over at me before answering.

"Boss, should we really talk business in front of Malibu Barbie?"

Julian slams the bowl in his hand down on the table so hard that everyone flinches, including me. "I asked if there was any word on the Montreal shipment."

The man ducks his head. "We're waiting for confirmation. As soon as we get the green light, I'll let you know."

Julian nods, and the table falls silent again. No one seems

interested in small talk about what a beautiful day it was in New Hampshire. Do these people even notice things like leaves beginning to change color? I'm guessing not. What *do* they notice?

When still no one deigns to speak, I say, "How many people live in this house?" I don't know who I'm asking, maybe Julian, maybe no one. Everyone at the table pauses, glancing over at me. Something about their shock sends a tiny thrill through me. They thought I would just roll over. Instead, I lean forward and meet all of their eyes. I don't know what it is about them that makes me want to push them. I'm afraid, but the anticipation of what *could* happen feels worse than just forcing something to happen myself right away.

On the other side of the man seated beside me, I see her. A woman. And not just any woman. Professor Murphy. Tyler had her for a low-level business class last semester. And here she is, the perfect little traitor herself. She's probably feeding Julian and his entourage information about the students, about Tyler. Is she how they met? Is that how Julian knew he could prey on Tyler, because she sold him out? Does she hold her position at the school just so she can let Julian know who to come after? Pay close enough attention and you can smell who has money.

Julian grunts, cutting into a piece of steak. The meal in question is steak and potatoes, and since I don't eat either of those things, I've settled for a serving of the roasted corn that someone put far too much salt in.

"Seven, not including you." His eyes meet mine with the expanse of the table between us. "I trust your room is to your liking."

"Don't you mean my cage?"

His cold, lifeless eyes burrow into me, but I don't look away. From here, they're so dark they look almost completely black. "I actually have a rather large dog kennel in the basement if you'd prefer that." He holds my gaze for another long moment before setting his fork down on his plate. "Sloane, no one at this table wants you here any more than you want to be here, so why don't we all just play nice until this is over?"

I can feel the press of everyone's eyes like fingerprints on my skin, but I hold Julian's gaze, testing him. "What do you get out of this arrangement?"

Julian chews and swallows, then leans one elbow on the table, lowering his face so he can look me right in the eye. "I'll do anything to watch your boyfriend suffer."

I can see in his eyes that he means it, which just creates so many more questions. How long have he and Tyler known each other without me knowing about it? What did Tyler do to Julian to make him hate him so much?

Julian straightens back in his chair. "And I suspect he's been using you to create the perfect image. Well-behaved frat boy with a steady girlfriend, both of them on the fucking honor roll. It's a pretty good cover."

Each word hits like bricks. "Cover for what?"

He snorts. "Shut up and eat your dinner."

SLOANE

At three in the morning, I'm curled against the headboard in my room, watching the door, wide awake, my knees pulled up to my chest. I've always found it hard to fall asleep in strange places, especially when those places come equipped with security cameras watching my every move. I keep waiting for the doorknob to turn, for someone to come in here and...

He told me I could do whatever I want to you.

I throw aside the blanket and stand. It's been quiet for hours. If I can't sleep, I might as well explore the compound. The faster I can get Tyler what he wants, the faster I can get out of here, right? They agreed on a month, but if Tyler can take this place apart as quickly as possible, I won't have to stay.

I sneak out of my bedroom as quietly as possible, surprised to find the building silent and empty. It's hard to imagine people like the ones who live here ever really going to sleep. But I guess they have to sometime. I don't want to know what will happen if I run into one of the men somewhere. I have to hope they're all hidden away somewhere.

I don't bother investigating upstairs. The second floor is clearly just a hallway of bedrooms. At least, I'm assuming they're bedrooms. I don't even want to think about which of the brooding men from dinner is in them, about the fact that they're just feet from my own room. I take the stairs down to the foyer.

I find the decor of this place slightly odd. For a normal person, it wouldn't be, but for a group of men that seem like they could be dangerous, it seems too bright... too simple. Instead of the glass and black-painted walls I was expecting, it's a lot of old wood and white paint, exactly what an old house in New Hampshire *should* look like.

I walk around the foyer, look at the rug beneath the chairs, the patterns along the fabric of them. I just can't imagine these guys picking out rugs. Maybe it's the work of Professor Murphy.

When I get to the dining room, I decide to take a left, moving into the hallway opposite the large staircase. I slip through a doorway and lean into the room that opens out from it. It looks like a sitting room, with a fireplace and two long couches. Above the fireplace hangs a framed portrait of Julian and a very stern-looking man. The man has his hand on Julian's shoulder, and they're both wearing suits. Tailored, black, expensive.

I step further into the room to get a better look at the portrait. It's an old photo, several years old, based on the child-like features of Julian's face, his slightly rounded cheeks and spots of acne. Just the two of them. No one else. I turn to leave, even though the room looks cozy and exactly the kind of place I would normally like to be on a night like this. But I can't stop moving.

When I'm back at the door leading into the dining room, I go the other way. Under the stairs, a long, dark hallway stretches far. It certainly looks like the kind of place you would hide something, like the kind of place I'm definitely not supposed to go.

I glance up at the ceiling, looking for security cameras, but oddly enough, I don't see any, not in the hallway itself. Maybe they're just hidden better here. Here's hoping that whoever watches the cameras takes a break at night. I mean, there aren't people watching the cameras at all hours, right? There's no way. Why would it even be necessary?

I take a step down the long corridor but don't even make it to a second one before a voice behind me says, "You don't want to go down there."

A shiver runs up my spine, and I spin around. It's Professor Murphy, the woman from dinner. She has a hint of a smirk on her face and bags under her eyes. She's old enough to be Julian's mother and doesn't fit in with the men at all. Where does she belong in all of this?

"I wasn't trying to—"

"I know what you were trying to do." She nods her head in the direction of the staircase, and I move back out into the foyer, into the light. She watches me the way she did at dinner, like she's trying to read my motives on my skin. Let's hope she can't.

"Am I not allowed in there?" I ask. "I'm not trying to infiltrate. I just want to know so that I don't accidentally end up where I'm not supposed to." I keep my voice light. Maybe I can make an ally here. There's something about her that's far less terrifying than the men.

When her mouth twists, I realize she's wearing lipstick. And a dress. Who is this woman that she's fully decked out at three in the morning? I cross my arms over my chest. I'm not even wearing a bra. I really didn't think I was going to run into anyone. Julian said there's always someone up, but this place is pretty big. What were the chances I'd end up in the same spot as one of them?

"No," she finally says, "you're not allowed in there." Her smile falls then. "And if you get caught, you might never make it back out. Do yourself a favor and stay where he can keep an eye on you."

Hmm. Confirmation that there aren't cameras down that hallway. Does she think she's deterring me? She basically just dangled a carrot in front of me, and even knowing it's poisonous, I still want it. I need it.

I nod to Professor Murphy and head toward the stairs. Before I start up the steps, I grip the banister and lean over it. "Goodnight, Professor Murphy." I want her to know that I know exactly who she is.

This time, she really almost smiles. "A word to the wise..." She comes over to the stairs slowly, her heels *click clack*ing as she walks. She reaches up and takes hold of the banister, right next to my hand. "Don't show any weakness. If you do, he'll use it. That's what he's good at."

5

Bang bang bang.

I jerk awake and groan at the pain in my side. I push myself up in the tub and look at the door. My bathroom is the only place that has a lock, and even as I stare at the knob, it rattles.

"It's time to go!" someone shouts on the other side of the door, a voice I don't recognize.

I toss my pillow down into the foot of the tub and climb out, rubbing my eyes. I can hear my phone out in the bedroom, beeping loudly to try and wake me up. I can't believe I left it in there. I'm probably late for class.

I rush to get dressed, pulling my hair back into a bun and deciding on very light makeup before throwing open my door and finding Hugo—the tall one—on my bed, arms crossed, scowl in place.

"Jesus, it's a classroom, not a church service. Let's fucking go," he says, standing and stomping out the door.

What would he even know about a church service?

I follow Hugo out to the car, the same one they retrieved me in before, and find that, just like yesterday, Magnus is in the passenger seat, eyes slanted halfway closed against the early morning sun. I open the door, but before I get in, my eyes catch on a group of people out past the side of the main house. Julian and a few other men are standing in the field beside the house, talking and gesticulating with their arms.

In the dark last night, I didn't even notice there are at least two other buildings on the property. From where I stand, the one they're beside looks like a garage, with several bay doors, and out beyond it, what looks like a barn.

It's a long commute back to Dartmouth from the compound, and we spend the first half in silence. I stare at the backs of their heads, their expensive, immaculate haircuts.

Maybe the best idea is for me to be a good little hostage, cooperate and see if I can get into the good graces of some of these people, kindly coerce information from them, even if there's no way I'll get into the good graces of Julian himself.

"So, what do you two do? You know, for a living." I lean forward as much as possible between the seats before the seatbelt starts to choke me.

They look at each other and then back at the road. Neither makes eye contact with me.

"We're mechanics," Magnus says.

"Oh, cool. I used to spend weekends watching my dad work on this old Buick Riviera he had when I was a kid. I hated the look of that thing. Have you guys ever worked on one?"

There's a beat of silence.

"No," Hugo answers.

Okay. Not giving me much to work with. "Are either of you married? Kids?"

This question, they don't even bother to answer. At least,

I tried. But we fall back into our original silence, and I watch New Hampshire fly past the windows.

"So, what's the plan here?" I ask when we pull up to campus, the car swinging around in front of my first building. "Are you two going to follow me around campus and make sure I don't skitter off?"

Hugo meets my eye in the rearview mirror. "Why would we do that?"

I shrug. "Because I might... skitter off..."

He shakes his head. "No, you won't. Because you made an agreement, and you're going to stick to the agreement or there are going to be consequences."

I resist the urge to clarify that Tyler made the agreement, not me.

Such a simple answer. I'm just so easy to control. I snatch my bag from the floorboard.

"We'll see you back here at two," Hugo says. I don't ask how they know my schedule. They seem to know everything about me. Tyler probably gave them all the information they wanted when he decided he was going to hand me over like cattle.

"Yeah, okay," I say, pushing out of the car and walking up to the building where my first class is. It feels strange to be here now after the night I had. My entire world has been turned upside down, and somehow I'm still right back where I am every morning. I glance over my shoulder as the black Cadillac pulls away from the curb.

I use the bathroom before class, and when I push the door of the women's room open to leave, I find Tyler waiting outside in the hall, leaning against the wall. He knows my routine better than I do. Better than Julian Shaw seems to.

"Baby," he says as soon as the door falls shut behind me, stepping up to me and taking my face in his hands the way he always does. They're soft and cold, which bothers me for some reason. "Are you okay?"

I pull his hands away, glancing around to make sure nobody is watching us. All I can think about is what Julian said, that betting me in the race was Tyler's idea. *He told me I could do whatever I want to you.* He had to be lying. He *had* to be. Because if he wasn't...

"I'm fine," I lie, hiking my bag up on my shoulder and turning toward our classroom. The door is open, people already filing in. I'm not going to tell him about sleeping in the tub. Maybe he expects me to cry and clutch at him, beg him to protect me. I won't. $100,000. Eyes on the prize.

He frowns at me, falling into step beside me. "What happened? What did you get?"

I spin around, my hand shooting out to block the doorway so that he can't go inside just like he did to me yesterday. My teeth grind together. "It was twelve hours, Tyler. Did you think I'd come back with all his secrets?"

He looks confused at my anger, incensed by it, like he can't fathom why I wouldn't want to throw myself on my own sword for any cause he finds worthy. "No, but you had to have gotten something."

I shake my head and let my arm fall away from the doorway. "Just let me breathe, Tyler." I walk into the classroom and take a seat in our normal row. He follows me and tosses his bag onto the ground at his feet. "Are you really mad at me about this? Don't you get that I didn't have a choice, Sloane? I wanted to race for money, but he just wanted you."

Our professor is already putting notes on the board, and I take my textbook out, trying to pretend that Tyler's comment doesn't feel like a knife. God, I wish I could tell if he was lying. "What do you mean, he wanted me?"

"I offered him a car my dad has in storage, a Jaguar that I

didn't think he would miss, and he asked for you. Said all debts paid if he won you."

He puts his arm along the back of my chair, and I fight not to flinch away, desperate to put distance between us. "And after you knew he had some reason to want me in that compound, you still took him at his word when he said he wouldn't lay a hand on me?"

His eyes flick toward me, unreadable under the fluorescent lights. "Did he?"

"No, but–"

"Then I don't know what you're complaining about." All his gentleness is gone. His eyes are full of anger, his jaw clenched tight. "You're getting what you want. You want money? Get me what I need."

Class starts, the professor cutting off any chance I might have had to respond. I have that disconnected feeling I get when my life has changed too much too quickly. I don't do well with change, much less the kind of change that puts me in a situation like the one I'm in currently.

Back in California, I was used to life being unpredictable. I was used to being unsure where my next meal was coming from or who I was going to find every day when I came home from school. Tyler changed all that, but now he's thrown me back into the thick of it in full force.

"What did you get from them?" Tyler asks as he walks me out of the technology building later that afternoon and into the parking lot where I'm supposed to meet Magnus and Hugo. They're leaning against the side of the car like they're my dates for prom or something. The day has been busy, and since we only have the one class together, Tyler and I haven't had a chance to talk.

I resist the urge to roll my eyes, at them *and* at Tyler. "Nothing yet. They live in a big compound out past Lyme, close to the interstate. There are half a dozen of them living there. They have a barn and some other building, probably a garage. I didn't get a chance to look at them. They have surveillance everywhere, including my room." I think about the long, dark hallway that I'm forbidden to go down. "Well... everywhere except this one hallway."

Tyler stops me before we get to Hugo and Magnus, and both men take note of this. They straighten away from their car when Tyler grabs hold of my arm, like they take personal affront to him putting his hands on me, as if they wouldn't do the same thing.

"What hallway?" he asks.

"There don't seem to be cameras there. I tried to go last night, but I didn't make it two steps before someone stopped me."

"You need to get in there." Tyler's eyes go over my shoulder, and that's all the warning I get before an arm snakes around my stomach and lifts me off the ground. "Hey!" Tyler shouts, but whoever has a hold of me—Hugo, I'm guessing, from how high up he's holding me—ignores him and carries me over to the car. Several people stop to look, but no one says anything. Good to know no one in this town is concerned about kidnapping.

I'm tossed into the backseat and my bag is thrown in after me. The door slams and the car starts.

I sit up in the backseat in a huff. "You can't just toss me around like that," I growl. "I'm supposed to be allowed to live my normal life. You guys are making it impossible."

"You're to go to class and then get back to the compound," Hugo says.

"Okay, and what happens when I want to have a social life? I have friends, I have a boyfriend. It's not healthy for people to be locked away inside all the time. And that goes for the two of you, too. Are you both getting enough sun? Vitamin D is very important for your mental health."

Magnus looks over his shoulder at me. "You don't have to make small talk with us. We would prefer your silence."

"That's rude." I cross my arms and watch New Hampshire disappear in the distance.

As soon as we're back at the compound, Hugo and Magnus take off, leaving me in the foyer. I drop my messenger bag on the floor and then just sort of... stand there. I don't want to go up to my room. I don't think I can take any more of sitting in there, even if it is the size of a small apartment. During a normal week, I would spend hours in my dorm room reading and studying, but it's different when you're in a place where you're comfortable and no one is telling you that you *can't* do anything else.

"Oh, good. You're back."

I recognize the guy coming down the stairs, but I've seen so many faces in the last twenty-four hours, and not all of those faces were presented with names, so I have no idea who this guy is, but I'm deeply aware that we're alone. The house appears to be empty, everyone off living their lives.

"Sorry, do I know you?" I ask him as he slowly saunters down the stairs, long hair pulled back into a bun, a gold chain around his neck. I get the feeling he thinks he looks cool, but he really just looks like one of those dogs in the online videos that aren't sure how stairs work.

He has a smirk on his face that makes me feel dirty. It makes me want to back out the front door and follow Hugo and Magnus wherever they're going. "My name is Frankie. I'm pretty much in charge around here."

I reach for my bag, figure it could be a good weapon.

"That's interesting because I was pretty sure that Julian was in charge and that Bram is the second-in-command."

He finally reaches the ground floor and stops right in front of me. "Well, you'd be wrong, wouldn't you?" His eyes scan down my body, stopping pretty obviously on my chest on his way back up. "With the exception of Claudia, we don't generally allow women to hang around unless they have something to offer. Otherwise, they're too much of a distraction."

"If you're that distracted by a set of boobs, maybe you should see a doctor. Seems like an inability to focus. Might need to have your head examined."

He gives me that smirk again. "Cute. Don't worry, I'm sure Julian will put you to good use sooner rather than later."

My skin burns, but I make sure not to let it show. Is that a threat? Even if Tyler is telling the truth about Julian agreeing not to touch me, if this guy is somehow convinced he's running the show, would he care at all what Julian has to say about what he does? How much control does he have over his men when he's not looking?

"If you so much as breathe on me, I'll slice off all three of your favorite appendages."

He grins at me. "Looking for an excuse to grab it, sweetheart?"

"If I needed something that small in my hand, I could go to the grocery store and fondle some grapes and a baby carrot."

He nods, runs his thumb along his bottom lip before pushing his long, dirty blonde hair out of his eyes. When he does, I see that he has a long scar on his cheek. Internally, I'm cheering for whoever gave it to him. "Okay, buttercup. Don't get your panties in a twist. If you'll excuse me, I have work to do."

"All that scum isn't going to suck itself."

He laughs, but it isn't a pleasant sound, as he vanishes

around a corner. As soon as he's out of sight, I rush toward the back of the compound. Logic tells me there's another door back here, and it only takes me a second to spot it through a window in the hall behind the dining room. I need to move quick, before anyone can see me going and ask any questions.

I push through another door and find myself in a pool room, inundated by the smell of chlorine. Before I can get distracted, I keep moving, throwing open a door in the giant wall of windows that spits me outside. I don't know what I was expecting, but this insane yard wasn't it. I wouldn't even call it a yard. It's a garden. From where I stand on a stone overlook, I can see down into it, flowers everywhere. I take the steps down and then press my back to the stone wall at the bottom.

Even though I know there are cameras out here too, I still feel like no one can see me. I take a deep breath and close my eyes, listening to the sounds of the birds. When I open them again, the first thing I see are the mountains. Standing where I am, surrounded by blooms and blue skies and miles of green grass, I can almost believe I live a charmed existence, that this place is some kind of gift. But that couldn't be further from the truth.

6

I'm going over the numbers for the Montreal shipment when someone knocks on my door. I don't answer immediately. If I can't get this car packed as cheap as possible, we're going to lose the sale, which means I'm paying out of my pocket for the man hours we've put into this, including the long drive, which is going to be hell on pretty much any of my guys. I could save money if I just did it myself.

"Yeah, what is it?" I call out.

Bram comes into my office and shuts the door behind him. "We have to do something about the girl."

Goddammit.

I toss the paperwork down on my desk and sigh, shoving my hands into my hair. "What did she do now?"

"Nothing. That's the problem. I found her sitting in the garden by herself, looking dazed as all hell. It's only been two days, and she's already bored out of her mind." He comes to stand by the desk, leaning on the back of the chair in front of me.

"And why should I give a shit if she's bored?"

"If she's bored, she starts poking around."

I go back to my work. "She won't find anything."

"Are you certain of that? We never have people inside the compound. You sure there isn't anything incriminating anywhere that she could stumble onto?"

He knows I can't be sure of that. Even with eyes on her at all times, which I can't really afford—the guys already hate cam duty as it is—who knows what she might stumble upon. The men are careful, but they're also just human. I toss my papers back down on the desk again. "Okay, so what do we do about it? Buy her a puppy?"

One side of Bram's mouth tips up. "I'm not sure yet, but I wanted you to know so you could be thinking about it."

I wave him off. "Sure. I'll be thinking about it. Because I have absolutely nothing better to do than worry about whether or not that shitbag's little girlfriend is entertained. Call me if she gives anyone dirt on Tyler."

Silence settles over us for a beat and then Bram says, "I was wrong about her. I don't think she's a spy. I think she's an innocent. Which might be worse."

I don't look up from my paperwork, but my eyes don't focus on the scribbles on the page anymore. *An innocent.* When was the last time anyone in this place was innocent? Maybe I could have said I was as a teenager, before my father croaked and left it all to me. But I always knew what he was involved in, and I never so much as blinked an eye.

"She's not our concern. She's a device, a tool to get to Tyler. That's it. Stop worrying about her so much and get back to work."

An hour later, I step out of my office in the back and head down the hallway toward the meeting room. Some of the guys have their own offices back here—Claudia, Bram, Frankie—but the rest of the guys, when they aren't working, hang out in the meeting room or the dining room to have lunch, talk, or get paperwork done.

Today, both the downstairs meeting room and the dining room are empty. While not impossible, it's statistically unlikely that everyone would be gone at the same time, especially on a day when there are no meetings, no pick-ups, and no deliveries. Where the hell is everyone?

A loud voice from upstairs catches my attention. I walk out into the foyer and look up toward the second story. Across from the open door of Sarge's room, Frankie is leaning against the railing, his arms crossed, staring at something.

"What the hell is going on?" I shout up to him.

His shoulders tense and he turns to look over the railing at me. "They're playing poker."

I scowl. "*Who's* playing poker?"

Frankie waves dismissively toward the open door without actually answering my question. I growl and stomp up the stairs. I ignore Frankie as I move into Sarge's room. He has the biggest one since it doubles as an infirmary, and in the main room, a round table is set up. I've seen that table hold bullets freshly extracted from flesh and bloody bandages. Bram, Sarge, Ronny, and Sloane sit in a circle, cards and chips scattered between the four of them while the rest of the men watch.

"What's going on?" I bark.

I'm only half surprised when everyone in the room jumps, the men at the table rising to their feet, except for Sloane, who stays seated. She doesn't even stop dealing cards. "You want in?" she asks me, tapping her cards on the table to straighten them.

"No," I growl at her. "I want my staff to be getting shit done in the middle of a work day. I'm not paying all of you to sit around and play poker. Jesus Christ." When no one moves, apparently waiting for clearer orders, I shout, "Get the fuck out!"

They all scatter, filing out of the room until the only ones left are Sarge, Bram, and Sloane. Sarge because it's his room, Bram because he's not scared of me, and Sloane because... well, because she's Sloane. Getting a read on her has proven difficult. Either she's afraid and not showing it, or she has a steel backbone.

She sighs and sags back into her chair. She's wearing a damn sundress like it's the middle of summer and not halfway through October. "Was that really necessary? They weren't hurting anybody."

I march over to the table, leaning across it to get in her face. This close, I can just make out her turquoise glitter eyeshadow, though it's hard since she's clearly trying not to blink. "I run a tight ship around here, Miss Moretti, and for good reason. Everybody has a job. If they don't work, we don't get paid. This is what they signed up for."

"And what about what I signed up for?"

I couldn't keep my eyes from dropping to her plump mouth if God himself was standing in front of me telling me I would burn in Hell for it. "The only thing you signed up for was being in my pocket until I decide you're free to go. I'm feeding you. I'm putting a roof over your head, and I'm keeping my men away from you. All I ask in return is that you stay the hell out of the way."

And just because I enjoy seeing her lose the upper hand, I slam my fists down on the table, satisfied when she flinches.

I straighten away from the table and look over at Bram. "You're on thin ice."

He doesn't respond, probably because he knows I'm full

of shit. I would do away with every single person in this building before I sent Bram packing. Nevertheless, I send him a deadly look before stepping back out into the hall to find Frankie still waiting. The bastard is watching. He likes seeing people get what's coming to them.

I smack the papers that I forgot were in my hand against his chest. "Run these numbers for the Montreal shipment. I want them by dinner."

$$7$$

JULIAN

Sitting at my desk in the middle of the night, I press my face into my palms. What to do with this thorn in my side. Tyler Price. I can't fucking do anything about him. There should be a solution. There should be an answer. But I don't know what it is. I don't know how to take this fucker down without my men getting caught in the crossfire.

I growl, swiping my hands over the papers on my desk in frustration and watching them flutter into the air and then land haphazardly on my floor.

I haven't slept in weeks. Every time I close my eyes, Leo's face flashes in front of me like strobe lights in a fun house. I dream about finding him in that dumpster, already gone. His lifeless eyes. His cold, pale skin. The foam still curling up around his mouth. Hands dragging me away.

I don't realize I've closed my eyes until they slam back open. Beyond my open door, the hallway is silent. Some of the guys are off with their women, on jobs, at the bars. The house is quiet.

Without second-guessing, I slide open my drawer and grab my gun.

I'm at my fucking wit's end as I stomp out of my office and through the dining room. I don't even care if she hears me coming. Let her hear it. Let her fear for her life.

At the top of the stairs, I glance at the door next to hers. Sarge's room.

I put her in this hallway because he's the only one I trust with her. Completely trust with her. Him and Bram, but Bram gets his own wing. Downstairs, far from everyone else.

I wanted to protect her when she got here. I wanted to treat her like she was made of porcelain and then smash her and watch Tyler see her break into a million pieces.

But my plan is not going to work out the way I wanted it to. He offered her up. He's not tortured over her absence. I told her she was here to make him suffer, but for fuck's sake, I was wrong. He's not suffering at all. So why the fuck is she here? Why the fuck am I still keeping her safe? Why did I put her in this fucking hallway? Should have just let the guys have her.

My stomach roils at the idea. I don't want to know which ones would lay hands on her if I gave them the freedom to. That's a question I don't need answers to.

I turn for her door. Claudia told me she caught her roaming the grounds last night. I'm not surprised. I fully expected her to go looking for things. I fully expected Tyler to have sent her here to tear apart my wiring from the inside.

When I set up the race, I just wanted to put pressure on him. I never could have imagined he'd offer her up like property. He didn't even blink. And that infuriates me. It infuriates me that I thought she was a precious jewel to him. She's not. Not even a little bit.

What does he think we're doing to her here? Why doesn't he fucking care? I slowly open her bedroom door. The light is on in her bathroom. It's the first thing I see, the door open, the light slanting across the hardwood floor. I think maybe she's in there, but when I step in, I see that she's asleep. She's using the bathroom light as a nightlight to keep the monsters away.

King-sized bed and she's pressed against the very edge. Maybe back in California, she was used to tiny beds. Twin-sized. Things that could barely contain her.

As I walk over to the bed, she doesn't move. Fast asleep.

All that sleep she lost last night must have caught up with her. Hugo found her sleeping in her tub this morning, but whatever happened at that poker table today must have put her at ease. Stupid. Letting her fucking guard down. I may not be interested in taking what she doesn't want to give, but I *want* to kill her right now.

I watch the slow rhythm of her breathing. The steady pulse in her neck. Under her soft, creamy looking skin. The kind of skin that you take care of because people care to look at it.

I lift my gun.

There's nothing I want more than to take something from him. To rip something he loves from his hands. If I shoot her right now, will he cry? Will he care? Will he have someone else on his arm in a week?

My finger tightens on the trigger.

And then her eyes open slowly. Just like that, she's as awake as if it was morning and sunlight was sweeping into her room. I see the moment the sleepiness wears off and the awareness settles in.

She doesn't move. She doesn't jerk away. She doesn't sit up. She just lays there, her eyes on the gun, the pulse in her neck kicking up even faster.

And we stay there for a long moment. Me trying to decide

if I should pull the trigger and end it all, and her holding as still as possible.

I lower the gun to my side. Angry at myself for being weak. Angry at myself for being half the man that my father was. He always did what he needed to do. He always took out the weak links. The rats. The loose ends.

Without a word, with her eyes still on me, I turn back to the door and walk out, leaving it open behind me.

⑧

SLOANE

Unknown Number
Get any sleep last night?

The text comes in the middle of class. My phone sits on the table between Tyler and me, and when the notification flashes across my screen, it comes and goes so quickly, that little bar across my lock screen that shows me what the message says, but I see Tyler's eyes trip down to it and then back up again.

He keeps his gaze trained straight forward, his pen still moving as he takes notes, but I can see the wheels turning in his head. There's a tic in the corner of his jaw that goes again and again.

My blood boils. He did this on purpose. I snatch up my phone and look at the unknown number. I know it has to be Julian. He's the only one who would push my buttons like this, that would taunt me, that would try to stir up trouble. To Tyler, that text could look suggestive or flirty.

Bastard.

Sloane
Who is this?

Unknown Number
Who do you think it is, princess?

I glance sideways at Tyler. He's still pretending to pay attention to the lecture, but I know he's watching me just like I'm watching him. If Julian wanted to rattle the cage, couldn't he have just texted Tyler directly and left me out of it? I'm already in the middle of all this shit.

I don't know why I didn't tell Tyler about last night. About waking up to Julian standing over my bed, his gun pointed at me. I've never been so scared in my life, but I also felt it deep down that he wouldn't do it. He *couldn't*. Not because he has some heart of gold or whatever, but because too many people know I'm staying with him right now, and if I turn up dead, well... I didn't tell Tyler about it. How could I? If he gets angry enough to yank me out, I lose out on the money. And if he doesn't care... It's honestly better if I don't know what he would do.

Sloane

I'm in the middle of class. What do you want?

Unknown Number
When Hugo and Magnus pick you up today, I expect you to be waiting on them. My men don't have time to chase you around.

Sloane

They wouldn't have to chase me around if you would let me drive myself like an adult.

Unknown Number
Adults keep their word. Prove yourself
trustworthy and you can have as much
freedom as you want.

I scoff out loud, and my professor pauses, looking over his shoulder at me with an eyebrow raised before going back to whatever he was doing on the Smart Board.

Sloane
I don't owe you anything.

Unknown Number
Don't forget I own you. Tell your
boyfriend I said hi.

I slam my phone down on the desk and take a deep breath. It's only when I look up that I realize I've made a ruckus and everyone in the room is looking at me. I sit up straighter and clear my throat. "Sorry," I say quietly and wait for class to resume before I slump back down into my chair again.

"What's going on?" Tyler whispers to me.

I cross my arms as tight as I can, like I can somehow strangle him if I just cross them tight enough. "Nothing."

Leaning over, he presses his mouth directly to my ear and says, "Don't fuck around with me, Sloane. There are no secrets between us. Tell me what he said to you."

Anger courses through my veins. I'm surrounded by men who think I belong to them, men who think they can toss me around like their plaything, and I have no choice but to do what they say. Sometimes, when I weigh all the information in my brain, I think maybe it wouldn't be so bad to be poor in California again. But I've spent my whole life wanting more than what my old life could offer. And it wasn't like I was any safer or happier there than I am here. Greener pastures and whatnot.

I push my phone over to Tyler and watch as he slowly reads through my messages. His face gets angrier and angrier as he reads, the vein in his neck beginning to throb and his cheeks turning red.

When he's done reading, he tucks my phone into his back pocket.

Without thinking, I lunge for it. "What are you doing?" I hiss at him, trying to reach into his pocket and take my phone back.

Under the desk, he grabs hold of my wrist, squeezing tight, until I have to hold in a cry of pain. "You don't need it anymore," he says. "He carts you around like a child, putting you on your little school bus in the morning and the afternoon, and then he has cameras on you all the time. What could you possibly need with your phone?"

"I can't make him angry," I tell him. If Julian can't get a hold of me when he needs to, what will he do to me? Have one of his henchmen throw me in a trunk?

His hand tightens around my wrist, and I wince, knowing he'll leave bruises. Tears prick the corners of my eyes. "It doesn't matter if you make him angry. You should be worried about making *me* angry. He thinks you belong to him? He's full of shit. You belong to me and nobody else."

I press my nose to his. "Maybe you should have thought about that before you gave me to him like a pair of used shoes."

Tyler releases me, and I gasp with relief, rubbing at my wrist. I seem to have won this round, but I can feel Tyler's attention on me all throughout the lecture.

After class, as we're walking out into the hallway, Tyler turns to me and says, "We should go back to my place."

Is he serious? After all that?

I glance at the clock hanging on the wall over his head. It's not like I can check my damn phone. "I can't. I have to study for midterms before my next class." It's not even an excuse, although going back to the frat house to spend quality time with him isn't high on my priority list after what he just pulled.

"Skip it," he says, and the way he says it makes it very clear it's not a suggestion.

"Tyler..." I *want* to study. I *want* to do well on my midterms. I didn't come to college to screw around like Tyler did.

But Tyler ignores me, wraps an arm around my waist, and steers me in the direction of the other side of campus. I don't fight him. I don't even know why. Maybe because I'm tired of fighting him. Maybe because I know if I just give him what he wants, he'll let up.

It takes a while to get to the frat house, and the whole way, I consider reaching into his back pocket and taking back my phone. He's right. I don't really need it. But it's mine. It's one of the few things I have that connects me to my mom, and even though she doesn't generally check in with me very often, I like knowing the connection is there.

But I don't want to start yet another fight, so I keep my hands to myself.

The frat house is empty. It's almost noon and most of the guys are in classes or practices or whatever else they have going on. Tyler doesn't even offer me water or a snack. He just takes me upstairs.

I've always hated Tyler's room at the frat house. He shares it with this guy who uses too much cologne, so the place always smells like a mixture of Drakkar Noir and ramen noodles. They live in the attic bedroom, so the ceiling is kind of low, and even as short as I am, I always feel like the ceiling is going to cave in on me.

Tyler doesn't even take me to his bed, one of the two pushed against opposite walls and covered in laundry and open boxes of snacks. Instead, he just shoves me against the wall, his mouth crashing down onto mine. He kisses me with enough passion to push me up onto my toes, and I moan.

I wish it could always be like this, him wanting me, *actually* wanting me, instead of wanting someone on his arm to show off and boss around. Even if other things between us have become tarnished over time, the sex has always been nice. Enjoyable. Tyler was my first, my only.

Almost as quickly as he started kissing me, he stops, pulling away and spinning me around to face the wall. I don't even have a moment to tell him to slow down, to come and kiss me some more because I was enjoying it, before he shoves my skirt up and pulls my panties down.

"Oh!" I say as he bends me enough to give himself access and starts to push inside. "Wait. Tyler, I'm not–" *I'm not ready*, I mean to say. *I'm not wet.*

But he clamps his hand over my mouth and keeps going. I clench my teeth and let him, biting my tongue to hold in any sounds of pain. It hurts, but it's not anything I'm not used to. Most of the time, I don't get wet, get to a place where I really think I could come, until he's almost done, until he's been pumping into me for a long time. I know I won't get anywhere near finishing today. I can already tell it's going to be over too quick.

"You need to remember who you belong to," he growls in my ear. He grabs on hard to my hips and pumps into me. I look for something to hold onto, anything, but there's only the wall in front of me, solid and blank. I press my hot cheek to it and let it cool my skin.

When Tyler is done, he pulls out of me, letting his cum run down my leg. I kick my shoes off quick so they don't get soiled and go into the bathroom to clean up. That's really the only thing I like about the frat house: I don't have to share a bathroom with six other girls, just two kind of messy boys.

Once I've cleaned up as best as I can, I open the bathroom door to find Tyler in bed, shirtless and already half asleep.

"I should go," I whisper to him, thinking I can still make it for the second half of my class, but he shakes his head.

"No. Stay here with me. Come lay down."

I shouldn't. I know I shouldn't. I'm going to miss my last class of the day if I lay down with him now. But I know his bed will be warm and that his chest will be, too. And all I can think about is how nice it would feel, after all the stress and the chaos, to just be held, to just be somewhere familiar for a little while.

The circumstances of my relationship with Tyler are complicated. He's a good guy. He's just not always the *nicest* guy. What guy is? Maybe he's not the same person he was when we met, but neither am I. We started dating junior year, and when he said he wanted to go away to Dartmouth and that his dad would foot the bill if I wanted to go with him, it wasn't like I could turn down the opportunity. Because I *got into* Dartmouth. Tyler's dad bought his way in, but I actually got accepted on my own merit. I couldn't say no.

And maybe Tyler has gotten meaner. Maybe he's kept secrets. But I made my choices. I can't back out now, can't lose my only path to a real future. Everyone has flaws.

I crawl into his bed, just barely bigger than a twin, and let him put his arms around me. In that moment, I feel safe, despite all of it. I wish I could just stay here. I don't want to think about going back to the compound, where I have to be around people I don't know and have eyes on me all the time. I just want to be comfortable. I just want to be myself.

9

SLOANE

Bang, bang, bang.

I shoot up in Tyler's bed, clutching his covers around me. Outside the door, loud voices argue, getting louder as someone rattles the knob.

"What the hell?" Tyler says, sitting up beside me. He's immediately out of the bed, his sweatpants hanging low on his hips as he throws open the bedroom door.

And there's Hugo and Magnus, looking angry enough to kill. My blood trembles as they stare me down.

"Get dressed," Hugo growls. "Be down in the car in ninety seconds, or I'll come back up and drag you down." They turn and go back down the stairs, leaving Tyler's roommate standing in the hall looking furious.

"Who the fuck are they?" he asks, but Tyler ignores him and slams the door. I'm already scrambling out of the bed, pulling my shirt and skirt back on.

"How did they find you?" Tyler demands as I tug on my

shoes. He's looking at me with blazing eyes, the muscles in his bare chest pulled taut. "Did you tell him where you were?"

I don't have time for his possessive bullshit. I don't really feel like being thrown over Hugo's shoulder and getting carted down the stairs while Tyler's entire fraternity watches.

I shove by him, a bit surprised when he just lets me go. "No," I say, throwing open the door. "You have my phone, remember?"

"Fuck," Tyler says as I step out into the hallway. "He bugged it." His tone stops me, the furious lilt of it that warns of impending reaction.

I grab onto the banister and turn to him, watching as he pulls my phone out of his pocket. He still has it on him. I know he was planning to go through it later, read every text message I've ever sent. The idea doesn't worry me. That text from Julian earlier was the only one I've ever gotten from him, so it's not like he's going to catch me doing anything that would piss him off.

Although, he may find a bunch of text messages from my mother talking about how much she doesn't like him. Serves him right.

"When would he have–" I start to say, but before I can finish the thought, he's holding my phone over the stair railing, dangling between his index finger and his thumb. "Tyler!"

He drops it, and it falls three stories down to the main floor, shattering on impact.

JULIAN

I pace across the foyer and back again, trying to calm myself before I speak. My eyes flicker over to Sloane, and I can practically smell the fear coming off of her. Good. If she's going to act like a fucking brat, she's going to be treated like one.

"When I told you that you were to be exactly where you're supposed to be exactly when you're supposed to be there, what did you think that meant? Was I speaking another language?"

She gives a weary sigh and looks away from me.

I stop in front of her and run a hand down my face. "You'll spend the rest of the week in your room."

Her eyes shoot to me and her mouth falls open. "Excuse me? I'm not a fucking teenager. You can't *ground* me. I have midterms."

It takes everything I have not to smile. Yes, I *can* ground her. She may not be a child, but if she's going to keep shooting her mouth off, I'm going to ignore her the same way I would a child throwing a temper tantrum.

"You'll be expected at dinner every night as usual, but you'll now be escorted to all of your classes since you can't be trusted to go to them on your own. You will not be allowed to wander the grounds, and you'll have a guard posted outside your bedroom at all times."

She throws her hands up. "Don't you need your men to actually work? Seems like a waste to have them babysitting me all the time."

"It *is* a waste," I growl. "But until you can learn to cooperate–"

"Cooperate?" she says on a laugh, her frustration as palpable as my own. "I don't have to cooperate with you, asshole. I just have to be here. I don't have to bow to your every fucking whim, the way everyone else in the house does. I'm not going to lick your fucking boots."

My temper is really starting to rise. It's not like I thought she was going to go quietly, but does she have to be such a pain in my ass? My eyes meet Bram's over her shoulder, and I see him bite back a laugh.

"I'm merely asking that you uphold your end of the bargain," I say, trying to be civil.

"Your bargain is bullshit," she spits back at me. She has no intention of being civil. Fine. If she wants to go to blows, let's fucking go.

Stepping up to her, I take her throat in my hand. She gasps. I feel her throat contract under my palm, but when she realizes I'm not gripping tight enough to cut off her air, she looks up at me with fury in her eyes. Using just enough pressure, I turn her and press her back to the wall beside the stairs.

I lower my face until we're so close I can taste her breath as she huffs in anger. "I didn't ask your opinion about it. You were told to be where I could keep an eye on you, and you weren't. If this is going to be a problem, I will chain you to your bed, do you understand me?"

I feel the way she sets her jaw in anger, but I also feel that she's trembling, either from anger or fear. Her skin is soft and hot under my palm, and I want to squeeze tighter, the instinct part rage and part arousal. Finally, she opens her mouth, pink with gloss that she most likely reapplied in the car. According to Hugo and Magnus, she was half-dressed when they found her, so I can only assume he didn't leave any behind on her mouth. "Yes."

"Yes, what?"

Her eyes widen, and the shock is like a hit of a very potent drug. I love catching her off her guard. I can tell how much she doesn't want to say it, how much she's fighting it, even though she knows I'll only squeeze harder until she does.

"Yes, sir," she says through gritted teeth.

Fuck. She just made me a little hard.

I nod and step away from her, letting my hand drop and then holding it out to her. "Give me your phone."

She scowls. "What? Why?"

"Because you need phone numbers, people who might need to get a hold of you. I'll give it back after dinner."

Her eyes fall to my hand. "I don't have it."

I wait, and when I don't say anything, she sighs.

"Tyler took it, okay? He smashed it because—" She snaps her mouth shut, but she doesn't need to tell me. I get it just fine. He smashed it because he saw my texts. I was hoping he'd see them, hoping he'd remember that she's mine now, that she belongs to me because he was too stupid to handle his shit properly.

I hold out my hand to Bram. He passes me a burner phone. We always have some lying around. I can't afford to not have a tracker on her. Hugo had to sneak the last one onto her phone while she was sleeping in the bathtub, and it didn't even last forty-eight hours.

I hold the phone out to her.

"What's this?" she asks without taking it.

I wave it in front of her face, satisfied when her mouth tightens into a line. "What, you don't know what a phone looks like? What is it that your punk-ass boyfriend smashed anyway? Besides you?"

She rolls her eyes. "He's not a punk-ass."

I snort. "Look it up in the dictionary. I think his picture's in there."

She rolls her eyes again, this time much more exaggerated. "What are you, a fifth grader?"

The brat clearly didn't learn her lesson.

She reaches up for the phone and my eyes fall on the bruises on her wrist. Not a punk-ass? She has to be joking because only some punk-ass piece of shit motherfucker would lay hands on his own girl.

Snatching the phone out of her reach, I grab her arm right below the bruises. "He do this to you?"

She yanks her hand out of my grip. "It's none of your business." She won't meet my eye. She crosses her arms and scuffs at the ground with her shoes. I can't avoid the curiosity coursing through me. I want to know how the hell this girl got wrapped up with Tyler.

"Go upstairs," I tell her, handing her the phone. "Ronny." I motion over my shoulder for Ronny, the youngest of the bunch, to go upstairs with her. He's still trying to prove himself, so I know he won't bug her, but I also know he won't go soft on her either. Like Bram has.

Like he's reading my mind, Bram steps up beside me, eyes on the two of them as they ascend the stairs. "We could kill him," Bram says. "Make it look like an accident. Cars blow up all the time."

"Too dirty. You know that's not an option. All fucking eyes are on that kid right now and he has a human shield around him." I look sideways at him. "Don't worry. He's going to get what's coming to him."

10

SLOANE

I'm twenty years old, not a child, not some elementary schooler, but here I am, locked away in a bedroom.

I tried to leave at breakfast time, but there was a guard sitting outside my door, and when I took one step into the hallway, he growled at me to get back in and slammed the door shut. So, here I am, a prisoner, even though I was told I wouldn't be.

I walk over to the window and look outside. From where I am, I can see a stretch of field. And off in the distance, the mountains. I wonder who gets the garden view. It's beautiful, really. I've been living in this town for over a year, and I haven't really paid much attention to the sights. Sometimes, Tyler and I will go hiking, but it's less about the actual hiking and more about getting away from his roommate so that he can fuck me. And after I got poison ivy from the knees down, I told him we weren't doing it in the woods anymore.

Behind me, the door opens, and I'm surprised when Xander, who I've been told is the cook here, steps into the room, a tray carried between his two muscular arms. He has the short sleeves of his t-shirt rolled up, like a greaser in a 1960s gang film.

"I hope you like oatmeal," he says, setting the tray down on the desk, sliding my open textbook aside as he does. He looks up at me with a smile like I'm at a Michelin-star restaurant.

"So that's it?" I ask him. "I make one mistake and I'm not even allowed to eat at the table like a civilized human being?"

Xander's shoulders fall, and he looks at the tray and back up at me. "Sorry to say it, missy, but yeah. Everybody here knows, and maybe you'll learn too: you don't fuck with the boss because he won't fuck with you. He's not a three-strikes-and-you're-out kind of guy. He's a one-strike-and-you're-out kind of guy. So I suggest you be on your best behavior, and maybe he'll let you out of here."

He turns for the door.

"He said he wouldn't keep me prisoner."

Xander turns back to me. "Very technically, you aren't. The door's not locked, after all. And if you decided to walk out of here, it would be just fine." His eyes darken, fixed on me. "But don't forget that he and your little lover boy made a deal, and you're here for a reason. If you take off, the boss is going to go sniffing after his money."

"That doesn't mean I should be treated like a dog. I'm not his property."

Xander laughs, a breathy little sound. "Whatever you say, sweet cheeks." He steps closer to me, and I'm surprised when his voice drops, going deep. "If I were you, I'd be grateful. Your little boy toy was pretty clear that you're on the menu." His eyes drop, and I'm made aware that I'm not wearing a bra. I resist the urge to cover myself. I'm not going to give him the satisfaction. "You're lucky we're not those kinds of men." He takes one step closer, and now he's so close to me that I can feel the heat radiating off of him. "At least, I'm pretty sure. So why don't you just simmer down, huh?"

My eyes flicker up to the camera. Part of me wonders if Julian has told all of them to do this, to try to frighten me, to scare me into behaving. I turn my face toward Xander's.

"I'm not afraid of you," I say. A lie. I'm so scared I'm trembling. But I'll never show it to him or any of them. Especially Julian.

Xander smirks. "Of course not. What do you have to be afraid of? You're the boss's. None of us are allowed to touch you. So if I were you, I'd be kissing the ground he walks on." His words, the implication of them, make my stomach turn.

"Over my dead body."

He smiles. "Oh, we'll see, Barbie." And with that, he turns and leaves.

I wait for the door to close, and then I walk slowly and deliberately toward the bathroom. As soon as the door shut behind me, I break, leaning against it as I cry.

I've never expected good things out of life because I've never gotten good things out of life. All I ever wanted was stability. A roof over my head. A chance to make my own way. Someone to love me.

Instead, I've been put in a room like a lapdog during a party, after being sold to someone who's probably a mob boss by someone who I didn't exactly think was my soulmate but who I at least thought cared enough not to sell me to the highest bidder.

I've never asked for anything. But could I not have been given something better than this?

SLOANE

Luckily, I'm escorted to dinner at the same time as always. My guard—Ronny, I heard Xander call him, with bright red hair and freckles—doesn't bother to knock, just pushes open my door as I'm lying in bed reading and motions me out of the room with the tip of his chin. If they want to treat me like a dog, then maybe I should start growling and biting like one.

I sigh and toss my book on the bed before getting up. Following him down the stairs, I get the feeling from the look on his face that he's not any more excited to be escorting me around than I am to be escorted.

At the dinner table, Ronny motions for me to take a seat. Only, instead of my normal spot, he's pointing at the seat that's always empty, right beside Julian. I pause, but Ronny just pulls the chair out, nodding at it before sauntering over to his own. I slowly walk over and sit, finding myself eye-to-eye with Bram on the other side. For the first time, I'm not the last one at the table. We all sit quietly as we wait for the chair at the head to fill.

Julian storms into the room and sits down. He's still wearing his coat and looks kind of silly sitting at a dining room table with it on, the collar obscuring the tattoos that go all the way up his neck.

His eyes find mine, seemingly just as surprised as I am to find me seated beside him. They're full of fire as he looks at me. I wait for him to say something, but he doesn't.

Instead, Xander comes out of the kitchen, setting bowls and plates in front of everyone. Sometimes, we serve ourselves and sometimes Xander does it. It seems to depend on how complicated the meal is. The room is silent as everyone eats. I stare down at the steak in front of me.

My stomach is rumbling. I've been subsisting off of

oatmeal and vegetables since I got here, seeing as how these people don't believe in having a meal where the focal point is not a slab of meat.

I poke at the asparagus on the side.

"You're going to hurt Xander's feelings, you know."

My eyes meet Julian's, and I make a point of holding his gaze as I spear another asparagus head. "If Xander's so worried about it, then maybe he should make me something that isn't cow."

At this, Julian's chewing slows. "You don't eat cow?"

I roll my eyes. "I'm a vegan."

His nostrils flare. "Fucking California girls."

I can feel that everyone is listening to mine and Julian's conversation. They're like children, desperate always to hear what their father has to say. Ears perked, mouths closed.

My eyes find Bram across the table. He's definitely older than Julian, even if it's only by a few years, hair always slicked back, but Claudia has to be twice his age. Why isn't one of them in charge? Bram has a glimmer in his eye, the beginnings of a smile on his mouth.

"Xander!" Julian shouts, not taking his eyes off me. I watch the muscles in his neck move as he swallows his food.

"Yeah, boss?" Xander says, emerging from the kitchen and stopping beside Julian's seat. Xander has a spot at the table too but often doesn't sit down until more than halfway through dinner.

"Get Sloane something to eat that isn't meat."

Xander looks at me, and I can feel him processing what Julian just asked. It's been days, and I've been fed almost nothing but meat and oatmeal. At least oatmeal sticks to the bones.

"What, Her Highness too good to eat what I put in front of her?"

I gasp when Julian fists a hand into Xander's shirt and

yanks him down so they're eye-to-eye. "I didn't ask for your fucking lip," he says. "I said, get her something to eat that isn't meat."

Something like pride bursts in my stomach, and I have to bite back a smile. After the shit that Xander said to me earlier, the things he implied, I rather enjoy watching him get put in his place. The fucker's practically trembling in his boots.

"Yes, sir," he says.

Julian lets him go with a hard shove, and Xander stumbles away. Julian reaches over and uses his steak knife to spear the giant hunk of meat on my plate and transfer it to his own. "Fish?" he asks, not looking at me, focusing on cutting his steak.

"No," I say.

He groans. "Make it easy on me. What do you like? Salads? Chickpeas? Beans? Vegetables?"

I feel off kilter at the way he asks, almost gentle, genuinely curious, like two friends at a party. What exactly is happening here? One minute, he's locking me in my room and the next, he's building me a custom menu. "I eat a lot of corn. Big fan of bread. Cauliflower tacos."

Julian raises an eyebrow in my direction and down the table, someone snickers. "What do you think this is, a five-star resort?"

"You asked."

He chews his meat, holding my gaze. "The fuck you do with a cauliflower taco anyway?"

"You put pumpkin seeds in it. Spicy ones and coconut yogurt."

"Yeah, we'll see," he says. "Xander's a good chef. He may not be that good."

"Tyler always made sure I had vegan food." The words slip out before I can stop them. It's true. Jessica, Tyler's cook, used to make me cauliflower tacos all the time back at the

Prices' house. She'd make me elaborate meals. Desserts. She used to love to feed me, said it was a fun challenge. She would research these intricate vegan meals, surprise me with them.

Tyler had always made a big deal about keeping me fed, but he stopped worrying about whether or not I was taken care of when we got here. Whether or not I had baked potatoes with vegan cheese and fake bacon bits. Whether or not I got cauliflower tacos and Mediterranean chickpea salads.

He was more concerned with the guys and his frat. And I just kind of swallowed it because I get it. This happens to a lot of people. You go to college and you start spending time with new people and you just drift apart. If the situation was different, I could have just dumped him, found someone who was interested in me. But when you're at college on the dime of your boyfriend's dad, you don't have the option of a breakup.

"I see," Julian says, pulling me back to the present. He crosses his arms, leans back in his seat. "Tyler the doting boyfriend, huh?"

I grit my teeth. "You really think you know anything about him?"

"I know enough."

I don't like the way he says it. There's this implication that Julian knows something about Tyler that I don't. Which is impossible, right? The thought settles behind my ribcage that Tyler has some kind of secret life. Something that he's doing that involves Julian. In the back of my mind, I already knew it; have known it since the race. But it's a truth I haven't wanted to look directly at.

I thought we were normal. I thought we were just regular people. College students. Away from home for the first time at an Ivy League school. And instead, Tyler knows *this guy*. This man who I can't prove is a criminal. But I know he is. Because why else would all these people be living in the middle of nowhere in this compound? Why else would they all whisper behind their hands all the time? I just want to know what's going on here. But I can't just ask.

I shake my head. "Whether you want to believe it or not, Tyler is not the bad guy here."

Julian smiles. "Are you implying that the bad guy is me?"

I don't say anything, just clamp my lips together.

He leans across the table toward me. "Oh, princess. You're not telling me anything I don't know. I never claimed to be a good guy. Never claimed to be the hero of this little tale that you've spun in your head. But don't you think for one fucking second that your boyfriend isn't a villain, too." His eyes fall to the bruises on my wrists.

I tuck my hands under the table.

Like he knows I need an out, right at that moment, Xander appears. He sets a bowl on the table in front of me. Spaghetti in red sauce.

"That's all I could do on a moment's notice," Xander tells me. "But give me some time and I'll do some shopping for you."

My stomach growls so loud I'm certain everyone in the room hears it, even if no one acknowledges it. "Thank you." I'm not sure if I'm saying it to Xander or to Julian—feel strange saying it at all—but it doesn't matter. I'm too hungry to be prideful.

I feel like everyone's watching me as I take the first bite, like I'm a judge in a cooking competition. It's almost frustrating how delicious it is. As I swallow, everyone goes back to their own food.

11

SLOANE

I'm brushing my hair, getting ready for bed—because what else are you supposed to do when you're locked inside a bedroom other than go to bed at eight o'clock, as soon as the sun goes down—when my door bangs open, slamming into the wall.

"Fuck," I hiss, my heart pounding. "Do I really not deserve any kind of privacy?" I shout at Julian as he comes into the room. His eyes sweep my body, and I hear what he's thinking even though he doesn't say it. He was hoping to catch me off guard. Maybe in my underwear. Maybe naked. Prick.

"Put your shoes on," he says. "We're going out."

"What? Maybe I could put some clothes on first?" I ask, aware of my small tank top, my short shorts.

He holds my gaze. "I don't have time to wait for that. No one's going to see you. Put your fucking shoes on." He walks out of the room.

Anger slams through me, and I clench my teeth to keep

from screaming. I'm tired of being tugged around, told what to do, threatened.

Bram's words come back to me. *Just do what he tells you. Just make it through this without getting yourself tossed out a window.*

As I put on socks and trainers, I see Ronny in the hallway watching me. His eyes are on my chest, where I'm sure he can see my tits through my shirt.

They already have cameras everywhere. They really need someone standing outside my room, too? They act like I'm Captain America or something, and I'm going to barge through doors and fight groups of muscled men to escape. I'm not getting out of here unless someone lets me go.

Ronny ushers me downstairs and out onto the U-shaped driveway. I'm surprised when he stops. I stop, too, but he just motions for me to keep going. To keep walking toward the Beast, parked at the bottom of the steps. I take a deep breath, pulse kicking up a rhythm.

I know I said I wasn't scared of him. And I wasn't. At least, not when we were in the compound. Not when there were other people around. But now he's waiting for me in his car. Where is he going to take me? What is he going to do? Did I make him so angry that he's going to shoot me and bury my body somewhere?

I look around, hoping maybe I missed something. Maybe Claudia's coming, too. Or Bram. But I see no one.

The driver's side window rolls down slowly. "Get in the car," Julian says calmly.

Well, at least if I die, I'll die in a cool car.

When I get inside and buckle my seatbelt, Julian says, "You certainly know how to talk the talk. Acting all big and scary. But you're fucking terrified. You're like a little chihuahua, trembling in your skin."

I don't deny it. It's useless at this point. Someone like Julian Shaw doesn't become who he is because people back down to him. Or because he doesn't know how terrifying he is.

People like him, they curate this kind of personality. They know it scares people, and they prey on them.

My eyes slide over to him as he puts the car in drive. A predator. That's exactly what he is.

"I was thinking about what you said," he tells me as we roll down the gravel lane, the private road that leads to the compound.

"About what?" I ask.

"About your perfect little angel boyfriend."

I sigh. "I never said he was a perfect little angel."

"No, you didn't," he says. "And that's because, despite what my men seem to think, you're not a fucking idiot."

I feel like I should be flattered. I think that's the closest he's ever going to come to complimenting me. Even though I don't know if not-a-fucking-idiot is really what I've always hoped to be.

"The thing is..." He shifts, then shifts again.

He's going well over the speed limit through the dark, empty streets, towering trees on both sides. And I try to cool my blood a little. Men like him don't get to be reckless without knowing what they're doing. I have to trust that he's not going to careen us off the road.

"...now that I know you're not a fucking idiot, what I don't understand is what you actually are."

"What?"

He shifts again and I'm caught, watching his hand. His long, slender fingers. Smooth skin. A tattoo on the back of his hand, two lines of script that it's too dark for me to read, the shape of something on his pinkie, two thin lines around his middle finger. I can't help but wonder if he's covered in them. Even though I would rather put a tire iron through my eyeball than ask him.

"If you're not stupid..." He glances over at me. "...and you're not a coward, then what the fuck are you doing with that human shit?"

All my anger comes careening back. "You don't get to call him that."

"Oh, don't I?" he says, sarcastically. "Haven't I earned the right?"

"You think you've earned the right to call him human shit? Look at you."

He laughs. "Yeah, look at me. Maybe I am human shit, but I don't walk around pretending that I'm not. I don't wait until the door closes and then put bruises on my girl."

"You don't fucking know anything about it."

"And I never will," he shouts.

I flinch.

"I never will know anything about it. You want to know why?" He doesn't wait for me to answer. "Because despite what both of you want to believe, you are my property now. And that twat doesn't put his hands on my property anymore."

I glare over at him, the implication of his words settling in. "You can't keep me away from him. That was the agreement. I get to go to school. I get to see him."

"That wasn't part of the agreement. I was just being nice," he hisses. "But I'm done being nice. If he wanted to keep touching all over his girl, he shouldn't have sold her to me."

I hate the way he says it, like I'm some object in the next room. "That's not what happened. Tyler didn't sell me. It was a bet. So, what are you going to do?" I ask him. "You're going to forbid him from touching me? Or what? You'll kill him?"

He snorts. "Give it a rest. Your boyfriend can go a little

while without your pussy." The word sounds so disgusting coming from his mouth.

I grimace when he says it.

"Though I'm sure it will be quite the sacrifice. Should have fucking thought about that before."

It never occurred to me that he might try to keep me from Tyler. How angry will that make Tyler? If he has to be celibate for a whole month, will he start shit with Julian and wreck the plan? Will he try to get me back?

"I don't think it's going to be a problem though," Julian says.

"Is that so?" I ask, embarrassed when my words crack. I keep my eyes focused out the windshield, watching the road cycle by in the dark.

"Nah. Not after what I'm going to show you."

Even as he says it, my mind becomes aware of the scenery, of the fact that I recognize where we are. The street, the houses, the trees and the cars. "What the hell are we doing here?" I ask Julian.

He pulls up against a curb down the street from Tyler's frat house without a word. It looms up ahead in the shadows. What is he planning on doing to Tyler? Maybe he's going to kill him and not me. Maybe he's going to take his gun in there and end this whole thing right now.

"What, tired of me already? You returning me to the store?" I pray he can't hear the panic I'm trying to mask.

Julian opens his door. "Would you get over yourself, Blondie? Come on. Get out of the fucking car."

I don't want to get out. If I stay in here, nothing bad happens. I know that whatever is coming won't be good. Nevertheless, Julian has climbed out and is waiting for me, back to the car, broad shoulders in a black coat. I get out of the car and walk over to him, shivering in my shorts. He gestures for me to lead the way.

"What?" I demand. "I don't even know what we're doing here."

"But you know the way to your boyfriend's house, yes?"

I sigh loudly. "Yes."

"Then after you, ma'am."

I've walked this path a million times. There are bushes on either side of the walkway, the long walk that leads up to the rather ominous house. It's never looked so foreboding before. Once I've gotten close enough to approach the door, haloed in the glow of the porch light, Julian stops me with a hand at my waist. The touch startles me. It's too...familiar.

"What are you—" I start to say.

He cuts me off with a hand over my mouth and drags me toward the side of the house. It's ironic that a moment ago, I didn't want to be here at all. And now, I'm fighting him as he drags me away, his arm a bar across my stomach.

"Would you stop?" he hisses in my ear, lifting me off my feet and pulling me behind a tree. He removes his hands and I spin on him.

"What are you doing?" My defenses are up. I'm vulnerable. It's dark, the streets are empty, and I'm half-dressed. Did he bring me out here to attack me within Tyler's reach and then rub it in his face?

"Would you just fucking pay attention?" he says between clenched teeth. "Stop being such a brat."

"Pay attention to what?"

He grips my face with the tips of his cold fingers and lowers his voice to a growl. "You were trying to defend him earlier. You said he was a good man. Isn't that what you said?"

I clamp my lips together, not giving him the satisfaction. His fingers tighten on my jaw when I refuse to speak.

"I have a feeling you don't know what he gets up to when you're not around."

My stomach turns. What does he mean by that?

His mouth curves up on one side. "I've had someone watching him since I won you, princess. Standing right here every night. And every single night, Tyler's spent his time doing the exact same thing."

"What are you talking about?" My voice has lost its anger. Now it's just hesitation, fear, sad anticipation.

Using his grip on my jaw, he turns my face toward the house. I'm looking right into the living room through the big side window.

At Tyler and two women. They're naked, half draped over the couch, right there where anyone could see. He kisses one of them while the other is on her knees, his dick in her mouth. On instinct, I start to turn my face away.

"No. I want you to watch. Watch what your knight in shining armor does while he thinks I'm doing whatever I want to you." He takes me by the shoulders and turns me back toward the window.

At first, all I feel is numb. Scraped raw. Exhausted like a rock on a cliffside rubbed smooth by wave after wave. I don't even know if I'm really surprised. I am, but at the same time, I'm not. Not really. Deep in the pit of me, I expected this.

And then all the numb is washed away by anger.

Anger that Julian knew exactly what he would find here. Anger knowing that every night, someone has been watching this happen and been reporting back to Julian. Anger because while I was sitting there at Julian's dining room table, he knew. Maybe they all knew. The butt of the joke, as always.

Why am I even here? In New Hampshire, in Tyler's life. Why does Tyler bother being with me? I've asked myself that question so many times when things weren't good, asked myself long before they got bad. Why doesn't he just break it off?

Now that I'm standing here, watching him, the answer feels obvious. Tyler is with me because of his father. Because someday, Tyler is going to want to take over his father's empire, and he knows that his father won't let him do that unless he has a good woman on his arm. Someone to keep him in line. Someone who would be a good wife. A quiet wife. An obedient wife.

While I'm still trying to breathe, still trying to sort through a range of emotions as wide as a canyon, the three of them reposition. The girl he was kissing bends over the arm of the couch and Tyler stands behind her, pushing in.

My skin burns at the reminder that Julian is witnessing this, too. That he's forever burned into this awful, sickening moment with me. I feel so fucking humiliated. I can't watch anymore.

"Okay," I say, choked. "You proved your point. Can we go?"

I start to turn, but he grabs my hips. Holds me in place, fingers digging in.

"No," he snaps. "I want you to understand. I want you to *really* understand, Sloane."

I thought I hated all of the little names he and his men call me, but it turns out I hate this even more. The way he says my name, so condescendingly, like he's better than me.

"We're going to sit here and we're going to watch. Because this is it. This is the man—the life—that you insist on defending."

Tyler pumps into the girl, and I'm shocked when the other girl lays down between their legs, her face just below where Tyler is plunging deep. The girl who's being fucked lets her mouth drop open, and I imagine that the girl between her legs is licking her.

"You see, this is the problem," Julian says in my ear. He's standing too close to me now, his front pressed to my back, his hands still clutching my hips. His breath is hot against my neck.

I want to move away, but I feel paralyzed. Watching what's going on through the window. Feeling him against me.

"This is why we're all here," he goes on. "Because you and your boyfriend, you get to look away too easily. You got bad shit happening right in front of you, and instead of looking at it, you look away. But you see, princess, I need you to fucking *look* at it. I need you to fucking understand—for once in your pathetic life—that this is what you have to look forward to. This is what you get, being on the arm of this colossal fucking prick. And it only gets worse from here."

His hands shift, pressing against my stomach. I hold my breath. He's fucking with my head, confusing me. I'm nauseated at the display in front of me and furious that his hands feel good. I want him dead; I don't want him to stop. Maybe he thinks if Tyler hurts me bad enough, I'll turn to him. That I'll let him fuck me to get back at Tyler. Well, he's fucking wrong.

"Imagine yourself five years down the line. Married to a man who goes off on business trips regularly, spending your money on whores. A couple of rug rats come along and you get to raise them all by yourself because he doesn't give a fuck. Before you know it, you're middle-aged and no one wants you. Not even your husband. Not your kids. Not anybody. And all you have left is the money. The money he sold you out for. It's not going to keep you warm in the winter."

Like they know that it would be the grand finale of Julian's little speech, Tyler chooses that moment to pull out of the girl he's fucking, point his cock down, and come on the face of the other girl.

I close my eyes, breath stuttering. But it doesn't matter. Julian knows it doesn't. Irreparable damage has been done.

"When you sit at my table with my men," Julian says, low

voice carving itself into my eardrums, leaving scars, "and you tell them that Tyler doesn't deserve all the shit that's coming to him, I want you to remember this moment. Whatever we thought you were to him, we were all wrong. You're just the woman who sits at home and waits on him and apologizes for his bad behavior while he gets his dick sucked."

He thinks he knows what he's doing to me, but he doesn't know that as soon as I get what I need, as soon as I get my money, I'm out anyway. Does it matter then if he fucks every girl in the northern hemisphere? A thought lingers, as potent as Julian's grazing fingertips: what if Tyler doesn't let me leave?

I watch the lights go out in the living room, the show coming to an end. But we're still here, back to front, crumbling like a castle that's been cannonballed. There's nothing left in me. Just a void, just white knuckles, just a beast fighting for survival.

Julian is wrong. He thinks he understands me but he doesn't know how hard I'll fight not to go back to my life of hunger and my mother's predatory clients, and a fictitious future that I can't make real. Tyler can't break me; I've been broken my whole life. Julian thinks this proof will be enough to shatter me. All he's done is harden me further, turning me to rock and steel and bone.

"I'd like you to take me home, please."

He hums in the back of his throat, taking his hands off of me. "Home, huh?"

I ignore him and walk back to the car. As we pass through the night, I sit silent. A realization begins to sweep over me like a quiet summer breeze. I'm not getting out of this. Tyler's not coming for me. Wouldn't even if he could. No one's going to save me. And there's no end in sight. I'm here and I'm at the mercy of this monster. And there's nothing anybody can do about it.

$$12$$

SLOANE

"Excited for school today, princess?"

I fight not to flinch at the sound of Julian's voice, the deep tone of it that my brain now associates with a discomfort in my diaphragm. Julian speaks, and I suffocate.

He steps up next to me in the driveway under the still rising sun. I meet his eye, even though it's painful to. I know he's feeling me out, trying to gauge my mood after last night. My mood is fucking *murderous*.

"Is it necessary for you to be such an asshole?"

He ignores my very rhetorical question. "Ronny's going to escort you to your classes today."

At this, I finally turn to look at him. "What do you mean, *escort me?*"

He puts his hands in his pockets. He's in all black, of course, and I'm fairly certain his dress pants and button-up are tailored. It's seven in the morning and the man looks dressed for Sunday service. Doesn't anyone in this house believe in loungewear? "I mean that you clearly have a problem doing what you're told. If you can't be where you're supposed to be when you're supposed to be there, then you'll have someone babysitting you at all times."

"Why Ronny?" Like I've summoned him, Ronny walks out the front door, Hugo and Magnus on his heels. They all go straight for the car.

He tips his chin up, looking down his nose at me. "He's a baby. He can pass for a college student. I hear those Dartmouth kids are smart. They're going to get antsy if they see Magnus lurking through the halls."

I keep my eyes on the trio getting in the Cadillac. "I'm surprised you're even letting me go."

"Oh, trust me. If I had my way, you wouldn't be. But I'm a man of my word, and I wouldn't want to be responsible for turning you into a flunky."

"Let me guess, you expect me to be grateful?"

He moves in the corner of my eye. I turn just in time to see him reach out and take a strand of my hair between his fingers. I don't jerk away, even though I want to. He rubs it like he's trying to make out the texture of it and then lets it fall. I can feel my body trembling, and I don't even know anymore if it's fear or anger or just the sheer anxiety of everything in my life turning upside down.

"I expect you to be smart," he says, dark eyes meeting mine.

"What do you want from me, Julian?" I can hear the surrender in my own voice. I'm exhausted playing these games, and after what he showed me last night, I'm also emotionally drained, like an empty bottle someone keeps squeezing.

One side of his mouth lifts in a devious smirk. "I just want you to *see*, princess."

See what? I want to ask him, but I know there's no use.

Everything that comes out of his mouth is cryptic, and for all I know, it might all be lies.

Except he wasn't lying last night. And he wasn't being cryptic. He showed me the truth, and there was no way for him to lie about it. It was right there in front of me. It was right there in front of anyone who cared to look.

"Ready?" Ronny asks, sticking his head out the back window. At the same time, Hugo and Magnus turn to look at us from where they're standing by the hood of the car, smoking.

"Why do they go everywhere together like the twins from *The Shining?*"

The smile is back, a ghost of a thing that isn't really there. "They work best together. Ever heard of friends, Sloane?"

I sling my backpack up on my shoulder and scowl at him. "I don't believe for one second that you have friends, Julian. Only henchmen. If you have to buy your friends, they're not your friends at all."

He puts his hands in his pockets and looks out at the driveway, the muscle under her jaw tensing. "Tell it to your boyfriend."

"You're quiet today," Tyler says, copying down the notes from the board. My eyes slide over to him, watching his hands move. I think about him jerking off into that girl's mouth, and bile rises in my throat.

"We're in class," I tell him, my teeth clenched tight. What does he expect me to do, carry on a conversation with him in the middle of the lecture?

"So you just get to ignore me? You didn't even kiss me

when I came in." I'm surprised by how much levity there is in his tone. This whole thing is a big joke to him. Everything's coming up Tyler on his side of the fence.

I grit my teeth so hard, I'm afraid I'll crack one. "You were ten minutes late."

He scoots his chair closer to mine and puts his arm around me, gripping my hip. "So? Give me a kiss."

I turn to look at him, aware of all the students around us, people who actually care about getting an education. He has to be kidding. He wants to, what, make out in the middle of class? Apparently, he's very much into exhibitionism.

He's leaning toward me now, like he's going to plant one on me, and I have to fight not to gag. It hasn't even been twelve hours since he had his mouth on some random girl, since he had his cock in one of them.

"Stop it," I hiss at him, shoving my elbow into his side. Maybe a month ago, this would have been cute; now, it's revolting.

He grunts, not a pleasant sound, and takes my jaw in his rough fingers and turns his face toward mine, all the humor gone from his voice. "I said, kiss me," he grunts, his voice dangerous, and then he waits. He's going to make me come to him. I think about Julian saying Tyler should have to live without touching me since he gave me away. I wish it were true now. But apparently, we've stepped into a realm where Julian's law doesn't apply. Tyler is touching me, and there's only one way to make him stop.

I lean into him and kiss him, making it long and wet so that he won't force me to do it again.

When we part, my eyes instinctively go to the row behind us, where a girl is watching us with wide eyes. I turn away from her quick and try to focus on the rest of the lecture. My chest burns. I feel cemented in place. This is my life now: from one cage to another and back again.

"Got anything for me?" Tyler asks when class is almost over.

Right. It's been a week. He wants information. Evidence. Proof.

"No." I keep my voice low. "After what we did last week, he grounded me. I'm not allowed to leave my room."

His blonde eyebrows furrow. "What the hell are you talking about? I thought you said you had free rein of the place."

Our professor is outlining materials for the midterm on the board, and I wish Tyler would just shut the hell up. "I told you he has cameras everywhere and now there's someone posted outside my room twenty-four-seven. When I didn't show up when I was supposed to, he decided I needed to be locked in my room twenty-four hours a day. I'm just lucky some of the other guys take pity on me and play games with me."

"*What*? What kinds of games?"

"Oh, for God's sake," I snap at him, trying to stay quiet. "Poker. Rummy. Chess. They're not passing me around like a blow-up doll."

"I didn't think—"

"Yes, you did, Tyler." I jerk my head toward him so fast it startles him. "Did you think I'd end up fucking someone? That I can't control myself?" *Like you,* I want to say. How many women has he had? How many times has he fucked someone without even a thought of me?

His eyes roam over my face. He doesn't look angry anymore, just contemplative, like he doesn't recognize me. "He said no one would touch you. I trust him to keep his word."

"Why? You don't even know him. How can you trust him?"

He shrugs. "Guys like him, their shit is built on honor."

"You sound like an idiot." As if he knows anything about honor, or about Julian, for that matter.

Our professor dismisses us, and everyone around us stands, gathering their stuff. I reach for my own bag, but Tyler stops me, hand wrapped around my arm so tight I wince.

He yanks me toward him, until my face is close to his. "Show me some god damn respect, Sloane."

"You first, Tyler." Maybe I can't break up with him, and maybe I can't call him out for cheating—not until this is all over—but I don't have to let him talk to me like this.

Over his shoulder, I spot Ronny, standing in the hallway as people file out around him. I never thought I would be happy to see anyone from the house of horrors, but if it'll get me away from Tyler right now, I would leave with Satan himself.

"I have to go. Let go of me." I tug at where he's still holding on to my arm.

"You're not going anywhere until you tell me what I need to know. You've been in that fucking house for a week. I know you've heard things." His hand digs in harder until a sound travels up my throat. "You owe me information."

When Ronny steps into the room, dark eyes focused on Tyler's hand, something in me breaks. It's like someone sticking a pin into a balloon. I look into Tyler's eyes and I remember why I'm doing this. Tyler is all I have. His money and his dad and this school.

So before Ronny can get to us, I take a deep breath and say, "I'm still working on it," in as agreeable a voice as I can manage. "Give me time."

His eyes narrow. He's still on the defensive, so I set my hand over his, the one clutching my arm, and stroke my thumb back and forth. I just need to diffuse, even if it makes me physically ill.

Ronny waits just inside the door, watching us. Tyler catches sight of him, and his hand finally drops. "Who the hell is that?"

I sigh. "That's Ronny. He's my nanny."

Tyler snorts and grabs his stuff before heading down the stairs of the lecture hall toward the exit. Ronny can't be much older than either of us. He still has acne and holes in his jeans, even if they are the required black.

"Better keep his hands to himself," Tyler mutters, loud enough for me to hear, before slamming his shoulder into Ronny's as he goes by.

To his credit, Ronny does nothing. Just watches Tyler go with a blank expression.

JULIAN

"*Shit.* Fuck. I don't have time for this shit."

I toss my phone into Bram's lap, and he grunts. I might have gotten him right in the dick. His body bucks and he smacks his head on the underside of the Rolls Royce Ghost he's under.

"Jesus Christ, Julian," he says, reaching for the phone. "What the fuck is it?"

"It's Barbara. She's got cold feet. I told you we shouldn't have kept the contract when her old man croaked."

He slides out from under the car. He has a streak of grease across his face, right under where his hair flops over his forehead. "She inherited his fortune. You want to lose out on three hundred grand just because you don't want to deal with someone's widow?"

I sigh and drop down to sit on a tire beside him. "Don't make this about the fact that she's a woman. That's not what this is. You know better than anyone that our clients are selected carefully. We need time to construct our house of cards. And now we're going to sell this car to someone who doesn't even know what's under the hood?"

He loops his arms over his knees. "Maybe she does know. Men tell their women things, you know."

I shake my head, thinking of the way her voice trembled over the phone. "Nah. He didn't tell her. It's obvious." I run a hand down my face, almost suffocating myself with the grease fumes on my hands. It probably looks like I have war paint on now.

Bram shrugs with his hands. "Why not cancel the deal, Julian? It's just money. You'll get another buyer. If you don't want to put this woman in harm's way—"

"I don't give a fuck if she's in harm's way," I shoot back. He watches me. I hate it when he pulls that Superman x-ray vision shit. I look away from him, grab a rag off the ground and rub at my hands, though I'm fairly certain I'm just making them dirtier. "It's fine. I'll have one of the guys do it. I was only meeting with him because he knew Dad. She's a nobody. I'll send—" My brain comes to a halt, an idea sparking. My eyes meet Bram's. "Why don't we send the girl?"

His brow furrows. "Who, Sloane?"

I shrug. "She's starting to doubt her prick of a boyfriend. If we offer her a little freedom, maybe we can get her on our side."

"Do we want her on our side?" He asks this like he wasn't in her room half the weekend playing card games with her. He thinks I don't know.

I nod slowly. "She could be our best asset. He doesn't care

enough for us to be able to use her to barter with, but after what she saw last night, maybe I can get her to work for me."

He laughs.

"What?"

He sets his head back against the car, Adam's apple like a spike. "She hates you. She's not going to work for you. She'd sooner drop dead."

I smile. I can't help it. I find her hate amusing. I love getting under her skin. "I'll make her think it's her idea."

He raises an eyebrow at me and lowers himself back down to the garage floor as the guys come in from lunch. We have three cars going out this week, and we're on a time crunch.

"Just keep me out of the line of fire, boss."

13

"You're needed downstairs," Ronny tells me when I open my door.

It's strange the way he says it, so formal, so professional, like I'm the President of the United States or something. His eyes dip down and then spring back up to my face. I want to sigh. Is he going to do this every time I'm in front of him in my pajamas? The ogling is getting pretty old.

"Why?"

He doesn't answer my question, just backs up to let me out of the room.

I grab my sweatshirt off the bed and throw it on. It's one thing to be practically bare-breasted on the security cameras—they're far enough away that whoever's watching probably can't see anything substantial—but it's something else entirely to be downstairs in the bright lights in front of God knows who with full-on diamond cutters.

I follow him downstairs and past the dining room. Since I've been grounded, I haven't had a chance to roam the grounds again. I mostly just see my room and the dining room. Sometimes Ronny lets me sit on the porch for a little bit because I told him if I didn't get some sunlight, I was going to fall into a depression, which wasn't even a lie.

So I don't know what's beyond the dining room—have never been back here—until we're passing through to a back wing of the house. Another hallway stretches out before me lined with doors, this one all wood paneling, warm from the finish and the lighting, a red rug rolled out on the floor. Down at the end of the hall, a door stands open, and a few of the guys sit around a circular table, drinking and watching something on a flatscreen on the wall.

One of them looks up and sees me—Frankie—and then kicks the door shut.

"Sir, she's here," Ronny says into one of the rooms, and guides me into an open door to my left.

Once inside, I hesitate. This house feels like Mary Poppins' magic bag. I knew it was huge, but every time I walk into a room, thinking it has to be a small one because there can't be *that* much floor space, it's actually ten times bigger than I anticipated.

It's an office. And from the way Julian is sitting reclined in a chair with his feet up on the desk, I'm going to assume it's *his* office. He motions for me to take the seat across from him. I glance around as I do, taking in all the model cars and books and expensive-looking trinkets on the shelves that line the walls.

"Drink?" He nods toward a bar that's built into the bookcase beside the desk, dark wood and filled with liquor bottles.

"Thought you said you were on the up-and-up." When he sends me a confused look, I say, "Can't be going around offering alcohol to minors."

One corner of his mouth tips up. I look away.

"I need you to do a job for me."

My eyes shoot back to him. "What do you mean, you need me to do a job for you?"

He sighs and leans back in his chair, lacing his fingers together on his chest. I didn't notice until now, now that he's tipped back in this position, now that I'm examining him in the light without averting my gaze, that he has a tattoo that spans across the length of his neck. From here, it looks like an angel.

"We have this customer. She's hesitant about pulling the trigger on a sale. But we can't afford to lose the money. It's already spoken for. I think she's a bit antsy because she doesn't like men." His dark eyes are steady on mine. "And who can blame her, right? So I figure sending a woman in to talk to her might get her to ease up a little bit."

I raise an eyebrow at him. "Spending money you don't have? Sounds like you need an accountant."

He doesn't say anything, just watches me.

He's serious. For all his sarcasm and his biting wit, he's not kidding this time. He really does want to send me in to convince some woman to do business with him. I try to keep my face blank. I don't want to give away just how shocked I am. He doesn't deserve my surprise, not when he's asking me for a favor. Is that what this is? If I do it, does he owe me one? Or is this what I do in exchange for not ending up with my head on a spike?

"What do you want from her?"

He shrugs. "Money. The money she owes me, to be exact. She's under contract, and I don't do well when people try to back out of arrangements. She's already been hemming and hawing long enough. The payment date has come and gone, and I've been patient, but my patience is running out."

I have so many questions, but I know I can't ask any of them. I can't ask him what she's so afraid of or how she entered into this agreement to begin with.

"Why can't you have Claudia do it?"

"Claudia and I have some business to take care of. We need you."

We need you. How can this person who has an entire town in the palm of his hand need me? How can this person who commands all these people, who takes what he wants, who goes around trading women and money in car races need me?

Taking hold of myself, I lean back in my leather chair and cross my arms. I try to make myself seem as solid as he is, but I don't think it's working. "You know, you would think you would hire some women, keep them around for this sort of thing. You might discover they actually have value."

He doesn't hesitate. "Women are a liability."

"How kind."

"You don't understand."

"You're right. I don't." Except that I think I understand some of it. My brain is processing everything he's telling me, going through the facts that I know just from the few days I've been here. Tyler's right. Something doesn't add up. "What car are you selling her?"

"1970 Chevelle SS 454 LS6."

I nod. "That's a nice car. If this woman backs out, someone else would surely snatch it up. Why are you so invested in this sale?"

He doesn't answer. His eyes are steady, not giving anything away. He knows I'm onto him.

"I know more about these things than you think I do."

I see the tic in his jaw, the way his skin pulls taut. "We're not bringing you here to ask questions. We just need you to talk to this woman. Got it?"

"That's certainly no way to ask someone you hardly know and are currently holding captive to do a favor for you."

"It's not a favor."

There it is. He may have asked me here under the guise of giving me a choice, but I know I don't have one.

"I want a lock on my door."

"A lock." Monotone. Not a question.

"I'm a human being. I deserve privacy. I'll do the job, but I want a lock."

There's a long stretch of silence. We stare. Neither of us is going to back down.

Until, finally... "Okay."

"Okay?" I can't let my disbelief show. I don't want him to know that I never thought my negotiation tactic would actually work.

Any amusement on his face is gone. "Go get dressed."

JULIAN

It takes the woman twenty minutes to get changed, and when she comes downstairs, she looks like she's getting ready to go to the senior prom. Her hair's all done up, half her head braided, and she's wearing a violet summer dress and six-inch heels. She looks like someone ate a bunch of Halloween candy and threw up on her.

Jesus Christ, maybe Bram had a point. Maybe we *don't* want her on our side. But my options are not good if I want to move this car *and* fuck with Tyler.

But asking the fairy princess to go in and talk to Barbara Sanders might be a huge mistake. I look past her to Bram. He always fucking looks like he's trying to hold back his glee on his kid's wedding day when he looks at her, and I can't tell if it's because he genuinely likes her or because he loves to see me in pain.

"You can't wear that."

The fairy princess scowls, hitching her little black purse higher on her shoulder and glancing down at her dress. "These are my clothes."

"Well, you're not going to a sorority mixer, so we'll find you something else."

I snap in Hugo's direction, and he takes off toward my office. Sloane and I watch each other silently while we wait for him to return. She had to know this wasn't an option. She's just trying to fuck with me because she's mad I'm forcing her into this.

And technically, I *didn't* force her. If she had said no, I probably would have let her off the hook. It's not her fault we got into this mess with Barbara. But I liked making her think she didn't have a choice, and I'm not sorry about it. Plus, she's getting a damn lock out of the deal.

She's doing a pretty good job of holding her own, even if she's not intimidating me the way I'm sure she's trying to. She lifts her chin a little higher, but I see the sheen of sweat that's starting to shine on her cheeks and her long neck. She's wearing purple eyeliner, for God's sake. It shimmers every time she blinks at me.

Hugo comes stomping back and shoves something into Sloane's arms so forcefully that it almost causes her to stumble. I grit my teeth and glare at him. His eyes go wide and he shrugs.

"I'll be back," Sloane says, rushing back upstairs with the clothes in her hand.

When she comes back down a second later, she's wearing a navy-blue hoodie and a pair of sweatpants, and when I think she'll complain, she doesn't. She just sticks her hands in the big pocket on the front of the sweater and says, "Lead on."

Outside, I head away from the driveway, toward the Beast, ripping the door open and hesitating. I'm putting too much trust in her hands. I know I am. She doesn't know what Barbara's husband was buying off of us, but she still knows something's up. And on top of that, she hates me. She could go into that meeting and tell Barbara not to do business with me, that I'm a bad man, that she should call the cops.

My heart pounds. People have tried to take me down before. Hell, Tyler has been trying to take me down since the moment he rolled into town. And somehow, it's this five foot, hundred-pound Playboy Bunny I'm most afraid of.

I look over at where the guys are loading her up into the car. Her eyes swipe over to mine, and she stops, her own car door wide open. *Please, God, don't let this tiny woman be the end of us all.*

SLOANE

We drive so far out of town that I'm not even sure where we are by the time the car pulls into the parking lot of an all-night diner off I-91. I'm not even positive we're still in New Hampshire.

Hugo pulls the car around to the side of the building, and Frankie, who, according to Julian, is the one actually running this particular operation, turns around in the seat. His eyes are bloodshot, and he doesn't look overly excited that I'm here. Well, that's fine. I'm not overly excited that I'm here either, so he can suck it.

"You think you can handle this, Blondie? You remember everything Bossman told you?"

I roll my eyes. "Yes, I remember everything because I happen to have an IQ higher than a hamster, if you can believe it."

He just blinks at me. Maybe *he* doesn't have an IQ higher than a hamster. My phone beeps. The phone that Julian gave me. I look down at the screen and see that Hugo has just sent me a text with a photo attached. I'm looking at a middle-aged woman with short blond hair and wrinkles around her eyes. It's...a mugshot photo.

I'm staring so intently that when Frankie speaks again, his rough voice startles me. "Go in, find her, order some eggs, put her fears to bed."

I stare down at the mugshot. Put her fears to bed. *Her* fears. What are they, and do they involve future prison sentences? Can I do this when I don't know what the hell is going on behind the curtain?

"What are you waiting for?"

I take a deep breath and tuck my phone into my sweater pocket. "Nothing. I'll be back." I throw open the door and get out before leaning back in. "And I don't eat eggs." I slam the door shut.

It doesn't escape me that these men are putting a lot of faith in me. They put a mic on me, but it only goes one way, so no one will be able to stop me to make sure I don't ruin this sale *and* their business. Julian is trusting me to go in and say what needs to be said.

Or...what if there are cameras or cops or something in there and I'm being sent in as bait or a scapegoat?

My steps falter, and I think about turning around and running. What am I even doing? Why am I letting him do this to me? Why am I letting *them* do this to me?

Because I don't have a choice. It's either this or California, in a dilapidated trailer with my mother, men coming and going and sometimes overstaying their welcome, and a job at the burger joint around the corner, if I'm lucky.

Inside the diner, I smile at the man behind the register, who looks up long enough to greet me and then goes back to his work. My eyes scan the place, and I spot her. She's sitting in a booth against the front window. I feel like I'm in some kind of bank heist movie, taking a seat across from her and glancing around to make sure no one is paying attention to us.

A crease forms between her eyebrows. "Who are you?" she asks, her voice scratchy from years of smoking.

I don't tell her my name. I may not know how this whole thing works, but I know that I don't want my name associated with her or Julian, even if this does turn out to be completely legal, which I highly doubt.

"I'm a friend of Frankie's."

She's clearly hesitant, like she's about to tell me she doesn't know who Frankie is. Maybe I wasn't supposed to say his name. Nobody *told* me not to say his name.

Barbara's face stays skeptical as she says, "Why did he send you?"

I sit up straight and smile. "Because I'm the best they have."

She raises an eyebrow at me, some of the tension seeping out of her features. "Is that so?" Her eyes scan over my face. "How old are you?"

"Twenty."

She glances over my shoulder and then turns to look behind her. When she's facing me again, her brow is furrowed deeper. "Is this a joke?"

My heart starts to pound in my ears, and a voice niggles at me. *You can't do this.* Yes, I can, goddammit.

"Nope! Listen, Barbara. I'll tell you the truth. The guys thought you might be a little nervous about this whole car-buying business—I get it, it's a big commitment—so they wanted me to come talk to you to let you know that you're in good hands."

She laughs. "Good hands? Have you seen those men? They look like they were sent from the devil himself. The one I was supposed to meet today, the one my husband has been talking to, Julian?" She shudders.

I snort. "You don't have to tell me. I don't think he's all that scary, but he walks around snarling like a dog." I roll my eyes. "Men, am I right?"

Her demeanor changes slowly. Her posture loses its tension and her expression softens. "I'm not scared, you know. I've dealt with men like Julian Shaw my whole life. I just..."

Surprisingly, her eyes start to glisten. She scrubs at her face and looks away from me. When she turns back, her chin is trembling and her face is flushed. "This was my husband's thing. He worked with Shaw Senior long ago, and it was his dream to own a Chevelle. He was finally doing it. And now... well, now he won't even be here to drive it." She sobs, and I reach for the napkin holder against the window. I hold one out to her and she takes it. She blows her nose and sighs. "How embarrassing."

"It's not embarrassing."

She finally takes a steady breath and leans across the table toward me. "I know these men might be shady and that my husband might have been neck-deep in something I don't even want to know about but...do you think I should get the car?"

I also think the men are shady, but I feel for Barbara. I know what I would do in her shoes. I smile. "Yeah, I do. Live a little." I don't know if this car will get her in any trouble, and I don't know what the chances are of her going back to prison. But I know what's like to wish you could keep a piece of someone who's gone.

She laughs. "You're young and optimistic. Life is a cruel thing. It'll come for you eventually."

I fight not to let my smile fall. If only she knew. "So what do you think?"

She nods.

"Great!" I take the slip of paper that Julian gave me and slide it across the table to her under my palm. "Someone will meet you there on the date the two of you arranged. I'm supposed to bring back half the payment, to cover the shopping costs." I get a thrill when I say it. I sound like I know what I'm talking about. For just a moment, I don't feel like someone's puppet.

She nods and plants her elbow on the table, trying to look casual as she slides me a manilla envelope that's thick and misshapen, obviously full of cash. I have to wonder if Julian has paid off the staff at this place because there's no way this is going down under everyone's noses and without them noticing.

I push out of the booth, but before I leave, I say, "I hope you feel better, Barbara. I'm sorry about your husband."

She gives me a watery smile.

14

JULIAN

Claudia and I agree to meet at the cemetery. I can already tell by the time I get to her that she's been drinking. I wouldn't be surprised if she started as soon as she woke up this morning. She has an odd tilt to her as she waits just outside the wrought-iron gate, curved wickedly in the fading sunlight behind her.

"Were you down at Rowdy's?" I ask her, taking her by the elbow and turning her toward the gates.

She nods. "He's raised his prices again. And the place was empty. I don't think business is good."

"I'll reach out." I look down at her. On a normal day, Claudia is a force to be reckoned with. The guys in the house are almost as afraid of her as they are of me. But here, in this awful place, she looks so small. "Ready?"

She nods and we start walking.

The cemetery is silent. Beside me, Claudia is picking at the bouquet of flowers she brought. I know she's trying not to cry, but I can hear the way she swallows every few seconds, choking back the tears.

We move to the headstone on instinct. We've both been here so many times, but it's different tonight. Because tonight, it's been a year. One year since he died.

"I'll do it," I tell her, holding my hand out to take the flowers, but she shakes her head.

"No. I should do it," she whispers. She takes a deep, quivering breath, walks slowly to the grave, and sets the bouquet at the foot of it. She stands and looks up at the marble angel, the way she always does, like she's looking right into Leo's face, like he's looking down at her through its eyes.

Claudia stays at the grave for a long time, her head bowed, most likely praying, either to God or Leo himself, I'm not really sure. I glance at my watch, an old Omega that belonged to my father. It was about this time a year ago that I got the call about Leo, some grizzled voice on the other end telling me where to find his body. Sometimes I can still remember the feel of his doughy skin under my hands, pliable with death, cold to the bone.

When Claudia comes back to me, I walk her over to the stone bench that we had placed beside Leo's grave, and we sit there in silence, listening to the incessant chirping of the crickets, to the traffic on the highway nearby. The universe has always felt too quiet without Leo in it.

"This girl..." Claudia says, pulling a tissue from a package in her purse. "Are you sure it was a good idea to send her?"

I'm not sure what to say. No, I'm not sure it was a good idea. And I can't tell if she's asking because she's genuinely worried about the sale or because she's still sitting by Leo's grave, her mind making connections. "If we want her to trust us, we have to trust her."

She turns her head in my direction. "What good does it do if she trusts us? I'd rather see her burn."

Her words are like a million tiny bugs under my skin,

crawling and buzzing. I look back at her, at the way wrinkles have started to form around her mouth and eyes. "Do you want to take down Tyler Price?"

Her jaw goes stiff and her eyes shift over to the angel. "You know I do."

"Then we need her to trust us."

"*Okay.*" Her mouth forms the words but no sound comes out. I put an arm around her shoulder and pull her toward me, letting her rest her head on my shoulder and cry.

15

JULIAN

"Hey, boss. What's up?" Ronan says when I step into the surveillance room later that night. It's almost three in the morning, but I can't get my mind to turn the fuck off so I can go to sleep. Not that sleep has ever been something I was very good at. Ronan is even worse.

"How's the pillow princess?"

Ronan snickers, peering up at me from under the hood he always has pulled over his face. "You think she is one?"

I shrug. "Who the hell knows?" I don't want to think about what Sloane is like in bed while Ronan is in the room with me. If I start to contemplate whether or not Sloane is the type to lay back and take it or climb on top and ride a man, I'll get hard. She may be a pain in the ass with a boyfriend I want to kill with my bare hands, but she still has a body that could end someone.

"I need to hear the recording from the sale tonight."

He nods and queues it up on the screen beside the security feed.

I jerk my chin toward the door, and he gets up without questioning me.

"I'll just take a coffee break," he says, tapping the inside of the door frame with his palm.

I know how it must look. Maybe Ronan thinks I'm going to sit in here and jerk off watching Sloane toss and turn in that tiny outfit she wears to bed, but I have bigger concerns.

I start the recording, listening to Sloane and Barbara's conversation. It surprises me, to say the least. The fierce little bird that's always stamping around the compound, needling at everybody constantly and kicking at her door because she's not allowed to leave her room, is nowhere in sight. Instead, she's a bubbly little cheerleader, talking to Barbara like they're old friends telling secrets over milkshakes.

It's impressive. There are dangerous people out there buying from me, people who have bad intentions and have very bad plans. And then there are people like Barbara, who are just trying to get by and aren't sure how to do it.

Who the hell does?

In the recording, it certainly seems like Sloane does, the way she coaches and coaxes Barbara.

There are over a dozen screens on one of the computers that shift between the myriad of cameras all around the compound. This late at night, it's mostly the cameras outside the compound, watching to make sure no one is roaming around that shouldn't be. And while my eyes flicker to those cameras too, I'm mostly just looking at one.

Up in the right-hand corner of the bank of feeds, Sloane is lying in bed. In the week she's been here, I've found she's about as good a sleeper as I am. She spends a lot of time reading, a lot of time with her beloved textbooks. Now, she's in bed on her phone, the one we provided for her, the screen of which is also recorded and monitored. She figured out pretty quick that she can't access social media or the internet, but she texts her mother a lot, mostly telling lies about how great her new life is that the screen recordings pick up and deliver to my email every hour on the dot.

She gets out of bed and walks over to the door, her arms crossed. She's wearing an oversized t-shirt that hangs off one shoulder and a barely-there pair of shorts that make her ass look incredible. She reaches forward and tries the knob on her door. When she discovers it's locked, her eyes go straight to the camera. There was always a lock on it, just not one she can control.

I know she has no way of knowing if she's being watched right now or that it's me watching her, but she doesn't seem to hate anyone else at the compound quite like she hates me, and she's glaring at the camera like she wishes whoever is watching her was dead.

She sighs and turns back to her bed. Reaching out, I press a button on the keyboard in front of me, unlocking the door. Sloane spins back to it, her arms still crossed and her blond hair fanned out across her shoulders. She must have heard the lock click open.

Ronny, take a break, I text him and watch in the hallway camera as he looks from the now-open door to his phone and turns toward his own room, around the corner from Sloane's.

She tries the door again, easily opening it this time. Sloane takes a step toward the hallway, slow, tentative steps, and when she sees that Ronny is gone, she looks back at the door, like she's afraid there might be a ghost. I guess she decides she doesn't care about the risks because she heads for the stairs.

She holds onto the banister as she goes down, her hot pink manicured nails shimmering in the light as she stops at the tall grandfather clock at the bottom. She watches it for a long time, and in the silence of the house, all the way down the hallway, I can hear it ticking in real time, something I've filtered out over years of hearing it constantly in the background.

From what I've been told, that first night she got here, she was particularly interested in the sitting room at the front of the house. She lingers there now, fondly brushing her fingers across the fabric of my dad's old wingback.

But she doesn't stay long. She heads for the dining room, her feet slowing as she passes the security wing. I can hear her footsteps outside the room, hear them hesitate. I'm guessing she's figured out there are no cameras here or in the back hallway. While I never expressly forbade her from entering either hallway, all the rooms are locked when no one is in them, so it isn't as if she's going to find anything.

She ambles through the dining room and over to the back hallway. She tries the first door—I can see from the camera in the dining room—and when she finds it locked, she keeps moving. I'll give it to her, she's fearless and persistent. My guess is that she's more afraid of what her boyfriend will do to her than she is of simply being executed by one of my men. As far as she knows, we don't even kill people. She hasn't seen anyone do anything questionable. Is it a false sense of security or a certainty that whatever he'll do would be worse? To her, a ruined life might be worse than an ended one.

She goes out the back door and into the pool room, completely glassed in. She stops by the billiard room off to the left, where she unceremoniously knocks all the pool cues off the wall, the dartboard following immediately after.

I'm surprised, even though I know I shouldn't be. She's mad that I grounded her. She's mad that I asked her to take that meeting for me. She's mad that she's here at all, mad that I can control her, that I own her.

My cock stirs. Fuck, even if she is currently wreaking havoc on my house, she's fucking sex on a stick, her tits on display like ripe peaches under her shirt, her long legs smooth and ready to be spread.

On the screen in front of me, she walks over to the bar by the pool that I let Frankie put in last year. A big screen TV that's easily bigger than her hangs on the wall. And when I think she'll throw a barstool at it or something, instead, she steps up to it, peers beneath it, and reaches her skinny arm up behind the TV. Cords start to fall one at a time. Girl can't even bring herself to do any real damage. That's what happens when you grow up in a house where every tiny luxury is precious.

Stepping over to the bar, she picks up a bottle of expensive liquor. She might not know how expensive it is. Just like that, she lets the bottle slip from her fingers. I don't hear it crash to the ground—the pool room has been soundproofed—but I don't miss her flinch when it does. She stares down at her feet, and I want to tell her to be careful, not to step on the glass. But I think the safety of her feet is the last thing on her mind.

She picks up another bottle, examines the label, and throws it at the wall. Her breath heaves out of her, and she stares at the place where the bottle shattered. She reaches over and picks up another. She throws that one, too, and doesn't hesitate before picking up the next one.

That's it, baby. Get it all out.

When she throws another one, I see the shape her mouth takes, and I can imagine the pitch of the savage scream that comes out of her, even if I can't hear it.

When she's smashed half a dozen bottles, she walks over to the pool and stares down into it. My hands clench into fists, and I start to rise from my chair.

Don't even think about it.

She knows she's being watched, I have to remind myself. She's not about to put rocks in her pockets and throw herself in when she knows someone can see her, right? She has to know I'll just go in after her.

Or maybe she's counting on me letting her drown. Maybe one of the other guys would.

She stares for a long time, teetering on the edge, and then steps back. She crosses her arms and looks up and out the window. I know exactly what she's seeing. I've sat in that room and stared out that window hundreds of times. A long stretch of open land, the tree line around the property, and past it all, rolling hills.

She stomps toward the door, and I'm surprised at how fast she moves, how determined she seems, until I remember that the other thing that can be seen from that window is the garage.

Damn. If she has any chance of actually finding anything, she's going to find it in there. I don't want to chase her around. I'm not a fucking babysitter. But I know I scare her, even if she would die before showing it. I see the tremor in her every time I get close to her, the way she has to focus not to look away when I invade her personal space. It's satisfying, that's for sure. Maybe catching her off guard would be fun.

I know she's testing me, like a toddler trying to figure out if her parents would punish her. Oh, I would punish her alright. The question is, can she handle what I would do to her if she tried to take us down?

She already has a pretty hefty head start, but it doesn't take me long to catch up to her. The side door to the garage is still wide open, and from where I stand, I can see her inside, staring down into the exposed guts of a car that Magnus is working on.

She stands there with her hip cocked and her arms crossed as I lean against the doorframe and silently watch her. I can tell she's not just staring blankly. She knows what she's looking at. It's written all over her face. She wears a pensive look as she braces her hands on the front end and leans under the hood, moving this way and that. Fuck, it makes her look good. The shape of her body, spine curved, ass out, tits up. She looks like a pin-up, all legs and blond hair.

A single light shines down on her as she steps around the car and over to the Beast. I try to see it from her perspective, just another car in a long line of them. She doesn't know that that car is my lifeblood, that I love it more than I love almost any human being that's living and breathing. To me, the Beast breathes.

She runs her fingertip along the hood, opens the driver's side door, and gets in. My body tenses, remembering what she just did to the inside of the house. If she so much as scuffs the leather... But I keep myself still. Watching. Waiting.

She wraps her hand around the steering wheel over the spots where my fingers always rest. When she lets out the tiniest of sighs, I can't hold myself back.

"What are you doing?" My voice is like a bullet in the silence.

She drops her hand from the steering wheel so fast that it hits the horn, and the sound seems to vibrate through the empty garage. She looks over at me, but she doesn't get out of the car like I thought she would. She just sits there, the door open and her hands in her lap.

"Did I say you could touch my car?"

She crosses her arms tight over her body. Instead of answering my question, she raises one eyebrow at me. "Did you unlock my door?"

I take one step into the garage, and even though she tries to hide it, I see her flinch. She pretends to just be adjusting herself in the seat, settling further into the leather of *my* car. I slowly walk over to her, past the other cars that are on the lifts. Grabbing onto the edge of the door, I push it open all the way and feel satisfaction worm into my gut when her eyes widen the slightest bit.

"You've been in a cage your whole life, haven't you, Sloane?"

Her chin jerks up. "Don't act like you know me."

"Oh, but I do." I reach down to wrap a hand around her upper arm. We're not having this conversation while she's sitting in my car. I pull her out of the seat, and she grunts but doesn't resist, stumbling out and then spinning to face me when I let her go. "Sloane Mackenzie Moretti, a cute little name for a future cheerleader. Born and raised outside of Fresno, California. Absent father. Hard-working mother who fell in with the wrong crowd. Got a scholarship to, what was it, Garrison Prep School during your sophomore year of high school? Met one Tyler Price—"

"Yeah, okay, I get it," she snaps, her face flushed. "Am I supposed to be impressed that you had your cronies do some research on me? That doesn't mean you know me."

She's right. I don't really know anything about her, but I'm starting to learn. I take a few steps forward, until I'm close enough that she has to tip her head just a bit to look at me. I can smell the cherry Chapstick on her lips. I want to bend forward and taste it.

"You know what I know, princess? I know that when people get locked in cages, one of two things happens: they submit, turn docile, become domesticated and tame and broken." I pause, taking a second to bask in the way she's hanging on my every word, her eyes dropping to my mouth. "Or they turn into feral animals. You lock them in once and every time you threaten them with a cage again, they're all teeth and claws. Which one are you?"

I already know the answer to my question. Nobody does the bidding of someone like Tyler unless they've turned into a house pet. Whatever he's got on her, whether it's love or brainwashing or something else, it's a leash that's getting tighter and tighter around her neck.

When she opens her mouth to speak, her warm breath puffs against my face. "If you're so powerful," she says, "why are you out betting on car races like some backwoods hick with a gambling addiction?"

"Lot of stupid people around here with a lot of money to throw around."

She narrows her eyes at me. "Doesn't betting on races just make you one of them?"

"I got what I wanted, didn't I?"

Her eyes are blank for a moment, and then a crease appears between her brows, giving away her confusion.

Because she can't fathom being anyone's prize.

But she's sure as hell mine.

"You don't need me," she says, assuming, like she has since the moment she walked in the door, that all she is to me is information. Just someone I need to break to get what I need. I wish she was right—it would be so much easier—but if I want to take down Tyler and keep it neat and clean, I *do* need her.

I stay silent, which seems to infuriate her more than my words do.

She clenches her teeth and steps around me. I watch her go, but just before she walks back out into the autumn-cold night, she says, "What could you possibly want with him?" She grips the doorjamb, her fingers sinking into the paint. "This stinks of a turf war, but Tyler isn't a threat to you. He's just a college kid who spends too much money on stupid shit."

She's either an excellent liar...or she doesn't know what her boyfriend is up to.

"Goodnight, Sloane. Better hope none of the guys want

their pound of flesh for all that perfectly good liquor you wasted in there."

She sighs, shakes her head, and walks away.

16

SLOANE

My door is still unlocked the next morning, Ronny still not standing guard in the hallway. Is my sentence...over? Now that Xander knows I'm a vegan—and now that I'm allowed down in the dining room again, for some reason—breakfast is something to look forward to.

When I walk into the dining room the next morning, I'm so distracted by the smell of tofu scramble that I've completely forgotten about last night.

About what I did. About the conversation I had with Julian.

It isn't until everyone looks up from their plates—at least half the compound sitting at the long dining table—that I remember. I open my mouth to say something, though I'm not exactly sure what it's going to be, when there's a loud clatter.

My head whips to the side, and I watch through the open doorway that leads into the bar at the back of the house as someone with their back to me uses a tall broom to brush all the broken glass I left behind into a pile.

When he reaches down to grab the dustpan, I realize it's Bram. I recognize the slope of his broad shoulders. He must catch sight of me out of the corner of his eye because he turns his head toward me. I can't read his expression. He just holds my eye for a moment and then goes back to what he's doing.

"Maybe you should try *not* biting the hand that feeds you."

My eyes find Julian at the head of the table. He raises an eyebrow at me, and I look away from him and take my normal spot at the table. It's odd to even fathom that I *have* a normal spot, that I've been here at this table enough days in a row now that everyone expects me to sit here, in this spot beside Julian.

As soon as my butt hits my seat, Xander appears beside me, setting a bowl of tofu scramble on my placemat, along with individual bowls of nuts and berries and granola.

"Thank you," I murmur to him before he goes.

At the head of the table, Julian snorts. "Oh, now you're grateful."

I glare up at him. "I get it," I snap.

Beside me, Magnus shoves his chair back, but Julian holds up a hand to him. "It's fine," he says, and Magnus watches me with eyes burning with anger for a long moment before sitting back down. What, exactly, was Magnus planning on doing? Guard dog protecting its owner, I suppose.

I don't expect any of these men to understand what I'm going through. They're not trapped here. They aren't being forced to be here by someone they thought they could trust. They chose their lives. They follow their leader because they *want* to. And I do it because he hasn't given me any other options. Kill or be killed.

I start stabbing at my food when, out of the corner of my

eye, I see Julian nod over at someone. Hugo stands and appears at my side. The thing about Hugo is that he's unnaturally tall, maybe over six and a half feet, so when I'm sitting down and he's standing up, it's sort of like observing Everest from the very base of it.

Without a word, he drops a stack of hundred-dollar bills on the table beside me and stalks off.

I just stare down at the money, neatly tied together with a blue rubber band. I don't understand what's happening. Why did he just put this here? No one else seems surprised. They don't even seem to have noticed this odd happening. I look over at Julian, but he's cutting all of his bacon in half with his fork, focused on it like it's a math problem.

"What is this?" I finally ask.

"It's your cut," Julian answers, still not looking at me, buttering his toast.

My fingers brush the stack of bills. I've never seen this much money in real life. And even when I touch it, it feels fake, like money isn't meant to be so crisp and perfect. "Cut of what?"

Julian meets my eye, leaning back in his chair and peering at me over the rim of his glass of orange juice as he takes a long drink. "The Chevelle sale."

Barbara, the woman at the cafe on the highway.

Julian holds my gaze. He sets his orange juice down and puts his hand flat on the table. I can see the dark ink on each of his fingers, a different symbol in the spaces of each finger. "It would have been more, but all the bourbon you wrecked last night came out to almost a grand. Maybe remember that the next time you want to throw a fit."

I'm still waiting for the other shoe to drop. I'm waiting for him to tell me there's some reason I can't have the money, some reason he's going to lock me in that cage in the basement and set the money on fire while I watch instead.

But he just goes back to his toast. It has dark seeds and raisins. As people finish their food, they push away from the table, going off to mystery places to do mystery business, until it's just Julian and me left.

I slowly reach out and take the money. Folding it in half, I put it in my pocket. I feel like a squirrel with a big juicy nut. I need to hide it somewhere. Bury it so no one can take it from me.

I shove back my chair. There are a lot of things I want to say, but everything going through my brain right now would either piss him off or stroke his ego, and I'm really not here to do either of those things. So instead, I say nothing and leave.

❶❼

SLOANE

"What do you mean, you can't find anything?" Tyler says, keeping his voice low as he leans across the table toward me. "There's no way those guys are clean."

I start to shake my head but Tyler grips my thigh under the table harder. I glance over at Ronny, who's sitting a few tables away from us in the dining hall, pretending to read but keeping a keen eye on us. It took me some time to convince Ronny to let me have lunch with Tyler. The rule is that I'm not allowed to take off alone, but no one can honestly expect to keep me away from my boyfriend for...however fucking long we're all playing this game.

"Don't let these guys fool you, Sloane," he says between his teeth. "Don't even for a second think that they aren't doing shady, illegal shit because they're not hurting you. Don't think for a second that they *won't* hurt you the second you do something that threatens them."

I narrow my eyes at him. "You mean like playing spy and snooping through all their stuff?"

My comment goes right over his head. He anxiously taps his fingers against the table and glances over his shoulder at Ronny. Watching him puts my hackles up. Ronny is just a kid, but I know that all Tyler can see is a mobster or some kind of criminal. It's not like I think Julian and his men are upstanding citizens, but I don't think Tyler knows any more about them than they do about him. Painting pictures from shadows.

"What makes you so certain about all this?"

Tyler turns back to me, voice going even lower. "What do you mean?"

I want to ask him about what Julian said, that Tyler isn't who I think he is. If Julian and his crew are doing bad things while looking pristine on the surface, then could Tyler be doing the same thing? And if he is, what kind of bad things is he doing? I feel certain if I ask him about it, he'll just lie to me. I'm starting to think all he's done since we met is lie.

"I mean, you're so fixated on this guy. Why? There's no sign of him being a criminal, and even if he is, what do you want with him?"

He looks at me for a long time and then leans back in his seat, crossing his arms. "What has he told you about me?"

"Nothing." I shake my head. "And even if he had, it's all lies, right?"

I can see the way he's calculating things in his mind. It makes my stomach turn. For a long time I thought Tyler was a nice guy, but I'm not stupid. I'm not delusional. I know he hasn't treated me well lately.

I also know the universe is not a magic genie, and I don't get to make a wish on a star for a better life and have it fall into my lap. Tyler takes care of me. He always has, even if he isn't always quite sure how to do it well.

There are worse men out there, and if Tyler is concerned about Julian, maybe Julian is one of them.

Looking at Tyler now, I can't help but wonder what he's gotten himself into. What he's keeping from me. How bad could it be? I have to do what I can to keep this relationship on track. I have goals. I have plans for the future. I can't let what's happening derail it.

I glance over at Ronny. "Listen," I tell Tyler, keeping my voice low, "I met one of their clients."

His eyes pop wide. "What?" he hisses, keeping his voice low. "Are you fucking kidding? And you waited until now to tell me?"

"I'm not even sure it's worth telling you about at all. This woman we met with, she was an older lady. Totally harmless. She was just buying a car for her dead husband." I think of Barbara's face, the way she gulped back tears while telling me about what the car meant to her. I may not know anything about her past crimes, but I don't think she's doing anything questionable in the present.

Tyler apparently disagrees. His eyes narrow. "They're duping you, Sloane. No one is harmless."

I shrug. "Maybe you're right. But I was there. It was just a car, and she was just a widow. There's not some secret. And even if there was, they've clearly got it under lock and key, and no matter how much I snoop, I'm not going to be able to find it."

"So you're throwing in the towel? You don't—" He peers over at Ronny, who doesn't seem to be paying attention to us, eyes on his phone. "You don't want the money?"

Bastard. He knows I want it.

"I'm not throwing in the towel." I stand, reaching for my bag and hoisting it up over my shoulder. "I'm going to go to the library, spend some time getting ready for this midterm next week."

I wait for him to say something. His eyes are low and unfocused. But then he looks up at me and says, "You know the bathroom on the fourth floor? The one that's always empty?"

His question comes out of nowhere. In the corner of my eye, I see Ronny stand, following my lead.

"Yeah."

"Meet me up there. I'll go in first and leave the door unlocked." He tips his head in the direction of Ronny, already making his way over to us. "That guy won't even know I'm in there."

"I don't want to fuck right now, Tyler." I'm too exhausted to pretend with him. I know I won't be able to hold him off forever, but I think if he touched me right now, I would scream.

"It's not that. I just...want a little privacy." His voice is almost a whisper now.

"In the bathroom?"

"Sloane." I can't read his tone. A little demanding, a little desperate, a lot aggravated.

"Fine. Okay."

He gathers his stuff quickly, taking the back hallway so that he can walk behind the buildings to the library while I meet up with Ronny and let him walk me out the front exit. He doesn't speak to me, just walks a few steps behind me, like he's been doing all day.

I don't know if he's not speaking to me because Julian told him not to or because he thinks I don't want him to bother me. It's bothering me far more that he's not speaking to me than if he was. It's like being followed around by a pet that doesn't actually like you.

"I don't have another class until one," I tell him over my shoulder. I can only imagine what someone would think if they were actually paying attention to us. How strange that this girl is speaking to a man so far behind her, craning her neck like a giraffe. "I thought I'd study in the library for a little bit."

"Whatever," is all he says back, his hands in the pockets of his black jeans.

I spin around, stopping in the middle of the walkway between the buildings so that students have to go around us. Ronny comes to a halt too, looking uncomfortable as he dodges people, standing at least eight feet from me.

"Why are you doing that?" I demand.

Ronny grimaces, his shoulders slumping like an annoyed teenager. "Doing what?"

"Keeping your distance like I'm a leper. Did Julian tell you to treat me this way?"

I think invoking the name of his boss does something to him because he seems to stand taller at that, to pull his shoulders back and lift his chin. "Julian doesn't have to tell me how to treat you."

With a frustrated groan, I stomp up the steps to the library, walking quickly, halfway hoping that Ronny will get lost in the crowd and have to search me out.

He doesn't, of course. I'm not that fortunate. I settle in at a table and open up my Sociology book. It's my hardest class, and at the rate I'm going with all this Tyler and Julian business, I'm worried I won't be able to keep my grade up.

Ronny sits at the end of the table, doing something on his phone once again. He's not even trying to fit in, and I guess by this point, it doesn't really matter. No one is watching us. And while Ronny may not exactly look like a studious social sciences major, he does just look like a normal kid.

"I have to pee," I whisper to him.

Without looking away from his phone, he nods and stands.

I pause, halfway out of my own seat. "Are you really going

to come with me? I'm just going upstairs. Who's going to watch my stuff?"

Ronny finally looks up at me and shrugs. "Take it with you. Boss says I'm not allowed to let you out of my sight. You're lucky I'm going to let you go into the bathroom alone. If he was here, Julian would probably insist I watch you piss."

I shove my stuff back down into my bag and sling it onto my shoulder. There may not be a high crime rate at Dartmouth, but I'm not going to risk leaving my stuff unattended.

And just like he said he would, Ronny walks me up to the bathroom. If he's wondering why we bypassed another set of bathrooms to go to the fourth floor, he doesn't say anything about it. Maybe he understands wanting a quieter place to do your business.

In the hall outside the bathroom, Ronny leans against the wall, still staring down at his phone. I drop my bag at his feet with a "watch this" and go into the bathroom. The second the sunlight streaming in through the high windows hits me, so does a hand, wrapping around my arm and shoving me against the wall.

I grunt when my back slams into the exposed brick and watch as Tyler reaches over to lock the door.

When his eyes meet mine, I know I've misunderstood this entire situation. He didn't bring me here to talk. Tyler is angry. "What the fuck is this?" he asks, digging his hand into my front pocket and coming up with the stack of cash that Julian gave me.

I want to kick myself. I'm so stupid, leaving it in my pocket like that. Even if Tyler hadn't found it, someone else was sure to. If Tyler was able to spot it, then any common pick-pocket would have been able to as well.

"It's just some money," I say, and Tyler's hand tightens on my arm. He pulls me away from the wall, turning me to shove me against the opposite one, so that his big, muscular body is between me and the door.

His hand moves from my arm up to my throat, his fingers getting tighter and tighter. I reach up to claw at him. I can't breathe, but he's looking at the money in his hand, and I don't know if he *knows* I can't breathe.

"Tyler," I gasp, but he ignores me.

"Did he give this to you?"

He finally lets go of me, and I gasp and choke as he paces away from me. I'm seeing stars at the corners of my vision. I focus on not passing out. He's blocking the door. If I called out for Ronny, would he come? Would he hear me? Would he care? Surely Julian wouldn't want me dead, right? Otherwise, he wouldn't have gone through all this trouble. He would have just killed me that night in my room.

Tyler seems to read my thoughts on my face because he reaches over and slams his hand against the big metal button on the hand dryer. The loud rush of air covers all the noise in the whole universe, it feels like.

Tyler stalks back over to me and growls, "I asked you a question. Did he give this to you?"

I nod, trying not to meet his eye. I'm like a dog, cowering at his feet. As slowly as I can, I reach into my back pocket and pull out my burner phone. It buzzes against my palm as I try to unlock it with my fingerprint.

"There's five grand here, Sloane. What did you do for five grand? Did you suck off every guy in that building?"

"How dare you ask me that?" I shove him away from me with one hand and start tapping on the phone screen behind my back with the other. I roughly remember where the text app is. I think I can text Ronny...

He comes right back, like a deranged boomerang, so close that when he speaks, his spit lands on my face. "Then what, Sloane? A guy like that doesn't just hand you five thousand dollars. Does he have you doing shit for him? Doing jobs? You said you met one of his clients. Is that what you are now, a common criminal, kissing the feet of some white trash gangbanger?"

"If you were so concerned, maybe you shouldn't have pawned me off on him."

He makes an angry, animalistic noise and slams his open palms into my shoulders so hard that my whole body jerks back and my head bounces hard off the brick wall.

My head starts to spin, and my phone clatters to the floor.

"What were you–" He bends like he's going for my phone, but before he can, someone bangs on the door.

"Sloane?" Ronny's voice comes through muffled, but I can hear the surprising amount of concern in it.

Tyler spins back to me. "Your fucking guard dog is here for you," he snarls.

Even though I'm still seeing stars, I reach down for my phone. I'm running on instinct now, an innate desire to just get help fast, even if I have to fight him while doing it.

"Give that to me," he says when he sees it in my hand. He lunges for it as Ronny begins to throw his body against the door, but I pull it away, holding it behind my back. I'm just so goddamn tired of him taking things from me.

Bang. Bang. Bang.

"Give me the damn phone, Sloane. If you can't get me anything from that fucking building of theirs, this is the least you can do. Seeing as how you've become his little lapdog, doing his bidding and taking his money."

He grabs my wrist, and I flinch, feeling him dig into the bruises that were already there. He forces my thumb out and presses it to the screen. Once it's unlocked, he lets go of me, forcing me back.

I stumble, tripping over the big metal trash can. And before I can catch myself, I slam into the edge of the sink, the porcelain corner hitting me in the cheek so hard that my vision goes dark.

JULIAN

I've probably had one too many for a Tuesday afternoon, especially a Tuesday afternoon where I've decided to oversee a potential sale. I can always tell I've had too much when I start to think Bram's jokes are funny. He leans on his elbows on the bar to see around me.

"You should see the Camaro in person, Joey. I swear, you've never seen anything so beautiful." Bram is good at sales. It's why I always give him the high-priority clients. After a drink or two, everyone starts treating Bram like an old college buddy. It's something I've never been able to pull off. Bram says I'm not "approachable."

Joey, who doesn't seem overly intimidated by Bram or myself, snorts. "I've seen a Lamborghini Revuelto in person, my friend. There's truly nothing else like it." He shoves all my glossy photos back into their folders and slides it across the bar to me. "I gotta think about it."

I lift a shoulder and take the photos. "You can think about it all you like, but Bram's right: the Camaro is pretty, and I can't guarantee it'll still be waiting for you if you don't pull the trigger today."

He seems to find my choice of words funny. One side of his mouth quirks up. I really hate a wise guy. "Calm down. You're going to get a sale out of me. I just have to check with my people, make sure we have funds for the extras."

"You do that."

My phone buzzes, and I look sideways at Bram. His eyes have fallen to my jacket pocket. Everyone who has my phone number is either sitting at this bar or knows not to bother me while I'm with a client.

I glance at my screen, confused when I see Sloane's name—or rather, *Princess Pain in My Ass*—in my notifications.

When I open the text, it just says one word.

Princess Pain in My Ass
Help.

18

JULIAN

My blood spikes. What the hell does that mean? Where is she? What's going on?

I pick up the folder with the photos in it. "You'll have to excuse me for a moment," I tell Joey. "I have a phone call to make. Bram will run you through logistics."

I already have my phone to my ear when I stride out the front entrance of Rowdy's. It rings once and then again and again. I growl, knowing she isn't going to answer. I rip the phone from my ear, the agitation starting along my jaw. I call Ronny next, and he doesn't answer either.

Fuck. I don't have time for this. Just like I told Sloane, women are liabilities, especially women like her.

I storm back into the bar and toss some money onto the bar top to pay for the drinks. "Sorry, gentlemen. We've had something come up." I open the folder and flick the picture of the Camaro over to Joey. "We'll be in touch."

"What's going on?" Bram asks as soon as we're in the car, but I don't have a chance to tell him I don't *know* what's going on, that I'm running on gut instinct and pure fury, when my phone rings.

"What?" I snap. At this point, it doesn't matter who it is. Everyone is fucked. I've reached my limit.

"It's the bitch," Frankie says in my ear. I grip the steering wheel tight, wishing I could squeeze blood from it.

I keep my voice calm. "What happened?"

"Ronny says her boyfriend attacked her in a bathroom. Sarge says she's got a concussion. She needed a few stitches. And Tyler's got her burner."

A concussion. What the fuck did he do to her?

"We're on our way back. Have Ronan wipe the burner remotely before he can do any damage. We'll be there in twenty."

I drop the phone into my lap and lay on the gas pedal.

When we pull up to the gate, Magnus is in the booth, which tells me Sarge is still inside tending to Sloane. It's his shift. I don't bother pulling into the garage, just swing the Beast to the end of the long driveway and shut it off.

Bram is right beside me as we head inside. The place is silent. A dead kind of silence. I look up to the second floor and see that the door to Sloane's bedroom is open. I motion for Bram to go up and see her. He'll report back to me. I have business to take care of.

I storm through the door to the dining room and down the hallway to my office. The guys know me well enough by now to know that there's no way out of consequences. That every person under this roof is responsible for the job they've been given.

And that's why Ronny is already waiting in my office when I get there. He already knows what's coming. He's sitting in the same chair she sat in last night when I asked her to talk to Barbara, but he looks massive against the leather. Ronny is all arms and legs, gangly, to say the least.

I take a seat, putting my feet up on the desk and crossing my arms over my chest.

I wait.

I watch him.

He starts to fidget, running his hands through his embarrassingly red hair, until he finally leans forward in the chair, elbows on the desk. "What are you going to do to me?"

"Here's what I don't get," I say, ignoring his question. I pull my feet down, sitting up straight so he'll sit up straight. I hate it when people fucking slouch, especially my guys. "You spent a lot of time trying to convince me that you could be one of us. That you could handle responsibility. That I could trust you. That's the thing, right? This job is a game of trust. And the first time I give you an important assignment, you fucking blow it. Tell me exactly what happened."

Just like I thought he would, he sits up straight in his chair, squares his shoulders, tries to pretend that he can be the man I am when he's just a boy still. I can smell his cheap body spray from here. I may be twenty-five to his nineteen, but it feels like a lifetime separates us.

"Everything was fine. Boring, even. I walked her to her

classes. I watched her while she had lunch with her boyfriend."

I put a hand up to stop him. "What happened during the lunch?"

"What do you mean?"

I have to rein in my temper. "*I mean*, what happened during the lunch? What did they talk about? Was Tyler acting suspicious?"

Ronny's face turns red under his freckles.

I sigh. "How far away were you sitting?"

"A couple of tables away."

I nod. "That one's on me, I guess. I didn't give you any parameters. Sort of thought it would be common sense. If we let them talk to each other, she spills secrets."

A line forms between Ronny's eyebrows. "She doesn't know any secrets. She doesn't have anything to tell him. We've been careful."

I throw my hands up. "That may be true, but we don't know for certain."

He continues to watch me with that perplexed look on his face. And I get it. I'm giving the girl too much freedom. Gave her way too much freedom the other night when she destroyed half the house. If I had left her alone in that garage, if I hadn't been watching her, would she have found what she was looking for? It was clear to me last night; Bram was right: she came here to spy on us. Not that it comes as a surprise.

"Boss, you said you wanted her to trust us. If we listen in on her conversations, she never will."

I did say that. That's exactly what I told him when I put him on this assignment. Be nice to her. Be her friend. For this to work, she has to think she has friends in the compound. Somebody who she can be herself with. She'll never tell me anything because I'm the big bad wolf. She needs a confidante. Ronny, Bram, whoever. Someone she feels safe with.

I motion for Ronny to go on.

"So they have lunch and she says she wants to go to the library to study before she goes to her next class. She had some time so I didn't see a problem. We settle in for a minute, then she says she has to go to the bathroom. So I follow her upstairs and I wait outside."

"You wait outside."

He can't meet my eye anymore. Instead, he eyes the liquor on my shelf. "I didn't think I needed to follow her into the bathroom. She's certainly not going to trust us if we can't even let her pee in private. You're the one who didn't even put a camera in her bathroom."

"Yeah, because I'm not a fucking pervert. A public bathroom is different. You should have gone inside if she was the only one."

"I didn't think her boyfriend would already be in there."

"What, he was waiting for her?"

"They must have coordinated it at the lunch. He probably went up to the bathroom first, hid inside, waited for us."

They coordinated it. Meaning Tyler convinced her to meet him just to attack her. The anger is starting to ripple through me now. Two-faced piece of shit bastard. I pull my hands under the desk, clench them in my lap.

"What happened next?"

"She was in there for a little while, but you know, you gotta do what you gotta do. So I didn't really think anything of it. But then there was a loud noise. I banged on the door. I was calling for her, trying to get in, throwing my body weight at it. And suddenly, her boyfriend rips the door open and runs down the hallway right past me. Takes off like a fucking fire alarm has gone off, and she's in the bathroom unconscious.

He was just going to leave her there. He *did* just leave her there, her face bleeding."

I take a deep breath. What does he have on her that he can do that to her and still keep her devotion?

But I don't need that question answered. I know what he has on her. The only thing she's never had on her own: money. But is there enough money in the world to pretend to love somebody who breaks your face open and leaves you there on the floor, hoping somebody else will take care of you?

"I wasn't even thinking about going after him," Ronny goes on. "I just grabbed her, snuck down the back stairs. Brought her straight here to Sarge."

It's not his fault the way things went down. Of course not. Tyler was going to get what he wanted either way. But I can't let Ronny go unpunished. If I do that, people will think I've gone soft.

"You're on clean-up. House, garage, warehouse, everything. One month."

His shoulders sag. "Great," he says, his voice laced with sarcasm. "She lets her boyfriend use her as a punching bag and I'm the one who gets punished for it."

I hold very still to get my temper under control. "Listen, Ronny," I say. Calm, cool, collected. "That woman is far more important to this organization than you ever will be. You see, you're disposable. You want to sit around and pretend like you're important enough to have a role here when you can't even keep your eyeballs open, much less use your fucking brain. But her, she's going to help clean up this mess if we play our cards right. If you think for one second you're going to earn a place here while refusing to acknowledge that, you clearly have no idea what's going on. Maybe *you* don't deserve clean-up. Maybe you should be sitting in the fucking cage."

At this, his eyes go wide. "I didn't mean it," he says, suddenly sounding very much like the seventeen-year-old kid who came to us two years ago begging for a place to stay, a place to be, because his older brother, who was taking care of him, got thrown in jail and he didn't have any skills. I made him beg. Maybe I'll make him beg now.

"I don't know, Ronny. I think you need some time in the cage because you've clearly become far too comfortable. You think you're worth more than you are. You think you can run your fucking mouth off at me and you're not going to see any consequences. I'm not your brother. I'm not here to make your life easy. I'm not here to fucking raise you. So get your shit together or you're going down to the fucking basement."

"I'll do clean-up. A month, a year, whatever you want."

"Yeah, I thought so."

He gets up to leave. I let it slide even though I didn't dismiss him.

"Hey, Ronny," I call.

Ronny stops right inside the open doorway and turns to look at me.

"You talk shit about her again, you'll be in pieces in the river instead."

He doesn't say anything, just watches me. I gesture with my chin for him to get out.

Far down the hall, I can hear some of the guys talking. I think maybe they're less concerned with her actual well-being than they are with how things went down. What it means for us, what it means for Tyler. But none of us will know anything until she wakes up. The ball's in her court right now. Maybe it always has been. She's the one who has to make the decisions here. What's the next step with Tyler? Is she going to help us or not?

How long has he been doing this to her? And if she's been letting him do it this long, does this change anything? I try to think back. Medical records, police reports, hospital visits, anything like that. I think about the bruises on her wrists last week. Maybe it's all new.

Someday, I'm going to have Tyler under my thumb and I'm going to make him count while I give him as many bruises as he's given her. And then I'm going kill him the way he killed my best friend.

19

JULIAN

I don't know how long I've been sitting here. My eyes ache, my body is sore, and my neck is stiff as shit. I can't stop staring at the screen that looks into Sloane's room, waiting for her to wake up.

I tell her in my head, *wake up, wake up*.

We're all impatient, all chomping at the bit. Right now, she's like Schrödinger's cat. As long as she's asleep, we're both fucked and not fucked. Maybe she told Tyler something that could take us out and maybe she didn't. Maybe she's on our side, and maybe she's not.

Sarge swears to all of us that she'll wake up, and he's the best doctor I know. He's been here since I was a kid. My father trusted him, so I trust him, too. But she's been out all afternoon and well into the night. We all ate dinner in mostly silence, and now the house feels like a graveyard, haunted by us all.

Ronny swears she hit the sink hard enough that he heard

it through the door. Sarge says her cheek isn't broken, but he did say a quarter of her face is fucking purple with bruises.

I watch on the screen as Bram sits at her bedside. He's the only one I trust with her. He's the only one who wanted to sit next to her, to stay at her side the whole time, make sure that if she needed anything, someone was there, that Sarge was called if things went south.

He has his feet up on her bed, his head back. I know he's not asleep. He's not dumb enough to sleep on the job, but he'll have to be relieved soon. He's already been at it for twelve hours. And she's just still like fucking Snow White in her glass coffin.

If I hold still, I can see the gentle, slow movement of her chest as she breathes in and out. In and out.

With a grunt, I shoot up out of the chair and go down the hall to my room. In the back of my closet, I have a box of tools. I don't have much as fixing things around the compound is generally Bram and Frankie's area, but I have what I need for this particular job.

I head upstairs and throw open the door to Sloane's room so fast that Bram jumps, pulling his feet off the bed and turning to watch me.

"What the hell are you doing?" he asks, his voice full of exhaustion and not anger.

Bending down, I put the drill to one of the screws holding the doorknob in place. Without looking up, I say, "I'm giving her her damn lock."

SLOANE

I wake up in the dark. My body feels sore, all of it, like if someone touched me, the pain would radiate into every cell under my skin.

My eyes find the light of the bathroom first, and I realize where I am. Julian's compound. Turns out it wasn't all just a bad dream.

I turn the other way and find Bram. He's just a shape in the dark, but I can see his eyes on me as I push myself up. I regret it immediately. My whole head feels like an open wound, throbbing steadily.

"How do you feel?" Bram asks.

"Is that an honest question?" The words come out little more than a croak. Geez, how long was I out?

"Yes." His voice is serious as he leans forward to plant his elbows on his knees, maybe more serious than I've heard it since we met.

"I don't feel good," I tell him.

When my voice breaks, I feel pathetic, like a child with a fever who's going to cry because they vomited. I need to put myself back together, but it hurts. It all hurts. One of my eyes is swollen shut. I didn't realize until they started to adjust to the dark that I couldn't actually see out of it at all, no matter how long I stared straight ahead.

"What happened?"

Bram looks down like he doesn't want to tell me. "Your boyfriend. We think you hit your face on the sink."

"Yeah, that was part of it," I tell him. That part, at least, I remember. "He sort of shoved me, but it was mostly just me tripping." But I wouldn't have tripped if he hadn't shoved me.

"Well..." Bram goes on. "You got knocked out when you hit. Pretty bad, from what Ronny says. And... Tyler left you there. Ronny probably would have gone after him, but he decided to help you instead."

"How sweet of him," I say, and then feel bad for aiming my bitterness at the wrong person. It *was* kind of him, but it's also basic decency to help someone who's out cold in a bathroom, someone whose boyfriend left them to rot. Ronny shouldn't have been the good guy in that story. "Is there a reason I'm not at the hospital?"

Bram's face finally starts to take on the characteristics I'm used to, gentle eyes and exasperated eyebrows. "Hospitals aren't really a thing we do here," he says.

"Why?"

He doesn't say anything else for a long moment, and I can feel him considering what to tell me and what not to. Can't get too close to the truth. I might have something to take back to Tyler. Some kind of evidence or confession.

"We've got a guy. He's been the doctor here at the compound longer than you've been alive."

"He's an *actual* doctor, right? Not some guy who knows first aid?"

One side of his mouth ticks up. "He was a military surgeon. He knows what he's doing. He has everything he needs to take care of you. You needed a couple stitches on your cheek."

"Stitches?" I gasp. "Does that mean I'm going to have a scar?"

He smiles ruefully at that. "Probably nothing you can't cover up with some makeup. I feel certain of it."

My hand goes to my cheek instinctively. I have other scars, ones given to me by my father and various men who stumbled about in our home. But this will be the first one on my face, and through all of it, that's the thing that makes me want to cry.

"I want to talk to Julian."

Bram purses his lips, takes a deep breath. It's like he knew what I was going to say before I said it.

"I'm sure he wants to talk to you, too."

I try to adjust on the bed and realize I have to use the bathroom. As I start to carefully get out of bed, I mutter, "I'm sure he would have been a lot happier had I not woken up."

When I have my feet under me, I see the look on his face. Like confusion, but laced with upset.

"Julian?" he asks.

I roll my eyes and regret it. Geez, that was unpleasant. Like having bruises behind my eyeballs. "I'm just a thorn in his side, right? Just this thing that he has to drag around now. I'm not stupid, okay? I know he's waiting for me to give something up so he can go for Tyler, on accident or under duress. I know that all I am to everyone is a database to be hacked. And if I don't give him anything, what then? His little anchor, slowing everyone down. Is he going to do this forever, or is he going to kill me?"

"Kill you." His voice is laced with amusement now. He tips his head back to look up at me, now that I'm standing over him. How long has he been sitting in that chair? "What do you think this is? Julian's not an assassin."

"I'm serious," I say, crossing my arms and trying not to let on how woozy I am. "Is he going to torture the information out of me?"

His smile falls.

"Whether Julian is a good man or a bad man, an assassin or a mobster or whatever, he needs something from me, and if I don't give it to him soon, is he just going to take it?" I realize my voice is quivering. I hate that, but I hate it less because it's Bram. "I don't even have whatever he thinks I do. I don't know what Tyler is hiding. Whatever it is, I don't know anything about it. Just like I don't know anything about what's going on here. Everywhere I go, I'm just being kept in the dark. And when Julian discovers I'm useless, he'll have to decide what to do with me. If he really is a bad man, like Tyler thinks he is, what's keeping him from disposing of me?"

I clamp my lips shut. I can't believe I just trauma dumped on him like that.

Bram doesn't act like it's odd at all. He just calmly says, "I can tell you one thing. Julian wanted you to wake up."

$$20$$

SLOANE

Within just a few moments, Julian Shaw has arrived in my bedroom. As he sits in front of me in the chair Bram vacated, I work to compartmentalize all of the events of the past twenty-four hours. I'm trying to understand. Tyler abandoned me in a bathroom, while I was out cold and could have been dead. Julian, hoping I would wake up. Ronny, saving me. Bram, sitting at my bedside.

A week ago, I might have been beside myself. Today, I'm just angry and bitter.

Tyler and these men, they've all buried their hearts in a cold grave. Maybe it's time for me to do the same.

I look at Julian, eyes steady, breathing slowly. A statue in a black button-up, elbows resting on the desk behind him, tattooed hands dangling.

I have to stay confident. I can't let him intimidate me anymore. If he wants something from me, I have to recognize my own power in this game.

"You wanted to talk," he says, voice low and calm. He

doesn't seem to know what Bram told me, which means there are no microphones in the cameras. This is not the face of a man who cares whether someone like me lives or dies. Maybe he just knows that if I die, he doesn't have a bargaining chip anymore and whatever he's trying to get from me about Tyler is out the window.

"I've been thinking…" I say.

"Oh yeah?" he says without letting me finish. "Is that what happens when you're concussed? Thinking through your life choices?"

"Would you just shut up?" I snap at him. It's bad enough that we're having this conversation while I'm tucked in bed without him turning it into a show of masculinity.

He grins. "Glad to know that head injuries make you feistier." I don't miss the way his eyes dip down to my chest. I'm only wearing a thin t-shirt. I hike up the covers so he can't see that I'm cold.

I take a deep breath, gathering my wits. "I've been thinking about what happened with Barbara."

His smile falls. "Barbara?"

"The woman with the Chevelle."

His expression doesn't change. "Go on."

"I want in."

Again, his expression doesn't change. "You want into what? The sorority? The chess club?"

I ignore his annoying comments. "I have things to offer. You need a woman on your team. For a lot of reasons. To make your female clients rest easy. To use my cleavage to convince your male clients."

His mouth quirks up.

"I can fix cars."

I'm surprised by the look that takes over his face now. Contemplative. Calculating. "Is that so?"

"Yes," I tell him. "Before my father ditched, he taught me everything. And I'm a good driver."

"How good?" he says.

"Really good."

"Good enough that if you had been driving that car instead of your boyfriend, you wouldn't be sitting here right now?"

I hold his gaze. *Not exactly.* I don't say it out loud. Tyler's Audi still isn't enough to beat the Beast, even with me driving.

When I don't say anything, Julian stands, putting his hands in his pockets. His earrings sparkle in the light of the beside lamp. "I don't need anyone else. I have a crew."

"You can't grow unless your crew grows. I'm here anyway," I tell him. "You're feeding me. You're keeping an eye on me twenty-four hours a day. You might as well put me to work."

I throw the blanket off myself and stand. I can't let him tower over me. I don't miss the way he watches my legs, either because he likes the way they look or because he's afraid I'm going to tumble back down at any moment.

"You asked me why I'm with Tyler. That scenario that you painted for me the other night, you were right." Admitting it tastes like acid, but I have to swallow my pride, or I don't get what I want out of this. "That's what Tyler wants from me. To be miserable, and to take care of his offspring, and to be his trophy wife."

He doesn't respond.

"Tyler said he would give me $100,000 if I found out what you're selling."

One of his eyebrows perks up like a fishhook.

"His father is paying for me to go to Dartmouth, but I thought if I got the money from this, I could be done with Tyler for good."

He doesn't react. Maybe he already knew that.

"I did love Tyler. When we started seeing each other, I...I loved him. And he loved me, I thought. His father agreed that as long as we were together, he would pay for my school. So, that's why I'm with Tyler. And that's why I'm not going to leave him."

"You're not going leave him?" An emotionless question. He asks it like he's asking my thoughts on the price of eggs.

I feel my face flush, feel the tears threatening to come loose. "No, I'm not going to leave him. At least, not publicly. I don't know why you're at war with him, but whatever the reason is..." I take a deep breath. "I think I can help you. But I can only help if he thinks we're still together. I'm your inside source. I need him to think I'm still his, even if I'm not."

Julian tips his chin up. "Aren't you? Still his?"

"No. Not anymore." Not after what he did to me today. I want a Dartmouth education. I want something to hold in my hand that could lead to a real future so I don't have to follow in my mother's footsteps. And I was willing to tolerate a lot for it. But what Tyler did today? It terrified me. *He* terrified me. He hurt me, left me.

So, no. I'm not his anymore.

I'm nobody's.

Starting today, I belong to myself.

"But once you get what you want from him, I'm going to need money to pay for school."

"So you want to work for me."

"Yes."

I almost tell him about the money Tyler stole from me, but I don't think I could get it out without my voice breaking. Five thousand dollars down the drain.

"And I'm just supposed to trust you? You seem to be an

awfully good liar, Sloane, and I don't take well to being lied to."

I nod. "I understand."

At this, his thick, dark eyebrows raise. He thought I was going to argue with him. Maybe if I wasn't practically begging him to do this for me, I *would* have argued.

"Only tell me as much as I need to know in order to benefit you. Need-to-know only. I can do whatever you need me to and you can teach me to do anything I don't already know. Teach me how to use a gun. Teach me how to sell cars—"

"You really don't know, do you?" He leans forward, planting his hands on knees and looking up at me. I'm surprised he hasn't stood, hasn't tried to use his height to get the upper hand. If anything, he's made himself smaller.

"Know what?"

"What makes that boyfriend of yours a bad guy."

And here it is. The thing I've been dancing around. The thing I promised myself I wouldn't believe, even if Julian told me. The thing that's put him and Tyler at war.

"No."

He nods and leans back, making himself comfortable, his long legs splayed out in the space between us. "In the year and a half your boyfriend has been here, he's become the most dependable and non-discerning drug dealer in the county."

In a split second, my mind tries to make sense of so many things at once. I try to remember if I've ever seen Tyler do drugs, or even any of his friends, anything harder than weed. I try to think if I've ever seen drug paraphernalia anywhere around his room, if I've seen him with suspicious characters, if I even think he's smart enough to pull something like that off.

"Is it that hard to believe?"

I'm not sure how long I've been mulling this over. But no, it isn't that hard to believe. Not really. Maybe it would have been before all this, but now that I know what Tyler is capable of, I don't know if anything could surprise me now.

"It doesn't make any sense. Tyler's dad is loaded. What does he get out of selling drugs?"

He sighs, and I can see he's trying to decide what he should tell me. While he's trying to decide, his eyes dip to my clothes, and I think maybe I should put on real clothes since apparently no one in this compound can function in the presence of tits.

I turn for the bathroom, where I've stashed my suitcase in the closet. When I'm inside, his voice carries in to me, half muffled through the door that I partially close behind me. "Tyler's father lost his company. His family is going broke."

I stop in the middle of the closet, looking at myself in the floor-length mirror on the wall. *His family is broke.* When was Tyler going to tell me that? How long was I going to be shackled to him under false pretenses, letting him cheat on me and abuse me, before I found out that the Dartmouth money is gone?

Stop. Compartmentalize. I can't deal with this information while Julian Shaw is right outside the door. I carefully bend down and rifle through my suitcase for something appropriate to wear.

"So, what, you want to take Tyler out because he's messing around in your territory?" I grab some fresh clothes and as I'm standing, a thought occurs to me, a thought that has my stomach sinking, even though I guess it wouldn't be all that surprising either. "Wait," I say, rushing back into the bedroom, "do *you* sell drugs? Is that what's in the cars?"

A wave of vertigo hits me like a truck. My vision starts to go spotty around the edges, and I lose my balance. Two big hands wrap around me, holding me up. "Hey," Julian says, bending to meet my eye, where the stars that were closing in are starting to dissipate. "You should sit down."

I don't move. All I can do is look up into his dark eyes, made even darker by the fact that we haven't turned on any lights, are just having this conversation in the subtle light of the bedside lamp. He looks soft in the light, all rounded edges and silky skin.

His eyes take me in, and then he turns us and settles me on the edge of the bed. He takes his hands away and shoves them in his pockets. "No. We don't sell drugs, and we don't want anyone else selling drugs in our market."

"Then what do you sell besides cars?"

His eyes dip to me. "Need-to-know only, princess."

The stupid nickname comes out a little softer than it has in the past.

I settle back on the bed. I *did* say I wouldn't ask for more information than was strictly necessary. It makes me nervous to work for people who are probably breaking laws without knowing exactly what laws they're breaking, but it's a chance I have to take. The choice, it would seem, is between one criminal and another, and this particular criminal hasn't almost killed me, so he's the better option.

My money would be *my* money.

"Let's talk about my cut."

He goes back to the chair by the window and leans back, pressing his fingertips to his mouth in a thoughtful gesture. "You're an enterprising young woman, aren't you?"

I don't respond to that, just wait to see what he'll say about the money. It's not as if I know what percentage I should ask for. I don't know how much money he makes or how much my skills are worth. All I know is that Dartmouth costs approximately $80,000 a year. My first year is all paid up, which means I have to scrape together $60,000.

Julian stands. "We'll talk about your cut tomorrow. Sarge

will kill me if he knows I kept you up with a concussion. You're grounded until you're healed."

"What? I have midterms."

He stops with the door open, the knob in his hand. My eyes are caught by it. Something is off, and it takes me a second to realize the knob has a lock. "Don't argue with me. I'll have Claudia sort it out. A make-up exam or an online test. She'll let you know. You need to rest, and we have plans to make. I'll see you bright and early."

With that, he's gone, and my whole life has changed. Again.

21

JULIAN

I want to have this conversation with the men about as much as I want to rip all of my own teeth out with a pair of pliers. I know my men well enough to know exactly how this is going to go.

I watch them settle into their seats around the dining room table, and I sort of wish that I had invested in a conference room extension the way Bram is always suggesting I should.

"We need to have a little discussion," I tell them. "I know that no one here is going to like what I have to say, but I also want to make it very clear that while I value the opinions of the people in this room, this is not a democracy." I glare at them and they all look back. I can see the hesitancy in their gazes. "I've made a decision, and it's not up for debate. I'm bringing Sloane into the operation."

I watch every expression at the table change in a fraction of a second.

Only two people don't react. The two people that I would expect not to react. Bram, who for some undecided reason seems to have a soft spot for Sloane and who already knew this was a possibility. And Claudia. Claudia doesn't react to much. Maybe because she isn't surprised by much. She's always a step ahead of everyone here anyway, myself included.

The first person speaks, and it's exactly who I thought it would be. "What the hell are you talking about?" Frankie asks. Frankie is a fucking pain in my ass. He'll never get over not being recruited to lead the business, or at the very least, being named second-in-command.

Bram is my second-in-command, just like I was my father's. I never wanted to be second-in-command, but that's how it goes. I never wanted to be involved in this shit at all, but when you're eighteen and your father says you're going to be joining the family business, you're not left with a whole lot of options.

I wanted to be a lawyer. But here I am, and needless to say, some of the old crew aren't all that excited about my dad naming me his second-in-command over them.

And even though we've never had any real conversation about it, Frankie has always made it very clear that he isn't happy with the fact that I'm leading the charge. Frankie is one of the old crew. Along with Sarge and Bram. I hired everyone else to my own satisfaction.

There are days I wish I could kick Frankie out, but these are the men who know my secrets and there's no getting rid of any of them without risking myself. It's one thing to let someone leave of their own volition, but kick someone out, and you have an angry dangling thread on your hands.

If I was my dad, I'd just put a bullet in his head. That was how he handled organization members he got tired of. I've never been a big fan myself.

"I said it wasn't up for debate," I growl at Frankie. "I didn't bring this to the table to ask for anybody's blessing. I don't give a fuck. Not today."

Frankie clenches his jaw, stares at me like he's trying to burn me alive with his eyes.

"But you have to understand how big a risk it is," Claudia says. Her eyes on me are steady. She knows she doesn't really have a say. Claudia is only here because of Leo, because of the promise I made to him. But out of everyone in the room, her opinion is the only one I would respect in this matter. She has just as much skin in this game as I do when it comes to Tyler.

"I understand the risk," I tell her. I look around the table at everyone, one by one. "She wants to help us take him down."

They're quiet. They're finally listening.

"I don't know if she trusts us. And obviously we don't trust her. But she's offering us assistance that we can't afford to turn down. We can't let this thing go on any longer. We've got her for now. I suggest we utilize her. I was trying to get answers out of her subtly, and then I tried to get answers out of her not so subtly. And then I found out that she doesn't have answers at all."

"What do you mean she doesn't have answers?" Xander asks.

"I mean that sweet, innocent little cupcake upstairs didn't know that her boyfriend was dealing."

Bram grimaces, Ronny lets out a snicker, but Frankie just scowls. "How could she not know? Is she blind?"

"She's trusting. Forgiving. Maybe expected the best out of someone she thought she knew. She'll never make that mistake again. The thing is..." I tell them, "she doesn't know anything. But she *could* learn something. She has access to him that we don't have. We just need her to snuggle up to him."

Frankie sighs. "That's bullshit."

"Again—" I start to say, but he cuts me off.

"I'm not talking about letting her in. I'm talking about the fact that she doesn't know what he's into. I don't believe her. I think she's lying."

"You can't fake that kind of shock." The shock on her face when I told her. It wasn't surprise that he could be some bad version of the guy she knew, and it wasn't surprise that he was managing to keep it a secret from her. It was shock that he would *need* to do something like this.

"Look, we all know she came here to spy on us. I'm not looking the other way. I'm not being blinded. I'm seeing the situation for what it is. She didn't get the information she needed. Her boyfriend got mad. He tried to beat the shit out of her."

I meet the eyes around the table. Most of them don't really know what happened yesterday, but I know word travels fast around the compound, from one sector to another.

"He sold her to me, he's threatened her, he's fucked around on her, and this was finally the last straw. She has no reason to go back to him. He doesn't have anything to offer her that we can't."

"What are we offering her?" Claudia asks.

"We're offering her a cut."

"A cut for what?" Frankie asks.

"For whatever she can do around here." I lace my fingers together, set them on the table top. "She says she can drive. It's a simple enough job, driving the deliveries."

Frankie scoffs, and I'm almost frustrated that all the other guys are letting him speak for them. I'd be happier if anyone other than Frankie was putting up a fight. It's not like I wasn't expecting it.

"She doesn't even have to know what's in them. I'm also going to teach her how to shoot."

"What?" This time, I can't even pinpoint where the outburst comes from because everyone at the table reacts so loudly, all speaking over each other.

"I said," I say over all of them, "I'm teaching her to shoot, not that I'm giving her access to guns. If you're worried about your safety, getting your balls blown off, don't fucking go near her. If you give her a reason to shoot, maybe you fucking deserve it."

My temper settling down, I take a seat at the table and sigh. "I'm open to suggestions, if anyone has them, about how she could be useful around here."

"Oh, I know exactly how she can be useful," Magnus says from the end of the table.

I slam my fist down, satisfied when all the breakfast dishes rattle. "I'm done with the fucking jokes. If anyone lays a hand on her or suggests to her that she should lay a hand on them, I'll start removing body parts."

I watch Magnus shrink into himself, so angry I'm vibrating in my seat.

"She's offered us a certain amount of loyalty, and we're not in a position to scoff at that. We take the risk because she could help us end it all. No one ever won by playing it safe. We need to take care of business."

"Let me take care of business," Xander says, eyes hard.

"No bullets," I tell him. "Not until we can neutralize the bigger threat."

They all nod.

"You're dismissed. Get to fucking work."

They all scramble off. I had to interrupt most of them in the middle of business for this meeting, and the last thing anyone wants is to stop workflow to hear news like this. Now they all have to play catch-up for the afternoon.

When I turn for the hall and my office, I hear Frankie follow me out. I know it's him because he's the only one in the compound who stomps everywhere he goes, like he has beef with God and is taking it out on the earth itself.

"What the hell do you think you're doing?" Frankie demands as soon as we're in the hallway.

"Enough," I growl back, stepping into my office and pouring myself a drink. I'm not going to get through this day without one.

"She comes in here, flashes her pretty smile—"

I spin around. "I said, enough. I didn't ask for your fucking opinion."

He shakes his head. "Pretty princess rolls up in here with her pretty blonde hair and her pretty blue eyes, and you turn into a fucking pussy. Should have known that when your daddy passed everything off to you, you would be too fucking soft."

"Who's been keeping you fed?" I demand before throwing back the drink in my hand. It can't hit my bloodstream fast enough. "Who's put a roof over your head, Frankie?"

"Your daddy never would have stood for this shit."

"Do you want to end up like him?" I shout, the words echoing off the walls. "Because he wouldn't have put up with *this shit* either, Frankie. He put bullets in his men for a lot less than the way you're mouthing off right now. Get in line or you'll spend the rest of your days down in the cage finding out just how soft I am."

There's rage in his eyes, but I can see him backing down.

"If you can't trust me, then maybe you don't belong here."

Something shifts in his eyes, and I'm surprised to find hurt there, of all things. Frankie has been part of this organization far longer than I have. Some of these men, this is the only family, the only home, they've ever known, and being told they don't belong, well, that might be the worst thing Frankie has ever heard.

If he wanted my respect, he shouldn't have come here gunning for a fight.

"Get the fuck out of my office."

22

JULIAN

I take a seat in the dark room, do my best to look around as inconspicuously as possible. Everything is awash with purple light. When a woman wearing nothing but a thong and glittery stars over her nipples bends over and asks me what I want to drink, I order a whiskey straight.

This is a mistake.

If I've learned anything over the last eight years, it's that you have to trust your instincts. My instincts are telling me that meeting one of Tyler's pawns whose face I won't be able to recognize just because he says he'll give me information for a substantial paycheck is definitely the wrong move.

I've done this enough times to know when people are trustworthy and when they aren't. And I have absolutely no reason to trust this guy.

But I also feel like my options right now are very limited. He wants to give me information about Tyler, so I'll take it. His men are starting to get hungry. Maybe if I just wait things out long enough, I can get them to turn on him one by one. That's what animals do, after all. When they're starving, they eat their young.

My eyes are on a woman on stage who has her legs wrapped around a pole when a body drops into the seat next to mine. "There are closer and better strip clubs," the guy says, reaching for the whiskey on the table between us. My whiskey. I don't stop him. Just watch him take a drink. He's pale and gaunt, lanky, with long, greasy hair that he runs his hand through as he drinks.

Once he's finished half the glass, he looks over at me. "These girls won't suck your dick. Did you know that?"

"No. I've never asked any of them to."

He scoffs, leans back in his seat. "You got the money?"

"It's in my car."

He throws his hands up. "Well, what good is it going to do me in there?"

God, this guy's an idiot. "Did you think I was going to stick fifty grand into my pocket and walk into a strip club?"

He shrugs. "Sure."

If I wasn't sure before, this man is proof that Tyler is hiring anyone he can find on the street. I've seen the men he works with over the last year and a half. People come to him begging for money, begging for a job, and he gives it to them and then tosses them aside at the first opportunity. Human shields and warm bodies, the lot of them.

These are no criminal masterminds he has working for him. They're just mindless thugs who don't have anything better to do and need money or a hit.

"Tell me what you've got."

He shakes his head. "No, not until I see the money."

I clench my fists, resist the urge to fucking put this guy on the ground, my boot on his fucking neck. I don't have time for this shit. I don't have time for people with no honor who assume that I also have no honor. He's lucky I'm not a fan of needless murder because all it would take is getting a message to Tyler that he's got a leak and this guy would be dead by morning.

"Fine. Let's go."

He grimaces. "What a waste of an evening, sitting in a strip club, not even getting my dick sucked."

"Well, I'm not going to do it for you," I tell him.

He stumbles out into the parking lot, and I follow behind, watching him go and feeling even more than before like this was a bad idea. This guy is barely coherent. Can I even trust whatever information he's about to give me?

"Aha, the Beast," the guy slurs, walking up to my car. He knocks on the trunk twice and leans an elbow on it. My eyes drop to his arm until he slowly straightens.

I just want to get this over with. Half the guys are on a job that should be finishing up across the border any moment, and the other half are down at Rowdy's waiting for them. I want to know how the job has gone, and then I want to go drink with my guys.

I do not want to be standing here with this fuck face. I pop the trunk, pull out the envelope I have stashed in one of the compartments there. "Here." I hand it to him and like the moron he is, he opens it and sticks his hand in. "Not fucking here," I growl. God, please send me someone who has a goddamn brain cell.

"How am I supposed to know it's all here?"

"If it's not all there when you count it at home, you can come and retrieve the rest. You know where I live. Now, fucking talk. I've got places to be."

"Sure," he says. "Mr. Important, Mr. Busy." He tucks the envelope into his back pocket. I'm not convinced the guy could count to 50,000. "So here's the deal, about this time last year, Tyler's daddy's company went tits up. He went from billionaire status to unemployed like that." He snaps his fingers. "Apparently his endowment to Dartmouth will get Pretty Boy through college, but once that's done, he's going home to nothing. So he decides he's going to start dealing to try and save the family. As if anyone ever became a billionaire by slinging coke to rich college students. But whatever. Not my business. That kid couldn't grow a brain in a lab. He figures he'll make a bunch of money and go back to California a hero."

"I hope you don't think this information is worth the money I just gave you. Tell me something I don't already know."

He nods impatiently. "Don't get your panties in a twist. I'm getting there. Last year, when that kid died…"

The whiskey that was sitting in my esophagus threatens to come back up. "Yeah," I say, letting him know to carry on quickly.

"It really drummed up shit for us. The cops were on Tyler's ass. They were on everybody's ass. They were asking around all over the place, and more than one person points them in the direction of Tyler."

Jesus. This is why you have to have discernment in your hiring process. Because when the cops show up, and they inevitably will, you can't just have some fucking rando drug addict on the side of the street knowing all your business. But Tyler doesn't know that because Tyler's a fucking moron.

"Tyler comes up clean, but now he's gotta lay low."

"Yeah, I could tell as much."

"He's outsourcing the work," he goes on. "He used to have suppliers here in the city, but now he doesn't know who to trust. So, he hires a guy out in east New Hampshire, in Lebanon. But he's got people like me carting it into town."

That's a fuckin' drive. Here in the city, I have the benefit of my name. People here know me, and they're scared of me. People out there don't give two shits who I am. I can't just go out to Lebanon and start asking questions without starting yet another war.

"You don't have names?"

He scoffs. "No, I don't have names."

"What about the guys who snitched?"

His eyes come up slowly. He raises an eyebrow. "What about them?"

"What did he do to them?"

He scoffs again. "You want that kind of information? It's gonna cost you a whole lot more than fifty grand."

I clench my teeth. "What you gave me wasn't even worth fifty grand."

He seems to consider this, tapping one dirty finger against his chin. "Tyler might be hiring half of Hanover to run for him, but he's keeping dirt on everyone."

I take a menacing step toward him. This could be interesting. "What kind of dirt?"

"He records everyone. They don't know it, but a friend of mine caught him out a while ago. He's recording everything so that if anyone else snitches, he can put them down..." His eyes shoot to me. "...the easy way."

So, Tyler kills one person to get him out of the way, learns that murder has consequences, and then to avoid having to kill anyone else, starts collecting blackmail material.

"Get me recordings and I'll give you an easy million."

I swear, I see dollar signs in the guy's eyes. "Come on, I can't pull that off."

I shrug. "Guess that's life. I'll get the recordings with or without your help." I turn toward the driver's side of the Beast, but when the guy steps toward me, I spin back. He stops advancing, a frustrated clench to his jaw.

"That's not fair. You can't just dangle that shit in front of me."

"Get me what I want."

Anger burns bright in his eyes. He has no idea how to get those recordings. He steps up to me, his chin up, eyes scanning me from head to toe. "You better watch it, bud. I know exactly who you've got in that little castle of yours. He'll come for little mama next."

I grab the side of his head and slam it down on the trunk. "If *you* don't fucking watch it," I growl into his ear, "you're gonna go back to your master without a fucking tongue. You hear me? You have some fucking respect."

He grunts, and there's a sharp pain in my side.

The fucker knifed me. Without a second thought, I pull the gun out of my waistband, put it to his head and pull the trigger.

Fuck.

I glance over at the back exit of the strip club. Chances are good nobody heard a thing. No one's going to see me. No one's going to come knocking. I use this particular strip club because they don't have security cameras. It's not very smart business, but I have to get him out of here. And quick.

I yank him up. So much fucking dead weight, and the pain in my side is enough to make my vision go spotty as I pop the trunk and slip him inside. What the hell else am I going to do with him?

If I had brought the guys with me the way I should have, I wouldn't be in this situation right now. Bram would have seen a knife coming a mile away.

I reach into the rat's back pocket to take my money back before I slam the door closed.

What a mess.

23

SLOANE

I've just turned in my last test of the day—it's insane that Claudia and Julian were able to talk my professors into this— when I feel the whole house shift. I recognize the feeling from the years spent living in our trailer. The wind would blow the door wide open when it wasn't locked, and the whole building would shift, all at once.

The front door was just opened very quickly, and then I hear it slam closed.

No one is supposed to be home tonight. I was told that some of the guys went to a bar and some of the guys had a job. We're still figuring out this whole need-to-know thing, but at least they're giving me information now, handing me facts, not keeping me in the dark about everything.

I'm here virtually alone. The only other person here is whoever is down by the gate.

I knew it was a test as soon as Bram told me. I know they wanted to see if I snoop. I don't blame them. How can I? And so, I haven't budged from my room all evening, not that I would want to. I still get a little queasy when I move around too fast. My head feels like a bowling ball perched on a plastic straw.

"Sarge!" I recognize Julian's voice, so loud I swear the pens on my desk rattle.

I sit very still. I know I have to be careful about this whole thing, be really smart about it. I know that if I put one toe out of line, the guys will make a move, maybe throw me into the lake or ship me back to Fresno in pieces.

So I don't move, even though Julian's shout sends a ripple of fear through me.

No one answers.

No footsteps, no response.

He does it again, screams, "Sarge!" and grunts.

It's the grunt that gets me up onto my feet. I recognize that sound, too. The universal sound for, *fuck, that hurts*. And something about it coming from Julian makes me move. I look up at the camera and press my ear to the door, listen to the shuffling downstairs. Julian's shoes. Another grunt of pain. I have my hand on the knob, but I know I shouldn't. If there's one thing I've learned being here, it's that I should absolutely never stick my nose where it doesn't belong or anywhere they don't want me to be. Which seems to be everywhere.

Whatever's going on with Julian, he and his men should take care of it. Except there are no men.

Was he out somewhere on a job alone? Even while I'm contemplating it, I hear the sound of footsteps on the stairs. I step back away from the door and scramble back to my desk. If he's coming in here, I know he won't knock. Julian never has.

He throws open my door and looks around until he sees me sitting at the desk. "I need your help," he says.

Those are not words that I ever expected to come out of Julian Shaw's mouth.

"What? You need *my* help?"

He leans against the wall by my door. In the bright overhead light, I see there's a wet spot seeping through his dark shirt, leaving a red stain on his hand.

I jump up out of my chair and almost tip over. "Holy shit, are you bleeding?"

"Look, I don't have anybody else," he says through gritted teeth. "So would you fucking help me?"

I don't point out that he would attract more flies with honey than vinegar, like I might have in a different situation. "What do you need?" I ask him instead.

He nods to the open door and stumbles through it himself, leading me to Sarge's room next door. I already know the inside of Sarge's bedroom, accented in a sort of plum color, with a big table to the side, where he evidently likes to play cards. But what I didn't know is that on the other side of Sarge's bathroom, there's a door, and that door leads into a sitting room with a medical table. Over by the window, there's a long cabinet and a desk, one of those really fancy ones that's made of real wood and probably weighs two hundred pounds.

"He has all the supplies there," Julian says. He nods in the direction of the cabinet, and I realize he means *medical supplies*. My eyes travel over to a cot folded and pushed against the wall.

"How often is Sarge treating injuries in here?"

"Often enough for me to pay him for it."

He settles onto the seat by the window, electing not to sit on the table or pull out the cot. In my mind, whenever I see window seats, I always think of Jane Austen characters reading books in the middle of summer in the English countryside. Instead, I've got Julian, wearing all black, bleeding through his shirt.

He strips off his coat, doing his best to keep his hand over his side. "You ever stitch up a wound before?"

"Have I ever stitched up a wound before? What am I, a medieval nurse? Of course, I've never stitched up a wound."

He sighs as I move to the cabinet and open it, even though I don't know what I'm looking for.

"I wasn't sure, what with your boyfriend throwing you around the way he does."

I'm glad there's a cabinet door between us so he can't see the look on my face. I want to be angry at his comment, but how can I be, after what he witnessed? After what everyone in this house witnessed? My own stitches are currently on display, after all.

So I keep my mouth shut and look around inside. There are small bottles that I know hold injectable medications. There are orange bottles full of pills, boxes full of bandages and gloves and surgical masks.

"What am I looking for, exactly?"

He slumps against the window. "For fuck's sake," he says. "Don't you go to Dartmouth? You're supposed to be fucking smart."

I slam the cabinet door closed. "If I was smart, maybe I would let you bleed out. My life would be a lot easier if you were dead, you know."

I expect some kind of witty quip or insult in return, but instead, he just smirks at me, the asshole. "I'm not going to bleed out from this particular wound, so don't start the funeral arrangements just yet."

My eyes fall to his side. I would have assumed a wound to the torso would be dangerous for organs, but he doesn't seem too concerned.

I open the cabinet again. "Now tell me what I'm looking for or find someone else who's willing to help you."

He grimaces. "You're going to need scissors. I'm not going to be able to get the shirt off over my head."

He wants me to cut his shirt off? I don't ask the question out loud because I don't want to hear what kind of smart ass answer he's going to come up with.

"You're going to need disinfectant, cotton swabs, and there should be needles. Curved ones. And thread. Have you ever sewn *anything* up before?"

I find scissors and a plastic bag of cotton squares. I don't know how big his wound is, so I grab several. There is a lot of blood, after all.

"I understand the physics of sewing," I say as I search for needles. "My mom tried to teach me once, when I was a kid, and my teddy bear's foot fell off." I finally locate a placket of sturdy, curved needles. I hold them up to the light coming in through the window. I've never seen needles like this before.

"Did you manage to get the foot back on to your teddy bear?"

"No," I tell him, slamming the cabinet shut again. "He had one foot forever, and eventually, all of his stuffing fell out." I grab the small pair of sewing scissors and step over to the window, what's left of the fading sun casting shadows across his face. "Hate to ruin your nice clothes," I say.

He snorts. "I have approximately three hundred black shirts."

"And impeccable fashion sense." My voice is steady, confident, but my hands are anything but. I've never done anything like this before, and it would have been hard to do with a normal person, a friend, someone I liked.

It's much harder to do it with Julian Shaw, a man I hate who hates me right back.

I focus on keeping my hand steady as I press close to

him. I don't like being close to Julian. It feels like getting too close to a vicious dog. As long as I keep my distance, I can run, theoretically, if he starts to snap.

I take the collar of his shirt in my fingers, careful not to brush against his skin, and start to cut, ignoring the way the fabric under my fingers is cold and wet with his blood when I reach the bottom.

When it's cut all the way down, I step back and watch him remove it carefully. I can't stop my eyes from moving over his chest, his sharp clavicles, the lines and pictures of his tattoos, the long, toned plains of his stomach.

The wound on his side—obviously from a knife—slashes right through a tattoo of a tiger just below his ribs. On instinct, I almost tell him I'm sorry the tattoo will be ruined, but I don't want him to think I have any sympathy for him. If he got himself stabbed, he probably deserved it.

"This isn't a bullet wound," I say, very gently pressing around the wound, trying to make sure the bleeding has slowed enough for me to work on it.

"I never said it was a bullet wound." To his credit, he doesn't so much as twitch.

"I guess I just assumed," I say, reaching over to the cabinet beside me for the cleaning supplies. It's nice actually, having something to distract me, something to do with my hands while he breathes steadily in front of me.

I focus on wetting one of the bandages with alcohol. "Tell me, Mr. Shaw, how does a car salesman manage to get himself stabbed?"

When he doesn't say anything, I risk a glance up at him. He's watching me, his blue eyes careful. "A lot of dangerous people around these parts," he finally says.

"By these parts, do you mean New Hampshire, crime capital of North America?"

The corner of his mouth turns up just slightly. I trade the

alcohol and cotton swab for the needle, holding it up to the light and staring at the curved shape of it.

"It's very simple," he says, his voice coming out ragged. "It doesn't have to be anything fancy; it just has to keep things together so they can heal. The knot is the hardest part. The straighter the better."

I nod. Totally know what all that means. "How do you know so much about stitches?"

"Years of watching Sarge."

I have the needle hovering over Julian's skin. Piercing skin is not the same as piercing the cotton on a teddy bear. Teddy bears don't bleed. Teddy bears don't have thick layers that you have to poke through.

"I don't know if I can do this," I whisper.

He sets his head back against the window frame. "Don't think about it, just do it."

Even though I know he's being condescending, his words still help. *Don't think about it, just do it.* I don't want to do this, but I also don't want to show any weakness. I don't want him to think this is something I'm not capable of. If I've learned anything in my time being here, it's that I have to prove that whatever these men can do, whatever they're willing to do, I'm capable and willing to do it, too.

So I grit my teeth and I shove the needle into his skin.

"You gotta get it in the whole way," he says. "You're going to loop it while you're inside the wound."

"I think I understand the basics" I tell him. Which is mostly a lie. I don't really understand. But I'm prideful enough to not want to have to listen to him instruct me every single moment of the way. I don't want to contribute to his swelling ego if I don't have to.

After a minute, he glances down, squints at what I'm doing. "Looks good.

"Is that a compliment?"

"They're stitches. No one's giving you a medical degree anytime soon."

My eyes flicker up to his and I'm surprised by the steadiness I find there, the lack of hostility. I would have thought he would be angry at me for being the only person who could help him in this moment, that he would be angry about whoever gave him this wound to begin with.

Once I've started stitching, things get a little easier. I get so concentrated on what I'm doing and making sure the stitches are correct that I forget I'm dealing with skin, that the tips of my latex gloves are red with his blood, that it's him at all.

And before I know it, I've stitched him up completely. It's ugly and chances are good Sarge will have to fix them, but it looks pretty alright to me. I straighten away from him and remove my gloves. For good measure, I pour some alcohol in the wound. I've forgotten for a moment that the wound is, in fact, on a person until Julian winces, sucks in air between his clenched teeth.

I huff out a laugh. "You can handle a knife wound, you can handle the stitches without anything to numb it, but you can't handle a little alcohol."

He raises an eyebrow at me. "I'd love to see how much you can handle, princess."

My breath stutters out of me. His eyes are steady as he looks at me and I feel like a book he's reading, a problem he's solving. I'm surprised when his eyes drop. They seem to scan my neck, my collarbone, the skin that I'm showing above the collar of my shirt. His hand comes up, his fingers ever so slightly brushing the bruised skin on my face, caressing the spot just below the stitches on my cheek. His eyes slowly track back up to mine.

I suck in a breath right as the bedroom door opens.

JULIAN

"She didn't do a terrible job," Sarge says, poking at my wound with half the grace and gentleness that Sloane did. He has sausage fingers and hers were featherlight. "Never sewn anything up before," he adds in a contemplative tone.

"Would you like me to ask her if she'll blow you?" I say between my teeth.

Sarge ignores my anger, just chuckles quietly. He straightens away from me, takes off the glasses that he has perched on the end of his nose. "What are you so bitter about, Julian? She's offering to give you everything you want."

"Assuming I can trust her."

"Yes," he says, "assuming you can trust her."

It's quite the assumption. At this point, there's no way to know who can be trusted and who can't. Just because this girl's boyfriend tried to knock her head in doesn't mean she's trustworthy. It doesn't mean she's being smart, either.

She could be lying to my face, telling me a sob story about not being able to afford college and being stuck with a boyfriend she hates because he has money.

Or she could be telling the truth.

At this point, I don't know which would be more surprising.

"How'd you get it?" Sarge asks.

I consider that maybe I should just keep it to myself. If the guys don't know what happened, they can't be incriminated. They won't be suspects. But I know that kind of wishful thinking only goes so far.

I straighten up off the window seat, where I've been

sitting so long that my ass is asleep. It's odd to be having this conversation bare-chested, so I put my coat back on, foregoing the t-shirt, now split in two.

"It was one of Tyler's guys."

Out of the corner of my eye, I see Sarge freeze. He was cleaning his hands, but he stops, looks over at me. "What were you doing with one of Tyler's guys?"

"He offered me information for cash. It wasn't worth it, but it'll help. He was an idiot." I shake my head, honestly embarrassed at myself, but it is what it is. "He started talking shit. I grabbed him and he poked me."

"I'm guessing he has more than a knife wound."

I nod.

He sighs. "Fuck."

"No one saw me. We were outside. I went to that place off Highway 10 that doesn't have enough security."

"What did you do with him?"

"Took Pinneo Hill out to the mountains. Guy was a lowlife. By the time anyone knows he's gone, he'll be halfway decomposed."

He watches me pace back and forth across the dark room, the pain in my side a steady drumbeat.

"Tyler's going to know it was you."

I laugh. "And? He doesn't care about these guys. What's he going to do? I would love for that fucker to come at me so I would have an excuse to fuck him up, alright? But he's too fucking scared because he knows he would never win in a fight with me. Not one-on-one."

I can tell by the look on his face that he's disappointed. And I get it. Play stupid games, win stupid prizes, and all that.

"What's done is done." I head for the door, sticking my head back out into the hall and checking to make sure Sloane isn't hanging around. "We're not going to tell the guys."

"Don't you think they have a right to know?"

"No. We don't tell anybody, and we don't have to worry about any of them giving up any information."

His eyes are alight with rage. "Does the girl know?"

I shake my head.

He nods in turn. "Keep the stitches clean, please. I don't want to have to cut you back open if it gets infected."

I tap the doorframe. "Aye, Captain."

24

SLOANE

"Okay, I think that's good. Turn toward the window. Let me get a good look. You'll still be able to see the stitches through it, but the bruises will be invisible."

This is the most Claudia has said to me since she arrived at my door to help me cover up my face with makeup. According to Bram, she's a master. I didn't think there was anything anyone could teach me about applying basic makeup, but I was wrong. Claudia has shown me a few things.

Her eyes examine me carefully as she holds me at arm's length.

"How is a Dartmouth professor so good applying make-up?" I ask, partially because the silence is starting to feel like ants under my skin and partially because I'm genuinely curious. Not that college professors can't wear makeup, but Claudia seems particularly talented even though she doesn't seem to wear heavy makeup herself.

She sighs and continues to pat gently at my face with the blender I gave her. "My husband was never concerned with making sure no one knew what he did to me. Most people would go for the body, to remain secretive. He always went for the face. Liked to degrade me that way. Although, that was thirty years ago and in a small town, no less. No one wanted to rock the boat, even when they did see."

"I'm so sorry," I say, the words coming out barely a whisper.

Her hand drops and she takes a step back from me. She examines my face again, but this time, I don't think she's looking at the makeup. I've been staring at her face for most of the last half hour, her frown lines and the maroon lipstick she's wearing, the light curls that hang just above her shoulders. But now I see something that wasn't there before, gentleness in her eyes. "You are, aren't you?"

"Yes," I say, more confidently. "No one should ever have to go through that. I'm hoping, um, you meant *ex*-husband?"

She shrugs and tosses the blender on the table beside us, where the rest of my makeup supplies sit. "Nothing as fancy as all that. My son..." At this, she pauses. Swallows loud enough for me to hear. "He walked in once when it was happening. Pointed a gun at his father and said he would use it if he didn't leave. So he did." She smiles fondly at the memory. "He was seventeen at the time."

What kind of life she must lead.

"What's your role in all of this?" I ask. She seems less hands-on than any of the guys. I don't see her around the compound very much, and I almost never see her involved in business discussions. And other than that first night, she hasn't really spoken to me. She's like a shadow on the outskirts.

"I mostly just keep things organized for the boys. You know how men are. They can't keep a schedule to save their lives. And I've always had a very detail-oriented brain, so I keep everyone in line."

"Why the job at the university then?"

She steps away from me, her body already turned toward the door. "You're an inquisitive one, aren't you, Sloane?"

Normally, no. But since getting here, my curiosity has taken on a life of its own. "I just want to understand."

She puts one hand on the doorknob. "Not everything is some great conspiracy. I work for the men because I can. And I work at the university because I always have. No secrets. Just a bit of admin work." With a nod that is neither kind nor unkind, she leaves my room, and I'm left with more questions than when we started.

25

SLOANE

"You're sure about this?"

I tilt my head up towards Julian, taking in the lines of his face in the morning sun as we wait for my ride back to campus. "If I didn't know any better," I say, trying to ignore the pain in my cheek, now an ever-constant ache, "I'd think you were worried about me."

He looks at me out of the side of his eye. "I'm worried about my investment."

I turn away, biting back a smile. "Speaking of which, how am I supposed to do this?" I ask.

Hugo pulls the car up to us in the driveway and watches us through the driver's side window.

"You're a good actress," Julian says.

I spin to face him. "That may be true, but Tyler can't possibly be stupid enough to think I would go back to him after what he did, right?"

His jaw works back and forth as he considers what I've said. "I honestly don't know, but it's important that you make him believe it." He tips back on his heels, hands in his pockets. "Maybe you could convince him you don't remember what happened."

I huff out a breath. "I just don't think that's enough. It was bad before the fall."

He shrugs. "Tell him you have temporary memory loss or something. Like you don't remember anything that happened before 9 AM."

"Do you even hear yourself when you talk? That's insane. This isn't a soap opera."

His glares at me, his patience clearly waning. "If I've learned anything about your boyfriend, it's that he's kind of a moron. I don't care what you say to him. Figure it the fuck out."

I take a steadying breath. I don't want to lie anymore. I don't want to deal with these fucking men anymore. These men who just see me as a tool in their games. I'm tired of it. But this is what I have to do to get what I want.

"Tell me what I'm looking for."

He keeps his eyes forward, like he's watching the exhaust puff into the cold morning air. I think it's some kind of power play—everything is with Julian Shaw—strategically avoiding eye contact, but in a way that makes it obvious it's his choice.

"I don't want you to know too much."

"Because you don't trust me."

He spins to face me, bending just slightly to see me from his perch way up there at his six-foot height. Now the eye contact is the power move. This time, intimidation. "Because if you get questioned, I need you to not have any information that could get us all sunk."

I clamp my mouth shut.

He ushers me toward the car, watches as I put my seatbelt on. "A source told me he has recordings."

I jerk my head toward him, hovering in the open door. "Recordings of what?"

He shakes his head. "It doesn't matter."

There are only so many places something like that could be hiding. "Is this something that could incriminate him?"

"Yes."

"Then he wouldn't be carrying it around, right?"

He taps his hand on the doorframe, leans in closer to me. "You tell me. You say he's not a moron, but is he dumb enough to carry the evidence of his own crimes in his back pocket?"

I don't know. "Why would he have recordings of him doing something criminal?"

"Because evidence of him doing something criminal is also evidence of other people doing something criminal. Insurance."

I sigh. "Okay, I'll do what I can."

"Great." He slams the car door in my face.

I'm trembling as I walk into the building. Maybe I'm the real moron here, thinking I can play Tyler when he's the one who started the game.

He's waiting for me outside our classroom. I'm surprised he's here at all. The nerve of this man to beat his girlfriend up, leave her unconscious on a bathroom floor, and show up to class two days later.

"Baby," he says when I get to him. He takes my face in his hands, brushes his finger along the stitches I still have in my cheek. Sarge says they can come out tomorrow but the bruising will last weeks. "Fuck, what a mess."

I think about what Julian suggested. It feels ridiculous—melodramatic, like I'm in a Shakespearean play—but I do it anyway. "Do you know what happened?" I ask, keeping my eyes wide, innocent.

A line forms between his brows. "You don't remember?"

Would I be letting you touch me if I did? "No. Well, sort of. I remember us agreeing to meet in the bathroom. I remember arguing with you and then I think I tripped? I woke up in the compound."

He steps back, the crease between his brows growing deeper. I can see the wheels turning. Maybe he's trying to figure out if I remember how rough he was with me, if I remember him leaving me in that bathroom, if the guys took me to a hospital or not.

"So they didn't tell you..." He trails off, watches me carefully. "They didn't tell you that you got knocked out and I called for help? That bodyguard guy...he insisted on taking you with him. You were pretty out of it. I tried to argue with him, but—"

"It's fine." He's really banking on the guys not communicating with me at all. He's just as stupid as Julian thinks he is. My eyes find Ronny over his shoulder, hovering, this time watching closely. Julian insisted he come with me today to keep up the act. I don't need a bodyguard anymore, but Tyler doesn't know that.

"Baby," Tyler says, stepping closer. I can smell the cologne on him that I used to love. "I'm sorry for fighting with you. I didn't mean to—"

"It's okay," I tell him, trying to keep my voice gentle. "Don't worry about it. Things are weird right now. Tensions are high." I watch his eyes as he looks at me, trying to read whether he's suspicious at all. "I was thinking..." I say, turning toward our classroom. We settle into our normal seats. Today is the midterm for this class and then I can stop obsessively studying every waking moment of the day. "Maybe I could come hang out at your place after class."

His eyebrows furrow again. "I thought they wouldn't let you anywhere near me."

I shrug. "I think they're starting to trust me." I sort of wish Julian could see the stupid look on his face right now. Tyler truly buys that I would be loyal through this all. And maybe I've given him reason to think it. He still thinks his $100,000 is enough weight to hold me in place. Would it be, if it weren't for Julian?

"Why would you need them to trust you?"

I turn big eyes at him. "So I can infiltrate. Wasn't that the plan?"

His eyes find Ronny, visible through the still open doorway as he leans against the wall outside the classroom. It's almost unnerving how much more attentive he is today. "Not for you to be on their side."

I scoff, making sure my expression is particularly disbelieving. I hope Julian was right about me being a good actress. "I'm not on their side. It's just a ruse." I scoot my chair closer to his. "If they trust me, they'll say things around me."

"But what are you doing to make them trust you?" There's venom in his voice, and I'm certain he thinks he knows exactly what I'm doing. Fuck them, and they'll trust you. Let them gangbang you, and they'll give up their secrets. Because Tyler can't conceive of a woman earning anything any other way than showing her fucking tits to someone.

"I'm not sleeping with any of them, Tyler." I'm feeling less generous by the moment. My acting skills can't override this. "It's called being nice."

"Nice?" he hisses back.

"Yes. These men, they... they don't know a lot of kindness,

and I think if I show them that kindness, they'll trust me." The worst part is, I'm not even lying. I've seen the way these men are with each other, the way they are with the outside world. I think a little kindness could go a long way. And I really do need them to trust me, just not for Tyler's sake.

He rolls his eyes. "Whatever, Sloane. Look, just don't make yourself too fucking vulnerable, okay? They'll take advantage."

It takes everything in me to keep a straight face. *They'll* take advantage? Tyler's using money to convince me to do his dirty work for him. He uses me as a sex toy. He has sex with other women the second I turn my back. He throws me around, and not in a sexy way. And he has the audacity to say that Julian is the one taking advantage of me?

I stare straight ahead, schooling my expression. "I just wanted to spend some time with you," I tell him, trying to make it seem like I'm disappointed, all while wondering how he could possibly believe me. "But it's fine if you don't want to."

"I want to," he says, his hand snaking out to grab my thigh.

The desire to push him away is a raging inferno inside me.

"Of course, I want to. I just... is that a good idea with, you know, that thing?" He points at my face.

That thing? He's talking about my fucking face. And the wound on said face that he put there. I reach my hand up and touch it gingerly, remembering the feel of Julian's thumb there.

"Yeah, I think it's fine. You know...if you can stand to look at me—"

"It's not that," he says, like it's an unbelievable notion. "Come on, it's not like that. I just, you know... I'm worried. I don't want to hurt you."

He doesn't want to hurt me... says the boy who hurt me.

As our professor starts handing out tests, I whip my hair to the side, exposing my throat and my cleavage. No one asked me to dress provocatively today. Nobody asked me to seduce Tyler. I guess that's why I'm so comfortable doing it. They don't expect me to, and Tyler's easier than all of them put together.

"I mean, we haven't fucked in days. I'm horny," I say, my voice low.

His mouth spreads into a sickening grin. "Is that so?"

"Yes." The biggest lie I've ever told. If there's anything I haven't been thinking about, it's my sex drive. And even if I *was* horny, I wouldn't be asking Tyler to take care of it. Not that I could ask anyone else...

"Alright," he says. "Come after lunch. Your bodyguard's not going to make a fuss?"

I shake my head. "I made it very clear to Julian that I need to be allowed to spend time with you. I just have to be back when I'm supposed to be."

"Does he know you're not a dog?"

Do you *know I'm not a dog?* I want to ask.

But instead, I push Tyler and Julian and stitches and money out of my head so I can focus on my exam.

Tyler groans into my neck, grinding his dick against my leg as he tries to unbutton my jeans. I fight not to gag. My eyes fall to the dresser that Tyler shares with his roommate and then move over to the closet. If I could buy myself, like, two minutes, which one would be the better option? I'd rather not make a habit of seducing Tyler so that I can snoop. I have to find an easier way.

The closet definitely has to be the better option. More storage space. Here's hoping.

"Oh," I say, stiffening my whole body.

Tyler, who finally has my pants halfway undone, pulls back. "What is it?"

"Um, I have to go to the bathroom."

He sighs. "Okay, but hurry. We don't have much time."

"I'll be two seconds." I hop off the bed and go to the bathroom, shutting and locking the door.

I stand there a requisite fifteen seconds before saying, "Oh shit," as loud as I can.

"What is it?" Tyler calls to me through the door.

"I think I started my period."

I can practically hear him rolling his eyes. "This has happened before, remember? It's not real."

He's referring to the fact that the birth control pill I'm on sometimes makes me spot. It wouldn't be unusual for me to have a period, but I don't have them very often, and they're rarely heavy enough for me to be terribly concerned.

"There's a lot of blood," I tell him, feeling a little thrill at the idea that this will disgust him. Tyler never could tolerate the occasional discussion of menstrual cycles. I want him to be disgusted with me. Maybe then he'll stop touching me.

"Fuck," I hear him hiss. Because now, he's not going to get laid. Tyler would never touch me in the face of period blood.

"I don't have anything with me. Can you go see if one of the girls has a tampon?"

"Are you fucking kidding, Sloane?" he growls.

"What am I supposed to do, bleed through my clothes?"

There's a beat of silence. And then I hear the bedroom door open. I don't think any of the frat guys' girlfriends are currently here, so he'll have to go check bathrooms. It'll give me some time.

I scan the bathroom, tiny hairs all over the sink from where he trimmed his facial hair, dirty clothes piled up in a corner, pink mold growing in the shower. I don't think I'm going to find what I'm looking for in here.

I throw the door open and rush to the closet. There's not much in there either, just a mountain of shoes and clean clothes on hangers. There's one box on the shelf in the top corner, and I rip it down, rifling through it.

It has extra shoes, worn to the bones, and cans of spray-on deodorant. There's picture frame at the bottom. A photo of Tyler and his mother that I know she gave him before he left home. He would never display it. People like Tyler think that masculinity means not loving your mom too much.

I don't find anything else. A soccer ball and a stash of mostly full tequila bottles are shoved under an old Garrison Prep sweatshirt, but that's about it. No cell phone, laptop, device of any kind, anything that could hold video recordings. I run my hand along the top shelf, hoping maybe something is hidden up there that I can't see. But all I find is dust and a dead roach.

Gross.

I open up his side of the dresser. The top drawer has boxers stuffed into it and an open box of condoms. The second drawer is full of folded up t-shirts and random shit like scissors and his AirPods case and a phone charger. The bottom drawer is just socks, halfway empty, but at the very bottom, underneath a mountain of white athletic socks, I find, hopefully, what I'm looking for.

I hold up the zip drive. Who the hell is even using zip drives anymore? People who are trying to keep things off the cloud and their devices, I assume.

My eyes shift over to Tyler's laptop, sitting open on the desk, his cell phone beside it.

If Julian and his crowd have all that hardware and those security systems, they have to have somebody who knows technology. If I could steal his computer or his phone, even if he deleted things off of them, I wonder if somebody at the compound could dig deep into the hard drive and find copies.

But Tyler would know that I was the one who took them.

I stick the zip drive in my pocket and push my hand further into the bottom of the drawer just as I hear footsteps on the stairs. My fingers brush something, and I grab it.

My cell phone. I think about taking it, but that's probably too suspicious. Right next to it in my hand, the stack of cash he stole from me. If I clean out his dresser, he's going to know it was me. If I just take the zip drive, maybe he'll think he stashed it somewhere else and forgot.

I rush back into the bathroom and shut the door just as Tyler comes back into the room. I can practically hear the anger in his steps. Not that I give a fuck.

"Here," he says, knocking on the door. He opens it without waiting for me to answer and drops a tampon onto the floor. Such a gentleman.

I make a bunch of noise and spend as much time as I think it would take for me to put a tampon in before tossing it in the trash and stepping out with a sheepish look on my face.

"Sorry," I tell him.

He's reclining on the bed, scrolling on his phone. He shrugs. "Don't worry about it."

Why would he be concerned when the second I'm back at the compound, he's just going to call one of those girls he was with and make them suck him off, since now he has blue balls or whatever.

"I should probably get to class," I tell him, stepping back

and feeling the weight of the zip drive in my pocket. I think about the other day, when he grabbed the money straight from my pocket without a second thought.

I can't let him see. I shift away from him. "I'll see you tomorrow, okay?"

He nods without looking up. His plaything isn't useful to him today, so he doesn't care and doesn't even watch me as I go.

26

JULIAN

"You can't just go in and see him." I hear Ronny's voice on the other side of the door, his tone insistent.

I ignore it. Whoever he's trying to keep out of my office can stay out. I don't have any meetings on the books today. All of the men are busy, and I have shit to do.

We have three cars that are supposed to go out this week, but two of our guys at the warehouse are sick, which means I have to get some of the guys in the compound out to the warehouse. But in order to do that, I have to move schedules around in a big way.

"He wants to see me," a feminine voice says through the door. I drop my pen, moving to the door to yank it open. I find Ronny on the other side, his broad shoulders blocking the doorway. He's so large compared to Sloane that I can't even see her on the other side of him.

"Ronny."

He spins around. "I know you're working," he says, the words flooding out of his mouth. He's been working overtime trying to get back on my good side. "I told her she'll have the wait to talk to you like everybody else, but she's insisting she needs to see you right now."

"It's fine," I tell him.

Sloane steps out from behind him, arms crossed, and gives a little harumph sound. "See? I told you he would want to see me."

"I don't want to see you," I tell her. I just need to know what she found.

Her blue eyes find mine, and her arms fall down to her sides. God, I love pissing her off.

She's wearing a purple tank top with this weird ruching on it that makes her tits look incredible. But I know she wore it just to get Tyler's attention, which is enough to make it less sexy.

"You better have something good. You're interrupting business hours."

"It's business," she says and holds out her hand. In the middle of her small palm is a thumb drive.

There's no way. It could not have been that easy. A year I've been trying to get to Tyler, and she found dirt on him in one afternoon.

"Get inside," I tell her and turn to Ronny. "Nobody else knocks on this door until we're done."

He nods.

I close the door behind us. "Where did you find it?"

She still has the thing clenched in her fist. "It was in his sock drawer."

Some of my excitement fizzles. That doesn't make me feel terribly optimistic about what's on it. I hold my hand out for the little plastic device. Imagine putting your faith in something like that, the fate of your business and your freedom.

She doesn't relinquish it. She drops down in the seat in

front of my desk and tilts her face up toward me. "Let's talk payment."

The little bitch.

I take a deep breath. Can I really blame her? I made it very clear to her how important it was for me to take down Tyler. This is what happens when you show people your weak spots, your vulnerabilities. They learn how to leverage them.

I take a seat across from her. "How much do you want?"

"Five thousand."

I cough out a laugh. She has to be kidding. "Five thousand. For having sex with your boyfriend and rifling through his underwear drawer?"

She leans forward, voice like ice. "For letting a man I'm no longer sleeping with grope me so that I could steal information." She holds my gaze, unflinching. She doesn't waver for even a second. My pants start to get uncomfortable around the crotch, but I refuse to move to adjust myself. "You said I was in. If I was one of the men, what would you do?"

"None of my men would expect money when money isn't coming in."

Her eyes flicker down to the thumb drive. "I understand that, but this situation is different. I'm trying to help you, and I need you to help me. Tyler stole five thousand from me, and I need it back."

He stole her money. Of course, he did. I watch her for a long moment. No, I wouldn't do this for any of my men. If any of them were dumb enough to let five thousand get lifted, that wouldn't be my problem.

I stand and come around to her side of the desk. I lean against it, so close our legs almost touch, and put my hands in my pockets. "I'll make you a deal," I tell her.

One of her eyebrows lifts, giving me attitude without saying a single word.

"If what I need is on this thumb drive, I'll give you the five thousand."

She nods once.

"But if there's nothing useful on it, you get nothing."

She raises her chin just a bit, nods again. "Deal."

She shifts like she's about to get up, but I bend and put my face close to hers. "But I need you to remember who's in charge here. Make demands of me, and find out what it's like to be my enemy. Do you hear me?"

For the first time since she got here, I see real fear in her eyes. It's delicious. It makes me want to bend her over the desk.

"You're going to learn how to properly do business, and this is not it. You keep this shit up, I'll toss you back to Tyler. Let him do whatever the fuck he wants with you. Get the fuck out of my office."

I turn my back, listen to the door open. And when I turn back around, she's gone.

"What do you think the chances are that this is actually something?" Ronan asks me.

I stand beside him as he inserts the thumb drive. "Frankly, I think the chances are pretty slim. Tyler's an idiot, but I don't know if he's stupid enough to have a zip drive of every criminal interaction he's participated in in his sock drawer."

"Hard agree." He cranes his neck to look at me over the back of the chair. "I looked into his dad's business; it's entirely legitimate. If this kind of criminal behavior isn't inherited, I'm not sure that he would have any common sense around it." Ronan shrugs under his oversized sweater, but almost immediately after, he sighs and leans back in his seat. "But I definitely think you're wrong about Tyler not being stupid enough."

My eyes go to the screen, where the file for the thumb drive is open. He didn't even password protect the damn thing.

There's only one folder on it.

"Why?" I ask out loud, leaning down to read the title on the folder. *Untitled.*

"Guy's fucking messy," Ronan says. I watch as he clicks on the file and we're met with a screen full of images.

It takes me about half a second to recognize a face.

"Don't look," I growl at Ronan.

He swings his face away from the computer quick, looking up at me.

"Get out."

He's gone in an instant, and I take his place in the swivel chair.

On the screen are dozens of naked photos of Sloane.

I'm not a good man, by any stretch of the imagination, but I'm also not the kind of man to look at naked photos of women that weren't intended for me. I never would have considered myself weak, but in this moment, I am the weakest I've ever been. Because my eyes are glued to the first photo on the screen like my eyelids have been taped open.

Sloane on her knees, taking a selfie in a mirror. She's wearing underwear, but nothing else, her beautiful breasts on display for the camera. The hand not holding her cell phone is down inside her panties.

I look away from the photo before I lose my fucking mind.

I scroll through photos, hundreds of them, my eyes scanning over them quickly, looking for anything that isn't flesh-colored, that isn't blonde, that isn't pink.

Halfway down, there are pictures of other girls. Tyler's many women.

There are redheads, brunettes; some have white skin, some have black skin. There has to be a dozen or more of them here. And who knows if these pictures were intended for him, or someone else.

Finally, at the bottom, there are videos. Only five. They're dark, grainy.

I click on the first one, and the sound gets me before I can make out anything else.

Her moans. Sloane's. I know the sound of her voice so well, and now this sound will live inside my head until the day I die. Her long, sensual whine as Tyler fucks her in the dark. Her tits bounce on the screen, and I shut it down quick.

All the other videos have the same lighting, the same timestamps.

None of them are what I'm looking for.

Julian
Tough luck, princess.

I watch in the camera as she gets the text on her new burner. She's perched on the edge of her bed, and as soon as she reads it, her shoulders slump.

I open another message.

Julian
Put $5,000 in a checking account.

Ronan
Anything special?

On the screen, Sloane falls back on the bed, arms splayed across the mattress.

> **Julian**
> No.

$$27$$

SLOANE

Everyone is in a tizzy, and discovering a *tizzy* in the compound is like discovering a house on fire.

It's like they're preparing for something. I stand upstairs at the railing and watch them down below on the first floor. There's a strange energy in the house as people go in and out the front door, carrying boxes and bags.

I look over just as Bram's head clears the top step. When he sees me, he stops. "I was just coming up to find you," he says.

"Is it to give me some kind of job? It seems like everyone has stuff to do."

He sighs, his shoulders falling. He shakes his head. "No, you won't have anything to do." He comes the rest of the way up the stairs. "I came to warn you."

"Warn me?" My stomach turns as his words overlap Ronny coming through the door downstairs, a box of clinking liquor bottles in his hands. I imagine some kind of meeting with very important and dangerous people. I'm used to the threat level of the men who live in the compound. I'm not sure I can handle any more than that. Can I trust Julian to keep them away from me?

Bram's watching me closely. "You're safe within these walls, Sloane. I promise you that." He joins me at the railing. "Every so often, we invite some friends to the compound."

There's something about the way he says *friends*. Like I'm supposed to understand that it means more than it means.

"Bram, I'm not some wilting flower. Can you just tell me what you're talking about?"

He looks away from me, down at the first floor. Elbows on the rail, hands hanging over. "The men like to invite women to the compound. Most of the guys aren't interested in relationships and outsiders aren't allowed anywhere in the compound besides the pool room, so they get rather..." He wiggles his head a bit.

I turn, press a hip against the rail. "Horny?"

His eyes flicker over to me, then away again. "Yes. And you're the first woman who's been here in a very long time other than Claudia. It's making the men a bit antsy."

"Antsy?"

He shrugs. "You're a beautiful woman, and the men know you wouldn't let them touch you, even if they were allowed. But there's something about having your feminine energy here that's been driving them all a little crazy."

I bite my lip. "Do I drive you crazy, Bram?"

He snorts, the curve of his ears turning red. "I value my life. You may be gorgeous, but I'm not about to let it mess with my head."

This makes me smile. There's something about Bram that I find comforting, that makes me trust him—maybe his eyes, maybe the way he hasn't tried to intimidate me like the others have.

"The reason I came to warn you is because things tend to get a bit rowdy."

"Rowdy," I repeat.

He takes another deep breath and I bite back a smile. Is he nervous? "Because the women aren't allowed inside, the men don't really have anywhere to take them, so a lot of them just...do what they want by the pool. Others will take the girls outside."

I tilt my head to the side. "Are you trying to tell me there's going to be an orgy downstairs?"

He laughs, the smile going all the way to his eyes. "I wouldn't have chosen that word, but yes. I recommend staying in your room. But if you must come out, just make it quick."

I consider everything he's told me, roll it through my mind like an old penny. "What happens if I don't stay in my room?"

Bram turns his body toward me, gripping the railing. "Sloane—"

"Has Julian *ordered* me to stay in my room for the night?"

He hesitates, smile gone. Maybe he's considering lying. "No, he hasn't."

"Then I don't think I will."

He sighs, tipping his head back like he's praying to the heavens for patience.

If someone tells me I can't do something, the first thing I want to do is that exact thing. When they tell me I'm not allowed and lock me in a room, it just makes me want to claw my way out.

So I do what any hard-headed girl would do: I go to the party. Only this is not what I was expecting. I guess I thought that a bunch of grown-ass, capable men could throw a party cooler than the ones that Tyler and his friends throw, but here we are. It might as well be a frat party.

Booze, half-naked girls, and a bunch of drunk boys.

Everyone has convened around the swimming pool.

None of the guys are in the water. Most of them are fully dressed, some with their shirts off, watching the girls in the water, all of them in bikinis, splashing each other and laughing big, full laughs over the loud beat of the music.

Over in the corner of the room, Julian watches everything, leaned back in his lounge chair, in his black jeans and his black shirt. It must be ninety degrees in this room, and the guy is wearing dress shoes by the pool.

I'm lounging too, reclining in one of the lounge chairs, legs stretched out in front of me. I find the whole thing amusing.

Even in their twenties and thirties, men don't change.

"Are you using this towel?"

I look up at the feminine voice. The woman is blocking out the light from above, her long dark hair almost touching me as she bends over. I keep my eyes focused on her face, afraid that if I look down, I'll get the full display. She's pointing to the folded towel on the table beside me. One of the guys put it there and made a comment about how I might need it later.

I don't know if he thought I was going to eventually just strip off my clothes and jump into the pool, but that's definitely not happening. I didn't exactly pack a swimsuit. I didn't think, when I was sold off to this little gang, that I was going to be attending pool parties.

Either way, I will not be using that towel.

"All yours," I tell her.

"Great, thanks, hon." She picks up the towel and unfolds it. She's not wet and clearly hasn't been in the pool yet, but she wraps it around her body, reaches underneath it, and pulls off her bikini. She tosses the stringy thing aside, and I watch it go right into the pool, floating on top like a multicolored tangle of seaweed.

In the pool, Ronny cheers. He was the only one willing to actually get in, probably because he's the youngest and doesn't understand that *not* getting in is some kind of power play on the part of the other men.

The woman in the towel, who looks old enough to be Ronny's mom, gets down on her knees by the edge of the pool and opens her towel to show Ronny what's underneath. She clearly intended for this to be a private moment between the two of them, but she doesn't seem to realize she's flashing him in front of a wall of windows and everyone in the room can see her naked body in the reflection.

She figures it out pretty quickly when all the guys in the room cheer.

As one of the other girls cannonballs into the pool, I glance over again at Julian. He hasn't spoken to anyone, just observed from his spot, completely expressionless. If he's bringing in girls for the other guys, then why not for himself? Is this how he does it? Isolate yourself moodily and the women will flock.

I'm starting to get a bit bored. I've refused alcohol, so where everyone else is starting to get tipsy, I'm still stone-cold sober. I think my curiosity got the best of me. I've never been in the same room with anyone who was having sex before, and I kind of wanted to see it.

But it's already almost midnight, and the only thing I've seen is the woman with the towel's obviously fake breasts.

Over by the side of the pool, a girl in a bright orange biki-ni is having what looks like a very serious conversation with

Bram. To his credit, he's not staring at her mostly exposed breasts. He's leaning against the wall, his arms crossed, looking to all the world like a professor having a conversation about grading papers.

"You know what I think?" one of the girls in the pool says. "I think we should play truth or dare." She pushes herself up out of the water, propped on the edge of the pool on her elbows. She raises her eyebrows over at the girl talking to Bram and then at a woman standing close to my chair. "What do you think?" she asks.

"Truth or dare?" Ronny says, even as some of the other guys have started to gather around, the ones that aren't over by the bar, watching a football game and clearly waiting for the women to come to them. A few already have. "What is this, middle school?"

The girl who suggested the game shrugs. "Come on, we're college girls. We play truth or dare all the time."

"Is that what you're spending all of that hard-earned tuition on?" Bram asks, an amused smile on his face.

"What about you?" The girl directs the question at me. I'm surprised to find myself the subject of her attention. She must be my age, with freckles and blonde hair cut short at her chin.

"What about me?" I ask.

"How old are you?" She must be wondering if I go to the university, too. It feels weird to be so joyfully brought into the conversation. I'm much more accustomed to bitterness from the guys, who generally ignore me.

"Um, I'm twenty."

"See?" The girl looks over at Ronny, hovering at her side. "It's not that we're childish, it's that you're old."

"I'm far from old, babe." He does something to her under the water that makes her shriek. "I'll show you how not old I am." Apparently, Ronny is going to have his pick of female companionship tonight while the other men are focused on trying to look cool.

Several people have wandered over; intrigued, I think, by the possibility that a fun game with a bunch of college girls could devolve into sexual favors. This is what they're here for, after all.

Magnus and Hugo come over, both of them shirtless and wearing board shorts. The two of them seem to do everything together, and I can't help but wonder if that includes sex. Magnus is stocky and muscular while Hugo has a torso that goes on for days. Sarge hovers nearby, eyes wary. I wonder if he's ever had to perform CPR at one of these things. He's much older than the other guys, probably in his fifties, so his choices for the night are significantly fewer but not non-existent. The women in the room far outnumber the men and range in age from early twenties to Sarge's age.

People pull up chairs, and once they're all in a circle, the girl in the pool, still fluttering around, looks up at me, eyes as blue as the water. "Are you going to join us?"

I glance over at Julian and want to smack myself. Why do I need to ask his permission to have fun?

I hop off my chair and go over to join the party. One of the girls, with long straight brown hair and perfect bangs, even in the humidity of the room, scoots over on her lounge chair to make room for me.

"Thanks," I say.

I didn't realize how much I've missed this, being around people, chatting, being silly. On campus, there's always somebody around, always someone to strike up a conversation with. It didn't occur to me how isolated I've become here.

"All right, Eve," Ronny says, looking at the girl who started this whole thing. "The game was your idea. Truth or dare?"

She bites her lip. "Truth."

I wasn't expecting that, and I don't think Ronny was either based on the look on his face. "All right," he says. "How old were you the first time you sucked a dick?"

She rolls her eyes. "You are so unoriginal. I was thirteen. Okay, my turn." She doesn't give her answer any kind of oxygen, just moves on. I'm kind of starting to like this girl. Her eyes move around the circle and land on someone over Ronny's shoulder. "Julian," she calls. "Truth or dare?"

Everybody turns to look at him. I swear he hasn't moved in the hour that I've been down here, his hands laced together on his stomach.

"No, thanks," he says.

Eve pouts. She may have Ronny's hands on her, but I think she might be hoping to hook up with Julian. I can't stop my gaze from traveling back to him. He's looking out the big window, jaw sharp and eyes glazed.

"Fine," Eve says, catching my attention. She regards the circle again, and her eyes finally land on me. I'm surprised by the lightning bolt that goes through my stomach. I sort of *feel* like a middle schooler at a party, wanting people to like me, nervous what they'll ask me to do or reveal. "Oh, you," she says. "Truth or dare?"

The quiet that descends on the room is heavy. If there's anything I've been avoiding the entire time I've been here, it's the truth. But God, I don't want to know what the dare is going to be. I just know I can't resist it.

"Dare," I say.

I'm surprised by the thrilled expression on her face. "I dare you to make out with somebody in the room."

I should have seen it coming. The most basic dare that ever existed. I guess I thought maybe she would ask me to do something a little more scandalous. Maybe I should be grateful she didn't. However, now I'm sitting in a room full of people, most of which I hate, and I have to choose one to kiss. I could just walk out. I am not, in fact, a middle schooler who's trying to impress her friends.

Nevertheless, I'm curious. I don't make eye contact with anyone as I catalog everyone in the room. I don't want any of the men thinking they're even an option.

And I definitely don't look over at Julian. What would he do if I went over there right now? Would he let me kiss him? Would he kiss me back? Would it be good?

I turn to the very pretty girl beside me and raise an eyebrow at her. I'm surprised when she doesn't hesitate. She smiles and nods at me. I lean forward and kiss her.

At first, I think maybe it'll just be a quick thing, but she apparently has more in mind because her hands come up to frame my face. And when I would have normally pulled back, she opens her mouth and runs her tongue along my bottom lip. A shiver goes through me. I've never kissed a girl before, although the idea has crossed my mind and Tyler has brought up the idea of a threesome more than once.

I'm surprised by how soft she is. How good she tastes. Like vodka and something sweet. I just kind of sink into it. I slip my tongue into her mouth, surprised when she moans. I'm even more surprised when the sound sends an ache to my clit.

A voice somewhere to my left breaks the spell. "Holy fuck." Ronny, of course.

The girl and I break apart, and I feel a little embarrassed that I just made out with someone, and I don't even know her name. I've said a grand total of one word to her.

Nevertheless, she smiles, running her index finger along her bottom lip without taking her eyes off me.

I tear my eyes away. "Okay, it's your turn to ask someone," Eve tells me.

I scan the faces in front of me, landing on Bram. His eyes go wide. He shakes his head, and I slump, disappointed. He's not really playing, and I'm not about to torture him but forcing him to. I look over at the woman I just made out with. She has purple streaks in her hair. "Truth or dare?"

"Truth," she says.

I tap my chin with my index finger. "Have you ever had sex with a girl?" The question comes to me quickly because I'm curious. She didn't seem hesitant at all and the part of me that's still revved up wants to know if she's done more.

Unsurprisingly, she nods and looks around, realizing she has a rapt audience. "Once, in high school. My best friend and I were curious, so we did oral."

"Did you like it?" Ronny asks, and weirdly, it sounds less like a pervy question and more like genuine curiosity.

"Yes," she says. "I liked it a lot." She leaves it there, and then it's her turn. She looks over at a woman floating beside Ronny in the pool, dark hair slicked back. She's wearing pink, heart-shaped sunglasses.

"Truth or dare, Brittany?"

How do they all know each other? The woman in the pool looks too old to go to Dartmouth. Do they all come here together on a regular basis?

Brittany gives a devious grin. "Dare." This, of course, surprises no one.

The girl beside me hums in the back of her throat before her face lights up. "I dare you to give Julian a lap dance."

I suddenly feel very small, like I'm shrinking and could just disappear at any moment, as Brittany pushes herself up out of the pool, her bikini-clad body dripping. She pushes her wet hair out of her face, and while everyone watches, she saunters over to where Julian sits in his chair. He tracks her approach. I don't know if he heard what the dare was, but he's not giving anything away.

When Brittany gets to him, she leans over and plants both of her hands on either one of the lounge chair's armrests. She has to be about ready to slip out of that top at the angle she's bent over. To Julian's credit, he keeps his eyes on her face.

They have a quiet conversation that none of us can hear. Julian raises one eyebrow. There seems to be some form of consent between the two of them because she turns and presses her lap into his. He's still stretched out on the lounge chair, something I would have thought would have made the whole thing awkward, but it doesn't. He watches her ass move as she grinds and swirls it, settling her hands on his legs.

His eyes trip up the length of her spine, and then shift, traveling across the room to find the group of us, stares glued. But he doesn't settle on the group. He finds me.

His eyes meet mine, and my pulse rackets up. Watching Brittany grind in a rhythm on his lap, knowing he's probably getting hard beneath her, does something to my skin. As much as I don't want to, I wonder how good it would feel to be rocking on that hard length. I wonder how big Julian is.

And I know all of these feelings are only happening because the whole room is sexually charged. It's not just the lap dance going on in the corner. It's the kiss I just shared with the girl next to me. The kiss that involved tongues and hands, that was so unexpected.

When I manage to look away from Julian, I'm surprised to find that no one else is watching them. Not even Ronny. Not even the girl who dared Brittany to do it.

Because everyone else has started in on their own conquests.

Bram kisses the woman he was chatting with earlier, palming her breasts through her bikini top. And in the pool, Ronny has pulled Eve's top off, his mouth attached to one of her erect nipples. She throws her head back and moans.

I missed all of it happening, missed them shifting and pairing off. Because I was watching Julian.

With an unsteady breath, I look back over at him, and his cold, emotionless eyes are still on me as he grabs Brittany's hips and forces her down harder on him.

I shoot up out of my chair. Every cell in my body is throbbing. And while I'm sure I could ask somebody in the room to finish me off, there's no way in hell that's happening.

I don't excuse myself because no one would notice anyway. I just turn and bolt out of the room.

28

JULIAN

As soon as the door slams shut behind Sloane, I shove Brittany off of me.

"Hey!" she says, standing and crossing her arms over her bikini top. "What the hell? Why does she get to go inside the house, and we don't?"

"Don't worry about," I growl at her, already stomping away. I cross through the room, averting my gaze as I go past Bram, who's getting sucked off by a woman on her knees right by the door.

I barge through the house like a bull on a rampage. That's what I feel like. An animal that's crazed with lust.

I watched Sloane's eyes on me as Eve gyrated on my lap. Maybe she was jealous, or maybe she was turned on. Either way, she couldn't look away, and neither could I. And now she's just going to run off right before things get interesting?

I don't think so.

It's my first instinct to follow her right to her bedroom, but when I pass the hallway with the security room, I skitter to a halt. I know I shouldn't. She would think I'm still in the pool room with Eve. She wouldn't know I'm watching.

And that's exactly why I do it.

I want Sloane unfiltered, candid. What does she do when she thinks she isn't being watched?

There's no one in the security room. Frankie is meant to be watching cameras, but he must have taken a bathroom break.

I lock the door, settle into the swivel chair, and let my eyes scan over the cameras. My mind conjures up images of what I saw last time I was sitting in this chair. The pictures and videos of Sloane, naked and being fucked.

Fuck, I'm hard as a tent spike.

I should stay as far the hell away from Sloane as I can, but she's like honey. I'm helpless to resist the sweet lure of her.

When my eyes find the square of her bedroom camera on the screen, I almost choke on my own tongue. Part of me thought she might be hiding in the bathroom or getting ready for bed.

Instead, she's on her back in the middle of her bed, her panties pushed down to her knees and her hand between her legs.

My body goes up in flames. I swear, I turn into a rabid dog. I want to lick the fucking computer screen.

There's no sound, but I watch her throat arch and her mouth open and imagine the sound she's making as she fucks herself.

I know how wrong it is, but I can't stop myself. My hands tremble as I undo my belt and shove my pants down, gripping my throbbing cock. It doesn't take me ten seconds of watching her circle her pretty clit and pull the top of her dress down to pinch her own nipple before I'm exploding in my own fist.

It's pathetic, but it is what it is.

She's still going. She has her eyes closed, and I want to imagine she's thinking of me, thinking of Brittany squirming on my dick, and getting herself off to it. Does she wish she was Brittany, riding me on that pool chair?

With a smile on my face, I take out my phone.

Julian
Do you have any idea how much
money I would pay to watch you come?

On the screen, I see her phone light up, sitting on her nightstand. For a moment, I'm afraid she'll ignore it, but then she visibly sighs, the hand that was between her legs dropping to her side in frustration before she reaches for it. She must think it's her mother. Who else would be texting her?

I watch with satisfaction as she reads the message. Horror crosses her face, and her eyes look up to the camera. She starts to tug her panties up her legs, but stops. With her eyes on the camera, she shoves them back down in some kind of act of defiance, this time kicking them off. I reach for a nearby box of tissues, clean myself up, and grab my phone again.

Julian
Finger fuck yourself, princess.

My dick is already getting hard again at the thought, and I swear another shot of blood pulses south when she reads the text and she freezes. She's just staring at her screen, and I know she's deciding if she wants to give me what I want, or if she wants to punish me. I know she *hates* giving in to me.

So when she slips two fingers into that pretty pink pussy, I know it's because she *wants* to. But I still want to pretend it's all for me.

I shove away from the computer and step out into the hall. The door to the pool room is still cracked and someone is screaming so loud I can hear her all the way on the other side of the house. I ignore the commotion and hurry up the stairs.

Throwing Sloane's bedroom door open, I revel in the shriek she emits. She has her knees pressed together as I slam the door shut behind me. "Get out!" she shrieks. "You can't just come in here whenever you want."

"It's my house, princess. Please, don't let me interrupt you." I press my back to the wall in front of her bed and put my hands in my pockets like we're about to engage in small talk. "You want me to see you get off? I'm going to be in the room while you do it."

In the light of the bedside lamp, I can see that her fingers are glistening, and I have to clench my fists to keep from going over there and shoving those fingers into my mouth.

Our eyes meet, stick, hold.

"Spread your legs, Sloane."

In the silent room, I hear her small intake of breath. I expect her to fight. That's all she's done since she's been here.

Instead, she obeys.

Her knees fall open, and I can't bite back my groan when I see her swollen cunt up close.

"Touch yourself."

This time, she doesn't move. When my eyes move up to hers, I can see the fight in them. She wants to argue. She's *going* to argue, going to say no. I can't let her. I meant what I said before. If she asked me to pay her a million dollars for this orgasm, I would. I can't leave this room until I see the face she makes when she comes on her own fingers.

When enough time passes, I take a step forward. She holds very still as I set one knee on the bed. That's all I allow myself. If I get on fully, I know what will happen. I'll end up with my mouth on her or my cock inside her. I've already crossed too many lines.

She watches, waits, as I lift a hand and take hers, the right one, the one she was using to pleasure herself. I can smell her on her fingers as I wrap a hand around her wrist and move it down her body. None of my skin makes contact with any of hers, except her wrist.

I wrap my hand fully around hers, forcing her first two fingers together, and press them to her clit. I look up to find her watching me, so close I can see every bit of pigment in her irises. Her mouth drops open, like she's going to moan for me, but she doesn't. She's holding it in. I press a little harder, circle.

She lets out a grunt this time, her eyes never leaving mine. Going by feel, I move her fingers around, careful not to brush that wet flesh that I want to feel so bad, until I've got her two middle fingers instead. I push them lower.

"Finger fuck that pretty cunt."

Her eyes go dark at my words, losing all focus as she presses those two fingers into herself and sets a rhythm. I feel like a house on fire. I want to be doing it myself. I want to feel her inside and out.

I settle for hovering my hand over hers so she bumps my palm with her knuckles every time she brings her fingers out to plunge them back in. Her other hand comes down to pick up the rhythm on her clit, and her breathing picks up. I want to watch her hand move, watch what she's doing to herself, but I can't tear my eyes away from her face.

"Are you close?" I ask her, watching the way her brow twists, the way her lips part, the way a flush creeps up her cheeks. Goddammit, she's beautiful like this, right on the edge. "That's it," I tell her. "Give it to me."

Her eyes fall closed, her head tips back, and she lets out a magnificent little scream that rings in my ears long after her muscles have gone slack and her hands have stopped moving. Her eyes open and shift to me, all the heat gone. She doesn't need to tell me I've overstayed my welcome, that I wasn't really welcome to begin with.

I get back to my feet and watch her cover herself up with her blanket. "Til next time, princess," I say and leave her to her own devices. It isn't until I'm in the hallway that I realize my cock is throbbing all over again.

29

SLOANE

On Fridays, I don't have class. It was a strategic play that, ironically, was Tyler's idea. I'm not sure he imagined me spending the semester in Julian Shaw's mansion, reading. And by reading, I mean trying to distract myself from the fact that I masturbated in front of Julian last night.

Spread your legs, Sloane.

Someone knocks on my door. Electricity races through me. I'm not ready to deal with Julian yet. But then I realize that whoever it is actually knocked. Julian never knocks.

When I don't immediately answer, Bram sticks his head in. He's fully dressed, shoes and all, his hair pushed back out of his face. "You ready to go for a little ride?" he asks.

I toss my book aside and sit up. "Where are we going?"

"It's time for some training," he says. "You're gonna come along with me. I've got a deal to broker."

I scramble out of bed, not willing to miss out on the action just because I was moving too slow. If I go on this job with Bram, chances are good I'll get paid. "Let's go."

Bram raises an eyebrow at me. "Do you want to change?"

I sigh. "You guys really have to stop asking me that as if I own other clothes." I tug on my hot pink shorts. "Please don't put me in any more of Julian's hideous sweats. They'll think you're my sugar daddy. It'll be hot."

He laughs. "Alright, come on, pumpkin."

We drive north for half an hour, miles and miles of empty road. We pull off onto a dirt road, where another car is parked in a copse of trees. A man dressed all in black just like Bram turns to watch us. It's like it's their uniform, identifiers from one criminal to another.

"You know, if you all dressed like normal people, you'd be less noticeable," I tell Bram.

"Your job is simple," he says. "Stay here and look cute."

I scowl. "I resent that."

He puts the car in park and looks over at me with one hand on the door. "You don't think you're cute?"

I scowl harder. "That's not what I meant. How am I supposed to learn how to do this thing if I'm not allowed to speak to anyone? Why did you even bring me?"

"Because I was the only one willing to let you tag along. I just also happen to be the only one dealing with a guy like this today. These clients are carefully chosen. This man"—he points over the dash at the man waiting patiently for us, looking down at his phone—"doesn't want women mucking up his business. He'll talk to you like a child, make nasty comments." Down by the console, he passes me a little piece of plastic. "This is an earpiece. Put it in after I get out and listen to the sale, yeah?"

I nod.

He winks at me and gets out of the car, slamming the door behind him.

The man looks up at Bram as he approaches, his eyes dark. I put the earpiece in my ear just as he speaks, his voice coming out clear and angry. "We bringing our bitches to confidential jobs? Didn't know, or I would have called that girl at the bar that sucked me off last night."

I don't believe for one second that this mean, greasy and red-faced, got anyone he didn't pay for to go down on him. My mind briefly flashes back to last night, to the woman who had no problem getting on her knees for Bram. For a split second, I see an image in my mind: me on my knees for Julian.

"Nothing confidential about a car sale," Bram replies. "I heard word you were interested in the Ferrari. That's not an inquiry we take lightly, packed or otherwise."

Packed? What does that mean?

"I was under the impression I'd be dealing with Julian Shaw." There's an odd tone to his voice, almost mocking.

Even I'm smart enough to know that meetings like this are below Julian's pay grade. From what Bram told me, this is just a meeting with a potential buyer. No contracts have been signed. Why would he expect Julian to be here?

In a calm voice, Bram says, "You thought Mr. Shaw was going to meet you to talk contracts?"

I watch over the dashboard as the guy raises his chin. "I thought Mr. Shaw was man enough not to send in his men to clean up his messes."

I sit up just a little straighter in my seat so that I can see better what's going on. Bram puts his phone in his pocket, and I see him fingering something in there. I wonder briefly if he has a weapon—a knife or, I don't know, brass knuckles or something.

This conversation has shifted. I can feel it, and I know Bram can, too. The meeting has gone from professional to something tense. I don't like it at all.

"I'm not sure what mess you're talking about," Bram says, his voice level, controlled. "If you have some kind of business with Mr. Shaw outside of what we're here to talk about today, I'd be happy to let him know you'd like to speak with him directly."

"Oh, we'd like to speak with him directly," the man says, "but seeing as how you're the one that showed up, I think we'll go ahead and take care of our business now."

I gasp when someone appears in the corner of my eye. A second man. I don't know where he came from, not from the car that brought the other man. He came from somewhere behind us, somewhere in the trees, moving so quickly that he's just a blur.

He lifts a bat and smashes Bram in the back of the head.

30

SLOANE

I'm ashamed of the second I spend caught in hesitation, the second I spend watching Bram's body fall to the ground, watching his head hit the concrete.

It isn't until the man lifts the bat to hit Bram again that I start to search the car. I open the center console first, but it's empty, save for a pack of breath mints. I check the glove box next and find what I'm looking for.

I take the gun in my hand, a heavy silver thing that looks like it belongs in an old western and throw open the door.

The man manages to get in one more hit to Bram's ribs. I don't know if Bram is conscious or not because he doesn't move, even after he's struck again, but it doesn't matter because dead or alive, unconscious or not, I'm ending this now.

I lift the gun and approach the men. "Get the fuck away from him!" I shout.

I see the shock on their faces, even the one who knew I was in the car. I guess the outfit worked because they thought

I was just Bram's arm candy. Maybe they had plans to beat me to death next.

I point the gun at the one with the bat, but they're standing so close together that it would only take a millisecond to shift to the other guy if I need to shoot.

The man with the bat has the decency to freeze, but the other one doesn't. It happens in a split second—the flinch of his arm. I already know what's coming before he's pulled the gun out of his waistband and pointed it at Bram.

Something comes over me then, something I can't explain. I always thought I was the kind of person that would never be able to hurt anyone, but when I see that gun pointed at Bram, I pull the trigger.

It's not a very graceful shot. It hits the man in the shoulder, blood spraying out against the blue sky, and his gun hits the ground. I turn the gun on the guy with the bat and he drops it. "Get the fuck away from him," I say, "or I *will* shoot you."

He puts his hands up, backing away slowly. At least one of these guys takes me seriously. The guy with the hole in his shoulder groans, bent over. At first, I think he's crouched from the pain, but then I realize he's going for the gun he dropped.

I step up close to him and put the gun to his head. There's no way in hell I would ever shoot someone point blank, but I need him to think I mean it.

"Get in the car and go."

He moves as quickly as he's able, half bent around his shoulder, toward the car that the guy with the bat has already started. They squeal out of the parking lot.

I drop to Bram's side, take his head in my hands. He's out cold. I turn him onto his side so I can see the back of his head. There's blood. A lot of it.

"Okay," I tell him. "It's okay, everything's fine."

I reach for my phone, reflexes telling me to call 911 but remember what Julian said the other day. These guys, they don't go to hospitals, they don't talk to doctors. They have Sarge. Probably because the second someone walks into the hospital with a bullet wound, people get suspicious.

Like I'm some kind of badass who actually knows what they're doing, I start to shove the gun into my waistband, and then I remember the safety. I take the gun back out, search for the safety—which I only know how to locate because of TV shows—flip it on, and shove it back in. I have to move quick. I know head wounds just bleed a lot, even if they aren't severe. It's unlikely that somebody who got hit in the back of the head with a baseball bat and crumpled six feet to the concrete is going to die of a head wound, but I don't know that for certain. I need to get him to Sarge.

But first, I need to get him into the car. I take two big handfuls of his jacket, making sure I have his t-shirt too so I don't just slide the jacket right off of him, and drag him like a bag of dog food across the concrete toward the car. I may be doing more damage than good, but at this point, it doesn't really matter. I have to get him out of here. How does one get an unconscious body into a car with very little upper body strength?

I have the passenger side door open when Bram starts to groan.

"Bram?" I cradle his head in my hands. "I know you're in a lot of pain, and I know you're not really here and you're probably super dizzy, but if you could help me get you into this car, I can get you help faster."

His eyes flutter open, his chest heaving.

"I'm so sorry," I tell him. "I'm sorry to have to ask, but I need your help. You have to get up."

He manages to get up on his elbows in the passenger seat. From there, I just shove him in. It doesn't matter if he's sitting in the seat. It doesn't matter if he's comfortable. It just matters that he's in the car and that we get on the road toward the compound.

"What happened?" Bram croaks when we're almost there.

"Give me your phone," I tell him, ignoring his question.

He gives it to me without question, and I choose to ignore my own surprise. There's no time to digest that.

I keep one eye on the road while I hold the phone steady so he can press his thumb to the screen. As I race onto the highway, I scan through the contacts, find Sarge's number, and call it.

"Hey, Bram," he answers, sounding distracted.

"It's not Bram. It's Sloane. Bram was hurt. He's okay. He's awake...mostly. We're on our way to the compound, but I need help with him."

"Gunshot wound?" he asks, voice alert now. The fact that this is his first question tells me how often the guys are getting shot.

"Concussion. A head wound. Some guy attacked him with a bat, hit him in the back of the head, and then he fell on the concrete. He's bleeding." I glance over at Bram, see his eyes have fallen closed again. "I think he may have just passed out again."

"Shit," Sarge barks. "What's your ETA?"

I look at the signs on the road that are telling me which way to go. "Twenty minutes, give or take."

"We'll be ready," he says. and hangs up.

31

JULIAN

I stand to the side as the men carry Bram into the compound on a stretcher. This was supposed to be a simple job. It's one of the reasons I agreed to let Bram take Sloane. A training exercise. They wanted the Ferrari, the one I spent years acquiring and fixing to perfection so I could make a small fortune off it. Not packed. It didn't even have to cross the border. I should have known better, but we're running a legitimate business as much as an illegitimate one, and it didn't raise any red flags.

The guys race by me and I glance at Bram's pale face. Bile rises in my throat.

Leo's face flashes in my mind. Pale and cold on the wet concrete of the alley.

The room starts to spin and I take a deep breath, standing alone in the foyer. The parade moves upstairs to Sarge's room, the voices getting quieter and quieter as they vanish down the hall.

I hear footsteps and turn to see Sloane standing by the still open front door. She looks shaken, her face almost as pale as Bram's, aside from the purple bruise covering her cheek. There's blood all over her shorts. This is not the same woman I was with last night, full of fire and attitude. She looks like a ghost who's lost on her way to the afterlife.

I step up to her, grab her wrists, and turn her hands out. Blood on both of them.

"It's probably all over the car," she says in a monotone voice.

"Fuck the car," I say. "Go wash up, okay?"

Her eyes lift to mine. Ocean blue. "It was an ambush," she says. "They wanted you. The guy that got Bram, he was hiding in the trees." She's speaking quickly now, like she has to get it all out before she shakes apart. I still have her hands in mine, cold and trembling. "He came out of nowhere. I didn't see him. Bram didn't see him. And then he was just there, hitting Bram with a baseball bat. They said it was a message for you. They got him twice before I..." Her eyes dart away.

"Before you what?"

"Bram had a gun in the glovebox. I got one of them in the shoulder."

I grunt. "Good girl."

It had to be retaliation. Because who else would be looking to send me a message if not Tyler Price?

She's quavering in my hands, still wrapped around her dainty wrists. The adrenaline is leeching out of her. She had the steadiness, the confidence to get Bram out of there, to handle the situation on her own and get him back here in one piece. But she's still shaking like a leaf. Terrified.

"You're okay," I tell her. "Bram's going to be okay." I try to believe it. I wouldn't be able to live with myself if he wasn't. I know I didn't make his choices for him. I'm not forcing him to stay in this job. Never forced him to be part of it to begin with. But he does what I tell him to. He goes where I tell him to go. And out of everybody, I try the hardest to keep him out of the middle of shit like this.

I should have seen it coming. We look into everybody. Criminal records, whisper networks. I don't just go into situations like this blindly. These guys were clean. They were nobodies, came recommended through old connections of my dad.

Everyone's hands are filthy with Tyler's money.

Sloane's breath trembles out of her. It pulls at something in me. It urges me to hold her. To take her into my arms and console her. I shake it off.

If she's going to do this thing, if she's going to be one of us, she's going to have to learn how to get blood on her hands and keep moving.

Everybody walks into the fire.

"Go wash up." I tell her again. "You'll feel better after you take a shower. A hot one."

Her eyes meet mine. "What about Bram?"

"If you can survive a head wound, he certainly can."

Her eyes flutter up the stairs. "If anything happens, you'll come get me, right?"

My stomach clenches. This isn't some show she's putting on. She actually cares. She shot someone for Bram. "Yeah, princess. If anything happens, someone will come get you."

She nods. I watch her stumble toward the stairs. She looks like she's a moment from falling apart. Maybe I've made a big mistake. If she's not strong enough to handle this, maybe she doesn't have a place here.

But if I'm not paying her, she'll go back to Tyler. She's made that pretty clear. And once she's on Tyler's payroll again, what happens then?

She could identify clients. She could be a weak link. She knows just enough to be a problem. And then what? I have to take her out? Put her down like a sick dog?

I go upstairs to Sarge's room. The door's open, a whole troop of men in there helping him.

"What happened?" Sarge asks, glancing at me before going back to work cleaning Bram up.

"Sloane says a guy came up behind him. Hit him with a bat. I know the lot where they met. All concrete. Double damage.

"Look," he says, coming over to me. "I'm going to stitch the back of his head up, alright? I'm going to eliminate his chances of an infection. But without an MRI, if there's anything serious, like a brain bleed, I won't know until it's too late."

I look over his shoulder at Bram on the table. He's still unconscious. "We take him to the hospital, people start asking questions. If we're going to put ourselves in the line of fire, we need to be sure."

He considers the facts, eyes unfocused, hands on hips. "It was just a bat?" he asks.

"They were going to kill him slowly. One hit at a time. Said they were sending a message."

He nods. "I'll get him stitched up and let you know when he wakes up. It's going to be a long night."

I walk out into the hallway, look left down to the stairs for a long beat. I turn right, toward Sloane's room. I open the door, listen to the sound of the shower running. Steam curls out of the bathroom. I should make myself known, but when I stand in the doorway of the bathroom and see her through the frosted glass of the walk-in shower, I stay quiet.

She's on the floor. I can just make out the shape of her, her hands that she holds up under the spray like an offering, her head bowed.

When I first started looking into her, the things I found in her background...

The shit with her mother. The men her mother was involved with. It's enough to traumatize anybody. Enough to turn anyone into a quivering mess.

I turn and leave her to her own demons.

32

JULIAN

"What the hell is she doing in here?" Frankie barks, eyes zeroing in like a bird of prey.

Sloane doesn't look up from the ground as she comes into the dining room. She has her arms wrapped around herself, her head hung low. I think she's beyond caring what Frankie thinks of her. I know I am.

"Don't worry about it," I tell him as everyone else takes their seats. Sloane takes the spot to my left out of habit. Bram's chair on my right is empty. "We have shit to deal with."

Sarge takes a seat next to Sloane. He puts a hand on her shoulder, leaning over to say something into her ear. She nods. I can only assume he's telling her she saved Bram's life, which she did. I know how far that lot is, how fast she had to have driven to get back. She wasn't lying about being a good driver. That's the kind of skill I need her to have to get her in past the men.

"There was an incident," I tell the group. "Bram's going to be out for a little while."

"What happened?" Claudia asks. She wasn't here earlier when we carted him in.

"That's not what I'm here to talk about. Who set up the job today?"

They look around at each other. Everyone except Claudia. Her eyes are focused on mine. Settled. "Frankie," she says. "Frankie set up the meeting today."

Of fucking course he did.

I look over at him. He shrugs. "Yeah, so what? It was just a meeting. You've been wanting to unload the Ferrari, and they wanted it."

"It was a meeting that got Bram a cracked skull."

There's murmuring around the table.

"Cut ties with the connection who referred them. Frankie, pull the file on the sale. Find the guy who did this. Magnus, take care of the problem." Sloane's the only one who looks surprised by my command. I turn to her. "Can you get Magnus a description of the guy with the bat?"

She nods, cheeks pink.

"Good. Tyler's turning people. No one can be trusted."

Frankie scowls. "How are we supposed to do business?"

"Out in the open. Meet in crowded spots, due diligence on every client, and no packing, for the time being."

This sends everyone into an outrage, like I knew it would. Sloane watches me, lips clamped together. She looks worn out, bags under her eyes, but in the chaos, she's the only quiet.

"We're not scared of them," Magnus says over the commotion. "They want to come for us? Let them."

"We don't need a blood bath," I say, and everyone finally settles down. "We can't off these guys one at a time without getting ourselves in hot water. We're going to handle this in a way that keeps our hands clean of anyone's blood but the people on top." I take a deep breath, consider my next words. "I didn't tell anybody because I didn't think anyone needed to know, but now you do: I killed one of his guys last week."

At this, Sloane's eyes pop up. "What?" she says. I shake my head at her, telling her to back down. If she wasn't sure before that we're killers, she's sure now.

"I'm not going to get into it. All you need to know is that this was payback. They said they wanted to send a message, and they did. Loud and clear. If we start shooting, they will, too. Tyler didn't care about the guy I killed. This was a power play."

"Then why didn't they kill Bram?" Magnus asks.

"Because Sloane stopped them."

Everyone turns to her, but I don't look over. I don't want to soften, even though I can feel it happening in my bones.

I watch them watch her and keep talking. "Loyalty is the most important thing. And when it came down to it, she did what she needed to. Without her, Bram would be scrambled egg. So from now on, she's in the meetings. She has clearance." My eyes finally make their way over to her. She's steady as she looks at me, jaw hard, eyes confident. "The need-to-know stuff."

A smile tugs at one side of her bare pink mouth. She's fresh-faced. No makeup. Her hair not done. Just her and her memories, all of her wounds on display.

"So what do we do now?" The question comes from Xander, sitting at the other end of the table.

"There's nothing we can do."

"That's it?" This time, it's Claudia. "You're just going to let him take everything from you because you don't have the gall to fight back?"

I stay composed. Claudia isn't technically one of us, so even though I want to, I can't throw her out because of her mouth. I made a promise to Leo to care for her, and I can't go back on it, even when she talks to me this way.

"We're outnumbered, Claudia. You know better than anyone that if I could have my revenge, I would."

I don't miss the way Sloane looks at me when I say this. She's getting a lot of information she wasn't ready for here, and she's still in the dark about much more.

"We have to be smart about this. As much as I hate to admit it, Tyler is *someone*. He disappears, people notice. The new mob loses their leader, they show up with more than baseball bats."

"What about the man you killed?" Claudia asks. "Was that revenge?"

"It was self-defense. I didn't have a choice. The guy knifed me."

Frankie groans. "Oh, fuck's sake, come on."

"If we go out there and start a war, we'll lose it. They have protection, clean hands, and an army. We keep our cool until we have reason to pull the trigger."

"I told you we should have been bribing the fucking cops," Magnus says, more to himself than to me.

"Try to keep your fingerprints off shit," I tell them all, "but if any of them step a toe out of line, you take them out. Tyler can't protect all of his underlings. If we can shrink his circle without him noticing, we have a better chance." My eyes meet Claudia's. I know the pain she's feeling, but I can't undo it. "These people, they're lab rats to him. We can't start a war; we need to find a way to quietly take care of shit so he won't feel a thing."

33

SLOANE

Tyler reaches over and puts his hand on my bare thigh. I fight not to shudder. For the rest of my life, I'll remember the sound of that bat hitting the back of Bram's head through the earpiece. For the rest of my life, I'll remember the feeling of his blood slick on my hands as I drove across town.

I could stomach it when Tyler hurt me, but after what he did to Bram, his touch makes my skin crawl. I lift my chin and grit my teeth, because that's what I have to do.

Just before the end of class, as our professor is outlining materials for our next assignment, the door flies open, and when Ronny sticks his head into the lecture hall, my heart pounds.

"What the hell is he doing?" Tyler asks beside me, but I'm already out of my seat. Ronny motions for me, puts up an apologetic hand to the professor, and goes back out into the hallway.

Bram is the first thing on my mind. Lying on the concrete,

bleeding. What if it was worse than Sarge thought? What if he's dead?

The silence in the room is heavy.

"Sorry, professor," I say, gathering my things. If Ronny needs me, or Julian, I have to go. No questions, no hesitation.

"What the fuck?" Tyler hisses at me. The class is waiting, the professor refusing to move on until the disruption has ended.

"I have to go," I tell Tyler.

"What do you mean, you have to go?" he says, grabbing my wrist. "You're not a fucking dog on a leash."

I yank my hand out of his. "I have to go," I repeat firmly. I hurry down the stairs and throw open the door. "What is it?" I ask Ronny. The door slams shut behind me.

"Bram's awake."

JULIAN

"We're not letting them low-ball us on this. We can't go lower than 80 or we're going to be upside down on it, do you understand?"

My office door slams open. Ronan and I turn to see Frankie standing in the doorway.

"Boss, Bram is awake."

For just a beat, my eyes close, and I take a deep breath, all the weight coming off my chest. "We'll finish this later," I tell Ronan, sitting in the chair across the desk from me, and rush out of my office. There's a congregation of men in front of Sarge's door; they part to let me through.

Sarge is bent over Bram in his bed, checking his blood pressure.

"I'm sorry, Julian," are the first words out of Bram's mouth when he sees me.

I wave him off. "Don't fucking apologize to me."

He looks like shit. Deep purple bags under his eyes, skin sallow. He has bandages around his head. He had to have part of his ear removed, it was so mangled.

I glance at Sarge. He nods at me. "He's going to be fine."

"You worried about me?" Bram says, a cheeky smile on his face. Sarge steps away from the bed, lets me take the seat beside Bram.

"Fuck yes, I was worried. What the fuck am I going to do if I lose my right-hand man? No one wants Frankie as a fucking second-in-charge."

Bram smiles in that way he does when he thinks my anger is amusing. "Hire the girl. She'd be a good right hand."

I can practically feel the nervous energy coming from the men in the hallway, desperately clamping down on the obvious hand job jokes. I glare over at them, still lingering in the doorway. "Get back to fucking work," I growl, and they disperse like a school of fish.

"Go easy on them," Bram says. "How long was I out?"

"Just twenty-four hours."

He pushes himself up into a sitting position, his back against the headboard. "Just twenty-four hours?" His eyes track back and forth, deep in thought, and then shoot to me. "What about Sloane?"

"She's fine. She pulled a gun on the guys that attacked you. Shot one in the shoulder. Dragged you, bleeding, back to the car and booked it like a bat out of hell back here to Sarge."

He smiles in an overly fond way now. "I knew I liked that girl."

As if we somehow summoned her, a blur of pink flies across my vision. I'm suddenly looking at Sloane's very round, very pink ass as she's halfway lying across my lap so she can wrap herself around Bram. She's nothing but pink cotton and blonde hair.

"I was so scared," she says.

"It's alright, cupcake." He pats her on the hip, and I watch to make sure his hand doesn't linger too long, as if I have any right to. She removes herself, awkwardly pushing up to stand beside me. I can't decide if I'm relieved or sad to see that ass go. "Thanks for saving my life," Bram says to her.

She shrugs. "You would have done the same for me." I'm surprised by the assuredness in her voice. I knew Bram had a soft spot for Sloane, but I didn't know they had formed a friendship.

"I'm not sure how these guys slipped under the radar," Bram says as Sloane sits on the edge of the bed. "They were vetted. They came recommended by an old contact of your dad's."

I scoff. "Half the town belongs to him."

Sloane throws her hands up. "But how? What is he offering these people to stay loyal to him?"

"Money," Bram and I say at the same time.

"I thought you said he didn't have any money," she says to me, accusingly.

"My guess?" Bram says, grunting as he adjusts himself again in the bed. "He probably had a secret stash. Probably came with several million in a shoebox or something. He may be an idiot, but somebody on his payroll has good business practices. He's running a successful operation here. And since we don't hire outsiders, it makes sense that people looking to make a buck would go to him instead. He's out here taking walk-ins."

Sloane has a wrinkle of distress between her eyebrows. "He wanted to start a war," I say. "Let's go."

34

Xander is already serving dinner by the time Sloane joins us. Like usual, she's showing off enough skin to drive a man crazy. In short shorts and a tank top, she's clearly made herself at home here. She's even barefoot. I'm not sure I've ever been barefoot in the compound.

Everyone looks up when Bram walks slowly into the room, dressed in sweatpants, a bandage still around his head but his cheeks flushed with color.

"You should be in bed," I tell him, standing to help him into his chair, but he waves me away.

"I'm fine," he says. "I've been in that fucking bed long enough. Let me have dinner with my family."

I settle back into my chair as Bram pulls his out and gingerly takes a seat. On my left side, Sloane is grinning like Bram is a puppy that someone just saved from a shelter moments before it was put down. I have to look away from the smile, acid settling in my stomach.

"You look so much better," she says to him. "How do you feel?"

"Like I was beaten with a baseball bat by a gangster. Thanks for asking."

Xander serves the men ribs, and sets a few plates of something in front of Sloane that I can tell she doesn't recognize. One of the dishes is clearly filled with rice, but the other is a pancake hash brown sort of thing. She leans close to the plate, her hair pulled to one side by her small hand. She's smelling it but in a way I'm sure she would consider graceful.

"Satisfied?" I ask.

Her eyes pop up to mine. She didn't know she was being watched, probably because I shouldn't be watching her. When our gazes hold, memories hit me like a freight train. Her fingers in her pussy, her neck arched on a moan.

Fuck. I can't get hard at dinner. I never should have put my hands on her in the first place.

"Sure," she says. She leans closer to me. "I think it's tortilla," she says under her breath, eyes watching Xander carefully. He doesn't seem to notice we're discussing the state of her food.

"It doesn't look like a tortilla."

She shakes her head. "Not a tortilla for tacos. It's a Spanish dish. Potatoes and egg."

"I thought you were a vegan."

She cuts her eyes at me. "Plant-based eggs exist. Good thing Xander is the chef and not you." She leans back, her eyes on her plate.

I'm surprised by the casual way she's talking to me. Things seem to have shifted between us. And as my eyes move around the table, I realize things have shifted for everyone else, too. They're all talking, chatting. It's not as if dinner has been silent as the grave for the past week and a half, but it hasn't been like this.

They're all far too comfortable, and here I am, every muscle I possess wound tight, my mind and body unable to relax in the face of what she and I did two nights ago.

I've considered calling one of the girls. I have all their numbers. But it feels like too much work. The women who visit come from everywhere. We've had a few from the university, mostly grad students. Some of them are women who have come and gone from the businesses we own, others from various businesses around town. The cafe, the service station. Even, at one time, the woman who works the front desk at the vet.

The guys put out feelers, Ronan checks up on them, and then they're allowed to come for the night. They know what they're here to do.

I think maybe it's easier for the guys; anytime I invite a woman into my bed, it's as if they feel they have to conquer me. They want me to show them I like them. That I enjoy their company, and not just their bodies. Sometimes I do. Women are women. Some of them are funny, some of them are sweet. Some, like the veterinary assistant, are especially smart. These Dartmouth grad students aren't at Dartmouth for no reason.

But they're all just blurs after a while. It doesn't matter if I like them, and they know it. They just don't want to accept it. So I refrain as much as possible. But sometimes they're still useful. Like when I let them grind on my dick just to make Sloane jealous, so that I can watch her finger fuck herself in her room.

Like he knows where my thoughts are, Hugo turns to me. "Hey," he says, like we've been having a conversation this whole time, "when are we having another party, boss?"

I roll my eyes. "It's been two days. We have to be more careful than this."

"What's more careful than not letting them in through

the doors? They're not finding anything damning in the pool room." This comes from Frankie.

My hands ball into fists. He has the audacity to question Sloane, but he'll never question any of the women who come in to suck him off.

"And every single one of you is staying sober enough to know where those girls go once you've drained your balls and passed out?"

Out of the corner of my eye, I see Sloane startle. If she's going to hang around here, she needs to get used to this. If she can handle witnessing the guys getting laid, she can handle listening to them talk about it.

"That's what security is for." It's Xander this time, coming through to refill drinks before he takes a seat and has his own dinner.

"No," I tell him, "that's not what security is for. We don't pay the guys to stare at computer screens all night to make sure your half-naked hookups aren't wandering through parts of the compound they shouldn't be."

They all go quiet at that.

I need these guys to be at the top of their game. This is their home, but it's also where they work, and they only get to live here because of the money they bring in. They put that in jeopardy, they're out on their asses.

"I'll have Claudia put something on the books."

Frankie's right; there are cameras everywhere, and this is why. So that when people are at the compound, there are eyes on them. I pay the guys extra for pulling night shifts.

The guys cheer. I swear, they act like they can't spend time with women unless they're delivered to them like take-out. Lazy bastards. Magnus and Hugo fist-bump each other.

"You guys are like horny teenagers," I tell them.

Hugo, who's six and a half feet tall even when he slouches,

smiles over at me. "Sometimes, you just have a craving for pussy."

"You're so weird, man," Magnus says. I'm sure he thinks he's being quiet, but he has the kind of voice that carries across a room. "I don't know how you deal with Esme and all that squirting."

I fight back a smile when I catch sight of Sloane. She has a fork full of rice hovering halfway between her plate and her mouth, her curious eyes on Magnus.

Hugo says back, the whole table listening to their exchange, "You don't like getting flooded?"

Magnus gives a little shudder. "Nah, all that mess isn't for me."

"If you don't like mess, you don't deserve to eat pussy," Ronan says, leaning forward in the seat across from Magnus and Hugo.

"You say that like it's some kind of privilege."

The table goes silent, everyone turning toward Sloane. Her comment wasn't quiet, but I certainly don't think she intended for the whole table to hear. Her eyes travel from face to face until she gets to Ronan.

"It *is* a privilege," he says to her. I don't miss the way his eyes trace down her body, landing on her cleavage in her barely-there tank top.

My knuckles turn white on the tabletop. If he doesn't get his fucking eyes off her soon, I'm going to rip them out. My gaze catches Bram's beside me. His eyes drop to my fists. I loosen them immediately.

Sloane misses the entire exchange. She just shrugs. "Every guy I've ever known talks about going down on girls like it's a chore they have to endure so they can have head."

"Some men do think that way." I'm surprised when the comment comes from Bram. He's always done his best to stay out of these kinds of conversations with the guys. Is this a side effect of the head injury? "But a real man goes down whether they're getting head or not."

There's that smile again, like he just told her happy birthday instead of trying to educate her on oral. "Would you say that a real woman goes down without the expectation of return service as well?"

He pokes at his food. He doesn't seem to have much of an appetite. "Sure. Good lovers do things because they want to, not because they have to. Because they want to please their partners."

"And what about a woman who goes down even though her partner never reciprocates?"

My eyes fly to hers. I can't stop myself. I don't care if everyone sees on my face the filthy things I want to do to this woman. I feel like she just knocked me off a cliff.

"Let me guess," I say, "our good man Tyler isn't a gentleman in the sack."

She doesn't answer. She just stares at me, and it fucking frustrates me. She's happy to discuss oral with everybody else in this house, but the second I want to join the conversation, the only person here who knows the sounds she makes when she comes, she's going to keep her mouth shut.

I start to put things together in my mind.

Tyler and Sloane, based on the research I did before she got here, started dating the summer before her junior year. What are the chances that she was with anybody before Tyler? And if she was, what are the chances that some sixteen-year-old knew how to properly perform oral?

"What the fuck are you doing with that guy, Barbie?" Everyone laughs at Ronny's comment.

"Some men really know how to fucking waste their time on Earth," Hugo says.

Sloane has some pink to her cheeks, either from embarrassment or amusement. Her eyes slide over to me.

I want to ask her what's going on in that pretty head of hers. I want to ask her if she, like me, is thinking about my mouth between her legs. I've never wanted to devour someone's cunt as bad as I want to devour hers right now. I want to toss her onto this table, spread her legs, and eat until I fucking die.

"I guess I just didn't think it was all that common," she says. She seems to be addressing the table, but her eyes are still on me.

"What? Giving head?" Hugo asks.

She mirrors him, putting her elbows on the table. "I guess, specifically, men giving women head."

Hugo gives her a look like she just said she wants to run for president. "It's not uncommon, or at least it shouldn't be uncommon. I meant what I said, men who don't eat aren't men. And if Tyler's not eating, good fucking riddance."

Sloane smiles down at her plate, and I'm hoping we're finally ready to move on to a different conversation before I pop a stiffy, but instead, Magnus grins and leans forward.

"How often?" he asks.

I should probably stop this, but she wanted to be one of the guys. This kind of conversation comes up at the dinner table way more often than I'd like to admit.

"How often what?" she asks. She doesn't seem bothered. Maybe she's even curious.

"How often is your little boy toy going down on you?"

"Magnus," I growl. He really has taken it too far now.

"I just want to know, boss." When I don't reprimand him again, he grins at Sloane. "What's the ratio?"

Sloane's eyebrows pop up. "The ratio of how often I...?" She doesn't actually say it, just trails off. "Compared to how often he...?"

"Yes."

She hesitates, and for a moment, I think she's been

pushed too far. But then, in a loud voice, she says, "Zero to, like, a hundred."

The table goes quiet.

And in a show of true gallantry, Hugo stands, his chair scraping back, and plants both of his palms on the table. "Are you trying to tell us that fucking dick weasel was getting regular blowjobs from you and never reciprocating?"

I'm surprised when she smiles and throws her hands up in a cute gesture, like it's no big deal. "I'm not trying to *tell you* anything."

The guys seem to come to the same conclusion I did: if Tyler has never gone down on her, chances are good no one has. Everyone seems to be shocked into a stupor.

"Alright, enough," I tell them, watching them glance around at each other and finally fall into a conversation about the upcoming party.

As soon as I'm sure no one is listening, I lean over to Sloane. I can hear the gentle tremor in her breath when I say, my voice low, "Does that mean you've never had a man's mouth between your legs?"

Her big blue eyes meet mine, staring at me quietly for a moment. Then, her voice a breathy rasp across my nerves, she says, "Is that a problem?"

My voice is barely more than a growl. "Yes, it's a fucking problem. It's a problem we're gonna fucking take care of tonight."

$$35$$

SLOANE

My leg rattles up and down as I sit on the edge of my bed. It's after midnight, and even though my whole body is exhausted, I'm wide awake, adrenaline pumping through my veins.

It's a problem we're gonna fucking take care of tonight.

I glance up at the camera in the corner of the room. The meaning of Julian's words *seemed* pretty obvious, but maybe I'm reading too much into it. Do I *want* him to mean what I think he meant? What am I doing? I can't be *attracted* to Julian. He's basically holding me here against my will, and he's probably a criminal, and he *killed* someone.

But he also has all those tattoos and those dark, steady eyes, and those fingers that he pressed to mine while I fucked myself.

I groan and stand, swiping my book up off the desk. I just need a distraction. I should have been done with this book by now, the one that my mystery friend sent me, but I'm always so caught up in everything going on with the guys that I never finished it.

I wonder if the books are still showing up at my dorm. Krista hasn't said anything about any, but I only see her twice a week in our Sociology class.

Boss
Look at you, waiting for me like a good
girl.

I toss my book aside when I read the message and look up at the camera. I flip it off.

Boss
Not very ladylike.

Sloane
Yeah? Well, it's not very gentlemanly to
tease women.

Boss
Tease? I thought it was gentlemanly for
a man to keep his hands to himself.

I don't want Julian to keep his hands to himself. I want him to put his hands on me. This is *insane*. Technically, I still have a boyfriend, even if it's all for show. If Tyler found out I was letting Julian touch me, he would murder us both.

I decide to leave Julian's message on read, tossing my phone onto the bed. I'm not going to beg him to come in here, even if the thought of him making me no longer an oral virgin has me positively trembling.

Maybe I should lock my door. Then I could go to sleep and not continue to make bad decisions. The decision would be made and Julian wouldn't be able to change my mind. But I'm horny, hornier than I've ever been, so here I am, sitting on the edge of my bed in the sweats Julian loaned me to meet Barbara in. They're actually very comfortable to sleep in.

Because most of the guys are in their rooms and I no longer have a bodyguard stationed outside of mine, it's quiet enough that I hear Julian coming up the stairs. The man never takes off those boots he wears, and I've never even seen him without his coat in the house. Well, except for when I saw him shirtless while I stitched up his wound.

A shiver goes through me at the memory of his slick skin under my hands, the dark lines of his tattoos.

My bedroom door swings open and falls shut, ripping me out of my thoughts.

Julian leans back against the door, silent as his eyes move down my body.

I know I'm going to Hell for this, but I also know that if this man wants to offer to do something for me that Tyler never would, I can't say no.

So I hold his eye as I push myself up on my bed, until I have my pillow beneath me.

"You gonna let me taste you, princess?"

I bite my lip and nod.

"Thank fuck." The coat comes off. He drops it by the door and strides toward the bed.

Julian might hate me, and he may be about to do this to prove some point about Tyler, but he also made Xander cook for me, he's stood up to Frankie for me, he's kept any of the guys who might want to cross the line from getting near me.

That's enough for me.

Because it's more than anyone else has ever done.

Julian crawls up the bed toward me, and I have to hold back a whimper. I'm pulsing between my legs, and the need becomes unbearable when he hooks his fingers over the waistband of my sweatpants and yanks them down my legs.

When he realizes I didn't put anything on underneath them, he freezes, his eyes glued between my legs. I start to press my knees together, but Julian reaches out, planting his hands on my inner thighs and shoving them back open.

"No, you don't." His dark eyes meet mine, and somehow,

they seem darker than ever, all black. "You went bare under your clothes because you knew I would come. You knew underwear was a waste of time. There's no backing out now. We're not stopping until you come on my tongue."

My muscles squeeze at the idea. I've never felt this way before. I lost my virginity to Tyler, and even though he was perfectly adequate in bed, he thought going down on girls was gross and wasn't always particularly concerned if I had an orgasm or not. It was always just a bonus.

But Julian looks like he's been sent here by the FBI to complete a very important mission.

Keeping his eyes on me, he lowers his mouth and spits between my legs. Before I've even had a chance to react, he licks me.

My breath rushes out of me. I remember the first time I saw a video of a girl getting eaten out and wondered what it would feel like. It's the kind of thing you can't quantify until it's happening to you. I never expected it to feel like this. I never expected it to feel *this* good. As Julian flattens his tongue to swipe it up the center of me and swirls it around my clit, I'm certain that nothing has ever felt this good in the history of mankind. I'm mesmerized watching his tongue as he sets a rhythm around my clit, flicking back and forth, and when he slips one finger into me, I collide right into an orgasm. It's almost embarrassing how fast it happens.

When I come down from it, my back hitting the mattress, I'm disappointed that it's already over. Just like that.

I start to pull away from Julian, who's watching me from the end of the bed, but he wraps his arms under my thighs and drags me back. "What are you—"

He puts his mouth back where it was, and I cry out, reaching down to fist my hands in his hair. "Julian," I whine, but he ignores me, opening his mouth over my pussy and devouring me like the first time was just an appetizer. His tongue travels down, until he's licking up every drop that's spilling out of me.

I moan, tugging his hair in an attempt to get him back to my clit. The need to come again is intense, so much stronger than the first time. As soon as he has his tongue on my clit and his eyes on mine, I start to rock my hips.

"That's it," I hear him say against me. "Fuck yourself on my tongue, pretty girl."

"Shut up," I hiss, halfway off the bed trying to get his mouth back on me. He started this. One orgasm would have been enough for me, but now he has me wanting more.

He smiles, closes his mouth around my clit, and sucks hard.

Rockets go off in my head, the rest of the world going dark as I come harder than I knew I was capable of. I don't even realize I'm screaming until it's over and my throat is raw. Julian is still on his knees at the foot of the bed, watching me like he's afraid I'll pass out.

Maybe *I'm* afraid I'll pass out.

I throw my arm over my eyes, gasping for breath. "Thank you for your service," I gulp out.

Julian gives a breathy laugh.

I rip my arm away, getting a glimpse of a smile before it falls away. "I didn't know you knew how to laugh," I say.

He presses my legs to one side, and I yelp when he smacks my ass. "Don't start with the attitude now, princess, or I might be tempted to leave."

I scowl. "Isn't it time for you to leave? You, uh, performed your duty. You can go now."

A devious smile spreads slowly across his face. "Oh, I'm not done. I want one more."

"What!" I start to sit up, scrambling up the bed, but just like before, he grabs me, this time throwing my legs over his shoulders, the bottom half of my body fully off the bed and tilted up toward his mouth.

And then his tongue is inside me again. Julian watches me, and all I can do is moan out his name. He takes his mouth from me, his lips and chin wet. "That fucker missed out on the taste of you, Sloane. And now I get to be the first to feast on you. I'm not done yet."

My mouth falls open on a silent scream as he licks me. Everything is so sensitive, my skin swollen and tender under his ministrations. I grab onto the sheets to steady myself and let myself feel him, the press of his tongue against my clit again and again, until tears are leaking from the corners of my eyes from the pleasure of it and my thighs are pressing against his face.

Like before, he plunges his tongue inside me, this time settling his thumb over my clit, and I don't even have the energy to scream, only to whimper as he pushes me higher and higher and shoves me over the edge. My whole body goes taut as he holds me up to his mouth.

My back bows, and I feel certain, as I come and come and come, that not a single part of my body is touching the mattress.

My body goes slack in his arms, and he slowly lowers me to the bed, where I'm completely limp. I feel like a jellyfish, ready to sink right into the box spring. I watch through droopy eyes as Julian wipes his mouth on his black shirt and reaches up to fix the diamond stud in one of his ears.

He hasn't looked away from me once through this whole process, and he continues to hold my eye as he leans down and presses a soft kiss to the top of my thigh. "Don't say I never gave you anything." When he straightens away from the bed, standing at the foot of it, I can see that he's hard behind the zipper of his black pants, his cock thick and ready.

"Why aren't you inside me?" I ask, feeling high. My fingertips are numb.

He bends and picks up his coat. "Haven't you had enough?"

Yes, I have. At least, for now. I'm sure when I wake up tomorrow, I'll regret not asking him to fuck me. But for right now, the idea seems daunting. I'm going to be sore as it is. "What about you?"

Draping his coat over his arm, he smirks at me. "Don't worry about me."

He turns and shuts the door without looking back, and I lay there for a long time, naked from the waist down, thinking about how cold I am now that his warm arms aren't holding me.

36

SLOANE

I startle awake when Julian throws open my bedroom door. "Get dressed. We have stuff to do."

I push myself up in bed. "Why won't you knock?" It's my fault, honestly, for not locking the door when he left last night. Maybe I've gotten too comfortable with these men.

"Why the fuck would I knock?" is all he says before turning and leaving again.

I lay there, the blanket pulled up to my chest, halfway naked beneath it. I never got dressed after what he did to me, just crawled under the covers, boneless, and fell asleep.

I finally scrape myself out of bed and close myself in the closet, where I've taken to changing clothes. I throw on a t-shirt and a pair of white shorts that I dig out of the bottom of my suitcase. Whatever Julian has planned, this will have to do. What do these guys do about their dirty laundry?

I glance at the clock on my phone. It's six in the morning.

I find Julian in the hallway, leaning against the banister,

hands in his pockets. I hate the way he can look so unaffected, like he didn't give me three screaming orgasms last night.

He turns for the stairs, beckoning with two fingers over his shoulder for me to follow him.

"Can you at least tell me what we're doing?" I ask, trailing after him.

At my question, he spins around. I'm too close to him to stop, and I smash right into him, bouncing away. He reaches out and grabs onto my arms to keep me from falling backwards.

I can't seem to stop myself from reaching up and grabbing his arms in return. I regret it once I have my palms on the bulge of his biceps through his shirt. My eyes slide up to his, but if he's thinking the same thing I am—that we should skip whatever work we need to do so he can take me back to my bed and make me come again—it's not written anywhere on his face.

"You need to learn how to shoot," he finally says.

"Oh, um. Yeah. I mean, I guess."

He scoffs. "You guess? You shot a man with a gun in the shoulder."

"Yeah, but I don't even know where I meant to shoot him. Do you really think that I'm going to be able to shoot someone in the face?"

He bends so he can look me in the eye, and I narrow mine at him. I don't need him to treat me like a child. "You pulled a gun on someone who threatened one of your colleagues."

I sigh. "I definitely would not call him a colleague, but sure."

He straightens, looking down his nose at me. "What is he then?"

"Bram is my friend." It's the first time I've acknowledged

it to anyone but myself, but it feels right to say. Sometime since I got here, Bram and I have become friends.

"No, Bram is not your friend." At this, his hands fall away from my arms. "Let's go."

He walks me out the front door and around the side of the house, until I realize we're going to the barn. The barn is the only place on the property I haven't been yet. I heard Julian mention once that it's just overflow storage for the cars.

I've never been in a barn, but somehow I'm not surprised when he throws open the door and dust flies. It smells like cedar wood and must and is full of half-dilapidated cars with peeling paint and flat tires. Julian walks through it and throws open another door, leading right back outside. He nods toward something and I turn toward the open field behind the barn that stretches between us and the forest. Close to the tree line, there's a wooden table with several beer bottles lined up on it.

I sigh. "Could you be any more of a cliché?"

He twists his body toward me and raises an eyebrow. "You mean, more cliché than a California blonde with a rich boyfriend?"

I cross my arms and scowl up at him.

"More cliché than a girl who pretends she likes nice guys but what she really wants is to be tongue fucked by a guy with a gun in his coat?"

Ignoring the heat I feel crawling across my skin, I let my eyes drop to his chest. "You have a gun in your coat?"

He gives me that smirk I hate so much and pulls out a small handgun. I couldn't tell you if it was a pistol or a revolver or a fucking shotgun. I don't know anything about guns. He shoves it into one of my hands and takes the other and wraps it around it. "How does that feel?"

"Heavier than I thought," I tell him honestly. I was so full of adrenaline when I shot that guy that I can't even remember how the gun felt in my hands.

He nods. "Don't worry, your body will get used to it." The way his voice crackles—the way his words could mean so many things—makes my hands tremble so much I drop the gun.

When it hits the ground between us, his eyes bore into mine. I know he can tell exactly what I was thinking, that his words set a fire in my blood. He reaches down and picks up the gun, pushing it back into my hands.

"If you drop a gun when it's loaded, you're likely to take someone's foot off. Hang on to it."

The heat I was feeling before quickly turns to ice. I'm surprised by how much I want to impress Julian. I want him to know I'm competent. That I'm just as capable as any of the men that work with him, even if I'm a little less knowledgeable. But I can learn.

"I know it looks cool in the movies, but two hands at all times. Despite what some people want to believe, firing a gun isn't about proving you're a badass. It's about killing someone."

My glance sideways at him.

He throws up a hand. "Or maiming them, stopping them from killing someone else, it doesn't matter. The point is, it's not about looking cool. It's about taking care of your business. So when you have this in your hands, both hands, don't miss."

Don't miss. It seems so simple, especially for someone like him.

He pulls something else from his coat pocket. Bullets. Stepping closer to me, he says, "I'm going to show you how to load it." And then he does just that.

I watch and memorize.

When he's done, he unloads it and analyzes me as I follow all the steps. It's simple enough. It's actually disturbing how user-friendly guns can be.

Julian takes the gun from me, hands sure and aggressive. "You can't be scared or nervous with a gun, alright? You need to be confident. Fear will make you miss. Nerves make you tremble. There will be no shaking and no trembling. Only confidence."

I nod even though that's not something I can reasonably agree to. I think back to what happened with Bram. I wouldn't say I confidently grabbed that gun. I just didn't know what else to do. The adrenaline kicked in, not confidence. Either way, I would never dream of showing Julian anything but confidence.

He comes up behind me. I can feel the heat of him along my back. I fight down a shiver. He reaches over my shoulder and points to one of the beer bottles. "I want you to aim for that one."

I lift both arms, holding the gun in a tight grip. Like he can see right through my eyes, he reaches around me and pushes my arms up an inch.

"You really want to be just underneath what you're trying to hit. All guns have a little bit of a kickback. When you jerk, you're going to send the bullet flying somewhere you don't want. You'll learn to adjust to it. Be careful. Be deliberate."

I nod.

I feel him step back and am overcome by a wave of relief. I never could have hit a target with him pressed against me like that.

"All right," he grunts. "Give it a shot."

I will not give him the satisfaction of laughing at his joke. Instead, I focus on steadying my breathing.

When I fire, I don't hit the bottle. Not even close.

It turns out that very large men at close range make better targets than small beer bottles four yards away. Instead, I hit a tree somewhere between one bottle and the next.

"That wasn't bad," Julian says behind me, "but I can tell you're nervous."

I let my arms fall and turn to him. "If you know I'm nervous, then you must know it's because you're very intimidating."

One side of his mouth lifts. "Did it pain you to admit that, princess? Yes, I know I'm very intimidating. And thank you."

I groan and spin around. When I do, a loud noise rings out. One minute, the world is quiet and the next minute, the gun has gone off in my hand. I jump away from the sound and drop the gun.

"Fuck," I hear Julian growl. Then he has his hands on my upper arms. "This is what I'm talking about," he says in my face. Heat travels across my cheeks. "You take it fucking seriously or you don't do it at all."

I grit my teeth. I'm trembling from the shock and adrenaline. If I open my mouth, who knows what will come out.

"You don't point a gun at something unless you intend to shoot it. That includes your own fucking feet. You're lucky you didn't shoot your goddamn toe off. Pick it up," he says, nodding at the gun.

I bend down and take it, but I feel far less confident than I did a moment ago.

"Keep your finger off the trigger. Do you understand?"

I nod.

He tips his chin toward the bottles again. "Go."

I lift the gun again, but now I'm frustrated and angry with him for not having any mercy, even though I know I shouldn't have expected any in the first place. Just because he had his mouth on me last night doesn't mean he's suddenly developed any mercy.

When I miss a second time, it's no surprise. It doesn't seem to come as a surprise to Julian either. He sighs and crosses his arms, looking like a disappointed parent. "I have plenty of bullets. Keep going until you hit it."

"It's time for you to leave for class," Bram says.

I turn away from the targets with a sigh, remembering to put on the safety before I lower the gun to my side. "I can't leave until I do this. I just can't. He'll think I'm pathetic."

Bram, sitting in a chair close enough to the side of the barn that he can rest his head against it, chuckles. "He doesn't think you're pathetic."

"You're kidding, right? He thinks I'm incompetent."

Bram raises an eyebrow at me. "He put a gun in your hand. He doesn't do that with people he finds incompetent."

That may be true, but Bram doesn't know that I almost took off my own foot. I shake my head and turn back to the bottles, lifting the gun again. I've been out here for an hour and haven't hit a single target.

"Maybe you have him all wrong."

My finger, ready to squeeze the trigger, relaxes again. "What do you mean?" I ask without moving or looking over at him. Under different circumstances, I might feel cool, like a badass in a spy movie. But right now, I just feel unsure of myself.

"I've known Julian for a long time, Sloane. He's different

around you. He respects you. And maybe it even bothers him that he does. He wants to hate you, but he just can't."

"How flattering." My eyes focus on a beer bottle, amber under the sun. I pull the trigger, and the bottle shatters. A rush of excitement flows through me. I grin out at the empty spot on the table.

"Hey!" Bram says. "Look at you!" I turn and hand him the gun, trusting him with it far more than I trust myself. I did what I was told and now I'm ready to not hold a gun for a very long time.

"I think you're the one who has him all wrong," I say. "It must be the brain damage."

He grins up at me from his chair, his skin still pale, his eyes still sunken.

"Want me to walk you up to your room?"

"Sure," he says, standing slowly. He slings his arm over my shoulders, and we hobble together around the barn and up to the house. "Sloane," he says as we head up the driveway toward the house, "I know everyone thinks Julian is made of stone." He stops me right before we reach the door and turns me to face him, both hands on my shoulders. "But he's not. Don't shatter him, okay?"

I just blink up at him. He doesn't want *me* to shatter *Julian*? Julian Shaw, who has threatened my life more than once? Julian Shaw who *killed* someone? Julian Shaw who made me come three times and then walked out of my room like he had somewhere better to be?

Before I have a chance to respond, the front door flies open. Hugo stands in the doorway, one hand still on the knob. His eyes scan me and he scowls. "You better get ready to go, Barbie. You're going to be late."

Right. Class.

"You'll walk him up?" I ask, referring to Bram, as I rush past Hugo to get into the house.

"Sure," he says.

As I head up the stairs, Bram's voice carries up to me. "Can you stop treating me like a little old man?"

I shut my door behind me and strip my shirt off over my head before remembering the stupid camera. Julian might have seen me naked but the other men haven't, and I'm not about to be some kind of entertainment for them. I snatch my shirt off the bed, but realize I tossed it onto something sitting at the foot of the mattress that wasn't there before.

A box.

I press my shirt to my chest and step over to it. It's a brown paper box, and it has a little piece of string tied around it in a bow. My mind can't help but conjure images of severed hands or bleeding hearts. I reach out and tug on the string. It falls away from the box, and I lift the lid cautiously.

Sitting on top is a note, written on a yellow square of card stock.

Don't spend them all in one place.

I stare at the note, trying to decipher what it means. I move it out of the way to peer into the box. There are two things in the box. A silver pistol and a box of bullets. I drop the note on the bed and reach for the gun.

Someone bangs on the door. "Come on, Sloane! Let's fucking go!"

Hugo. Shit.

I slam the lid down on the box and run into my closet, stashing it in a dark corner before hurrying into a different outfit. I don't know what Julian was thinking. Did he honestly think I wanted my *own* gun? I don't want a gun at all! I can't shoot anyone!

Except I did shoot someone, and I know I would do it

again if someone came for Bram again, or Ronny, or Sarge... or Julian.

The thought sends a wave of heat through my stomach.

If someone came from Julian, I know without a speck of uncertainty that I could shoot them.

I don't have time to examine that thought process. I slip into my shoes and rush out to meet Hugo.

"What happened to you yesterday?"

Sitting in the dining hall, Hugo beside us at the table, a few seats between us and him, Tyler begins questioning me the moment he takes his seat.

Hugo looks so out of place, unnaturally tall and Scandinavian blonde and easily pushing thirty. A few people have glanced over at us, but he doesn't seem to notice. He's eating a BLT sub like it's his last meal. When he takes another bite with his cheek still full, like a squirrel storing up for winter, I have to bite back a smile.

"It was nothing," I tell Tyler, focusing down on my textbook.

"Nothing? You ran out of class like a bat out of hell. And that bodyguard guy, he was just summoning you out of class like he owns you."

"Well, Tyler, you sold me to Julian, so they *do* own me."

Hugo laughs with his mouth full. I guess I didn't think he was listening, but he is.

Tyler glares at him, but Hugo just goes back to scrolling on his phone. Every few seconds, it vibrates against the table. Bram told me the guys at the compound have a group text. I try not to feel jealous that no one has mentioned adding me to it, especially if it's particularly entertaining. I have to remind myself that I'm not actually one of them in any real way and that I don't want to be.

"Maybe I should talk to Julian about the fact that you can't be missing classes. You can't flunk out of Dartmouth when my father is footing the bill."

Anger threatens to blind me. He's sitting there across from me, acting like he doesn't know that, as far as he's concerned, the money train comes to an abrupt halt after this year. I'm paid up until summer and then what? Tyler thinks *he's* going to pay for both of us to go to Dartmouth?

I know I have to play along, but all I want to do is flip this table and tell him to fuck off.

"It really wasn't anything important," I say, attempting to placate him. My eyes meet Hugo's briefly and slip back to Tyler. He knows how important it was to me that Bram woke up. "It was just that Ronny had a family emergency and couldn't leave me here by myself. It didn't even have anything to do with me."

Tyler's face is expressionless. "Fine. But you're on thin ice. If you fail a class, we're going to have to re-think this entire arrangement. I can't have a stupid girlfriend."

Hugo stops eating, his eyes landing on Tyler.

Before he can say anything damning, I lean toward Tyler, giving him a perfect view down my shirt. "Haven't we established that the arrangement with Julian can't be amended?"

Tyler doesn't even spare me a glance. "I'm not talking about that arrangement. I'm talking about you and me."

My skin prickles. I fight the urge to look over at Hugo. Tyler is trying to humiliate me. He's trying to make me feel unwanted. As if his attention is something I should beg for. Maybe there was a time when I would have, but not anymore.

Images from last night flicker across my mind. The things Julian did to me, the same things Tyler always seemed appalled by. I don't need Tyler to want me. I don't need *anyone* to want me. All I need is the knowledge that I'm *worth* wanting. And that's something I know to be true. I know I need to stay close to Tyler in order to accomplish my goal, but I'm fed up with this.

"If you don't want this anymore, I understand. It must be hard that your girlfriend is getting so much attention from other men."

Hugo shifts. Out of the corner of my eye, I see him glance over. *Trust me*, I want to tell him.

Tyler's face scrunches into a scowl, just like I knew it would. I sit back in my chair. If we were in private, he would have a lot to say, but he won't say it with Hugo breathing down his neck. Tyler takes in a deep breath. He doesn't want to give too much away.

"Hugo?" I turn to him, and he glances up with a question in his eyes. "Can you be a dear and buy me a Diet Coke?" I smile, bright and kind.

He holds my gaze for a long moment and nods. "Sure thing. Be right back." He leaves his half-eaten sandwich on the table.

"I have information for you," I tell Tyler as soon as Hugo is gone. I need Tyler to think I'm so desperate for him not to break up with me that I'll do anything, which isn't entirely wrong, just not for the reasons he thinks.

"What information?" he asks.

"Julian showed me inside the barn and behind it. From what I could tell, the barn is clean. All I saw were old cars that I guess they're going to fix up and sell. But they have a firing range in the back. Why would they need a firing range unless they were shooting people?"

Tyler's scowl doesn't change. "That's not information, Sloane. I know they shoot people." He glances over his shoulder at where Hugo is standing in line to buy my soda. "A friend of mine went missing last week. We're pretty sure one of Julian's guys made him disappear."

I school my features so I don't give away that I already knew this. "What friend?"

Tyler waves me off. "Just a guy I know. Julian has made it clear that he doesn't mind killing people."

The same question keeps coming back to me—why did he send me in if he knew they were dangerous? I couldn't help him if I was dead. "Then why don't you go to the police? If you think Julian is doing something that serious..."

"I can't prove it, and I can't go to the cops without evidence. I need to know what he's doing. They're not just going to knock his door down because some nobody went missing." This seemed so valid two weeks ago, but now I see it for what it is. Tyler isn't going to the cops because that's not what criminals do. They handle things with their fists.

"I thought you said he was your friend."

This seems to bring Tyler back to attention. His eyes stop wandering and he settles on me. "He was, but not everybody is somebody, Sloane. Not even here."

I hate the way he says it, like there's some hierarchy for existence. Some people's lives matter and some people's don't. He makes me sick. I can't believe I ever thought I meant anything to him.

"Here you go," Hugo says, stepping up to the table and putting my Diet Coke in front of me.

"Thanks."

I stash my textbook in my backpack and pull out the book I've been reading, the one my mysterious gift giver left me just before I moved out. I make a mental note to text Krista and ask if I've gotten any more packages. I open the book and take out the index card I've been using as a bookmark, the same index card that was left with the book. My eyes move briefly over the handwritten words before I start to read.

But then, my brain catches up to my eyes, and I snatch the card back up. With the book open in my lap, I stare down at the handwriting on the card.

This one is an old favorite. Enjoy.

Don't spend them all in one place.

The handwriting is the same.

$$37$$

SLOANE

Over the next few days, I carefully learn the schedule of the guys who hang out in the security wing. I'm still not allowed anywhere near that hallway, but I know from listening when they think I'm not that Julian's room is down there. I've been inside his office. Short of going through his computer and his desk drawers, I can tell there's nothing there of importance. Julian is too smart for that. He knows that anyone who found their way in would go straight there and ransack it.

No, it's his bedroom where the real stuff is going to be.

I don't even know what I'm looking for. Proof of some sort. Julian has secrets, and I'm tired of being left out of them. He was sending me books before I came here, and I want to know why. Why me? I have no intention of taking information back to Tyler, but would it hurt for me to have that information for myself?

The first room on the left is where they're watching the security cameras. I've seen it in passing, walking close to the wall, turning at weird angles while being as inconspicuous as possible. From what I can tell, there's another room past that, on the same wall, and then at the very end, a door.

When I pass by, I get a good look, expecting to see a keypad. Something with numbers, maybe a thumbprint reader like Sarge has, but there's nothing. I guess they feel it's secure enough because there's always someone in the security room, always someone watching. Not everybody watches security cameras. Bram, for example, doesn't watch cameras. Below his pay grade, I assume. Neither does Frankie or Claudia. But Ronny does.

Ronny, who is a little bored, a little young, and maybe also a little flighty. This is how I know that my plan is going to work. If he's not paying attention, which I'm sure he won't be, based on past experience, I'll have time to set the fire in my bathroom and casually take off before he figures out there's smoke. I'll hide in the front sitting room while he goes to investigate. I'm hoping he'll see the smoke before there's too much damage to my room.

I learn the security schedule, and I learn when Julian will be out on a job. These guys, they run like clockwork, and it actually isn't that difficult to find out. Hopefully they're not as obvious with their outside endeavors as they are with what's going on inside.

Just like I planned, I set the fire with a lighter I found in the dining room and hide out in the sitting room. Once I hear Ronny curse loudly and make a run for my room, I take off to the security wing. I walk right past the room with the screen showing all the security cameras and into Julian's room.

It's dark, the only light coming from a very small lamp on a bedside table. I can't find the light switch. It's cold and smells good in here. It smells *really* good. Like cologne and fabric softener.

When something brushes up against my leg, I have to

clamp my teeth shut tight so I don't scream. I throw both hands over my mouth and look down, only to find a gray cat, long hair sticking out in every direction, looking up at me with blue eyes.

The cat meows softly, and I'm perplexed. There's been a cat back here this whole time and I didn't know about it?

It seems to be very friendly, so I bend down and pet it.

"Show me where to find your daddy's secrets," I whisper. It purrs and rubs its face all over the tops of my bare feet. "Yeah, you're no help." The room is mostly bare, not unlike my room.

This is ten times worse than going into Tyler's room without knowing what I'm looking for. I'm truly clueless now, with no leads.

I've been getting books for almost a year. I've never had any clue where they were coming from. They just started showing up at my dorm one day, and when I moved dorms, they followed me. And yes, it was a little scary, but I honestly just kind of thought it was someone in one of my classes, someone who had every reason to know where my dorm was. Some kind of secret admirer. It was almost flattering.

Part of me even thought it was Krista for a little while. That maybe she was doing it out of some kind of weird kindness of her heart. I once thought it could be Tyler when he mentioned visiting a bookstore in town, but that was short-lived. It took a five-minute conversation with him to figure out I was wrong. Not only was he not thoughtful enough, but when I asked him who his favorite writer was, he looked at me like I'd asked him to explain quantum physics.

My love for books came from my mother. There was a time in my life when I thought it was something we were sharing, something she was passionate about, but I realized when I was still fairly young that it was something she was doing to placate me. Other parents put tablets in their kids' hands, put them in front of TV shows and video games. My mom bought me books. It was cheaper than cable, more affordable than video games. She could buy paperbacks for a dollar at a thrift store and they would entertain me when she would disappear for a day or two days or a week, coming back just as the food ran out.

I think about that last package, the one that came the same day as the race... What was the point? That's the answer I'm looking for.

I go through all of Julian's drawers, go through his closet. I'm not all that surprised to find that his bedroom is devoid of personality. It has exactly what you'd expect from a bedroom, like a layout in a magazine. He has his own bathroom, shaving supplies, clean towels. He even has a special moisturizer for his tattoos, which I didn't know was a thing. But personal items? Not so much. No pictures or cards or books. Just vitamins and a half-empty glass of water on the nightstand. Lines of expensive-looking shoes in the closet.

The closet in his bedroom has every single black outfit he owns. Unsurprisingly, he *only* owns black outfits. He does have the occasional white dress shirt, but nothing more than that. Ties and jackets and whatnot. Everything's so neat and organized.

But when I'm in his bathroom, standing right beside the remarkably large walk-in shower, I see that there's another closet. It has double doors. And I realize by the shape of the handles, in keeping with the pattern of the rest of the house, that this is not a closet. It's a door to another room. And it has a lock. This explains why there's no keypad on the bedroom door. The keypad is in here. Which means there's something he's trying to protect.

It's not a fingerprint scanner like the one upstairs. It takes a code.

"*Shit.*" I'll never be able to figure out his code. It's probably his dead mother's birthday or something. I walk back through his room, searching for a clue. I know it's not like in the movies. I'm not going to conveniently find four numbers on the back of a picture frame.

The cat jumps up next to me on the bed, and I absently run my fingers through its hair. It's probably a boy cat. Julian *would* only want a boy cat. He steps across my lap, and I hear the faint jingle of a collar on his tag.

Maybe...

I snatch the cat before he can hop off the bed and turn him toward the light. *Winston*, his collar reads. But of course, there's no date of birth. I'm not sure why I thought there would be. I sigh and set Winston on the ground, falling back on the bed. I hate that it's so soft, that it smells so good. Julian's room shouldn't be comfortable. It should be cold, like the house of a dictator.

I watch Winston putter into the bathroom. He stands at the foot of the door and looks up at the handle. He crouches and then springs, grabbing onto the knob and slipping off of it so it makes a *boing* sound.

"Winston," I whisper, and then stop.

Winston.

There's no way.

I take out my phone and Google Winston Churchill. There's just absolutely no way.

Winston Churchill, born November 30, 1874, died January 24, 1965.

I go to the keypad and try the years first, then both full dates. I put in several different combinations, but I keep coming up empty. I knew it couldn't be that easy. I stare down at the keypad. I have to give up soon. I've already been in here too long, and I know I'm going to have to sneak back out of the hallway. Ronny already knows I'm not in my room.

I turn and stop, standing in the middle of Julian's luxurious master bathroom. Winston Churchill was pivotal in World War II. What if...

1945.

The door unlocks. When I throw it open and go in, I find a room at least the size of a walk-in closet. But when I flip the light on, I see I was right: it's not a closet at all. Where his bedroom was organized and immaculate, this room seems not to have a single bare square inch of space. Boxes stacked high against a wall. Piles of paper on a table. There are so many things to look at that it takes me a moment to even process what it all is.

Then I see myself. My own eyes looking back at me.

On the wall, there are dozens of glossy photos. I carefully step up to them. Since walking into the compound, I've felt angry. Nervous. Unsure. Confused.

But I didn't feel truly afraid until this moment. Because there are dozens of pictures of me on the wall. Pictures of me outside my dorm hall, on campus with my friends, at the grocery store, at a café.

I would have thought it was a shrine if any of it was flattering. But it isn't. It's clinical. Analytical.

I step back, taking in more of the wall. More photos. Photos of Tyler and some other person whose face I don't recognize. There are almost as many photos of him as there are of me. A guy about my age. In some of the photos, he and Tyler are talking, shaking hands. Who is he, and why is he so important?

I hear footsteps behind me, a low *meow* followed by someone gently clicking their tongue. I turn, feeling a crackle in my blood, knowing that somebody's about to walk through the door and that person is probably going to be Julian.

There's a gun on the table beside me. Without hesitating, I pick it up and point it right at the bathroom doorway, just as Julian appears in it.

38

JULIAN

I should have seen it coming. Sloane is too smart to have gone on much longer without asking questions.

She set a fire in her room, waited until Ronny went to check it out, and snuck into my bedroom. She doesn't know I have access to the security cameras on my phone and that I saw exactly what she was doing and sent Bram in to take care of the meeting without me. Pain in my ass.

The moment the smoke started, I got in my car, but I wasn't near fast enough to get to her before she got to me.

And did she ever get to me.

She's standing in the one place she shouldn't be, right in front of a wall of her photos, a gun pointed right at me. I put my hands up, even though I know she won't shoot me. She has too good of a heart. She won't shoot someone—even when they deserve it—unless she has really good reason.

I walk slowly into the bathroom, one quiet step at a time. She doesn't budge an inch, just keeps the barrel of my own gun pointed at me. It's my fault. I let my guard down. I thought between the security cameras and the fact that I trust everyone in the compound, that my secrets would be safe.

I was wrong.

"What the hell is all of this stuff?" she asks, not a quaver to be found anywhere in her voice. Good girl.

I take another step.

"You know, Ronny is facing a harsh punishment because of you."

This makes her falter, just the tiniest bit. She blinks. "What will you do to him?"

"What do you care? You're the one that put him in this position."

She grits her teeth, and it makes me want to smile. She's wearing a mini skirt that sparkles in the light, and she's actually considering shooting me. I want to put her on this tile floor and make her come. "*You* put *me* in this position. By lying to me."

"I never lied to you."

I see her consider this in her head. It was never me that was lying. It was always Tyler. I just never told her the whole truth. Need-to-know, we agreed.

"Tell me what all of this is."

I let my hands drop to my sides. There's no reason not to tell her everything now. "Okay. But you have to put the gun down."

She cocks her head to one side. "You know, I don't think I will, Mr. Shaw."

I bite back a smile. If one of the guys did this to me, he'd be hanging in the barn before the night was out. But I know I'll let her get away with it, just for having the guts. And because it's making me hard.

"I was twenty when my father was murdered and left me his empire. He made me get involved in the business as soon as I graduated high school, made me his Second, taught me everything I know. When he left the business to me, I didn't want it. Who wants to inherit a car trade and a gang from their father? Not me. So I asked my best friend, Leo, to run it with me. To be my right-hand man. Leo, he had a head for business. That was five years ago."

Sloane thinks she understands me, and maybe she does, in part, but not all of me. Not even standing in the middle of all my secrets.

"Leo was smart, he was logical. But he had one problem. Coke. Couldn't get him off the stuff. I tried. I succeeded, for a little while. He was in and out of rehab the whole time we were at school. When he started running the business, he managed to get clean. I was there with him through all of it. The business gave him purpose, distraction. And then Tyler moved to town."

The gun slips down an inch. Sloane's eyes soften, just like I knew they inevitably would. She can't help herself. She cares about people, even people like me.

"I've always kept drugs out of the business, even though the guys tried to change my mind. There's money in it, especially if you move the heavy stuff. But I knew what it would do to Leo, so I kept it away from us. I did everything I could to keep drugs out of this town. It's how I made my name. People brought it in, I threw them out, preferably dead. But Tyler rolled into town with a rich daddy and an army of people willing to work for him."

I don't miss the disappointment that flashes across her eyes. I still haven't told her about the guns. She's still trying to get answers, and for what? To take back to Tyler? She wouldn't. I know she wouldn't. Not now.

"A year ago, Tyler sold Leo some bad shit. It was laced with fentanyl, and it was too much for Leo's system. I got an anonymous call from someone who told me where to find

Leo's body. Tyler and his men had tossed him in a dumpster out on Highway 10. He had overdosed for sure, but they put a bullet in him so no one would be able to get him to a hospital in time for him to survive. He had to cover his tracks."

She lowers the gun, but I wish she wouldn't. I wish she'd just put a hole in my fucking chest. End it all. Instead, she looks at me with glistening eyes that make me want to hit something. I don't want her to cry for me. I don't want her to pit me. I want her rage. It's comforting, familiar.

"I'm so sorry."

"No, you're not. You're not. Stop apologizing for him. Stop trying to crucify yourself for his sins. He doesn't deserve it."

She sniffles but doesn't argue with me. She knows I'm right.

"Claudia, she's Leo's mother. I went to her after, offered her a place here because Leo was taking care of her. She wanted me to kill Tyler. *I* wanted to kill Tyler. I couldn't. I still can't. People like Tyler, they don't just disappear; they go *missing*. People search for them. That daddy of his will coming looking for him. I can't start a war with his people, with all his little minions. If I put a bullet in him, his men come for mine, and he has more men than I do, even if their collective IQ is lower. I'll put myself in the line of fire, but I can't risk anyone else."

"That's why you wanted me, right? He took something from you, so you were going to take something from him." She doesn't seem surprised by anything I've told her, just attentive.

I nod. "I thought taking you away from him would hit him where it hurt. And I guess it did. It hit his pride. It just took us a while to get there." I gesture to the room behind her, stepping around her to go inside, to look at everything that's been on the walls for a year. "I was going to take you."

She spins around to follow me with her eyes. "What?"

"I started watching you a little while after Leo died. I had eyes on you all the time."

"You were sending me books."

And just like that, she takes me by surprise. I don't know how she always does. There's a stack of paperback books on the table beside my laptop, and her eyes are glued to it. I'd honestly forgotten all about the books. When I figured out that Sloane was a reader, I pulled boxes of books from Dad's library and started mailing them to her. Maybe I wanted to seduce her. Maybe I wanted to scare her. I don't even know anymore.

"I was sending you books. I was coming up with a plan to snatch you, use you as leverage somehow. But I didn't even have to because I set up the race, and he showed up, just like we hoped he would. I got him enough in the hole and told him he could keep it all if I could have you. He offered you up like an ugly Christmas sweater his mother knit him."

She flinches, the gun still in her hand, pointed at the ground. "He lost the race on purpose to send me in here. At least, I thought he did. He's still bothering me for information. But maybe he *was* trying to get rid of me. Just like he's trying to get rid of you."

I lean against the table behind me. "Oh, Tyler's not trying to get rid of me. He doesn't want to destroy what I've built. He wants to steal it."

One of her blonde eyebrows cocks. "What?"

"He doesn't want to destroy me. He wants to *be* me."

$$39$$

SLOANE

Everyone stops talking when I step into Julian's office the next morning. My eyes shift from Claudia to Frankie to Julian, sitting at his desk.

It's hard to make eye contact with him after everything we discussed last night. In a way, it was easier for me to see Julian as some dead-inside non-human. Someone who cared about money and didn't care who he hurt. But knowing about what Tyler did to his friend? Knowing this wasn't a life he chose for himself? That's different.

Not to mention what he's done for me in my bed. But neither of us have mentioned that since it happened. It was transactional, a momentary lapse in judgment.

"You asked for me?"

"We have a job for you."

This significantly brightens my spirits, but I'm not going to show it. Julian is really good at being stoic. He seems to think that's where he gets his power from, constantly hiding everything he let me see last night. So I'll be stoic just like him.

"What is it?" I ask.

He knows what I'm doing. I can see it in his expression. His eyes wash over my face, and then he looks away. Well, that's a first. "You remember Barbara?" he asks.

"Of course, I do."

He laces his fingers together and sets his arms on his desk. "It's time for delivery."

Excitement bubbles up under my skin. "Do I get to drive the Chevelle?"

He gives me a sort of *are you fucking kidding me* look. "No, you do not get to drive the Chevelle. You'll be driving the Cadillac. I will be driving the Chevelle."

I scowl at him. "Why would you be driving it? You're not a driver."

I can tell he's exhausted with my questions. He breathes in and out through his nose. But before he can answer, Freddie steps between us, forcing me back a step. "Would you stop fucking talking back? Boss gave you an assignment."

"He's not my boss," I snap. "I'm my own person. I'm not going to be his little lemming like you."

He takes a step toward me like he might grab me, and I reach up to shove him back before he can get the chance. He stumbles and slams into Julian's desk. Behind him, Julian watches us patiently.

"Don't you ever fucking put your hands on me," I tell Frankie.

While we're still staring at each other, locked in a battle of wits, waiting to see who will crack first, Julian stands and sticks his hands in his pockets. "It's time for you to get ready, Sloane."

I'm forced to break Frankie's stare. "I can't miss class."

"I've already spoken to your professors," Claudia says. I

forgot she was even here. She practically disappears into the woodwork on Julian's expensive bookshelves.

"You can't keep dealing with my absences." I barely know Claudia and I'm not a child. How will it look to my professors if she keeps doing this?

"We'll get it better managed next semester. No one thought we would have to work around a class schedule when we planned meetings and deliveries."

Her words make me pause.

Next semester.

They're expecting me to stay. But for how long?

JULIAN

"We need to buy you some fucking clothes," I growl, stomping past Sloane to get into the front seat of the Chevelle. Out of the corner of my eye, I catch her assessing her outfit, a sundress that's distracting, to say the least. Fluttering around her knees in the breeze. I want to put her on those knees and watch her look up at me.

She follows me over to the car, puts one hand on the Chevelle's door and the other on her hip. "Don't you think it makes more sense for me to dress like this? No one's going to suspect a pretty blonde in a sundress of doing anything nefarious."

I narrow my eyes at her. "We're not doing anything nefarious."

She rolls hers. "I may not know what you're doing, but I'm not stupid enough to think you're doing anything legal." She leans down, and for just a moment, my brain is caught between her pink, glossy lips and the tops of her perfect breasts, all of it right in my face, like a buffet, her blonde hair cascading down between us. "Julian, you stink of criminal activity."

"This coming from the woman who couldn't tell her boyfriend was a drug dealer."

That takes the smug smile off her face. She wants to pretend she knows what's going on, but really, she's driving blind. I tug the end of one of her blonde strands, and she straightens away from the door.

"Head north."

SLOANE

I pull into line behind the other cars at the Canadian border and turn up the music. From the looks of it, we're going to be here a while. I glance into my rearview mirror, make sure Julian is still back there. I can see him in the bright sun, looking off into the distance, into the mountains. How did I even end up here?

I sing along with the radio, dance in my seat. Am I nervous? Sure. This is certainly new territory. I don't have the first clue how this is going to play out. I don't even know what's in the Chevelle that we're about to deliver to Barbara.

It's not drugs, I can be sure of that. Maybe counterfeit money? As long as he's not trafficking people, I don't know if I care all that much. I've never claimed to be some righteous saint. Maybe the guys rob banks and move the money out to some account in Canada.

That sounds idiotic, even as I think it.

The line moves forward one car length.

Maybe it's pharmaceuticals, but isn't medicine cheaper in Canada? That doesn't make much sense. Unless somehow, we're going to be bringing some back. But Julian has very specifically been calling these trips deliveries. I don't think we're picking anything up.

I glance at him again in the side mirror. Maybe it's guns. I walked all up and down that garage. I didn't see any guns. Plus, I'm pretty sure drug-sniffing dogs can smell guns too, but I'm not sure. Don't they x-ray vehicles at the border?

I have the radio so loud I don't realize my phone is ringing until I glance at it, sitting on the stand against the air conditioning vent, and see the word *BOSS* on the screen. I didn't program it in that way. Ronan must have.

"Shit," I hiss, turning down the music and answering as quickly as I can. I don't need another admonishment from him.

"What?" I say.

"We need to switch cars and we need to do it now."

"What?" I ask, my tone much different this time. I meet his eye in the rearview mirror, watch him speak into the cell phone pressed to his ear.

"You drive stick?"

"Yeah."

"Good. We need to not attract any attention, okay? I want you to get out of the car and come over to me. I need you to follow my lead."

I was nervous before, but now I can hear my heartbeat, like it's banging through my chest. He wants us to switch cars. I glance up at the booth and count the cars between us and it. Ten. We're ten cars back. If any of those border patrol officers see us switching cars, they're going to get suspicious.

I hang up the phone and slowly open my car door. I walk over to the Chevelle, trying to appear casual even though my skin is burning. Julian gets out, leaving the door hanging open. He glances over to the booth, where the officers don't seem to notice us.

"What's happening?" I ask him, keeping my voice low, as if they could hear me all the way over there.

"Don't worry about it." His eyes don't quite meet mine.

"I *am* worried about it," I say.

"Yeah, I know, and it's above your fucking pay grade."

I clamp my mouth shut, in anger and fear and something else I can't seem to name.

"I just need you to do what I tell you to do. Now, kiss me."

My eyes find his and drop to his mouth. It feels like it's a mile away, all the way up there attached to him. Half of me wants to refuse out of disbelief and rage, but the other half of me wants to taste him so bad I can't think straight. I wrap a hand around the back of his neck, yank him down to me, and slant my mouth across his.

This is entirely fucked. Julian has made me come numerous times with the very mouth I'm kissing, and yet, this is the first time we've done this. My heart is racing in my ears, but I can't tell anymore if it's from fear at the situation or excitement because Julian's mouth is finally on mine.

My skirt is short, and when he grabs my hips, his fingers digging into me, it inches even higher, putting me in danger of flashing anybody who happens to be looking over. Julian opens his mouth over mine, gentles the kiss, and it's strange the way it comforts me, if only for a moment, even though anxiety is like lightning in my blood. He slips his tongue between my lips, and I can't hold back the moan I let loose before I touch his tongue hesitantly with mine. I don't even know what we're doing anymore.

And then he's pushing me away.

"Get in the car," he says, wiping my lip gloss off his

mouth. He reaches over to hold the door of the Chevelle open for me as I get inside.

I don't like that he's ordering me around and that we're clearly dealing with some kind of situation he's not telling me about. While he might have told me the whole truth about Tyler and Leo, he hasn't told me the whole truth about his business. I'm tired of this need-to-know shit.

Something is wrong, and Julian just put me in the car with whatever contraband is not supposed to go over the border. Whatever has gone wrong since we left the compound, Julian is going to let me take the fall for it.

"Julian?" I say, my voice breaking. I sound pathetic, weak, everything they thought I would be.

His dark eyes meet mine. He just stands there, like the angel of death, with the door open and waits for me to get in. "Drive to the meeting point and don't look back." He closes the door.

$$40$$

SLOANE

I watch Julian walk to the Cadillac, feeling sick. I let my guard down. I was in the clean car. I was safe. There was nothing to even connect the two of us. And now I'm in a car with something in it that I'm not supposed to have, and there are four cars between us and those drugs-sniffing dogs.

He told me his secrets just to toss me to the wolves the next day? Why? To get rid of the person who saw him that vulnerable?

Julian pulls up to the booth, exchanges a few words with the Border Patrol officer, and drives on through. No questions. Nothing.

When I pull up to the booth, my hands are shaking. If there's anything that makes you look more suspicious, it's nerves. My eyes are on the dogs, the officers that are hanging out on the sidelines with their leashes wrapped around their hands. The man that comes to my window has short-cropped hair covered by a baseball cap and a bulletproof vest.

"How are you doing today, ma'am?" he asks.

"Good. How about you?" I smile up at him.

He grins big, showing me all of his teeth. I'm not even remotely surprised when his gaze dips to my cleavage. "Can I see some identification?" he says.

I take out my passport, try to still my shaking fingers. The only reason I even have a passport is because Tyler's parents paid for it so we could all go to the Bahamas last summer.

The officer looks down at it, looks back up, hands it to me. His eyes go to the empty car. "This is a nice car," he says, clearly impressed.

"Isn't it? It's my boyfriend's. He lets me drive it sometimes."

This gets a cheeky smile out of him, just like I knew it would. I can guarantee I know more about this car than he does, but boys would much rather you say you don't know anything, that you're just dating a boy who does. Makes them feel good about themselves.

He pats the hood. "Can you pop the trunk for me?"

I'm quivering from head to toe. I don't know what's in the trunk. My eyes flicker up, peering over the dashboard, but Julian's car is long gone on the highway. He left me here.

I'll admit the one thing I don't know about this Chevelle is how to pop the trunk from the inside. Instead of trying to locate it, I look up at the officer. "I'm so sorry. I'm not sure..." I shake my head.

"Let me see." He reaches in through the window, his face inches from my chest. "There it is." He pulls a lever under the steering wheel, and I hear the trunk pop. I ball my fists in my lap as he walks around to the back of the car and flips up the lid of the trunk.

I can't breathe. There's an elephant sitting on my chest. I try to focus, breathing in through my nose and out through my mouth in beats of three, like my mother once taught me. I can feel my face getting hot, the way it does just before I start to cry. I'm not going to cry. Even if he hauls me out of this car, I won't give him or Julian the satisfaction. I count to ten. And then eleven. And then twelve. Thirteen. Fourteen.

The trunk slams. The officer comes around the side of my car. He taps my window frame with one big hand. "Alright, you're all set."

I just stare at him. "I'm all set? I'm good to go?" I look back in my rearview mirror, like there might still be some threat waiting back there, rifling through my trunk, finding whatever illegal substance there is to be found.

"That's it?" I ask the officer again.

He smiles big at me, apparently, not finding my behavior peculiar. "First time through?"

I nod.

He leans down, crosses his forearms and sets them on the window frame. "If you ever need anyone to show you around..."

I smile right back, making sure my dimples come out, the ones that Tyler said make me look like I give good head. And I do, goddammit. "I don't think my boyfriend would like that very much," I say, pushing my chest out. "But thank you, Officer..." My eyes drop to his name badge. "...Morris. I appreciate your help."

I wait for him to very slowly remove himself from my window, like if he lingers, I'll change my mind. I take off.

I try not to drive too fast, but as soon as I'm out of sight of the border, I pull off on the side of the road. Shaking. Gasping for breath.

That asshole. That fucking asshole. I don't know what he was thinking, but he could have fucking warned me. He could have fucking just told me what the problem was. As my blood steadies, my terror turns to anger.

I put the car in drive.

JULIAN

We're meeting Barbara in a parking garage in Quebec, but Sloane and I agreed we should meet a couple of miles away first to re-group after going over the border. I know exactly how it's going to go. Sloane is all fire and I just tossed gasoline on her.

I pull into the meet-up point, a park about a mile off the highway, and wait.

Over the horizon comes the Chevelle, a red streak across the blue sky. I swear she speeds up when I'm in view, engine revving, racing toward me.

She slams to a stop behind my car and gets out, not bothering to pull into a spot. "Fucking bastard," she says, her breath steaming out of her into the cold air. She looks like a fire-breathing dragon. "You absolute fucking asshole."

"Alright," I say.

But she's not done. She walks straight over to me and shoves me with both of her hands. "You fucking piece of shit. You put me in that car to try and get me caught."

People are watching us, two soccer moms sitting together on a bench and a young boy perched on the end of the plastic slide. "Did I now?"

She shakes her head, and her chin trembles just once before she squares her shoulders. "Why did we switch cars? Was it because you were trying to set me up? Were you hoping I would get arrested so I wouldn't be your problem anymore?" She lifts her hands like she might shove me again, and I grab her wrists, holding them away from me.

"If you put your fucking hands on me again, you're going

to lose them, you hear me?" I drop her hands, and she doesn't argue with me. "If I wanted to get rid of you, there are a hell of a lot easier ways to do it. I think I've made it pretty fucking clear that the reason you're here is to help me get what I want. How would it help me get what I want if you're sitting in a fucking jail cell?"

"I don't know," she screams back at me. "But I know you did that on purpose."

"Yeah, I did it on purpose. Because I needed to make sure you would follow orders. I needed to know that you would do what I told you to without explanation when it came down to the wire."

She bites her lip. Her lip gloss is almost completely gone. I know I'm wearing a lot of it. "So it was a test?"

"Yeah, it was a test."

She shakes her head. "You put me at risk."

I snort. "At risk of what? There's nothing in the car, Sloane. This is a perfectly legal sale and the car is clean. Barbara doesn't know what her husband intended for that car, so we didn't pack it with what he paid us for. It would have been a waste of inventory."

"Inventory of what?"

I ignore her question. "That is what you signed up for. You wanted to be part of this. That involves risk. If you're not willing to take the risk, it's time for you to go home."

"I hate you," she hisses at me, her voice hoarse.

"Yeah, I know," I tell her. "Now get in the fucking car. We have a job to do."

She hesitates, her nostrils flaring as she gulps in air. But eventually, she does what I tell her to and gets in the car.

Barbara's car is parked in a spot facing out of the parking garage, and I see the front bumper from down the road. She drives some bright yellow thing like it's the 90s. I pull in a few spaces away. I can see her in the front seat, her big, curly gray hair making shapes in the shadows.

Sloane pulls up beside me and gets out. She doesn't wait for me before walking to Barbara's car. I have to grit my teeth and take a deep breath to keep from losing my shit. I have to remind myself that she doesn't know yet that she doesn't make a fucking move without my say-so. That she shouldn't be approaching people's cars without my permission. But I can't reprimand her here, no matter how much I want to. I don't want to do this in front of a client, especially one that's fond of her. I'll wait until we're back over the line. Things will be much easier then.

I get out of the Cadillac and head around the front of my car just in time to see Sloane spin away from Barbara's car with a gasp. Her face has gone pale under all of her makeup, her eyes glistening with tears.

"What the fuck is it?" I say, rushing over to her. I move her out of the way and look into Barbara's car.

She's there. But she has a hole in her head. There's blood everywhere. My eyes move up, scanning the area around us. I reach for Sloane without thinking, wrap a hand around her upper arm in case we need to take cover.

"Who would do this?" she asks, her voice quivering.

I don't see anyone. There's no place for anyone to hide. It's just an open, barren garage. I tilt my head down to her. Suspicion creeps in again, like a clawing animal under my skin. "You said you told Tyler about the deal..."

"I didn't tell him her name or that we were meeting her or anything." Her voice cracks. "All I said was that I met a client and that she was an old lady. I didn't—" Her mouth clamps shut and now there are tears streaming down her face. I'm surprised when she steps toward me and buries her face in my shirt.

I'm frozen to my spot. This is the same woman who not ten minutes ago told me she hates me. My stomach knots, and, not sure what else to do, feeling compelled to just get her through this, I wrap my arms around her, one hand going into her hair to stroke it, soft under my fingers.

"I'm sorry," I tell her. "But we have to go. Did you touch the window?"

She looks up at me with confused eyes. "No."

"Okay. We're going to park the Chevelle. I know a safe place nearby. I'll send Hugo and Magnus to get it tonight."

"Why?" Her eyes search mine, and I look away. I don't need her looking that closely. I don't know what she'll find.

"You're upset. You shouldn't drive."

She pulls away from me, her warmth gone as her face changes, discontent forming in the line between her eyebrows. "I can drive just fine."

"I just think—"

"I can drive, Julian." Her voice is hard, confident. She never fucking backs down. I want to put my hands back in her hair, taste her mouth again. But my eyes go over her shoulder to Barbara in the front seat of her car.

"Okay. Let's go."

41

JULIAN

"Why would he kill Barbara? How did he even *know* about Barbara?"

I hear Bram's voice in the back of my head, but my attention is focused on my phone. She's been like this since we got back from the delivery, curled up in her bed, her back to the camera.

"Isn't it obvious? She told him."

Claudia's comment finally rips me away from the footage of Sloane. She's standing over by the door of my office, her arms crossed, leaning against one of the bookcases.

"She didn't."

Her jaw tightens. "You're so set on trusting her—"

"Because she trusts us," I snap back. "She didn't have any information on Barbara. She didn't even know where the meeting point was. She followed me in." I don't tell her about Sloane breaking into my room. The only ones who know are Ronny and Bram. She was in there with confidential information, but she wasn't in there long enough to do anything with it. None of my files were even touched.

"I trust her," Bram says, his eyes on Claudia. "She's had plenty of opportunities to make a mess, and she hasn't."

I keep my mouth shut. I have no intention of telling either of them about the gun I gave her. I know everyone would lose their shit if they knew. But Bram is right. If she wanted to hurt us, she would have found a way to do it by now. We have things locked down here, and she doesn't even know about the warehouse, but that doesn't mean she couldn't have caused problems if she wanted to.

My eyes drop back down to my screen. She still hasn't moved.

"She'll have to get thicker skin than this."

When I look back up, Bram is standing close enough to my desk to see my phone screen. I would try to hide it, but it's too late. Besides, Bram is observant. He would have figured out already that there's something soft inside me for Sloane, that my desire to protect her is warring with my obligation to bring her into the organization. I'm stuck between giving her what she wants and giving her what I know she needs.

"No," I tell Bram. "She needs to stay how she is. She's compassionate. It's not a weakness."

Bram studies me carefully. "Then why are you always acting like it is?"

I ignore his question and go back to the matter at hand. "Maybe this will be incentive for us to move faster on this. Sloane already has her next meet-up with Tyler planned. She's going to bug his laptop. That should get us what we need."

Bram sighs. "You're putting a lot of faith into that little ladybug."

SLOANE

The compound is quiet. I don't know how long I've been laying here. Long enough for the sun to go down. Long enough for the guys to all go to bed. My muscles are stiff from being curled up, my eyes aching from staring into the darkness on the other side of my window.

I can't stop seeing images of Barbara in my mind. Her blood splattered on the car windows. Her body slumped awkwardly in the seat.

I knew I would never be able to outright kill someone, but I didn't think it would feel this way to see someone else killed. And I certainly never thought Tyler could do something like this. Though, in all fairness, he most likely didn't. He probably had someone else do it. The coward.

I push myself up in bed and stand, stretching my body. My stomach growls. I missed dinner, but thankfully, no one gave me hell for it. Even though I wanted to hide it, Julian knows how upset I was today. When we found her, I couldn't keep myself from turning to Julian, even with how angry I was about the stunt he pulled at the border. I just wanted him to hold me, the only person left who I think might get what's going on in my head.

He might act cold—might even *be* truly cold—but I know he understands what Tyler has done to me. He's done the same thing to Julian in a way.

I crack open my door and peek out into the hallway. I don't know if anyone is watching the cameras this late since it's just the guys in the compound tonight, but I still feel like I'm being watched as I move quickly down the stairs and toward the kitchen. I've never actually been in the kitchen before; I've only seen it when Xander holds the door open to go in and out while serving dinner.

The compound is colder than ever, like ice under my feet, now that the sun has set. But when I push the door to the kitchen open, I'm surprised to see the glow of firelight in the room. Everything else is dark, the fire the only illumination besides the moon coming in through the big windows.

My eyes catch on a kitchen nook first on the other side of the room, pressed against the windows, moonlight flooding down on it. A large room stretches out in front of me, cabinets and appliances and marble surfaces as well as a small sitting area in addition to the nook.

I startle when I see the shadow moving by the counter between me and the nook, overlooked at first glance.

He doesn't realize I'm here until the door swings shut behind me with a gentle *swish*. Julian stops what he's doing and looks over at me as my brain starts to piece together the scene before me. He's standing at the counter, preparing food of some kind, a butter knife in his hand. His hair is slicked back out of his face. Even in the low light, I can tell it's wet. And he's shirtless, wearing nothing but a pair of dark gray sweatpants. The only time I've ever seen him out of his usual put-together black outfit, he was bleeding out of his side.

"What are you doing up?" His voice is deep, barely more than a rumble.

"I was hungry," I tell him. I walk over to the counter, my eyes caught momentarily on the couch in front of the fire. It's like a little apartment in here. No wonder Xander spends all his time hiding out. "What are you making?" I step up next to him, surprised when he makes room for me at the countertop.

"Just toast. It's a comfort food of mine."

I reach over the dish of butter and the loaf of sliced bread on the cutting board to pick up a small bottle of cinnamon. I raise an eyebrow at him. "Were you making cinnamon toast?"

He sets the knife down on the cutting board and crosses his arms. "Maybe. Is that a problem?"

"No. It's not a problem at all... if you're eleven."

He shakes his head. "Things don't stop tasting good just because you get older."

I open my mouth to respond, feeling a flutter in my stomach at this new development, when my eyes catch on one of his tattoos in the light. Just above the outside of his wrist, he has a large tattoo of a lion. His best friend. Leo.

I reach out to touch it without thinking, run my fingers along the lines. When Julian doesn't pull away, I take a step closer. My hands travel from that tattoo to another, higher up on his bicep, a tattoo of the Beast. It occurs to me that maybe the car was his father's. Just above it, there's a tattoo of a flower, a lily, pink in the center.

My fingers drop to the spot on his side, where the knife wound is still red, still healing. My hand keeps moving up over his shoulder, following the lines of ink across his clavicle, up to his neck. I go up on my toes, cup him around the back of the head, and meet his eye.

His gaze is dark in the shadows the fire is casting. "Maybe I should put on some clothes," he says, his voice quiet, deep, but I just shake my head. The very last thing I want is for him to put on more clothing.

"Or you could take mine off."

I swear, his eyes get darker. They drop down to my mouth before he speaks. "As good as that sounds, we shouldn't do it like this. You've been through hell today."

"Please," I say, when his mouth is inches from mine. "You can take it all away."

He lets out a groan and kisses me. His arms come around me, hauling me up against him and bending me over backward as he opens his mouth over mine. I shove my hands into his hair, feeling the wet strands between my fingertips.

I didn't even know how hungry I was for this, to be wanted and lusted after and touched by a man, but especially *this* man. His tongue meets mine, and I moan into his mouth. I want him to do shameful things to me.

Like he can read my mind, he bends and latches onto my thighs, pulling me up to wrap around him. I'm so concerned with licking into his mouth, with rubbing myself against his stomach, that I don't realize we're moving until he's lowered me onto the couch in front of the fire.

I'm not there for more than a second before he's shoving my shorts down, never taking his mouth from mine. I reach for him too, trying to get my hand inside his sweatpants, but he pulls it away, pinning it to my side as he licks his way down my throat.

My gaze is fuzzy, my eyes not seeing anything as I focus on the feel of his tongue, on the grip of his hands, on the cool air touching where I'm now bare between my legs. His teeth latch onto my clavicle, and I buck against him.

"Why aren't you inside me yet?" I want him to push my legs open, shove deep and fuck me hard. But instead, he's hiking up my shirt so he can latch his mouth to my nipple and pull it into a peak with his teeth.

"Because," he says, pulling away, "I've got your gorgeous body here to do with as I please. I want to enjoy it."

I make a sound in the back of my throat when one of his hands finds the cleft between my legs. He rubs me with his palm, letting me feel the size of his hand, while he sucks at my nipple. My mind cascades back to when he put his tongue inside me, and the memory of that moment has me bucking my hips again.

"Please," I say up at the ceiling. "Oh, my God, Julian, please."

I don't even know what I'm asking him for, but he slips a finger inside me and gives my nipple one more hard, punishing suck.

My God, how does he know exactly what to do to me every time?

He raises his head, his intensely dark eyes meeting mine before he pulls his finger out and puts it in his mouth, sucking it clean. "Fucking delicious," he says, and then he's gone, his mouth on my stomach and then my hip.

"You don't need to do that," I tell him. "I'm wet. I'm ready."

He hovers between my legs, his face a mask of confusion. "I don't *need* to do anything. I'm going to eat this dripping cunt because I haven't thought about anything else since I got a taste of you. Now shut the fuck up."

I'm caught between laughing and arguing when he licks my clit and I forget my own name. He swipes his tongue up the center of me, swirling and licking and sucking. How the hell did I go so long without this, without the feel of a man's mouth between my legs? Girls I went to school with were doing this with their boyfriends long before I even started dating Tyler, and now that I know how damn good it feels, I'm doing it with the one person I can't be doing it with.

The thought burns in my brain, and I wipe it away, focusing on the magnificent things he's doing to my body.

I don't realize I'm pleading with him, whispering *please, please, please* over and over again, until he pushes up onto his knees between my legs and says, "Since you asked nicely..." He shoves his sweatpants down.

My mouth goes dry at the sight of his cock. It's not that he's all that much bigger than Tyler, the only dick I've ever had inside me. It's like he has a bigger...diameter. It looks smooth and swollen in the firelight, and I reach for it without hesitation, running my hand down the shaft and back up, giving the red tip a few squeezes as I stroke him.

"Fuck," he says, throwing his head back. "I thought you wanted it in you."

"I do," I say, voice louder than it has been all night. Now that I'm distracted, it's more than sighs and whispers. "If I don't get it inside me, I'm going to lose my mind."

He smiles and shoves me back on the couch, my head hitting the crimson pillows. "Wouldn't want that," he says, holding my gaze as he slowly strokes himself. I want him so bad I'm squirming. "You want me to wear a condom?"

I shake my head. "I'm on birth control."

He groans, pressing his tip against me. "I thought I would die before ever feeling you raw."

"Julian," I say, my voice sharp.

His eyes zone in on mine.

"Shut up and fuck me."

He smiles, looking positively villainous, and sinks into me in one smooth stroke. I swear, I black out for a moment. Every muscle in my body tightens and quakes, and I gasp for breath as, unbelievably, I come the moment I'm stretched around him.

I press my fingers to my clit, feeling like I have to somehow control what's happening to me, but when the orgasm finally ends, I press a hand over my eyes, unable to look at him.

I feel the heat of him on top of me, settling against my body. "Did you just come?"

"Jesus, your ego is already massive. I can't believe that just happened."

He pulls my hand away from my eyes and leans forward, running the tip of his tongue along my bottom lip. "Knowing you're so fucking worked up over this has me about to spill too, baby, and feeling you come around me like that didn't help matters."

Unable to stop myself, I wrap my hand in his hair and yank his mouth down to mine. Everything happens fast after that. He kisses me and begins to thrust, an even rhythm that pushes his pelvis against my clit with every inward stroke.

He kisses me and kisses me and fucks me and fucks me, and I swear that nothing in the whole world has ever felt as good as this: the slap of his hips against me and the press of his tongue against mine and the way we're wrapped around each other, like we're trying to crawl inside each other's skin.

"So fucking good," he says against my mouth, coming up for air. "I knew you'd be perfect. I knew you'd be tight and wet and hot. I knew I'd want to spend the rest of my life inside your perfect pussy."

I bow up off the couch, my toes curling and hips jutting as another orgasm crashes over me. Somewhere in the distance, I hear Julian groan, feel him empty himself inside me.

Then we're just a sweaty heap of limbs and breath. Neither of us speak, just lay against each other and gasp for air as the fire flickers and crackles.

When he does finally speak, his voice rumbles against my chest, his breath fanning out against my neck, where his head is pressed. "Are you okay?" he asks.

I snort. Of course, he thinks I'm somehow more affected by this experience than he was. I mean, yes, it was probably the first time I've had that kind of DNA-altering sex, but he thinks that just because I'm a girl, I'll see this differently than he will.

"Yes. Are *you* okay?"

He laughs quietly, like he knows exactly what I was thinking. He pushes up on his elbows and looks me in the eye. "I want you to understand that you're mine now."

A record scratches in my head. "What?"

He reaches up and takes the tip of my chin between two fingers. "As long as you're here, as long as we're together under this roof, you belong to me. No one else touches you, do you understand?"

I fight to keep my face straight. "Who else would touch me, Julian?"

He scoffs and lets go of my chin, turning his face away from me. "Give me a break, princess. You could have your pick of any man in this compound, and you know it. You're so goddamn beautiful, it's painful to look at you."

I grab his jaw and turn his face back to mine. "If you want me to belong to you, you have to belong to me, too. Put your hands on another woman, and I'll break all your fingers."

He grins. "But if you break them, how will I finger fuck you?"

I shrug. "Maybe I'll get one of the other guys to do it."

He throws back his head, and when he laughs up at the ceiling, all my insides clench. I've never seen him like this before, his mouth stretched into a carefree smile, his hair a mess, his skin warm in the light of the fire.

When his gaze settles back on me, I feel turned inside out. "I bet that cinnamon toast is sounding pretty good now, isn't it?"

I giggle as he pushes up off the couch and goes back into the kitchen, washing his hands before making two sets of cinnamon toast, stark naked.

42

JULIAN

"Why do you look like you're watching the hangman ready your noose?"

I glare over at Bram. He thinks because he's my Second that he needs to nose his way into everything. I ignore him and slouch down in the chair I'm already slumping in.

We're sitting in the parlor waiting for Sloane to get ready for Tyler's stupid fucking Halloween party, and I look like I'm walking to my execution because the idea of Sloane having to pretend to be Tyler's girlfriend after I was inside her last night makes my blood boil. As if I didn't hate Tyler enough already.

When I don't answer his question, Bram keeps talking. He's always had a problem with silence. "Do you think she's ready to go back in there? After what Tyler did, I mean?"

I grit my teeth. "She can handle it. She can handle anything."

I know I've said too much, but he doesn't comment on it, just watches me from the vintage suede couch I can't bring myself to throw out. "I've been thinking about this whole Barbara situation..." He leans forward, planting his elbows on his knees. "We were so certain that Tyler's endgame was figuring out the business and undercutting you to shut you down. But if he knows what the business is, maybe even has a client list—and I can't even begin to fathom how that happened—why isn't he doing what he set out to do and take over? Why kill a client?"

"He's angry, and he's emotional. He's not thinking about business strategy right now. He's just thinking about how to fuck with my head."

"Is it working?"

No. Tyler isn't the one fucking with my head. Sloane is. I feel like I can't see anything clearly now that she's in my field of vision.

"My question is..." a voice says behind me. I turn and watch Frankie come into the room, his arms crossed tight. "...how did he get Barbara's name?"

"I don't know," I tell him, turning away. I already know where this conversation is going. The same place it's been going since Sloane got here.

"Come on, Julian. You know. It was her."

My eyes meet Bram's. He's not quite as good at keeping his thoughts off his face as I am. He sends Frankie a dead-pan look. "Sloane didn't know a damn thing about Barbara or the delivery to tell him. Unless you have something useful to contribute, you can keep your mouth shut."

He holds my eye for a long moment. He can't honestly think he's going to win this one. "You're not seeing what's right in front of you," he finally says.

"And you have no clue what you're talking about," Bram says before I can.

Frankie shakes his head. "We're cooked if you can't get your head out of your ass."

I stand, making sure Frankie remembers that I'm much bigger and taller than he is. I'm not going to put up with this shit. He doesn't get to insult Sloane and tell me to get my head out of my ass and get away with it.

He tilts his chin up. I'm not sure what he thinks is going to happen. Maybe he thinks we're going to argue. We're not. This is not a debate.

I stop in front of him and punch him in the stomach, feeling satisfied when he slumps over. I doubt it was as painful as it was surprising. While he's still bent, I shove him to the ground.

"I don't know what you think is going on here, Frankie, but I've had enough of your mouth. I don't want to hear you question me again." I turn to Bram. "As soon as we're gone, stick him in the cage. He can spend the night down there."

Bram nods. I can see the doubt in his eyes. I don't enjoy putting my own men down there, but Frankie needs to learn.

Out of the corner of my eye, I see someone step into the room, someone bright pink. I look up from Frankie and hold myself still when I see Sloane in the doorway. She's wearing some kind of 80s-style, blue swimsuit over a pair of pink tights, a pink headband across her forehead. She even curled her hair. I told her she could buy whatever she wanted for this party, and she apparently went all out.

The fact that I can see every inch of her body through the skin-tight costume is almost enough to make me forget Frankie at my feet, until Sloane's eyes drop to him.

"Am I interrupting something?" she asks.

"No," I tell her, just as Ronan appears in the doorway beside her.

His eyes scan her. "Holy hell. You look like a walking wet dream."

I growl and reach down to wrench Frankie to his feet,

shoving him in Bram's direction. "Take care of him." I point at Ronan. "Get in the goddamn car."

He puts his hands up and turns to the front door.

Sloane moves out of the way to let Bram out, and I follow, stopping in front of her. She straightens the lapel on my coat. "You don't need to do all that," she says, peering up at me under heavily mascaraed eyelashes. "They can look. You're the only one who's allowed to touch, remember? Do you like it?" She steps back and gives a sexy little spin.

Do I like it? I'm going to spend the rest of my life trying to get the image of her tits in that swimsuit out of my head. "I want to rip it off you and bend you over my desk."

She grins. "I'll take that as a yes." Some of her humor fades. "What did Frankie do?"

"Don't worry about it. Stay focused on your mission."

All the humor is gone now, her mouth practically turned all the way down. "What if Tyler catches me? What if he attacks me?"

I'm surprised by the vulnerability in her eyes. Everything has changed between us. She never would have shown me this fear a week ago.

"You have your gun?"

With a small smile, she pats the shimmering pink purse in her hand. She even did her nails. Of course she did.

"That's why I taught you how to use it. Any guy gets handsy with you, you shoot."

She bats her eyelashes. "Even you?"

"Especially me."

SLOANE

The job for tonight is simple. Julian has given me one hour to get into the frat house, get upstairs to Tyler's room, and essentially bug his laptop. I have no idea how this kind of technology works, but according to Julian and Ronan, who I suspect knows far more about technology than I ever will in my entire life, all I have to do is download a certain software onto Tyler's computer. Then Ronan can search through everything for the files they're looking for.

I just have to get up to Tyler's room. On a normal night, this wouldn't be a problem, but tonight, I need to get up there alone. A seduction is not in the cards. And besides, every time I think about Tyler, Barbara's vacant eyes pop into my head. It's all I can see. I will never let him touch me the way he wants to again.

It was a strategic move to show up late to the party. Not only do I have to pretend I had to fight my way over here against Julian's wishes, but I also have to pretend he's put me on a strict curfew. And since I only have an hour, it's important that I be as efficient as possible.

I look at the clock on my cell phone and back at the car where the guys are waiting across the street. Julian said if I don't come back out in an hour, he's going to start shooting.

I can practically hear his voice in my head. *Go inside, princess.*

As I walk in, I look around at all the girls in the room. It's exactly what I expected. Like me, they're all half-dressed, mooning over boys. Most likely all tipsy or close to it.

The first thing I have to do is clock Tyler. Where is he? Is he drunk? Can I get him distracted long enough to sneak up to his room? Probably.

My eyes scan the first floor, taking in the number of

people who are currently making out and/or dry humping on various pieces of furniture.

My mind flashes back to that night with Julian, when he brought me here to show me what Tyler was doing behind my back. This thing with Tyler is almost over. I just have to hang on a little longer, and he'll be out of my life forever. But then what?

"Baby!" someone calls out. Several people turn, and I spin around to see Tyler coming from the kitchen, a beer in each hand, one a brown bottle, the other a tall can. I want to ask him why he needs two, but honestly, it doesn't matter. Maybe I won't have to do any work at all. Maybe he'll just drink himself into a stupor without me having to intervene.

"They finally let you out of your prison," he says. He stops, his eyes scanning down my body. I expect him to make some kind of lewd comment about the fact that my breasts are hanging halfway out, but he doesn't. Instead, he says, "Did they see you in that?" His face loses its goofy smile, and all that's left is anger.

"Well, someone had to drive me here," I say, trying to sound nonchalant, like someone who wasn't naked beneath Julian Shaw twenty-four hours ago. I would give anything to rub that in his face right now. To tell him about how Julian fucked me and tell him how he made me come just by putting it in me.

Tyler presses his mouth, wet and beer-scented, against my earlobe. "Let those fuckers look at what's mine."

Bile rises up in my throat, but I keep my mouth shut. About that, at least. "What's the big deal? It's just boobs and an ass."

He reaches forward and takes a handful of my ass cheek. "*My* boobs and *my* ass," he says.

I shove his hand away, trying to seem playful. "Can we just have a good time, please?"

"Sure," he says, and hands me the beer bottle before walking away.

I sigh and watch him go. I glance up the stairs. A lot of people are already hanging out on the steps, some of them talking, some kissing, some doing shots. It's not so much that I think I couldn't get up there unnoticed. The problem is that I need enough time to do what I need to do without Tyler walking in. If I don't have him distracted, I can't guarantee that.

Ronan says the whole thing should take five minutes, tops. The answer comes to me pretty quick. All I need to do is talk to the right person.

My eyes move around the room, looking for the face I know will be able to help me.

There he is on the couch, brown hair messy, eyes half-lidded. Weston. I know for a fact all of the car racing started with him. Tyler was always into cars when we were back in California—it's how we met—and he would race them sometimes, mostly just having fun with his friends. Nothing competitive, no gambling. But when he got here, Weston introduced him to the guys that take their cars out on the weekends.

In a roundabout way, Weston was the one who connected him with Julian. Though, now I know it was Julian who went looking for Tyler.

Unfortunately, Weston currently has a girl grinding on his lap. And from the way her dress is slowly riding up, I take it it's not going to be just grinding for much longer. I need to get to him before he goes up to his room.

I skitter over to the couch and drop down beside them, trying to pretend I'm not uncomfortable at the fact that I am between one couple dry humping and another couple who I'm pretty sure is getting to third base.

I make sure no one is looking before tipping the beer in my hand right between Weston and his female friend.

"Holy shit, I'm so sorry," I say as they break apart and the girl looks down at her ruined fake nurse's outfit. There's a huge, pee-colored stain down the front of it now.

"What the fuck?" she says. "That's never going to come out."

"Oh, come on," Weston says with a laugh. "It's a Halloween costume. It's not like you're going to wear it again. And besides..." He slaps one big hand against her bare ass cheek. "You're not going to be in it much longer anyway."

"You're such an asshole," she says, climbing off of him and rushing away.

"Melissa," he calls after her, but when he starts to get up, I put a hand on his chest. He doesn't seem concerned about the fact that he has beer in his lap. Probably isn't the first time he's ended up with beer in his lap at a party.

"I was thinking..." I say, setting the mostly empty beer bottle down on the floor by the couch. Behind me, someone's elbow bumps me in a rhythmic pattern and I scoot away so I'm not indirectly involved in a hand job.

"You were thinking maybe it was time for a three-way? Me, you, and Tyler?" Weston asks, his eyes dropping down to my chest.

I roll my eyes. Doesn't anybody think about anything other than sex? And like the hypocrite I am, my brain flies back to last night, to Julian pumping into me in the light of the fire. If I was living a normal life, and the guy that fucked my brains out last night was in the car out by the curb—like he is currently— I would be dragging him into the backseat and riding him for all he's worth instead of dealing with this dipshit.

"You know what would make this night perfect?" I say to Weston.

"Didn't I just tell you?" His idiotic grin is lopsided.

"A car race," I say, ignoring his comment.

His brow furrows. "What, are you kidding? I'm trashed."

"Oh," I say, scooting back. "I'm sorry. I thought men could handle a stick shift, even when they were drunk."

His eyes are suspicious. And maybe I overdid it a little bit with the acting. But it doesn't matter because a second later, his mouth spreads into a grin.

He leans in closer to me. "I know this neighborhood nearby where all the rich folks live, and they get so fucking pissed when we take our turbo engines over there."

I curl a lock of my hair around one finger. "But you don't want to get the cops called."

He shrugs. "They're not gonna bust up the party. Tyler has the whole fucking police department in his pocket."

His words slither under my skin like ice. I drop my coy, seductive act.

"What are you talking about?"

He shrugs again, throwing his arm over his eyes.

But I can't stop. Tyler might be good at staying tight-lipped, but apparently no one else is. "Is Tyler bribing the police with part of the drug money?"

He drops his arm and looks over at me. His eyes are fully open now. Ice blue. "He told you about the business?"

I shrug, as casual as he was a moment ago, making sure my boobs jiggle nicely to keep him talking. His eyes plummet, just like I knew they would. "He just wants me to be a part of things."

Weston leans close to me, until his hot breath lands on my neck. "Is the pretty little princess on drugs?"

I shove him away from me. I know Tyler isn't using, and he never once tried to get me to do any drugs. Is that the smart move or is it suspicious? "Get a life, Weston. I thought you were fun, but you're clearly nothing but a lightweight pussy."

I start to stand, but he grabs onto my wrist and pulls me back down. I fall halfway on top of him. When I straighten, my eyes meet Tyler's across the room. *Shit.* If he thinks something is happening between Weston and me, he'll probably kill one of us.

Barbara's face flashes behind my eyes again, and my hand drops to my purse, still halfway slung over my shoulder. I'm not using that gun in the middle of a frat party.

I stand, pulling Weston to his unsteady feet as Tyler heads our way.

"What the hell is going on here?" he demands, angry eyes on Weston. A few people look our way, curiosity in their gazes. Wouldn't want to miss a fight.

Diffuse. Act innocent. "Me and Weston were just thinking it might be fun to have a little car race."

The anger dissipates from Tyler's eyes. He glances over at me before turning back to Weston. "A race?"

Weston shrugs. "Sure, man."

"Outside that neighborhood over by the lake?"

Weston nods.

Tyler narrows his eyes at me. "You're okay with this?"

I shrug. "I just thought it would liven up the party a little bit. I mean..." I gesture around the room, where everyone is either hooking up or chatting quietly. Most of the rowdy people are out back. "I'm bored, and I want a show."

His eyes gleam. He's so fucking easy. "All right," he says. He reaches forward and grabs my ass, palming me roughly. "Get your ass out on the front lawn. I'll give you a show." He presses his mouth to my ear. "But afterwards, I want you on your fucking knees for me."

I pull back, trying to stay calm when all I want to do is

run, or gag. "Only if you win. Maybe if you lose, I'll get on my knees for Weston instead."

Weston cackles.

Tyler's jaw clenches. "Don't fucking talk like that."

"You better fucking win then."

It takes approximately five minutes for all the frat boys to go from making out with their girlfriends or playing beer pong to lining up on the sidewalk. I line up with them, staying as far back as I can manage. The second they take off, I'm going inside.

Weston and Tyler both roll their windows down, shouting something back and forth between the two of them as their cars idle in the street. The windows roll up, the engines rev, and they're gone.

As soon as their tires squeal away, I turn back to the house. No one seems to notice. They're all screaming and cheering, some of them getting closer to the street so they can bend and watch the cars disappear.

I try to move slowly, even though I know my time is limited. Just before I slip inside, my eyes find the Cadillac, parked across the street, dark against the shadows of the neighborhood.

At least three quarters of the party has moved outside. I head for the stairs with a kind of confident intent, like maybe I'm just running up to get something I left in Tyler's room or to find a clean bathroom. But as soon as I walk up one flight and realize nobody is paying attention to me, I run.

I'm huffing and puffing by the time I get up to Tyler's room. It didn't even occur to me that his roommate might be up here. I don't remember seeing him outside. Luckily, when I throw the door open, the room empty.

And luckily, Tyler's stuff is exactly where it was the last time I was in here. A long time ago, Tyler told me the password to his laptop. It was an in-passing thing, when I needed it to check my school email. I just pray he hasn't had the good sense to change it since.

I hit enter, and the screen changes, taking me to his desktop. Ronan showed me how to download the software and how to give him access. I try to carefully remember the steps as I go through them.

I hear the roar of engines in the distance. The guys are coming back, and I need to go.

Ronan's voice sounds in my head. *Don't forget, you have to get rid of any evidence that you were ever there before you leave.*

Just as the screaming and cheering starts out on the lawn, I slam Tyler's computer shut and leave the room, carefully closing the door behind me.

I'm out on the landing, half turned toward the stairs, when I hear a loud *thud* and stop. It wasn't downstairs. It was up here. There are only three rooms on the third story. Tyler's room, one more bedroom, and a bathroom.

I push the bathroom door open, but the lights are off. There's no one in it. My eyes fall to the closed bedroom door beside me. It's probably just somebody having sex or something.

From inside, I hear someone scream, "Help!"

● 43

SLOANE

In a split second, my mind runs over all the possibilities, landing, of course, on the worst ones. I crash through the bedroom door to find a girl kneeling on the floor. She looks up at me with red, tear-stained cheeks, and I finally see that she's kneeling *beside* someone, someone who is clearly unconscious.

Krista.

JULIAN

I know the race was Sloane's idea. And it was a brilliant one, if she can manage to get upstairs in the time it'll take these idiots to race through the neighborhood.

It baffles me, as I watch their taillights disappear and the college kids on the lawn start to turn towards each other to engage in conversation as they wait, how Tyler can be so conniving and such an imbecile at the same time. He must have quite the store of dumb luck.

"She's going in," Ronan says from the driver's seat, as if I can't see her with my own eyes. "We should move. When Tyler gets back, he's going to be far less distracted. He'll see us here."

I know he's right, but I hate the idea of letting Sloane out of my sight. "Take us around the corner."

Without turning on the headlights, he pulls quietly out of our spot and turns the corner to park in front of another house. Everything out here is student housing, so it's likely that this house is empty, its occupants back at Tyler's frat house.

My fingers drum on my knee as Ronan opens his laptop, clicking around before going still on the keys.

"Just have to wait for her. Please don't fuck this up, Blondie," Ronan mutters quietly.

"She's not going to fuck anything up," I growl. Sloane has proven herself just as competent as any of the other men, if just slightly less knowledgeable. But she'll get there, with some time and experience.

"I wasn't insulting her, boss," Ronan says, his eyes never leaving the screen. "I like Blondie. Is she, uh, gone once all this stuff is over?"

"She'll still need to work for us," I tell him, even though she and I haven't explicitly discussed it. "She needs the money."

He nods. "So she's really moving in permanently?"

God, I certainly hope so. The idea of having her in my bed every night makes my fingers tingle, and I have to focus on not getting hard while Ronan is sitting beside me.

Before I have a chance to answer, Ronan jumps in his seat. "I'm in. We've got it."

Seconds later, Tyler's car flies by us, followed by the other. I glance in my rearview, but I can't see the house from here. She's probably already out of the room, but she needs to get downstairs before Tyler realizes she wasn't there waiting for him.

Has he realized it already?

I want to go in. I *need* to go in. But I know I can't. We just have to wait and trust her to know where she needs to be. She set this whole thing up; she knew the risks.

Through the window, I can hear voices on Tyler's street, people laughing, talking, partying out on the lawn. Even if she was out, she still has a half hour before we can go get her and claim curfew. She has to look like she's still on his side, like she wants to be here.

Ronan is already clicking away, having a field day with Tyler's laptop, and I lean back and close my eyes, count the seconds until Sloane is back with us.

Off in the distance, I hear sirens.

I open my eyes at the same time Ronan looks up. The sirens are getting louder, coming right toward us.

"Oh, fuck," Ronan says when an ambulance swings onto Tyler's street.

I shove my door open and get out of the car, already halfway down the street before I hear Ronan's voice behind me, calling my name. I round the corner as the paramedics are going in. The crowds outside on the lawn part for them, and all I hear is buzzing in my ears as I move toward the house.

When I'm up on the lawn, through the haze in my brain, I'm aware of someone grabbing me, aware of turning to find Tyler, aware of him screaming in my face, even though the words don't process.

I shove him away from me, watch him fall into a group of people, and turn for the house, the buzzing in my ears getting louder. I try to reason with myself. Tyler was outside. He couldn't have hurt her. She was on Tyler's computer. She was conscious and okay.

But my head replays the memories of finding Leo's body in a dumpster, of watching Magnus and Bram pull him out, his body limp and cold.

"Out of the way!" someone shouts, breaking through the fog.

I dodge the stretcher coming down the stairs, move out of the way of medics as they rush out the door. I see the girl on the stretcher, take in her dark hair as she's carried out.

"Julian?"

Sloane comes down the stairs, her eyes on me, her face incredulous. I fight the urge to grab her, to kiss her and take her away from here.

"What are you doing in here?" She doesn't wait for me to answer, just keeps moving. "I have to go to the hospital." And then she's gone, almost as quickly as the stretcher was, climbing into the back of the ambulance.

A second later, Tyler storms into the house. He doesn't seem to have even noticed that Sloane is gone. "What the fuck are you doing here?" he says, beer-scented spittle flying into my face. "Stop being a fucking pervert and get the hell out of here!" He reaches out like he's going to shove me again, and I can't seem to stop myself as I cock my arm back and punch him.

People gasp, some of them watching from the living room while others peer in through the still-open front door.

"Don't put your fucking hands on me again," I sneer at Tyler and walk out the door. I have to get to the hospital.

SLOANE

I watch Krista breathe. All the research I did on overdoses said they can stop someone's breathing. So even though Krista is safe and being monitored, I'm still afraid she'll suffocate.

"Sloane?" Her eyes are heavy-lidded and puffy when they open and settle on me.

I bolt up in my chair. "Hey."

"Where am I?"

I take her hand, brush some hair out of her face. "The hospital. You overdosed."

Like someone flipped a light switch, she starts crying.

"Hey," I try to calm her. "Everything's okay. Your parents are on their way." I run a hand through my greasy hair. While they were loading her up onto the stretcher, I grabbed one of Tyler's sweaters to put on over my silly Barbie costume. It smells like him, which is sickening.

"It's not okay," she says, her voice breaking again. "My parents are going to know. Everybody's going to know that I tried E exactly one time and overdosed."

"Well," I tell her, "these things happen."

"But they rarely happen accidentally," a voice says behind me. I turn toward the door and watch Julian step into the room.

Krista scrabbles to sit up, like she's going to try and jump out of the bed, but I stop her.

"It's okay," I whisper to her.

Her eyes seem to question me, but she just nods.

"What do you mean, these things don't happen accidentally?" I ask him, but he doesn't answer right away.

He comes over to me and grimaces down at Tyler's sweater. "Take it off," he growls.

"Julian—" My words cut off when he starts to take off his coat. He slides it gracefully down his arms and raises an eyebrow at me. I comply, slipping the sweater off over my head. Julian takes it from my hand and tosses it on the hospital room floor. He lifts his coat and sets it around my shoulders, holding my gaze the whole time.

My breath stutters out of me when he steps back and admires me in his clothes before turning away. Krista's eyes are wide as she watches him move.

He stands at the foot of Krista's bed, a menacing figure. "I mean," he says, more to her than me, "that you weren't just given Ecstasy."

Krista's eyebrows furrow. "I wasn't?"

"No. You were given Ecstasy laced with something that very easily could have killed you if you had had too much of it. You didn't take the whole thing, did you?"

She shakes her head. "I split it."

"With who?"

"With my boyfriend, Liam."

"I believe the drug you were given was laced with fentanyl."

I jerk my head toward him. "How do you know?"

"Did you get it from Tyler?" he asks Krista without acknowledging me.

Krista doesn't answer but it's obvious in her eyes. I can only imagine she won't be telling the doctors or her parents where she got it from. She's protecting Tyler. She doesn't know he doesn't deserve it.

Julian seems to consider this. His eyes meet mine, and I can tell there's only so much he wants to say in front of

Krista. "Call it a suspicion, but I'm sure the doctors will confirm it as soon as they talk to you."

"You think Tyler was targeting someone."

"Wait, what?" Krista looks back and forth between us. "Like Tyler was trying to kill someone? He's your boyfriend!"

Julian sighs and glares over at me. He didn't want Krista to know that, but if she got caught in the crossfire then maybe she deserves to.

"We can trust her," I tell him. "She's not going to tell anybody anything."

"What would I tell them?" she asks. "Is Tyler some kind of hitman or something? Are *you* some kind of hitman?" Her voice gets higher with each word, more and more hysterical. When I see how pale her face is, I wonder if we're pushing her too hard. She just overdosed. She can't be feeling good. But none of the machines she's hooked up to are alerting us of any issues. No nurses have come running.

"No," Julian says, "I am not a hitman. However, Tyler has gotten himself into a bit of a mess." Julian laces his fingers together in front of his hips. I can't seem to take my eyes off him. "We would appreciate any kind of information you can give us." His eyes flicker over to me. "We're both very happy that you're alive and well, but there are other people who haven't been as fortunate. If we let Tyler continue on as he is, there might be more."

"I don't understand," she says, her voice quiet now. "What exactly do you think Tyler is *doing*?"

Julian doesn't answer, just presses his lips together and watches her.

I roll my eyes. Does he have to do his little intimidation act with *everybody*? "Krista, why wasn't Liam with you?"

"He was watching the race. He has more experience with all this stuff than I do because—" Her eyes go to Julian. He leans forward a little on the bed, pressing his hands to the mattress very carefully on either side of Krista's feet.

"Krista," he says, "is your boyfriend working for Tyler? Is he dealing?"

She looks at me and then back at Julian. "I don't want anyone to get in trouble." Her eyes shoot back to me. "You're Tyler's girlfriend. Why would *you* want him to get in trouble? He could get arrested. He could get kicked out of school."

Maybe Julian was right. Maybe I shouldn't have told her anything. But if she can give us more threads to follow, if she can help us get Tyler...

"Right," I say, leaning away from her and glancing over at Julian. "And I'm worried about him. This is scary stuff, and we need to get him to stop selling it."

"Then tell him to stop!"

"It's not that easy. He won't listen to me."

Her brows furrow. "What does *he* have to do with it?" she asks, nodding toward Julian.

"He's helping me," I tell her, surprised by how true the words are. "He got me away from someone who wanted to hurt me."

"And *he* doesn't want to hurt you?"

"I'd rather be fucking dead." There's not a single bit of emotion on Julian's face. His eyes are focused on Krista, the heavy darkness of them, his jaw, razor sharp, clenched. He can't see what his words just did to me, like someone tossed me off a skyscraper without a parachute.

"I've heard so many bad things about you. They say you're a bad man, that you've killed people, that you ship illegal things across the border, that you work with, like, gangs and assassins and shit. They say you wash money and use college girls like tissues. What about all that, huh?"

"I'm not going to argue with any of that," Julian says, his voice calm. "I'm not going to lie and tell you I'm a good man, but I'm here to clean this mess up and make sure no one else ends up in a hospital bed. Or worse."

"Clean up the mess? Are you going to kill people? What about my boyfriend? What about hers?" She jerks her chin toward me. "They might be in some bad shit but they're still people."

I reach forward, touch her hand again. "You have to understand that this is for people's safety."

She yanks her hand away, surprising me. "I don't care. No one made me take drugs. Tyler and the guys aren't forcing anybody to do anything. If people die, they're the ones who made that choice."

My heart jumps into my throat, thinking about Leo, looking at her here in this bed. And all she can do is blame the wrong person. "Krista—"

"You know," Julian says over me, "you're right, Krista. I'm a bad man. I don't care if your boyfriend is a good person or what he deserves. Tyler took someone from me, and I'm going to have my revenge. And if your boyfriend gets in the way, then so be it."

Krista turns toward me, her mouth hanging open. "You're just going to let him do this?"

I stand. "It's like you said: everyone makes their own choices. We've made ours and you've made yours. Look what he did to you. Look what he's doing to Liam. He turned you into a fucking statistic. And he's going to keep doing it. I hope you get better soon."

I turn away from the bed, but Krista's voice stops me. "Liam told me Tyler makes him record every time he distributes." I turn back. She pushes herself up a little straighter. "Liam knows more of the athletic guys, so he sells sometimes."

"Okay..."

"There was this one night he was at the dorm and I went

to the bathroom. When I came back, I heard him watching a video." Her fingers fiddle with the plastic tag on her wrist. "I asked him what it was because I thought it was like a social media thing, but I looked over his shoulder, and it was just a video of people. Nothing funny or weird happening, just talking. One of them was Tyler. He paused the video, like, immediately. I asked him what it was and he said Tyler makes him record when he deals just in case anything goes wrong. He sent it to someone."

"To who?" Julian is quick to jump in.

"I don't know." She sounds defeated now. Exhausted. We need to stop. "He didn't say. He sent them to a number that wasn't even saved in his phone."

I look over at Julian. He didn't send them to Tyler. Then who is he sending them to?

"So what now?" Krista asks.

I wrap Julian's coat tighter around myself and take a step away from the bed. "Now, you forget any of this happened. Don't talk to anybody about it and stop hanging out with Liam immediately. Put as much distance between you and him as you can. And if any of them start asking you questions, you let us know."

Her mouth drops open. "So, what, you can silence them?"

Julian steps around the bed, over to the door. "We're not going to silence anybody. At least, not yet," he says, and walks out of the room.

I move to follow him, but Krista calls out to me one more time.

"Sloane, you know you can't trust that guy. You're not safe with him." The sincerity in her voice cuts deep. If only she knew.

I shake my head, feeling a sadness deep in my bones. "None of us are safe."

44

JULIAN

"The damn computer is clean." Ronan leans back in his seat. He's still in his clothes from last night, which tells me he spent all night going through the laptop. And got nothing.

"We know Tyler has been trying to keep his hands clean," Sloane says.

"But why?" I pull out a chair at the table in Ronan's room and settle Sloane down into it. She looks like she's about to fall over, and I feel my skin heat when she smiles up at me lazily. "You said Tyler's paying off the cops. If that's true then what does he care if he gets caught?"

"The guy you offed," Ronan says, and Sloane and I both shoot him a look. He puts his hands up. "Sorry, *your contact* said Tyler was laying low after Leo. Maybe his police reach only goes so far."

"Or maybe he's trying to keep someone else off their radar. Some higher power? If he wants to be the king, wants to run his business, your business, own this whole town, eventually someone bigger than the Hanover PD is going to notice. Especially if people keep dying." She cuts her eyes at me, and I send her a look.

"He hit first, princess."

"Okay, okay," Ronan says. "So, what's next?"

"What about the number Tyler has his henchman sending the videos to? Could you find out who it is?"

Ronan sighs, running a hand over his face. "I don't have a name, I don't have a phone number, I don't have any way to track him. That's probably not even a real number. It's probably a third-party service or something. I can't search every goddamn phone and computer and Cloud storage in New Hampshire. We have to narrow it down."

"What if this is bigger than Tyler?" Ronan and I both look at Sloane. She has a contemplative look on her face as she stares at the rug beneath her. "We know Tyler is getting his supply from somewhere."

"You think he's sending the videos to his supplier?" Ronan doesn't sound convinced.

Sloane shrugs. "Why not?" Her eyes come up to us. "Tyler isn't smart enough to do any of this without help. He wants to act like he's the one calling the shots, but maybe he's not. If he has a supplier, he has someone to answer to, someone who handed him a piece of his business."

"Someone who would be far less bothered by putting a bullet in someone." I shake my head. "Tyler wouldn't stand for being someone's underling. He's made it very clear that he wants to be the apex predator."

"He goes to Dartmouth, right?" Ronan shrugs, runs a hand through his thick beard. "He's probably got a bunch of science nerds using one of those fancy labs to make more of what he has coming in. Probably E and designer drugs. That's why they're lacing it with fentanyl. They're holding some of it back. Once he's producing his own, he can take out the big guy and be king of the rock."

I nod. "The guy I met with, he told me Tyler's guy was in Lebanon. That should help us narrow it down."

Sloane straightens in her chair, pushing her shoulders back. She has this cute look on her face, all lit up like a child on Christmas. "What if we could get the phone number? With that and knowing his general whereabouts, you could find him, right?"

"Sure," Ronan says, looking about as patient as I feel to see where she's going with this.

"Tyler's phone connects to his car automatically."

I squint at her. "Okay. And?"

"If he's connected his phone to the car, then if we had access to the car..."

Ronan shakes his head. "Nah. His phone would have to be actively connected in order for me to break in."

"If he's close enough to the car, we could get that data before he even knows his phone is connected."

"How are we going to get in the car?" I say.

"That seems easy enough," Ronan says. "People fuck in their cars all the time."

"No," Sloane and I say at the same time.

Ronan rolls his eyes. "I'm not saying you actually have to fuck the guy. Just pretend like you're going to."

"No," I say, louder.

"Then how?" Ronan asks.

"I have an idea," Sloane pipes in, standing and pacing over to the door and back.

I want to be done with this meeting. I have plans for her tonight, and I'm ready for them, but she needs to get some sleep first. She looks like she's about to fall over.

"All you have to do is play him at his own game."

I share a look with Ronan, and Sloane grins.

"A car race."

Sloane heads upstairs, her shoulders sunken and her eyes tired. I follow behind her, taking her hand to stop her halfway up.

"Take a shower and get some rest. We have a party tonight."

Her eyebrows arch toward each other. "Tonight? I'm exhausted."

"Not much is expected of you. But I left something for you to wear on your bed."

I can tell she wants to argue, and I know it's selfish to ask this of her after the night she had, but I stand one step below her and take her face in my hands. "You'll enjoy it. I promise. And you can leave whenever you want."

She presses her forehead to mine and nods. "Okay. Do you want to fuck me before I nap?" She asks so politely, so casually. But I know she's not asking because she thinks she has to. She's asking because she wants it, maybe as a comfort after a trying night.

"Save it for tonight."

SLOANE

I shouldn't be surprised, but somehow, I am. I stand in front of the mirror, wearing the "outfit" Julian left for me to wear to the party. I didn't even see the tiny scrap of fabric when I fell into bed to nap. It wasn't until I woke up at sundown that I saw the bikini.

I stare at it now, holding tight to my body. It's a knit bikini, black to apparently match Julian's wardrobe, small enough that I feel naked with it on. It's not like I've never worn a bikini before, but I've certainly never worn such a revealing bikini to what I know is going to devolve into another sex party.

And I can't decide if that excites me or terrifies me.

Boss
Waiting on you, princess.

I roll my eyes at Julian's text. He's so full of shit.

But thinking about him buying this tiny thing in his free time has my blood pumping hot inside me. Did it make him hard to picture me in it?

I throw open my bedroom door and go downstairs, aware of the cold air on my skin. I feel like I should have put on a cover-up or a towel, at the very least.

I hear high-pitched, feminine voices when I get close to the pool room. With my hand on the door, I think back to the last party. So much has changed since then. But I think of Julian following me to my room, watching me touch myself. A shiver runs down my spine. I lift my chin high, toss my hair over my shoulder, and open the door.

At first, no one seems to notice me as I stand just inside the room, my eyes scanning to find Julian. But then Bram, on the other side of the pool, catches my eye. He pushes up off the bar and lets his eyes sweep down my body.

From there, one person after another turns in my direction, all of their eyes on me, both men and women. I try to act like I'm not affected by the attention as my gaze finds Julian, leaning against a wall, talking to Hugo.

Hugo spots me first and nudges Julian, who turns. When

he catches sight of me, he sucks his bottom lip into his mouth before beckoning me over. Part of me hates that he does this with everyone watching. I don't want anyone thinking they have control over me. I'm the only one who controls me, and the only reason I'm letting Julian do this now is because he clearly wants to claim me, so I go to him.

When I'm close enough, he reaches out and pulls me against him, his mouth hovering over mine. "You look good enough to eat, princess."

I plant my hands on his chest and push him back enough to meet his eye. "This is hardly what I had in mind when you said you got me something to wear."

He lowers his mouth beside my ear. "You could take it off if you'd prefer."

I shove him away again, this time walking over to the bar. Xander is on the other side, and when I lean over the bar top, I can see the effort it takes him not to look at my tits. "Can I have a bourbon on the rocks?"

"No," he responds, curt.

"Excuse me?"

He plants an elbow on the bar and leans into it. "You're underage."

"Oh, you *have* to be kidding. I'm old enough to fire a gun, old enough to work for someone like Julian, old enough to be wearing *this* in front of everyone. But alcohol is where you draw the line?"

"Correct." He winks at me, and I narrow my eyes back at him. Oh, he has no idea who he's messing with. I know this little directive came from Julian, probably because he doesn't want me getting drunk. Well, he can kiss my ass.

I march behind the bar.

"Hey!" Xander says, but I ignore him, grabbing a glass and swiping it through a cooler of ice against the wall. "You're such a bitch," he says, but there's no menace in his voice. He watches as I pull a bottle of Marker's Mark from the shelf and pour myself a double. I've never been close enough to him to see that he has a scar through one of his dark eyebrows.

I give him the finger and take a drink as I move back around the bar. And run right into Julian.

He wraps his hand around my throat in a gentle, almost affectionate grip. "I was going to wait until later to do this," he says into my ear, "but you're already causing trouble, so I think it's time now."

The bourbon settles at the base of my throat in an uncomfortable lump. "Time for what?"

He grins and kisses me. It's not gentle or slow. His tongue is in my mouth and his hands are on my ass, hauling me up toward him. His mouth moves to my jaw and then my neck, and even as I gasp at the sensation, I can see that everyone's eyes are on us. I'm not sure who already knows about us, who's pieced everything together and who hasn't. I guess everyone knows now.

Part of me cares. Cares so much I want to shove him away and tell him I can't do this. But the rest of me wants him so bad that I don't care, wants him to claim me and mark me and do it in front of everyone.

He pulls away from me, reaching out to take the glass out of my hand and set it on the bar top. "Get on your fucking knees."

I stare up at him, shocked. I know this is exactly what I was expecting, but I can't help the surprise that goes through me. We're really doing this.

He holds my gaze, and even without him saying anything, I feel the comfort of him, of knowing that he's got me. That I'm not alone.

I sink to my knees. Behind me, people murmur. From where I am, my back to the room, all I can see is Julian. I'm vaguely aware of Bram somewhere nearby, but I have to shut him out of my head before I can unbuckle Julians pants with my shaking fingers.

I keep my eyes fixed on his as I reach into his pants and take his cock out, already halfway hard. With one hand in my hair, Julian uses the other to grip his dick at the base. "Open for me. Tongue out," he says, and I can't help the high-pitched sound that comes out of me as I obey.

He sets the head of his cock on my tongue, and pump his hips, running the underside of it in and out of my mouth as I keep my tongue out for him, feeling him get harder and harder.

He hisses out a breath. "Suck," he growls, and I hungrily close my mouth around him, moaning as I lose myself in the taste and feel of him. He's so hard now, and I lick at him greedily when pre-cum oozes from his tip. "Greedy girl," he says.

I look up at him under my eyelashes, pleasure ricocheting through me when his lips fall open and he fucks into my mouth. I've always loved giving head, loved the way it made me feel wild, but this is different. Everything is different with Julian. He makes me feel like he would die if he couldn't touch me, so when he wraps both hands in my hair, I let my eyes fall closed and just enjoy the feel of him moving deeper and deeper down my throat.

"Oh, fuck," he says, when I take him as deep as I can and swallow. "Enough." He pulls me off of him, leaving me gasping for air. But before I can orient myself, he bends and scoops me up into his arms, wrapping my legs around his hips. When he walks, my pussy presses up against his stomach, and I can't keep myself from rocking against him, trying to find relief for the ache between my legs.

"Be patient," he says against my mouth.

"I can't," I whine. "I need you. I need you so bad."

He breathes a laugh, lowering us both down onto a lounge chair, the same one he sat in last time, far from the pool, from our audience. I pull back and meet his eye. I thought the blowjob would be the end of it. I thought from there, he would take me to his room or to mine and we would fuck there. But that's clearly not his intention. He's going to do it here, in front of everyone.

He kisses me as he settles me in his lap and hooks his fingers into the cups of my bikini top, pulling the fabric aside so my breasts are bared. His hands go there, cupping and squeezing me in a way that makes me rock against him some more. I feel like I'll go insane if he doesn't fuck me right now.

He sucks on my neck and one of his hands travels down my stomach and into the bottoms of my bikini. I moan loud when his fingers find my clit. *Oh, God. That feels so good.* My hips start to buck, and when his mouth surrounds one of my nipples, I become frantic.

"That's it," he says, tonguing my nipple into a peak. "Ride my hand, pretty girl."

I grip his shoulders, rocking harder, faster, as the pleasure builds. "Julian!"

"Yeah, baby. Come for me."

I grind my hips and throw my head back, doing exactly as he said, coming hard in his lap without him having done much of anything at all. How does he always manage to turn me into a wanton, horny pile of girl goo?

When it's over, I have my arms wrapped around him, breathing hard. My body is worn out from the last twenty-four hours. So when he whispers, "Turn around, baby," in my ear, I can't make my body respond.

I shake my head against his shoulder. "Sleepy."

He laughs and kisses me on the neck, a soft, chaste thing. "We're not done yet." He smacks me playfully on the hip, and I do as he asks, turning around in his lap, my breath catching in my throat when I find a room of people staring back at me. This isn't a sex party. No one else is indulging in pleasure the way they did last time Julian had a woman in his lap.

No, we're putting on a show. Everyone's eyes are on us as Julian tugs at the strings of my bikini bottoms. He unties the knot and pushes them away, tossing them on the tile floor, a strange anchor for my gaze to stick to as Julian lifts my hips and lowers me onto his cock.

I cry out, unable to hold the sound in as relief floods me. Being full of Julian is the greatest sensation I've ever known. He sits up behind me, wrapping his arms around me and pressing my back to his chest.

"We don't have to do this," he says quietly to me. "Say the word and I'll carry you out of here and fuck you in the dining room."

I'm already shaking my head before he finishes what he's saying. "I want this," I tell him, and I'm surprised to find it's true. I want everyone to see I'm his. This isn't about who owns me anymore. No one does. It's about where I *choose* to be. No one is keeping me here anymore. I'm staying because this is where I belong.

"Then ride me, princess." He grips my hips and tips me forward, until I'm steadying myself on the edge of the chair, and lifts me up and lowers me back down on him. It doesn't take us but a second to find a rhythm.

The very last thing I thought I would ever do in my lifetime is fuck someone in a room full of people. I'm not even processing their faces. They're all a blur as Julian fucks me from behind, until, when Julian tilts my hips forward and bumps right into my G-spot, my eyes lock on Bram's.

His gaze is heated. He still has a drink in his hand, but he's clearly forgotten it as his eyes watch us, rapt. I can see through the front of his pants that he's hard, and the idea that a man I'm friends with is watching me fuck his boss and is getting turned on by it pushes me even higher.

I hold his gaze as I thrust back on Julian, fucking him as much as he's fucking me. Even as Julian rearranges us, shifting back against the chair so that I'm no longer holding myself up, I can't tear my eyes from Bram's. He's like a lifeline in an ocean of pleasure.

"What's got your attention, huh?"

I know I should pull my gaze away. I know that the fact that I've somehow brought Bram into this will make Julian mad, but I can't stop looking, can't stop the knowledge that having him, specifically, watch is making me hotter.

Julian presses his mouth to my ear and wraps his hand around my throat. "He wishes he was me right now," he says. "He wants to be deep in this cunt."

I whimper in response.

"Do you want him to come over?"

This finally pulls me away from Bram. I try to turn my head, but Julian holds me still with a gentle hand around my jaw. "What?" I ask him.

"I would never let him fuck you. This pussy is for me and only me. But I'll let him touch you if you want. Would you like that?"

Oh, God. I have no idea if I would like that. The thought of it, of being with two men at the same time, has never even crossed my mind. One was always plenty. Julian is *plenty*. But I can't stop the thoughts that blow through my mind, of Bram coming closer, putting his hands on me, both of them touching me at the same time, giving me pleasure.

"Yes," I finally say because if Julian is going to make me an offer, I'm going to take it.

Julian raises a hand and gestures at Bram with two fingers. The same two fingers I rode to orgasm just a moment ago.

It's a silly impulse, but I have to close my eyes. I somehow feel embarrassed and powerful at the same time. I want Bram to come over, but I can't bring myself to watch it actually happen.

"Touch her," Julian's voice growls in my ear, and I open my eyes in time to see Bram right in front of me. He's in a black t-shirt and jeans, clearly having no intention of swimming, and my eyes meet his just before he straddles the long chair in front of me and puts both hands on my breasts.

It feels good. Bram's hands are different from Julian's, bigger and rougher, and when he pinches my nipples, the pleasure is too much.

"I need to come," I say because even though I've already orgasmed once, the need is so big, so intense, that I almost want to cry. I've never been this turned on in my life.

"You heard her," Julian says. "Make her come."

My eyes roll back in my head when Bram reaches down between my legs and starts to rub circles into my clit. The sounds I'm making are unintelligible now, garbled words and moans as I'm pushed higher and higher, Julian thrusting into me faster and harder as Bram settles into a quick rhythm.

Until all I'm saying is *yes, yes, yes* over and over as I come.

"Beautiful," Bram says when I'm done screaming myself hoarse. He licks my juices from his fingers and stands.

I think he's about to leave when Julian says, "Do you want to suck his cock?"

I'm not even thinking anymore. Everything is just sensation and desire as I nod and watch Bram undo his pants. Just like with Julian, I open my mouth and wait for him to use me. But this is so much different. Bram isn't commanding me, isn't controlling the situation. It's like he's...grateful.

"That's it," Julian says in my ear when Bram pushes into my mouth. "Be a good girl and suck him off."

I moan around Bram and he groans loudly in return. I would smile if my mouth wasn't otherwise occupied.

"You're so good at that," Julian says. I don't know how he can concentrate when he's fucking me this hard. How can he keep his wits about him when this is happening between us? Between all of us?

"I'm not going to last," Bram says, his hands coming up to settle on the back of my head. "Can I come in your mouth?"

I'm practically on all fours, and I have to twist a little to meet Bram's eyes so he can see me nod. As soon as I do, he starts to groan louder, starts to pump into my mouth.

"Don't swallow," Julian says. "Hold it in your mouth."

I barely have time to process his words before Bram is unleashing on my tongue, filling my mouth with cum. It seems to go on forever, and I wait patiently for him to finish, focused on holding it on my tongue until he pulls away.

As soon as I'm free, Julian takes my jaw again. He turns my face towards him, his pace punishing inside me. "Show me," he demands, and I open my mouth, careful not to let any slide out. "Good girl. Now, swallow."

I do, and as soon as Bram's cum is down my throat, Julian kisses me. The thought that he's most likely able to taste Bram has me feral. "Fill me up," I tell him. "Please. Come inside me."

He keeps kissing me, pumping into me, his hands gripping my hips hard, until I feel him spill inside me, filling me just like I asked him to.

We're both panting when he's done, and if I thought I was tired before, I'm completely unable to move now. I'm aware of things going on around me—Julian slipping out of me, Bram buttoning up, the rest of the party getting in the pool, making out, getting the night started now that the show is over.

But my eyes are already closed, my head on Julian's still-clothed chest.

"Alright, pretty girl. Let's get you to bed." His voice is already coming to me as if in a dream.

45

JULIAN

I'm not sure I've ever felt so... content. I run my fingers through Sloane's hair as she lies in my bed. I've never brought a woman here before. Partially because anyone not in the organization isn't allowed inside the compound, but also because I've just never wanted to. It's never even crossed my mind.

But having her here feels good. I've been watching her sleep for a while, my hand on her chest as she breathes in and out. I can't believe she did all of that for me.

Like she can feel me thinking about her, she shifts her face into my arm and opens her eyes. She stares straight ahead at my chest for a moment and then looks up to find my eyes.

And then she realizes Winston is nestled between us.

"Hey, there," she says, her voice soft as she reaches up to pet him. He purrs between us. He was immediately crazy about her and hasn't wanted to leave her side since I brought her in. "I still can't believe you've been hiding a cat in here."

"Technically, I'm not hiding him. He hides himself. Doesn't like being anywhere else."

She snorts. "Sounds familiar. Do you clean his litter box? I can't imagine you cleaning a litter box."

"It's self-cleaning."

This makes her giggle. There's a loud noise from downstairs, and her laughter stops. "Are they still going? How long was I out?"

"A few hours. And yes. They'll probably be going until sunrise. Look…" I move Winston out from between us and move a little closer to her. "I know you're pretty worn out, but I want to show you something. You feeling up to it?"

She grins and nods. So generous and eager. I kiss her once and get her some clothes from my dresser to wear. A button-up and sweatpants.

"These are cozy," she says, pulling up the sweats that are too big for her.

"Don't get used to it." I take her hand and lead her to the door. "If you stop wearing those sexy pink outfits, you would break my heart."

I pull her out of the bedroom, but when she starts back down the hall toward the foyer, I stop her. She turns and sees me standing in front of the only other door in the hallway. Her face twists in confusion, but she doesn't ask me any questions. That's a first.

She knew this door was here when she scouted out this hallway so she could break into my bedroom. She just doesn't know what's behind it.

I push it open, not surprised when we're met with cold air. The door is shut so much of the time.

She doesn't wait for me to escort her in. My curious little cat steps into the room, her eyes going to the red leather chair behind the antique mahogany desk and then roaming down the bookcase, fingers sliding along the spines. They're mostly business and law books, nothing she would read for pleasure.

"It's my dad's office. When we added the new wing, I stopped using it."

She stops and lifts her hand from where it paused on a bust of Mozart. "It's very sophisticated."

I snort. "Yes, that was Dad. He liked it when people *thought* he was sophisticated. He set up here because he went to Dartmouth."

"A breeding ground for criminals, it would seem," she says, walking back to me and putting her arms around my waist.

"It would appear so. He was so smart, my dad. But he figured out quick that if you really want to get ahead in the world, you have to be ruthless, dishonest, conniving." I take her by the shoulders and lead her back to the bookcase, sliding my own fingers along the spines. "He knew he could either do it in a boardroom or in a warehouse in the middle of nowhere."

I pull the bust of Mozart off its perch, and the wall beside us swings in.

Sloane's mouth falls open. "Are you kidding? People actually have those?"

I set the bust on the rug. "My father liked drama." I pull her through the doorway and watch as she realizes it's another library, filled with floor to ceiling bookshelves.

She lets out a sound that could only be described as a squeak, and I smile. "I thought you might like it."

She walks to one shelf and examines the books, careful to leave an ample amount of space between herself and them.

"You can touch them. It's okay." I understand her hesitance. The books in here are old, some of them shockingly so. One of the many reasons my father kept them in here. Out of the sunlight and elements, they're much safer. "My father loved fiction."

She reaches out and touches the leather spine of a book. "Why did he hide them?"

"There are some pretty expensive books in this room. A lot of first editions. It's all safe-keeping."

She pulls one off the shelf and smiles down at the cover. It's an old copy of *The Little Prince*. She turns to show it to me. "Have you read this one?"

I shake my head.

She bites her lip and looks down at it.

"Take it."

Her eyes widen. "I couldn't."

"Why not? All the books I sent you were from this library. No one else reads them. What good is a library full of books that never get read? Take any that you want. You know how to get in here. Clean the place out."

Her eyes stay locked on mine as she walks over to me. I half-expect her to make a crass comment, but she just says, "Are you sure?"

I tilt her chin up and press a kiss to her soft mouth. "He would have loved you, and he would have wanted you to enjoy them."

She looks up at me in this way she never has before, a way I can't even describe. Her eyes are soft, roving over my face, and she's frowning, but not in a sad way. It's like she's confused.

Before I can overanalyze, I say, "There's something else I want to show you, but you have to put on shoes."

There's a padlock and keypad to get into the warehouse and one guy at the gate. Sloane's eyes open wide in shock when we drive up to the little security hut I put on the property. Ryan gets paid a lot of money to live on site instead of at the compound. He gets time off during the day, when one of the guys can take over long enough to let him sleep.

But Sloane didn't know he existed until tonight. Just one more secret between the two of us.

I'm about to unveil the last one.

She waits for me to unlock the padlock and pull the chain before putting in my code and listening to the door unlock with a mighty, metal *clang*.

"What's in here?" Sloane asks as we step inside and I flip on the lights. Her blue eyes scan the room, taking everything in before they meet mine.

"It's what Tyler wanted you to find."

She holds my gaze as we walk toward the car in the middle of the warehouse. I can see her analyzing things, see the wheels turning in her head as she sees that the car is partially dismantled, that there are gun parts scattered beneath it, that there are safes stacked one on top of the other in the corner.

"Everyone knows where the compound is," I say, smacking the Corvette on the bumper, like an obedient horse. "This is what we keep off the radar. Only the guys and Ryan out there know how to find it."

"Why are you showing me?"

When I turn back to her, I'm surprised by the sincerity on her face. She doesn't understand why I would introduce her to our biggest secret. She doesn't understand why I would trust her.

"Because you're one of us now. We have a small crew of mechanics back at the compound, including myself. Once the cars are ready for delivery, we bring them here and pack them with guns. Under the hood, in the floorboard, the trunk, anywhere we can put them that the heat won't destroy."

"Guns," she says. "I had a suspicion it might be guns." She seems almost fascinated by the concept, running her hand down the side of the car. Her nail polish is chipped. I make a mental note to get her some extra cash so she can go have them done.

"I've got a guy at the border," I continue, the two of us circling opposite sides of the car. "The one you talked to."

She shoots me a look. Guess she's still mad about that. Can't say I blame her.

"He makes sure the cars get through security." I pat the safe closest to me, cold and rough. "After every job, I get a cut, the one who secured the contract gets a cut, the mechanics get a cut, delivery gets a cut, and the rest goes in the safe. Once things settle down and we're back in business, we'll find a place for you."

She walks toward me slowly, a sly smile on her face. She's swimming in my clothes, wearing my shirt like a dress, but she still has that little bikini on underneath it. I watched her throw my stuff over it back at the compound. As she walks toward me, she undoes the first button on the shirt.

God, she can't be serious, my greedy little girl. There's no way she can still be horny after what Bram and I did to her at the party. Hell, the party's still going back at the compound, and here she is, trying to talk me into more?

She undoes another button and perches one hip on the Corvette. "Show me what you'll do when you get home after a hard day. When you get back to the compound and you find me waiting there, what will you do?" She leans back on the hood of the car, and I get a glimpse of the tiny scrap of fabric between her legs.

"I already fucked you into next week today."

"That was *hours* ago. And I've slept since then, so it's basically tomorrow." She undoes another button as she lets her knees fall open.

And I'm powerless to resist. I'm on top of her in a second, my tongue in her mouth and my hands all over her. She kisses me back hungrily, wrapping her legs around my waist.

I lift her against me and walk toward the door at the side of the building.

"What are you doing?" she asks against my mouth.

I throw open the door and rush over to the Beast, setting her down beside the car that's still running on the dirt. "If you want me to fuck you on a car, it's going to be *my* car. Now turn around and bend over."

The world is dark around us, the only light the car's bright headlights pointed at the side of the warehouse, ricocheting off into the night. As far as I'm concerned, the rest of the world doesn't exist. Just me and this beautiful girl.

She spins around, and I don't bother taking the shirt off, even though half the buttons are undone. With a hand on her neck, I push her down onto the hood and reach under the shirt to shove the sweats and bikini down her legs.

"I've never felt like this before." I don't know if she means for me to hear her whispered words, but I do hear them, and in my head, I say back, *Me either, baby*.

I drop down to my knees and put my mouth between her legs, tasting her arousal against my tongue as she squirms and moans for me. I push my tongue into her and she reaches back to fist her hand into my hair, holding me in place like I'm going somewhere.

I reach up and circle her clit the way I know she likes, my eyes rolling back when she starts to come around my tongue, her internal muscles squeezing me. Her legs quiver and threaten to give out, but I wrap my arms around them, holding her up while she finishes.

I lick her until there's nothing left and then stand and rip my pants open to get my cock out. She has her cheek pressed to the hood of the Beast, her limp hands on either side of her.

But when I press into her, her mouth opens on a gasp, and she makes a high-pitched noise in the back of her throat.

I revel in the sound as I pull out and push back in, revel in the sight of her hands curling into fists. I know she's exhausted, even if she pretended she wasn't, but I know she can't resist this any more than I can.

Wrapping my arms around her, I haul her up so her back is to my chest. She turns her face toward mine, and I kiss her as I start to fuck. With my arms around her like this, one hand full of her breast, the other pressed to her rib, I feel like I'm holding the whole universe together. And if I let her go, it'll all unravel.

I pump into her tight, wet heat, lose myself in the sight and smell and feel of her.

"Julian," she whines against my mouth, her eyes squeezed shut.

"I know, baby. I know," I say. Because I do know. The world has gotten too big, too complicated, too everything. I bend us both over the hood, press kisses to the back of her neck while I pump, until we're both moaning and shouting and panting in the aftermath.

We're like that for a moment, pressed together, until I have to pull out of her and let her right herself while I lock up the warehouse.

I hold her hand all the way back to the compound, and we sneak back into my room while the party rages by the pool.

She falls asleep with her head in my lap while I read her *The Little Prince*.

46

SLOANE

"Everyone is staring," I tell Julian, watching yet another person walk by, eyes on the Beast. "You probably should have driven something a little more inconspicuous."

"I don't really own anything inconspicuous," he says, which I guess is true, but Hugo manages to get me in and back out of campus every day without causing this much commotion.

I smile over at him. I've felt like this all morning, like there's a buzz under my skin. I know I shouldn't be soft towards Julian—that he's not a soft man, and he doesn't want to be surrounded by soft people—but I can't help it. The things he's done to me, with me, in the last few days. All the anger, the resentment, it's all slowly leeched away.

"Well, at least don't come in the building," I say, reaching for the door handle. "Everything's fine. I can come up with some reason why I don't need a bodyguard anymore. Or I can just tell him you're waiting in the car, or whatever." I shove open the door.

"You should feed him something," Julian says from behind me.

I whip around to face him. "What, information?"

He shrugs. "Nothing too incriminating. Obviously, don't tell him about the guns, the warehouse, anything like that. Tell him we're letting you go on a sale soon and that you're sure to get some intel. It'll make his dick hard." He keeps his voice neutral, cold.

I can't tell from where I am, feeling like a sparkler crackling and popping, whether this is a show, or if he really still feels nothing toward me. It's hard for me to imagine, after the other night and everything he shared with me, that he doesn't feel *something*. I don't think I can believe it. I don't think I will.

He watches me get out of the car. I bend, satisfied when his eyes drop to my chest. If he doesn't want to admit he's emotionally attached to me, that's fine. But I know the truth.

"See you later, sugar," I tell him with a grin.

He says nothing, so I slam the door in his face. Let him sort out his own feelings. I feel lighter today, and it's not just because I got fucked silly over the weekend, but also because part of me believes this might all really be over soon.

It's my job to drop the idea of the race to Tyler today. To come up with some lie about how I overheard the guys talking about it at the compound and that Tyler getting involved would benefit him. Tyler has been the very center of my life long enough now that I can't imagine what it's going to be like to be free of him. It's like sitting at a red light and suddenly, the light is green and the road is open in front of you and there's no speed limit.

I bite back a smile as I walk into the technology building. I haven't felt this good in ages. Like I'm really doing something.

I've almost made it to class when I see him. Tyler is

leaning against a wall just down the corridor from our lecture hall, doing something on his phone.

"Hey," I say, hoping I sound pleasant. Tyler looks up from his phone, his dark eyes meeting mine. "I talked to Krista's mom yesterday," I say, a script I already wrote in my head on the way here. "She said that—" My words are cut off when Tyler clamps a hand over my mouth.

"Don't say a word," he grits out between clenched teeth. "Come with me." He wraps a hand around mine and pulls me down the hallway. My stomach turns. No, no, no, no, no. This is not how this was supposed to play out. I was supposed to see Tyler in class and maybe study time in between and that was it. No more frat house visits. No more seductions. No more faking periods. This is supposed to be over.

Tyler's grip on me eases as we move into an empty classroom on the other side of the building. He shuts and locks the door. My eyes are frozen on that lock as he comes over to me. The room is dark, the only light what sunshine can make it through the closed blinds, everything a muted gray.

I don't want to do this. I *can't* do this. But it's been long enough now since Tyler and I had sex that I guess I shouldn't be surprised. He steps over to me, sandwiches me between himself and the wall, while I try to figure out how to get out of this.

And when I think he'll lean in and kiss me or maybe try and stick his hand into my pants or grab my boob or something, he just looks at me, steady, like he's waiting for me to answer a question he didn't ask.

"What is it?" I ask. I can hear my pulse in a steady rhythm in my eardrums.

"I got an interesting message from a friend of mine last night."

Everything goes quiet in my head, sifting through his words. "Friend? What friend?"

He shrugs. "Just a friend. They sent me a video."

"Okay..." My fight or flight has started to die down, my hackles lowering. What the hell is this about? Tyler's never been one of those guys who shares memes and funny videos, but I can't imagine what else he'd be talking about.

Until he pulls out his phone.

When he turns on his screen, his face lights up and it hits me how much I feel like I'm in a horror film, waiting for the killer to strike. Sound erupts from the phone speakers and he turns the video toward me. It only takes me a few seconds to figure out what I'm looking at, what I'm hearing.

On his phone screen, I'm naked, getting fucked from behind by Julian on a lounge chair, Bram's cock in my mouth. It's like seeing a glimpse of another life. I wish I was back there, that place where I felt so safe with those boys.

But I'm not there. I'm here. And I can feel all the dread rushing back in a blaze across my face. I've already started to run through steps in my head, possibilities: screaming, even though Tyler has brought me to an empty part of the building and it's unlikely anyone will hear, banging on the windows. I know Tyler doesn't have a gun. Neither one of us would have brought one here. So even if he does try to kill me, it won't be quick. I'll have a chance to fight back.

I'm still moving through my options when he wraps a hand around my throat. "I knew you were a slut," he says, pressing his mouth against my ear. "I knew it because of how easy you gave yourself to me. Little sixteen-year-old virgin, begging to be fucked, but I didn't think you were a fucking whore, too. What a joke you are. A fucking cliché, giving yourself to men for money, or whatever the fuck they promised you."

On reflex, I wrap my hands around his upper arm. "Tyler," I gasp. "I can't breathe."

"He didn't even have to rape you," he says, ignoring my pleas. "You gave it to him willingly. You're not fighting him in the video. You're practically panting for it."

My attention is caught by a feeling in my back pocket. Tyler is sliding my cell phone out of it. I grab at it but he holds it out of my reach, his arms so much longer than mine, especially with his hand still pressed to my throat the way it is. He turns on the screen. When he sees that he needs my fingerprint to unlock it, he spins, pressing his back to me. I'm simultaneously gasping for air after he's let go of my throat and realizing I can't get any because he's putting so much pressure on my lungs from the front.

He presses my thumb to the phone screen and jerks back away from me. I gulp in heavy, deep breaths.

Inexplicably, Julian's voice echoes through the room. Tyler called him and put the phone on speaker. "Miss me already?" Julian says, his voice stoic, the way it always is.

"Julian," I gasp, like a reflex.

"Baby?" he says, the tone of his voice shifting so quickly. There's fear laced in it.

Before I can respond, Tyler speaks. "You don't get to fucking call her that," he says. "She's mine. She's always going to be mine. You fucked what was mine, and I'm going to take her back."

"Sloane—" I hear Julian shout just before Tyler tosses the phone.

I lunge for the door, but my fingers just barely grasp the handle before he has his arms wrapped around me and is pulling me back into the room. I struggle, trying to remember some kind of self-defense move to get me out of this, but my brain is like static. All I can do is pound my fists at his arm, kick at his legs, even though he's just ignoring me.

He tosses me onto the floor and climbs on top of me. He pins my hands above my head. "You're nothing but trash now. Used up fucking trash. I thought you were better than giving it to him. Now you're worth nothing." He holds both my hands in one of his and shoves the other up under my shirt. "Maybe if I fuck you," he growls, "he won't want you anymore."

Shoving the top of my bra down, he twists my nipple and I scream. He's distracted just enough that I'm able to yank one of my hands out of his grip and punch him. I doubt I hurt him in any real way, but he's surprised enough that I have a moment to wiggle out from beneath him.

I turn over onto my stomach and try to get my feet under me, but he's already there, crushing me into the carpet.

"You could have had everything, Sloane. A future, all the money you could ever want, security. And now you're a whore, just like your fucking mother. How does it feel to throw everything away?"

My fingers are still scrabbling at the carpet like there's some kind of salvation beneath it.

Tyler shoves my skirt up past my hips and a whimper falls from my mouth. I know Julian is coming for me. He would never give me a phone that didn't have a tracker on it. All I have to do is keep Tyler at bay until he can get to me.

Tyler is shoving my underwear down my legs. And there, right at my elbow, is my backpack. I hear the sound of his belt at the same moment that I wrap my hand around one of the sharp pencils in the side pocket. He's too heavy for me to be able to flip over, so when I stab him, it's blindly.

My arm swings out over my side, flying out behind me to hit whatever I can. Tyler lets out an ungodly screech and the door handle begins to rattle.

Julian. He's pulling at the handle, banging on the door as I scramble away from Tyler. I turn over and feel a burst of relief to see the pencil jutting out of his shoulder.

Julian crashes through the door, stumbling as he catches himself. I'm paralyzed, watching Tyler try to pull the pencil out at an awkward angle. I see Julian take it all in, process what he's looking at—me in a ball against the wall, Tyler howling in pain, my crumpled underwear on the floor between us—and then he's on Tyler. He shoves him down to the ground, landing on the pencil, and I watch with satisfaction as it goes all the way through the flesh of Tyler's shoulder, and he screams.

Julian punches Tyler again and again and again, and I want to let him kill Tyler. I know he would. He already wants to. He's said it so many times. He wants Tyler dead, but he's controlled himself for the sake of the men. I think if I let him right now, he would break every bone in his hand beating Tyler to death.

"Julian," I convince myself to say. "Julian," I say louder, my voice breaking.

He ignores me.

"Julian, you have to stop." I find the strength in my legs to go over to him, to wrap myself around him. "You can't do this," I say to him. "You can't, you know you can't."

This seems to break him out of it. I have my hands wrapped around his shoulders, my face pressed to the back of his neck. I can practically feel the anger coming off of him in waves.

Julian stands and looks down at where Tyler is bleeding. "You come near her again," Julian says, his voice empty, cold, "not even God will be able to save you." He takes my hand and leads me over to the open door. He stops and looks both ways in the hallway. Just before he pulls me out, I look back at Tyler, lying in splatters of his own blood.

JULIAN

I lean against the wall outside Sloane's bathroom, the scent of minted lavender wafting out on the steam. I glance inside, find her reflection in the mirror. She has her arms wrapped around herself, her forehead pressed to the tile wall.

She told me the whole thing on the drive back, voice monotone.

"He didn't manage to..." she said, the thought of finishing the sentence clearly causing her pain. As if that's the only thing that matters. As if he didn't hurt her. As if he didn't hit her. As if he didn't pin her to the ground. He doesn't have to rape her for it to leave scars.

She finally gets out of the shower and wraps herself in a towel. We meet by the door. I press my hand to her cheek. She turns her face into it.

"I'm okay," she says, her voice soft, small. "He can't hurt me."

"He can, though." If this doesn't end well and I'm gone, who protects her? What keeps Tyler from coming after her? "You should have aimed for an artery," I tell her, pulling her into my arms. I smell her skin feeling like I can breathe again with her this close. I don't know if any moment in my life has been as terrifying as listening over the phone to Tyler hurting her and not being able to get to her fast enough. The memories will play out in my nightmares forever, I know it.

"I have bad aim, remember?"

"You could have killed him." I hate to put this weight on her, but it's true. "You could have done it free and clear. Self-defense."

The shadows she was trying to hide reappear in her eyes. "Women have been thrown in jail for killing their attackers before. No one is on our side."

I know she's right. They would have made her prove it, and she wouldn't have been able to. History has not been kind to women trying to convince courts they've been attacked.

I run my fingers through her hair. "Can I hold you?" I ask her.

"You are holding me."

"In your bed."

She steps back, looks up at me, her face clean and her hair wet. "You better be careful, Julian Shaw. I might get the idea that you like me."

I know she wants to make light of this, but I can't. When I heard her yell my name over that phone, I went cold as death. I can't pretend anymore, can't keep trying to hold her at arm's length.

I take off my shirt, the one I changed into when we got home because mine was covered in Tyler's blood. I'm surprised when she takes it carefully from my hands and puts it on over her naked body. I strip down to my boxer briefs and we get into her cold sheets.

On the app on my phone, I make sure her camera is off. It's been disabled for a while now, but I check it out of habit.

"What do we do now?" she asks, setting her head on my chest. I sigh at the reassuring weight of her against my side.

"We keep you away from Tyler. Me and the guys will see this through to the end."

She sits up, shoving away from me, her eyes full of anger. "What? Absolutely not!"

"Sloane, he tried to *rape* you. He knows about us now. You can't be part of this anymore."

She bursts out of the bed, standing by the window, her hands in her hair like a medieval painting. "All the more reason for me *to* be part of it. If you think I'm not going to end this, you're wrong. Our agreement was that I would help take him down, and I'm *going* to take him down."

"Okay," I tell her. "Okay. We'll figure it out, okay? Just... come back to bed."

She hesitates, her chest rising and falling rapidly. She finally does get back into the bed, back to the spot beside me, where she belongs.

"We take some time to relax while Tyler licks his wounds," I tell her. "First thing next week, my guy sets up the race."

$$47$$

SLOANE

Tyler is gone for almost a week, and then, the day of the race, I'm getting ready for class when I get a text from Claudia.

> **Claudia**
> He's been spotted on campus.

I feel surprisingly calm. The calmest, actually, that I've felt since this whole thing started. I don't have to walk into that classroom today and pretend to be Tyler's girlfriend. The pretending is over, and I feel free.

I meet Julian down on the front patio, and even when I see the look on his face, that scowl he wears when he's particularly disappointed, my mood is unchanged. I knew this was coming, of course. I'm sure Claudia sent Julian the same text she sent me.

It's not like we didn't know this day would arrive eventually. It's why Bram has been coming to class with me since that awful day. Julian knows he can't come, that if he were to get anywhere near Tyler after what he did, he wouldn't be able to stop himself from killing him.

But Julian also knows I'm not about to bow out of my classes for Tyler. It's too late to drop the class, and I'm not wasting a fully paid-for semester. Tyler doesn't get to win that easily. He doesn't even care about finishing. Dartmouth means nothing to him.

Standing in the driveway of the compound, Bram right beside me, I say—and really believe it, all the way down to my bones—"Everything is going to be okay. This is so close to being over. The race is almost here."

Ronan has already shown me how we're going to get the numbers from the car as quickly as possible. Once we have the information we need, we find Tyler's supplier, we get the videos, and even if Tyler does have some officer in his pocket, it won't be enough to save him from his own horde.

I start to pull away from Julian but his grip on me is solid. I tilt my head to look up at him. "Don't forget why I'm doing this," I tell him.

He does that thing, putting on his mask, so that his face is unreadable. "If he lays a finger on you, I'm going to put a bullet in his head."

"I'm not letting you start a war over me, Julian."

"Too late."

Bram quietly sneaks into class with me, like he has all week. Technically, he has permission, as Claudia contacted all of my professors to tell them I would be escorted around campus for the foreseeable future. I know the boys are trying to be helpful, but I don't want this kind of attention. I don't want to be some special case. But Tyler has made it impossible to have things any other way.

Bram sits down beside me, even as our professor's eyes follow us. I don't think he likes Bram all that much, and I can't blame him, as Bram never bothers to listen to the lectures, just plays games on his phone during class.

Tyler comes in not long after us. I've chosen to sit far in the back of the room, far from where Tyler and I used to sit. But he heads to our normal spot. Just before he takes his seat, his eyes find me. His face is barely recognizable. One eye swollen shut, purple in all the important places. And just inside the collar of his shirt, I can see the edge of a white bandage. His wounds almost match mine. My own bruises have faded, the spot where I had my stitches nothing but a small magenta mark on my cheek.

I hold his stare. His one good eye flickers over to Bram. He turns and takes a seat.

Bram puts his arm along the back of my chair and leans in close. "Julian's handiwork looks good on him."

I turn my face toward his. "I'd like credit for the bandage, please. That was all me," I whisper.

His eyes scan over my face, and he squeezes my shoulder. "Nice work. I'm shocked he made it out alive. Now that you're Julian's, he'll do anything to protect you."

His words drive up under my ribs. *Now that you're Julian's...*

Bram and I stand as soon as class is over. We have our routine. I carefully gather my books and we head down the stairs of the lecture hall. I know I shouldn't be surprised when Tyler grabs onto my arm as I pass. I shouldn't be surprised by his audacity, but I am. Bram is dangerous. I don't know whether or not he's packing, but neither does Tyler. Tyler saw what Julian was capable of. He has to know that the other men are capable of the same things. And yet, he still has his fucking hand on me.

I spin around. "Don't touch me," I say between my teeth.

I've just barely gotten the words out before Bram has a hold of Tyler's hand. He twists his arm at an unnatural angle and Tyler whimpers. "I suggest you keep your hands to yourself before you end up with your head on a spike," Bram growls. I don't even realize I've never seen Bram angry before until I'm looking at someone unrecognizable from rage.

"She's my girlfriend," Tyler snaps, managing to wiggle out of his grip. I know he wouldn't have been able to if Bram hadn't let him go.

"Your girlfriend?" I ask, my voice hysterical. There are still a few stragglers in the room and they look our direction. I take a step toward Tyler and lower my voice. "Are you honestly so fucked in the head that you think that after you tried to rape me and called me a whore that I would still be your girlfriend?"

Even through the swelling on his face, I can make out the furrow of his brow. "We were supposed to be forever, Sloane. We came here together. I'm sorry for what I did, but I was just angry. I mean, how can you blame me? You—"

"I'm not sorry for what I did." My eyes drop to the bandage. "I wish I'd gotten you in your fucking neck."

What Julian said the other day has been going around and around in my head. I could have killed Tyler. I know he feels like he can't without putting a target on his own back, but I could have killed him. He was guilty of what he did to me in that room, and I know that Julian would have killed him with his bare hands if I hadn't stopped him. Maybe I should have just let him die.

Tyler's jaw visibly clenches. "You're nothing without me." Just like that, he abandons his fake gentleness. "What's going to happen next year when you need someone to pay for school, huh? You gonna get on your knees for him? Prove me right that you're just a fucking whore?"

Bram starts to lunge, and I step between them, pressing my back to Bram's front.

Tyler's eyes lock onto Bram, like he's really looking at him for the first time, and his mouth falls open. "You're the other guy!" he says. "From the video. You fucked my girl."

"Go to hell, Tyler," I say, before pushing back against Bram, a sign that it's time to go. I take his hand and lead him out of the room, Tyler screaming obscenities as we go.

"It's like he *wants* to get shot," Bram mutters behind me.

"Keep dreaming." I lace my fingers through his to steady my own shaking hands.

In the library, Bram settles in at the table beside me and gets out his phone.

I open my textbook. "Don't you have something you're supposed to be doing all day?" I ask him with a smirk.

"Yes," he says without looking up from his phone. "Protecting you."

I roll my eyes. "I mean, don't you have work you're meant to be doing back at the compound?"

His hazel eyes look up and meet mine. "Sure. My job is mostly communications. Some of it I can do from here." He lifts his phone. "And the rest I either delegate to someone who's looking for a little extra commission, or I handle it after dinner."

I feel guilty that this is the way the guys are spending their time, babysitting me, and all because Tyler can't be trusted to keep his hands to himself.

"I'm sorry I'm such a burden."

Bram looks up from his phone, his brow furrowed. "That's bullshit, Sloane. You're not a burden. The guys are happy to have you. *I'm* happy to have you. The house is...brighter, livelier. And Julian..." He shakes his head, looks down at his phone again. "I've never seen him like this before." He goes back to his business like what he said is no big deal, like his words don't have my throat tightening and my chest aching.

I wish they knew that I'm different, too. That they've changed me.

I need a minute to compose myself. I push my chair back and point in the direction of the stacks. "I'm going to go grab a few books for my Sociology essay."

He nods and doesn't even argue with me about going alone. Weird. It's not as if I'm planning on going far, but Bram has been so intense about not letting me out of his sight.

I wander into the stacks. I don't even know what section I'm in. I look up in time to catch a sign. Medieval Philosophy. Perfect. This aisle and the surrounding area are empty so I grab onto a shelf, press my forehead to it, and close my eyes.

What the hell am I doing? This whole thing with Julian and the guys and the compound, it was just supposed to be a means to an end, a way to make money so I can graduate. And now, what? I'm going to live with these guys for the next four years? What happens after that?

The air shifts, and I know I'm not alone anymore. Naturally, the one time someone is looking for a Medieval Philosophy book. I sigh and open my eyes, taking a step back from the shelf, realizing too late that there's someone behind me. Someone I knock right into.

"Oh, I'm so so—" I spin around, but as soon as I do, I'm backed into the bookshelf behind me.

My pulse breaks into a sprint, my hands coming up to shield myself, until I look up into dark, familiar eyes.

48

SLOANE

"What are you doing here?" I whisper to Julian.

"Just checking in, making sure Bram is doing his job."

I roll my eyes. "Don't any of you have *real* jobs?"

He smiles. "Are you asking me if I make an honest living? Because no, I don't." He bends in close to me, and when his lips skim mine, I glance sideways, making sure there's no one around.

"Julian," I breathe, "we can't."

"Can't what?" he asks, his voice sweetly innocent. I jump when his fingers land on my knee, just below the hem of my skirt. "I'm just rewarding you for being so studious."

His mouth descends on mine, and I'm lost. I can't say no to Julian. I've never been able to, not even when I hated him. I've wanted him since the second we met, and now that my emotions are involved—because I'm way past pretending they aren't—I have no hope of resisting him.

As his hand moves up under my skirt, pushing it up so he can fill his hand with one of my ass cheeks, he backs me up, until we're pressed against the wall at the end of the aisle, as far from the main aisle as possible. Back here, we're partially obscured where the wall juts out.

He doesn't take his mouth from mine as his grip shifts to my hip and then dives into my underwear.

A yelp escapes me before Julian claps a hand over my mouth. He glances over his shoulder and then turns those dark eyes back on me. "Shhh. This is a library, Miss Moretti." His mouth travels across my cheek, settling against the shell of my ear. "Be a good student, and you'll be graded fairly."

His fingers settle over my clit. I slam my eyes shut, bucking against his hand. I couldn't stop myself if I wanted to. Once he starts to make me feel good, I'm nothing but sensation and lust.

"Already so wet," he practically mouths against my ear, his hot breath caressing my skin. "I love that I can do this to you. That just me being near makes you so slick it's dripping on my fingers. I love knowing you're always ready to be fucked by me."

I grab onto his sleeve, fist it in my hands. I want to kiss him or bite him or worship him, I don't even know.

"You like that, don't you?" He's rubbing me in earnest now, trying to get me off as fast as possible, but then his fingers dip down, spearing into me. "Do you like knowing you're all I can think about? That I was sitting in my office, so hard thinking about being inside you that I couldn't even focus on my work? That I was so distracted that I couldn't get anything done until I touched you?"

Between his words, his fingers, and the smell of him, I'm rocketing toward an orgasm at an alarming pace. I'm moaning against his hand. I've stopped caring if we're on campus, if we're in the library, if people can see or hear. I just want him so bad I'm seeing stars behind my eyelids.

"That's it," he says. "I love how you respond to my touch.

I love that I can make you come this fast. I love that you soak my hand with how much you want it."

I love you.

I don't know if it's my own thought or what I want him to say next, but either way, it goes off in my head, like a siren drowning out his words.

"Come on my fingers, princess. Let me feel that squeeze I love so much."

Love.

It's all my brain can process as I'm pushed up onto my tiptoes and start to come, his hand clamped so hard over my mouth that I almost can't breathe, but I don't mind because I *need* the angry press of him. I need him to fill me and surround me and make me his.

And I know, even as the orgasm starts to fade, that I'm so fucked. Because I know I'll never want anyone this way again. Whatever this is with Julian, it's not *normal*, and if it goes away—if I leave the compound or if Julian doesn't want me like this anymore—I think I'll unravel.

He finally pulls his hand away from my mouth, letting me suck in a lungful of air, and slips his fingers out of my underwear. He presses his forehead into the side of mine.

"Bram told me about your run-in with Tyler. I thought you could use a little stress relief."

I imagine him and Bram worrying over me, discussing me. "You boys have got to get a grip."

"I'll get a grip," he says before wrapping his hand around my neck and forcing me back against the wall, his touch light but commanding. "He attacked you, Sloane. Not once, not even twice. The fact that you still stand up to him is why I can't even think your name without getting hard, but that doesn't mean you have to shrug it off. You're safe with me. If you need to feel something, feel it."

I'm so close to his dark brown eyes that I can only look at

one at a time. I do feel something. But it's not heartbreak over Tyler, or fear or even anger. Yes, Tyler hurt me, and I hate him for it. But he doesn't deserve my thoughts or my emotions.

Julian hasn't figured out that Tyler can't haunt me because he takes everything Tyler has done to me and makes it easier to face, lessens the hurt and bandages the wounds.

I hook my hand around the back of his neck and pull him down for a kiss. "Thank you. But you need to get the hell out of here and get ready for tonight."

He smirks. "Yes, ma'am." And then he's gone, a shadow in the night, like he was never here to begin with.

$$49$$

SLOANE

"How do I look?" I ask from the top of the stairs.

Julian, down at the base of them, turns and looks up at me. I do my best not to squirm under his analysis.

It's not that I'm opposed to the color black. I'm just opposed to the color black on me. But here I am, in a pair of black jeans, with a black shirt, and a black leather jacket, courtesy of Claudia.

Julian's wearing that expressionless expression again. But after a moment, he takes a deep breath, his nostrils flaring. "You look sexy as fuck. So sexy that, if we weren't on a very important mission, I'd have you bent over these stairs."

I blink at him. "Noted." I meet him at the bottom. When I get there, he wraps his hand in my hair, still down around my shoulders, and leans in to kiss me.

"I like you in your little pink dresses," he says against my mouth. My cheeks go warm at this, and he slaps me on the ass. "You ready?"

Under the cover of darkness, I can't see the look on Tyler's bruised face when we approach. He's standing in a group with his friends, or his minions. I'm not really sure who's who anymore.

I think he must see Julian first because he takes one big step back as we get closer. It's the most satisfying thing I've ever seen, watching him cower at the sight of Julian. But his eyes drop to me, and there's that anger again that I saw this afternoon.

"What the fuck are you doing here?" he snarls at me.

Julian reaches out to shake a guy's hand to Tyler's right. This must be the connection who set up the race. By the look on Tyler's face, he didn't know the two of them knew each other. He scowls at the other man.

"You're in my territory, Tyler," Julian says.

Tyler scoffs. "I'm not fucking racing you."

"Wow," I say, smiling up at Julian. "That was easy."

"The fuck do you mean?" Tyler demands.

I cock my head to the side. "Nothing," I say, trying to sound innocent. "Julian swore that you were too much of a coward to race him, but I thought you at least had the balls. And yet, here we are."

The fact that Tyler is so easy is almost comical. He's like a cartoon villain. His masculinity is constantly at peril in the most predictable way. You don't even have to work for it.

"Okay," he says to Julian over my shoulder. "Let's go! You want to put yourself up again?" he directs at me.

I cross my arms. "I didn't put myself up last time, Tyler, or maybe you forgot."

He shrugs. "You were already acting like a whore, so what

did it matter? You want to go around selling your body to the highest bidder? It's fine by me."

Julian is quiet behind me, carefully in control. We agreed that if Tyler did this, if he brought up the possibility of betting me in another race, we would do it. We knew that this is exactly what he would do, that he'd try to take me back. Julian didn't want to agree to the terms; he fought me all the way here, but in the end, he knew he didn't have the final say. Julian has to give me back the control that Tyler took away.

"Okay," I tell him, "if you win, I'll leave with you."

He narrows his eyes. "And if you win?"

"And if I win, I get the Audi."

He reacts exactly like I expected him to. His face scrunches in confusion. "The Audi? The fuck do you want with the Audi?"

A fast car that you would never let me drive. A car that's worth 120 grand.

I don't answer, just wait, face expressionless, the way I've learned from watching Julian.

He chews on the inside of his cheek for a second. I can see the hunger in his eyes. He wants revenge. Of course, he does. If he wins, he'll take me away from here. I don't think he'll try to rape me again. It's not about that anymore. It was before. But now he just wants to hurt Julian. I doubt he'll be checking for the gun I have strapped to me under my jacket. If he lays a finger on me, we'll find out how good my aim has gotten.

Tyler holds out a hand to me, and I shake it, bile rising in my throat at the feel of his skin on mine. "Get it set up," he says to Julian.

I wander back to Ronan's car, lean against it while he watches me from the driver's seat. "Are you ready to go?"

He smiles up at me, eyebrows wriggling. "Might surprise

you how nimble these fingers are. I can get a lot done really quickly."

"You better not hear your boss talk to me like that," I tease.

We hear engines on the road. While the cars are being put in place, the nerves start to ratchet up in my stomach. I wait until they look like they're done and head back over, my hands in the pockets of Claudia's jacket.

I deeply enjoy the moment when Tyler realizes I'm getting into the driver's seat of the Beast, not Julian. Because I can't help myself, I look over at him and give him a wink.

When Tyler first started participating in the races, I asked him a few times if I could drive. I learned how to drive a stick-shift at thirteen, having to regularly drive my mom home from the bars where she'd spend the evenings letting men buy her drinks. Tyler always said no. He wouldn't even let me drive to the supermarket. He was that kind of guy, the kind who thought if he let his girlfriend drive, it meant he was less of a man. Oh, to be so fragile.

I rev the engine, my hand on the gear shift, and watch in the glow of my headlights as a girl I don't recognize in a short skirt, even though it's getting colder by the minute, raises her hands above her head and lets them drop.

I slam on the gas pedal. I don't think Tyler has any clue what's going on under the hood of the Beast. There's no universe in which his cute little Audi could beat this car, and I'm going to make sure he knows it.

I pull out ahead of him and jerk back as I shift into second. The dirt road stretches out ahead of us in the dark. There's an S-curve at some point, something that'll throw both of us off our games. I keep my foot on the gas, let the needle rise and rise and rise.

Up ahead, I see the curve. It slants left and then a quick

right before going straight again. If you were going thirty miles an hour, it would be almost non-existent. But I'm sitting at 120, and it's going to be complicated. I can see Tyler in my rearview mirror. There's almost a whole car length between us, but I know the S-curve will slow me down. I downshift, start to turn left.

Tyler pulls left and goes wide on my outside into the grass to get around the curve to try and head me off, but when he pulls back onto the road, all he does is push me off of it. He's not ahead, but he's right beside me as my tires find the road again on the right-hand curve.

I take the turn too fast and my tires skitter. I feel it underneath me when the car gets purchase again. While Tyler is still trying to navigate the grass and the dirt, I slam the car into fifth gear and speed ahead.

All that work and he didn't come out ahead of me. All that work and he almost got us both killed.

He's in my blind spot now. I can hear the rev of his engine almost as loud as my own, trying to catch up with me. As we speed towards the people waiting further down the highway, they wave and cheer.

I don't want there to be any doubt, so at the last minute, I push the Beast to 140, pull ahead of Tyler, and slam left so that I'm driving directly in front him.

That's how we scream across the finish line.

Without even pausing, I pull left into the grass, go around the crowd of people, and pull back onto the road, going much slower this time but still fast enough that I feel like I'm flying.

Just like I thought he would, Tyler follows me in my rearview. He's not trying to overtake, but he's driving so close to my bumper that if I even tapped my brakes, he'd hit me. I speed up and he speeds up. I take the curve quickly and Tyler goes off into the grass to get in front of me, as if we're still racing.

He knows perfectly well he lost, but he's not going to pass up the opportunity to try and show me up.

When we get back to the start, the car isn't even at a full stop before Julian has the door open, his eyes roaming over my face. "You okay?"

"We need to move fast," I tell him and he nods. Someone else would have already told everyone down here that I won before we even made it back.

I walk around the Beast and meet Tyler in the middle of the road, our headlights still shining on us. Tyler holds out the key to the Audi. When I make a grab for it, he pulls it out of my reach, and I sigh. It's always imperative for him to act like a five-year-old. How is this the man commanding armies?

With his eyes on me, he dangles the key in front of Julian, who takes it. I make a split-second decision. The plan was to take the Audi and hope for the best, hope we could get what we needed before Tyler took off, but I think I can buy Ronan some time.

I turn to Julian. "Go," I whisper. He looks like he wants to protest, his mouth opening, but I just very subtly shake my head. "Go," I tell him again.

The door to the Audi stands open and Tyler watches Julian get in and take off with it, leaving me with the Beast.

"You said you wanted to talk this morning."

Tyler spins to face me, and I'm horrified by the hopeful look on his face. It has to be some kind of psychosis, the way he can go from beating me to acting like he loves me, the way he can do what he's done to me and think I'll still want him.

Maybe he thinks he *does* love me. Maybe he thinks this is love.

"I wanted to apologize."

"You're not sorry, and neither am I." His face is less

swollen than it was this morning, but one eye still refuses to open all the way. I wonder if it's infected.

Tyler's jaw clenches. He may be able to pretend to be soft for a moment, but the second things start to go wrong, he can't anymore. "You don't think I deserve to be a little angry?"

I cough a laugh. "Angry enough to try and rape me?"

He shakes his head and looks away from me like I've said something infuriating. "Come on, Sloane. That's not what that was. You can't rape a girl you've slept with a hundred times."

My dinner crawls up my throat.

"And besides, you cheated on me. You fucked another guy. *Two* other guys. How do you think that made me look? And you don't think I have a right to be mad?"

I take a step toward him, tip my chin up. "I'm not your girlfriend anymore, Tyler. Maybe you can heal your broken heart with one of those girls you've been fucking behind my back since we got here."

His eyes widen. He was so certain that he was going to be able to hide it all forever. He was so certain that I wouldn't ask any questions.

"Say what you like about Julian Shaw, at least he doesn't lie to me."

He snorts. "You think that guy isn't lying to you? You think he just likes to sell cool cars?"

I smile. It's almost impressive how he's deranged enough to think I still don't know what Julian and the guys are selling just because I never gave up the information to him. "Oh, I know he's not just selling cars."

His mouth falls open. "What do you have on him?"

I take a step back, hoping that by now, Ronan and Julian have what they need. "Everything. He's told me the truth of who he is and who you are, too." I look around at the people watching us. "Tell me, these races. Good place for dealing?" I can practically feel the rage coming off of his body in waves of heat. "Julian is going to end you. He's going to end all of this. And I'm going to sit back and watch it happen. I'm going to have a front-row seat."

50

JULIAN

The thing about drug labs is they tend to have shit security. This particular drug lab, hidden in the woods of Lebanon, New Hampshire, has two men with handguns at their front door. No back exit.

I'm not sure who masterminded this outfit, but the planning isn't there in any sense. There's no gate, no watchdogs, nothing.

Magnus has a hole in both the security guy's heads before they know what literally hits them. I walk up to the front door, attach the explosive to the beige metal, and step back. As soon as I'm out of the blast zone, Magnus detonates it. I watch as the door explodes, black smoke billowing out into the open autumn air.

The people that start filing out, workers, all of them, are too panicked by the smoke to notice the dead bodies, to bother with checking before they run out into the sun. Each one of them is picked off quickly.

The leader is easy to identify. He doesn't come out

coughing and sputtering. He comes out with an automatic rifle tucked under his arm, his eyes scanning. He's the only one who understands what's going on. He spots me immediately.

Before he can lift his gun, Magnus puts a bullet in his thigh. The man shouts and drops his gun. I march over to him, his blood a bright streak across the white gravel that the building sits on.

I don't have much time. Someone will see the smoke, call the police. If the police don't get to us first, whatever chemicals are burning inside that lab will. I motion to the men in the trees with two fingers.

Magnus, Hugo, and Bram. Their job is to assess the lab. Mine is to take care of this fucker.

I know him. His face is recognizable. Pale, ruddy skin, blue eyes, a scar down the side of his face that bisects the upside-down cross tattooed beside his right eye.

"Benedikt Boleslav," I say, kicking his gun out of the way so I can stand in front of him and put mine against his head.

He raises an arm like he's going to try and grab me. I lower my gun quick, the barrel of it meeting his palm, and shoot. His hand explodes, blood and bone and gore.

He screams, sweat running down his temples as I put my gun back to his head. "What has it been now?" I ask him. "Three years? Four?"

As soon as I saw his face, I remembered the man I met in a bar the day after my father's funeral. He heard that my dad was gone, and Leo, being the addict he was, set up a meeting I didn't know about. Benedikt wanted us to get into the drug business, and so did Leo.

"I seem to recall telling you to fuck off," I say to the screaming, quivering mass kneeling before me, clutching his destroyed hand. "I told you not to bring drugs into my town, and you fucking did it anyway."

He shakes his head. "I didn't know. I didn't know he was taking it back to your turf until it was too late."

"Too late?" I ask him, shoving the barrel deeper into his dark hair. "It's never too late for extermination. You should have taken care of your business. But now, you're my business."

I can't put a bullet in Tyler's head, but Benedikt's army is non-existent. He's not a gangster, he's a chemist. Just like me, he was never a fan of making people eat ammunition. There are rules though, boundaries, lines that he knew better than to cross. He got in bed with the wrong person.

"You have a wife, don't you?" I ask him

"Please," he sobs.

I'm not going to touch his wife, but he doesn't know that. He knows he's about to die, so I need to give him a reason to give me what I want.

"Where are the videos he was sending you?"

His red, teary eyes shift to me. "I don't have them."

"Yes, you do. Unless you want me to go see if your wife has them..."

He whimpers.

"You want to tell me where they are?"

"There's a safe," he says, his voice desperate. "It's not even locked. There's a hard drive."

"I'll find it. And just know, if what I need isn't on that drive, I will come for your wife."

"Please, no," he says.

"What were you thinking, Benedikt? That if I came for you, you could call on Tyler's army? Tyler's army doesn't belong to you; it belongs to him. Count yourself lucky that I got to you before they did." I pull the trigger.

The guys come out of the building hacking.

"It's exactly what we thought," Bram says, gasping beside me. "Coke, heroin, designer drugs, even some pot out back."

"Gotta cast a wide net," I say. "There's a drive in the safe." Bram starts to turn, but I stop him. "I'll get it."

"Julian—"

"No sign of meth?" I ask. He shakes his head. If there had been, the whole place would have blown. "Get to the car, I'll be back."

"Eyes up," he says. "There could still be someone hanging around."

I heed his warning as I move inside the building. The smoke has covered everything in a haze, but I can make out the long tables, the workstations, pills and powders.

It's a walk-in safe, some old school thing they must have inherited. There's plenty of money inside. Stacks of it. But that's not what I'm here for. I shove some of it into my pockets so the guys can get paid a little extra for their hard work and then keep moving.

In the corner, there's a shelf of electronics. Laptops, phones, walkie talkies, all kinds of shit. On top of a laptop, hooked up to wires lights flashing, there's an external hard drive. Hope it's the right one. Who knows what kind of shit is on these devices: evidence, data, or something much worse.

I have one more bomb in my gloved hand. I set it in the middle of the room, shoving the drive into my coat pocket. I slam the safe closed and detonate the bomb.

"Not all girls like flowers," I hear Sloane say out in the hallway.

"Well, do *you* like flowers?" Ronny asks, tentative.

"They can be nice under the right circumstances."

Noted, princess.

"Well, what are the circumstances if we've fucked a million times, but now I kind of want to date her?"

I drown them out and turn back to Ronan at his desk, bending down to see what's on the screen. "It's all here, boss," he says, scrolling through hours of footage.

"It must have really cracked Tyler's nuts that Benedikt was demanding this from him."

Ronan spins in his chair to face me. "He knew he wasn't in control. If we learned anything about that little fuck-face, it's that control is the only thing he wants."

I shake my head. "He hasn't earned it." I pat Ronan on the shoulder. "Thank you."

"What are you going to do with it?"

I shrug. "I'm going to spread the word. Tyler has an ulterior motive. That's a fuck ton of blackmail material. If no one else takes him out first, all we have to do is wait for everyone to decide they're done with him. Once he doesn't have a human wall to stand behind, we'll take him out ourselves."

The corner of Ronan's mouth turns up and his eyes slip past me.

Sloane is a sexy silhouette in the doorway. Her eyes go to the computer and back to me. "You got it?" she asks.

"We got it."

$$51$$

SLOANE

"Alright, now we just need to flush it. Go ahead and slide out."

I do what Julian says, sitting up on the creeper. I set my elbows on my knees, my hands out in front of me, and just sit there. When I don't move, Julian laughs and pulls my gloves off for me. We've been working on this Mercedes for hours. We're the only two left in the garage, as it's almost dinnertime, and the guys wanted to go in and shower.

"So, was your dad a mechanic?" Julian asks, not looking at me as he slides a drip pan under the car and opens the brake line.

I shrug. "Sort of. He worked a lot of part-time jobs, and he fixed cars on the weekends, mostly for other people living in the trailer park. It was something he was pretty good at, too. I don't know. He could be a mechanic now, for all I know. Maybe he owns his own garage somewhere."

Julian straightens. He's sitting on an empty plastic tub. He looks more delicious than ever, in a black Henley, the sleeves rolled up and grease smeared on his lower arms. He leans back against the car's bumper. "How old were you when he left?"

"Twelve. I always thought it was weird. It was his trailer. His money went into it. I'm not sure why he left it behind. He could have made us get out instead. One final act of generosity, I suppose."

He nods, tipping his face toward me, the light catching on the diamond stud in his ear. His eyes scan over my face, like he's trying to read me. There's nothing to read. I haven't felt anything for my father in almost a decade. He gave up on us, and even though my mother wasn't always the most attentive parent, at least she was there, trying to provide for me.

"My mom left, too," Julian says. "When I was just a kid. I never could bring myself to blame her. My dad was a ruthless man. I don't know if he was once kind or if she was with him because of the money or because she got pregnant with me. My father and I never discussed it. His business was his and mine was mine."

I hook my elbows over my knees. "That's awful. You deserved to know about her."

He shrugs. "She was gone. That's all my dad cared about. He had an empire to run. He did tell me about starting the organization though. *That* was my business, he felt. He was the CEO of some bullshit company in the city, and I guess he thought he'd rather steal from the rich than be amongst them. He started with embezzlement and then moved into insider training, then eventually landed on money laundering and..." He gestures around the garage. "... all this."

"Wait, so all this money comes from his previous thievery?" It's not like I thought they bought the mansion only selling cars, but I had no idea it went back that far or was so steeped in corporate crime.

Julian smiles. "Don't go developing a conscience on me now."

I roll my eyes. I guess he has a point. What he's doing is illegal, and the law is the law. What does it matter if it's guns or stocks?

"I think he would have liked you." His dark eyes hold mine. "He was a callous man, and he would have hated that I let a woman become a distraction, but...he would have thought you were funny and interesting...because you are."

I clamp my hands together. "Thanks. I think."

He puffs out a breath between his lips and leans forward quick, pulling at the band in my hair. "You're done under the car. Get this down." My hair falls around my shoulders, and he uses his fingers to brush it out, to position it around me like he's getting me ready for a photoshoot. "I've been thinking..."

Ah, there it is. He's refusing to meet my eye, still focused on my hair, like he can hide behind it.

"I think you should move your stuff into my room."

I take hold of his wrists, make him stop messing with my hair so he can look at me. And he does, hands falling into his lap. "You sure?" I ask. There's no doubt in my mind that I would rather be bunking with him and Winston than sleeping in that room upstairs alone. Although, I haven't really been sleeping alone, as of late.

Julian nods slowly. "You're a disgrace to everything I've tried to build, Sloane Moretti, and I would really appreciate it if you never left."

My stomach clenches, and I throw myself into his lap, mouth crashing down onto his, tasting all the desperation and vulnerability he tries so hard to hide on his lips.

52

JULIAN

I shut the door to Sloane's room and lean against it with a sigh. When I find her stuffing things into her suitcase, relief washes over me.

She's moving to my bedroom, straight into my clutches.

"How did it go?" she asks, coming over and taking my face in her hands in that gentle way she does. That gentle way I don't deserve, especially after a day like today.

"It's complicated," I tell her, wrapping my hands around her wrists and pulling them down to my chest. I've spent the last several days contacting everyone who made an appearance in any of Tyler's videos.

Dismantle, dismantle, dismantle.

"We should expect retaliation now that it's done," I tell her. "He'll start to realize soon that no one wants to work with him anymore. Probably already has a target on his forehead."

Her eyes search mine. "He definitely already knows. He hasn't been in class in days. Dealing with all the people you plotted to betray can be time-consuming." She starts to turn away from me.

"Where the fuck do you think you're going?" I say, holding onto one of her wrists and dragging her back to me. She giggles when our bodies collide and I bend down to kiss her.

Then someone has the audacity to knock on the fucking door.

"We're busy!" I growl, fisting my hand in Sloan's hair and tipping her head back so I can kiss her neck.

"Boss, it's Ryan."

There are few things that could have kept me from ignoring Magnus and taking Sloane over to the bed instead. This is one of them. I pull away from her and she looks up at me with worried eyes.

"Ryan, the guy at the warehouse?" she asks.

I move out of the way of the door so I can open it. "What did he say?" I ask Magnus.

"Cops."

And like he summoned them with that one word, there's a knock at the door downstairs. The gate stays open during the day as so many of the men are coming and going. If someone's knocking, it can only be someone who isn't welcome. I turn back to Sloane. "Stay here," I tell her.

"Are you serious?" she asks.

I ignore her, turning and going down the stairs. I'm shocked when I look back up to find that she's actually listened to me and stayed put, her hands gripping the railing of the balcony that overlooks the foyer.

The shapes of the officers are obvious through the frosted glass of the front door. Two of them, one taller, one shorter. Magnus and I get there just as they knock again.

"Police," they say through the door, as if it wasn't obvious.

Magnus reaches out to open the door, but I put up a hand to stop him, opening it myself.

"Good afternoon, officers," I tell them with a kind smile, even though in the back of my head, I have a lot of choice words for a police department that would take bribes from a rich college boy dealing drugs.

I scan both of their faces, two women. The first thing Ronan and I did when we got those videos was watch every single one to find familiar faces. Not only did Tyler record everyone he did deals with, but he also recorded the cops he bought.

Neither one of these women were in Tyler's videos.

"Are you Julian Shaw?" the shorter woman asks.

"Yes," I say simply.

The other one nods and steps forward, reaching for something on her belt. "You're under arrest."

"Excuse me?"

I hear Sloane coming down the stairs before her voice rings out in the foyer. "Julian!"

I don't fight as the officer turns me around and handcuffs me while I'm staring into the house, watching as my men start to file into the foyer to see what's happening.

Bram steps forward. "There must be a mistake," he says, as if I'm some kind of innocent party, just a law-abiding citizen.

"It's okay," I tell him as they affix the handcuffs around my wrists.

"It's not okay," Sloane says, stopping next to Bram. "What is he under arrest for?"

"I'm afraid we can't discuss that with you, ma'am," the shorter officer says.

Sloane's eyes meet mine, wet with worry. They start to pull me away, and she takes a step forward, like she's going to grab onto me and not let me go. I hold her eye until they spin me around and force me down the steps.

They put me in the back of the car, and Sloane's distraught face, her cheeks pink, her eyes watery, is the last thing I see before they drive me away.

"Tell me, Mr. Shaw, what are you using the warehouse for?"

The detective across the table from me is very professional. She has her hair pulled back, wearing a jacket because it's cold even inside the police precinct. She has a file in her hands. She laces her fingers on top of it on the table.

"We sell cars," I tell her. "We use the warehouse to store and work on some of them."

"And the safes?" she asks.

And that's how I know we got lucky. There were men working on a car today, but when Ryan saw the cops descending, he must have had enough time to warn them to load up and lock the safes.

"Why do you need to know what's in the safes?" my lawyer, Graves, asks. It's a stretch to call him my lawyer, I suppose. He was my father's lawyer, but we've kept him on payroll even though we don't generally need him.

Detective Coates puts her hands palms-down on the table, fingers spread. "It's very simple. We're investigating a missing persons case, and Mr. Shaw is a suspect."

"Based on what evidence?"

This has Detective Coates sighing. Not so much exasperation as defeat. "Based on an anonymous tip."

"An anonymous tip?" Graves scoffs. "I'm sorry. That's what we're calling evidence now?"

"An anonymous tip helped catch Ted Bundy," Detective Coates says.

"I'm not a serial killer." I chime in. Graves puts a hand on my arm, telling me to shut up.

"He doesn't have to open any safes for you without a warrant."

Her eyes shoot back to him, sharp as daggers. "We've already searched the grounds."

"And what did you find?"

She clenches her mouth shut and looks back to me. She didn't find anything. I didn't bury the guy on our property. I disposed of him far from the warehouse and the compound, out in the mountainside. But I guess Tyler thinks I just keep bodies around where they can be discovered. I guess he thought the warehouse was hidden enough. It's not hidden anymore.

"Just because we didn't find a body doesn't mean you aren't still responsible."

"That's fine," Graves says. "Even though my client is innocent, obviously, we'll be happy to talk to you again when you have some actual goddamn evidence."

She narrows her eyes at him. "Don't take that tone with me, Graves."

Ah, so they know each other.

"I'll take whatever tone I want when you're arresting perfectly good men in their own homes based on nothing."

I want to tell Graves that maybe he shouldn't exaggerate so much, but I keep quiet.

"Based on nothing?" Detective Coates says. She leans back in her seat. "You have quite the reputation, Mr Shaw. This is not based on nothing."

"A reputation is not a record," Graves says.

She nods like she agrees. "I'll ask one more time, Mr Shaw, what is the warehouse for?"

This time, Graves stays quiet, letting me answer. "It's for working on cars."

"Why do you need four safes taller than me?"

I shrug. I don't have to answer her. Without a warrant, they can't get into those safes.

Graves leans forward, steeples his hands on the table between us. "You may have been able to search the grounds unlawfully because you thought there was a body. But now that there isn't one, you're going to need a warrant."

They stare each other down for a moment. It would be amusing if not for the circumstances.

"You know you won't get one," he goes on. "Because you don't have any substantial evidence. You have no reason to suspect my client. And therefore, we are leaving."

We start to stand but her voice stops us. "And what about Benedikt Boleslav?"

I raise an eyebrow at her. "Who?"

"Benedikt Boleslav," she says more aggressively. "He was found dead on a property twenty miles from here three days ago, the house he was living in burned to the ground and half a dozen men killed around him. We found drugs. We found money."

"Sounds like he was into some bad shit." I keep my voice light.

"So your official statement is that you didn't have anything to do with that?"

"I didn't know the guy," I tell her before Graves steps in.

He grabs his briefcase from where it sits on the table. "So you're arresting him for one missing person but now you're bringing up somebody else that has nothing to do with him or this case?"

"Maybe if I dig a little deeper..." she says.

I stand, surprised when she stays seated. "I'm going to dig

a little deeper too, detective. Tell me, do you know Tyler Kent?"

Her eyes go wide. Beside me, Graves makes a humming noise in the back of his throat.

I lean across the table toward her. "Detective Coates, I know you're too much of an upstanding citizen to take bribes from a drug dealer, but I also know that there are people in this building who aren't. And you know it too or you wouldn't be looking at me like you swallowed a wasp. You make my life miserable, I turn your precinct inside out. Sound good?"

Her lips clamp together again. It's a satisfying expression, at least for me.

"Hmm. Good luck with your warrant, Detective Coates." I keep my eyes on hers as we walk out of the room.

"Who's this guy you're talking about?" Graves asks me as we walk to his car.

"Just a cockroach I'm trying to crush. You mind giving me a lift?"

53

SLOANE

"Breathe, Blondie," Magnus says as I drum my fingers on the dining room table.

"Shut up," I hiss at him. "Has this ever happened before?"

He shakes his head. "Not while I've been here."

I shut my mouth, leaning back away from him. Bram is sitting across the table. We're the only three left standing. It's been two hours since they took Julian away. According to reports from Ryan, the cops came in, searched the warehouse, and left. They demanded that the men open the safes, but none of them did.

I'm just about to ask Bram what our next steps are when we hear the front door open. I'm the first out of my seat, running toward the foyer.

Julian comes in, looking exhausted, his face pale.

"Oh my God." I throw my arms around him. "Oh my God, what happened?"

He squeezes me back tight once and lets me go, keeping a

hand on my hip. "All the men here now," he barks at Bram, who nods and leaves.

"What's going on?" I ask him. He looks angry. I can't imagine what's going on in his head right now, but I want to know every detail of what happened at that police station. I get the feeling he's not going to give them to me, at least, not right now.

He puts his hand on the back of my neck, skin to skin, and I can't tell if he's trying to reassure himself or me as we wait for the man to file in. Once the foyer is full, Julian takes his hand off of me.

"The warehouse needs to be stripped," he says. "Everything comes back to the compound until we can find a new place."

"What happened?" Ronny asks.

Julian waits a beat, his jaw clenched. "We have a rat in our midst."

The men look around at each other, eye suspicious, analyzing.

"Only the people in this room know the location of the warehouse, but somehow the cops got the address."

"Tyler," I say.

Julian just said earlier that we should be prepared for retribution. Well, here it is.

"Yes," Julian says, not looking over at me. "But how did Tyler know?" His gaze travels around the room, emotionless, stopping on each man individually. "We don't keep the address anywhere. We don't tell anybody. That information has never left this property."

Ronny, standing at the front of the group with his arms crossed, shouts, "Fucking hell. So you're saying one of us went to Tyler?" When he says this, there's heartbreak in his voice. It's surprisingly vulnerable.

"If it was an accident, there will be punishment, but we can move past it. And if it wasn't..."

No one says a word.

"Everyone's room will searched. Everyone's car will be stripped. And business is shut down until further notice."

"Isn't it obvious?" a voice comes from the back of the room, and like the Red Sea, the men split, turning to look at Frankie, leaning against the wall.

"Do you have something to say?" Julian asks.

"It's obvious who did this," Frankie says, pushing himself off the wall and walking toward the center of the room. "Everyone knows you took her out there."

His words are like a bucket of ice water over my head. "What, you mean me?"

Julian shushes me.

"It's in the logs," Frankie says. "We all know you took her out there the night of the party."

"She's one of us. She should know where it is, just like everyone else does."

"Yeah, and a week later, her ex-boyfriend is there." Frankie's face is red, veins popping out of his neck, while everyone watches him like an animal in an exhibit. "You can't honestly tell me you're this blind, boss."

I wait for Julian to put Frankie in his place, to defend me like he always does.

But instead, he turns to me, and the look in his eyes makes my skin burn.

Suspicion.

$$54$$

SLOANE

Pain crawls up my throat and chokes me as I say, "Julian, I didn't. I swear. You know I would never."

He doesn't say anything. The room is silent as the grave as he watches me, his dark eyes steady.

"Julian," I whisper. I hate that it comes out like a plea.

He looks away from me, up at someone I can't see because my eyes are on the floor. "Ronan, search her phone. She doesn't leave the compound until I say so."

I'm embarrassed by the sound that bursts out of me, a painful sound I can't swallow back. I can't bring myself to look up at anyone, to see the looks on their faces as Julian humiliates me in front of them, as he turns me back into someone that can't be trusted.

Bile rises up in my throat when Ronan steps in front of me. He holds out his hand. I take my phone from my pocket and set it in his palm.

"I'm sorry," he whispers, but I just shake my head, never looking him in the eye.

I turn and run up the stairs, feeling like a child when I slam the door behind me. I have to stuff my hands against my mouth to muffle the scream that comes out of me. When I pull my hand away, it's covered in hot tears.

After everything. After *everything*, he still doesn't trust me. He still thinks I would go back to Tyler after what he did to me. After everything that's happened between *us*.

I thought I was home, but I'm right back where I started.

JULIAN

She's packing her things. But she's not packing to move in with me anymore. She's packing to leave. I watch her on the camera, watch the angry jerking movements with which she shoves things back into her suitcase. She picks up the stack of books she took from Dad's library and sets them on the desk, shoving them away from her, like it's their fault we're in this position.

"You're an idiot, Julian."

I don't look up at Bram. He's the only one I would let talk to me like this. He can spout off at the mouth if he wants to, but the facts are all there. Tyler didn't know where the warehouse was until now, and what Frankie said makes sense. Days after I took Sloane out there, Tyler led the cops right to it. *No one* knows about the warehouse but us. It's a rule as solid as a brick wall.

Two hands slam down onto the desk in front of me. "Wake up, Julian!"

I glare up at Bram, his dark hair, normally slicked back,

falling into his face. "What do you want from me? I'm trying to protect my men."

Bram snorts and straightens, standing to his full height. "Give me a break, Julian. You're trying to protect yourself. You don't like that a girl came in here and turned your world upside down."

"Do you really think I would let my personal feelings dictate something like this? I'm trying to be sensible here."

"You're trying to be heartless." He turns away from me, walking over to the bar and pouring himself a drink.

"As much as you might hate it, what Frankie said makes sense. Sloane has been a double agent from the beginning. Is it really so impossible to you that she might still be one?"

"For what?" He takes a long pull of his drink. "For Tyler? For a man who abuses her? I saw her with him yesterday. You can't fake that kind of disgust."

"So maybe she was doing it for the cops or for someone else entirely that we don't know about."

He coughs. "Keep trying to justify the mess you've made. You're not going to convince me. That girl up there trusted you, and you destroyed her."

"I've had enough." I slam my fist down the desk. "If you don't like the way I do things, you can get the fuck out. This is why Dad put me in charge and not you."

"You're right," he says, throwing back the rest of his drink with a grimace. "You're right. This is why he gave it to you. Because I'm not willing to be a heartless bastard."

"I'm not heartless."

All I can hear in my head over and over again is, *It has to be true, it has to be true, it has to be true.*

Because why else would she be doing any of this? Why would she be here working for me, living with me, if not to get something from me? She was doing it to Tyler. She was staying with him even through it all. First for money, success, a future, and then to take him down. Why couldn't she do it again?

Maybe someone else made her a better offer than I did.

But if it's true... I've lost the last piece of humanity I had left. It's gone. It's over. I have nothing left. Maybe I am a heartless bastard because I'm fucking numb watching Bram pace my office.

I've been running through it all in my head while we wait for Ronan. If she did tell him, it would have had to have been on the phone. There would be a trace of it.

Bram sets his empty glass down on my desk. He turns for the door like he's going to storm out, but when he opens it, Ronan is waiting on the other side, his hood pulled up over his head like it always is. His eyes go to Bram first and then find me beyond him.

I am an empty tomb. There's nothing inside me but the echoes of what used to be a heartbeat.

"Tell me," I say.

"I should come in." Bram steps back and Ronan shuts the door behind himself. "Her phone was clean."

I should feel relief. This clenching in my chest should give way. But instead, dread threatens to drown me. What's worse, her betraying us all, or me accusing her of betrayal when she was loyal the whole time?

I crushed her. I turned on her. I suspected her when I didn't deserve her to begin with.

I clear my throat. "There's a chance she could have told him without using the phone."

"Stop this," Bram says.

"That's not all," Ronan says.

"What else?"

He sighs, clenches his fists. He seems to be trying to steady himself. "When I didn't find anything on her phone, I went through everyone's."

"All of them?"

He shrugs. "The software makes it easy when everyone's in the compound at the same time. I didn't have to look very far."

"What's that supposed to mean?"

His eyes scan over to Bram, and they seem to have a silent conversation before Ronan turns back to me. "Frankie."

I do my best not to react, not to show my shock. Maybe my lack of shock. I don't even know anymore. "What about Frankie?"

"He sent the address of the warehouse yesterday to an unsaved number."

The silence that descends on the room is deafening, pressing in against my eardrums until I feel like they might burst.

"For what it's worth," Ronan goes on, "he also sent the video. The one from the party. To Tyler."

"What else?" I ask.

"They've been talking for months, it seems. Mostly Tyler trying to convince Frankie to give him information, and Frankie refusing."

"Barbara?" I ask.

Ronan nods. "He got paid for that one. He didn't think it would be that big a deal. He didn't care about Barbara. He figured she was just collateral damage. It's all in the texts. Tyler tried to delete them, but it's not that simple."

Sloane cried in my arms for that *collateral damage*. Cried in my arms because Frankie wanted money. More than what he already makes for me.

"So he was working for Tyler." I try to keep my voice steady. Professional. I need to get through this conversation. Assess the damage.

Ronan shakes his head. "Not exactly. He wouldn't give

him much. Tyler kept asking him what we were putting in the cars, but Frankie wouldn't tell him."

"Why not?" Bram asks. "He was going to betray us either way. Why not just tell him?"

Ronan shrugs. "He knew Tyler wanted to take down the business. He wasn't ready to lose his income yet. He probably didn't trust Tyler to keep him on if he took over the business."

I can't help but laugh. A sardonic, empty thing. "Of course, Tyler wasn't going to keep him on. As soon as he got what he wanted, he would have put a bullet in Frankie's head. No one would put up with that fucker if they didn't have to."

I expect Ronan to laugh but he doesn't. He just watches me with sad eyes. Because he's been betrayed by his brother. Because he knows what will happen to Frankie now.

"So what about the video?" Bram asks. "What was his motivation there?"

Rage pumps through my body at the idea of it. He sent that video to Tyler, and Tyler went ballistic on Sloane for it. He almost raped her because of Frankie.

"Frankie really hates Sloane," Ronan says. "He knew what would happen. He detonated a bomb hoping that she would catch the strays."

"And then the warehouse," I say, baring controlling my anger.

"He's had enough," Bram says, reading my mind. I can see the anger in his eyes, too. "He decided to just end it all. What do we do now?" He already knows the answer to that question.

"Get Magnus," I tell Ronan, pushing my chair back. "Tell him to get Frankie and toss him in the cage and to wait until I come for him."

"Where are you going?" Bram asks.

"I have business to take care of."

●55

SLOANE

I eventually decide to take a shower, not because I need one, but because it's the only place I can go where they can't watch me. It's either that, or sit on the floor in my closet. Maybe I'll drag the blankets in there, sleep in there tonight.

I don't know how long I'll have to wait for them to decide my fate. They're not going to find anything on my phone, but that doesn't necessarily mean they'll trust me when this is all over. They'll see that I didn't make any phone calls to Tyler, or to anyone that doesn't live in the compound, but maybe they'll think I whispered secrets into his ear while we were in class.

Will they think that, despite everything Tyler has done, I want to go back to him? Or that it was all a show? Will they convince themselves that I did it all for money? That I didn't care about anyone, as long as I got what I wanted, my ticket to Dartmouth?

I turn the shower up as hot as I can stand and get in. I suffocate under the steam. Now that I'm away from prying eyes, I start to cry. I feel stupid for crying, because I should be angry. I should be angry at Julian for believing any of it, for not believing in me. We made it this far, and I thought we finally understood each other. I trusted him and he trusted me, and that was all we needed.

But it was a lie. Like a dog that falls asleep but still has one ear listening for threats. I trusted him with everything I have and everything I am, but he was still waiting for the proof that I was going to turn on him. I should have known.

I know I should be angry, but all I feel is the emptiness. I feel like I found my someone just to have them taken away, just like that, in seconds. Because of fucking Tyler... again. A man who shouldn't have so much power over me but somehow does.

I cry until I'm gasping for air. I set my forehead against the hot tile, touch the slick surface of it under my fingertips.

I gasp when the bathroom door opens. I spin away from the intruder, trying to cover up, when I hear the unmistakable pattern of Julian's shoes on the tile.

"What are you doing?" I shout. I don't know if he can even see me behind all the steam, but it doesn't matter. It's the principle of the thing. I don't want to be naked in the same room as him right now.

"I need to talk to you," he says, his voice echoing through the room.

"I don't want to talk to you. Get out."

"It's my house, my bathroom."

He's not going to leave. I don't even know why he's here. I keep my arms crossed over myself, like I can create some kind of shield, a barrier. So he can stop hurting me. So I can make myself not so easy to hurt.

"What do you want?" I ask the tile wall.

There's a long silence. When I look over my shoulder, I'm shocked to find that he's undressing.

"What are you doing?" I shriek.

He ignores me, and I feel a panic in my blood. He can't come in here, because if he comes in here, I'll be too helpless, too vulnerable. I won't be able to bring myself to push him away. He can't do this to me.

"I'm sorry," he says.

My thoughts go quiet. "What?"

He opens the glass door between us, stands in front of me in all his glory. I keep my back to him, looking over my shoulder. "I said, I'm sorry. Forgive me, Sloane, for not trusting you."

In a way, it's exactly what I want to hear, but I have to hold my ground. "It's not enough," I say, turning my face away. "It's not good enough. You don't just get to do what you did to me and then apologize."

"I know," he says. I hear him step into the shower behind me, his feet padding softly in the pools of water. He shuts the door, shuts us in.

There's a riot of emotions inside me, anger and fear and sadness, but also a desperate need to have his arms around me again. I don't want to want that.

"I'm sorry," he says again. "I'm so sorry." His hands come up to my shoulders, and then into my hair, pushing it aside before his mouth finds the skin of my neck.

I spin around, finally letting my arms drop because what does it even matter? "Who cares if you're sorry? You believed it so easily. And even if you changed your mind and you think I didn't betray you, what happens a week from now or a month or a year? When something else comes up, are you going to question me again?"

His eyes are sad, and that makes me even more mad because he has no idea how sad he made me. "I know I can't be perfect for you."

"I never wanted you to be perfect. Do you know why I do

all of this, Julian?" I gesture to myself. "The hair and the makeup and the dresses and all of it?"

He watches me quietly, silently.

"I do it because I noticed when I was younger that girls who did that, who spent hours in front of the mirror and picked out the right outfits and did all the right things, they got attention."

He grimaces but I can't quite figure out why.

"I realized that even though my mother ignored me and my father left, even though no one else paid attention to me because I was poor, that if I just dressed the way they wanted me to, acted the way they wanted me to, people would look at me. So I stole makeup and I stole clothes and I made myself look pretty because I didn't want to be invisible anymore."

I take a deep breath, feel stupid for ranting at him like this. I don't even know why I am. I just need him to hear it. Need *someone* to hear it.

"I just thought you dressed that way because you wanted to."

"I *do* want to," I say, practically shouting. "I do want to dress this way. I like it. That's why I keep doing it, even though no one sees me the way I want them to. Because everyone was looking at me and everyone was giving me attention but no one could *see* me." I pause, breathless. "I thought you saw me, Julian. I thought you *saw* me."

"I do, baby." He steps closer to me, his hands finding my shoulders, my neck, my jaw, until he's tilting my face up to look at him. "I see you. But you see me, too."

I shake my head. "I don't understand."

His eyes take in my face. "I just can't fathom how you can see me the way I see you and still want to stay. How you can still want me."

A sob rises in my throat, and my hands grab at him, his

chest, his face, his hair. "You really think you're so impossible to love?"

His eyes widen, and there's one tremble of his chin before he schools his features, puts back on his mask. "You don't know what I'm capable of. You don't know what I've done."

"I don't care. I thought I made it clear. I'm here. I'm in. I'm with you. Even if you do bad things." I grip his hair, pull his forehead down to mine. "If you want to be bad, be bad. Just let me be bad with you. For you and only you."

He lunges, his mouth crashing against mine, wet skin and wet mouth slipping against me.

I fist his hair tighter, make him feel my anger, pulling his face away from mine. "Don't you ever fucking doubt me again, Julian Shaw."

He shakes his head. "Never." He pushes me hard against the wall at my back, hands going everywhere, finally settling between my legs. I moan into his mouth, desperate with need for him.

The whole day has felt like an earthquake, causing a rift that got wider and wider between us. Now, I need to be as close to him as I can get. I need to erase the last few hours.

"Inside me. Now," I whisper.

He doesn't hesitate. He bends and scoops me up, wrapping my legs around him. He holds me against the wall, hand pressed to the tile over my head, and lets me slowly sink down onto him.

When I'm full of him, we pant together, mouths open, and part of me thinks I could just stay like this, with him inside me, not moving, not letting go.

I lean my head back and close my eyes, holding in everything that wants to burst out of me. I can't do this now. I'm still too wounded to make myself that vulnerable.

He lifts and lowers me, and a high-pitched cry explodes out of me. He makes me feel everything I didn't know I could feel. He makes me feel steady and wanted and like everything I thought about the world was wrong. Because this is it, the whole world, right here in his arms.

He presses his mouth to my chest, sucks at my skin. "You feel so good," he says, his voice soft, breathless from moving me on him. "I love making you come." He leans back enough to take my breasts in his hands, his thumbs moving over my nipples. "Your body was made for me."

I whimper, the muscles between my legs tightening around him.

"Yes," he says into my neck. "Yes, just like that. Let me feel it." His hand dips, finding my clit. His fingers push me higher but the tension in my body won't let me go over the edge. There are too many emotions racketing through my body, too much distraction.

"Give it to me," he says in my ear. His fingers move faster, and my nails dig into his shoulders. His hips pick up speed at the same time as his finger leaves my clit.

I feel raw, too sensitive, close to tears as I hold onto him, as I try to force him to never hurt me again, to never leave me.

"You're holding back."

"I'm not," I say, the words coming out a whine.

"You are," he growls back. "Give me what I fucking need." As soon as the words are out of his mouth, I feel his hand on my ass, creeping up, until one finger finds my hole and presses in.

A sharp cry bursts from me when Julian tugs my hips forward, so that each forward plunge presses his pelvis against my clit. He latches his mouth onto my nipple. All the sensations together shove me over the edge hard, my vision going black. His finger presses deeper, prolonging the orgasm until I'm gasping for breath.

Julian spills inside me, setting his forehead on my shoulder as he pants.

Afterwards, he lowers me to the floor, my legs trembling, and I turn towards the water. "How did you know I didn't do it?" I ask him. He's quiet for a long time until I look at him over my shoulder.

"Frankie."

I piece together this information, everything I know about the organization, about Frankie, about Tyler, about the timing of each individual thing. It makes perfect, unfortunate sense.

"I'm sorry," I say. Because I know that if it was hard for him knowing that I could have betrayed him, someone he's only known for a few weeks, that it must be so much harder to know that someone he's trusted for years has done it.

"He was my dad's recruit," Julian says, picking up my bottle of shampoo and pouring some into his hand before lathering it into my hair absentmindedly, like he just needs his hands to be moving. "He's always hated me, but I was his meal ticket so he knew he couldn't walk away."

"Is walking away even an option?" I think about those mafia movies where the only way out is a body bag.

"Sure. We've had a few men come and go. A few who wanted to start a family, who wanted normal lives. Some who just didn't want to live this life anymore. I would never force anyone to stay."

"So what happens if they get caught selling secrets?"

"None of them ever have." He turns me toward him, tilts my head back just enough to let him wash the shampoo out. "Frankie he could have left. But honestly, he's too stupid. He doesn't have marketable skills. He doesn't have anything to offer anyone else. I guess he just had enough."

"Because of me," I say. He doesn't have to tell me. I've

seen it. The tension between the two of them just because I was here, just because I existed.

"It doesn't matter. He's always been angry that I was on top." He sets his hands on my shoulders, rubs circles into my muscles. "I think he was trying to figure out how to take me out on his own. But when he figured out he couldn't, he probably turned to Tyler. He has to know that Tyler will just take my place and put him in his. No matter what, he doesn't come out on top."

"What did you do with him?" I whisper.

"Nothing yet. He's down in the cage, but it's time to take care of it."

56

My hair is still wet, my stomach in knots, as we walk down the stairs, my hand in his. The men watch us with confusion in their eyes. They've all been summoned from their beds, from their homes, their offices. They're looking at each other curiously, looking down at where Julian's hand is connected with mine. Because just hours ago, he was having me locked away.

"What's going on, boss?" Hugo asks, his eyes blurry with exhaustion.

Julian doesn't answer. He doesn't have to. Because a moment later, there's a commotion somewhere beyond the dining room, the sounds of shouting and banging.

Magnus drags Frankie into the room by his hair, screaming, struggling, the men watching in horror.

I'm as far away from them as I can get, standing by the front door, but I can see from here that Frankie is sweaty, his hair stuck to his face, can hear the sound of his flesh hit the ground when Magnus tosses him.

Julian leaves my side and walks the length of the foyer to meet them. He looks up at all of us and I'm surprised to see that his eyes are red-rimmed, like he's trying not to cry, whether out of anger or sadness, I'm not sure.

He points at Frankie. "Your brother has betrayed you."

The silence is like a monster. It's wrapped its hand around everyone's throats as we watch Julian circle Frankie, take us all in, shudder with anger. I wait for Frankie to defend himself, but he doesn't.

"It's come to my attention," Julian finally says, "that Frankie has been in communication with Tyler. A conversation was found on his phone in which he divulged the address of the warehouse and other private information that should not belong to anyone but the people in this room. Because of Frankie, I was arrested today. Because of Frankie, we have to sell the warehouse. Because of Frankie, things will have to be sorted, arranged, taken care of." Julian lifts his chin, his eyes going from face to face.

He opens his mouth like he's going to say something, but instead jumps when Frankie grabs him, both hands around Julian's ankle.

"Julian, please," he says.

It's like a fire ignites inside Julian. He bends, pulls Frankie's head back by his hair and punches him once, twice, three times. A splatter of blood flies across the floor. "You were given everything," he says, bending down close to Frankie's face. "Everything you could have ever wanted. But it wasn't enough. You wanted power. Maybe you'll get what you want in Hell."

I suck in a breath when Julian takes out his gun and puts it to Frankie's head. We all knew this is exactly where we were going to end up. This is the only answer. And I know I can't look away, for Julian's sake. So I watch him, his finger on the trigger, gritting my teeth.

"What do you have to say to me?" he says, his voice rough, thick.

I've known Frankie for a month, and in that time, I've heard him spew more vitriol than anyone else in this house combined. He's threatened me. He's suspected me. He tried to frame me for something he did. He was perfectly content with letting me take the fall. The knowledge of that burns in my chest, makes me ball my hands into fists. I don't want to watch this man die, but I also can't feel bad that he's going to.

"I worked hard for your father," Frankie says, coughing, spitting some blood. One of his eyes is already beginning to swell. "I worked hard for him, and I felt like I deserved what you got."

"Yes, everyone knows. You haven't exactly been quiet about it." This from Bram, standing beside Julian. I half expect Julian to tell him to shut up, but he doesn't. "That was why he didn't give you the position," Bram goes on. "Because you made it clear it was all you wanted. He never trusted you, and we shouldn't have either."

"Enough," Julian finally tells Bram quietly.

Frankie, on his knees on the ground, lifts his eyes to Julian's. "I did everything right. I did everything the way I should have, and I still got nothing."

"You have money. You have a home. You had a family. That should have been enough for you."

"Is it enough for you?" Frankie asks.

Julians look over at me, catches my eye. I force myself to hold his gaze as he visibly steels his nerves. His jaw clenches. He tightens his hand on his gun, steadying himself, but I can see all the way from here that he's trembling.

"*It's okay,*" I mouth to him.

He sucks in a breath and pulls the trigger. I cling to his dark eyes like an anchor as, in my peripheral vision, Frankie's body hits the ground.

Magnus drags Frankie back out of the room, quiet this time, and Julian walks straight to me, his gun vanishing back wherever it came from. He presses his forehead to mine, and I take both of his hands. I press a kiss to his knuckles, where he's bleeding.

JULIAN

I'm still awake in the middle of the night when someone knocks on my bedroom door. Sloane and I ended up back here after everything. My limbs were too heavy after killing Frankie to make it upstairs.

She's warm in my arms, pressed against my side. When the knock comes, I slowly pull her arm away and slide out from under her. She isn't normally a heavy sleeper, but it's been a long day. She must be as exhausted as I am, emotions and nerves rattled.

I pull open the door, find Hugo on the other side. "If you wake her, I swear to God, I'll kill you."

Hugo puts his hands up. "I'm really sorry, boss, but... it's Ryan. He says the security system over at the warehouse is blacked out. He's..." He glances down the hall. "He's worried that it's an ambush."

I step out of the room and shut the door behind me. "Jesus, when will he give it a rest?"

Hugo crosses his arms. I'm tall, but Hugo is even taller, almost towering over me with his blonde buzzcut. "Maybe. Could also be a trap. He probably knows the compound has too much security and he would never be able to get anywhere. But he's probably hoping that if he hits the warehouse, you'll show up to check on things."

"You think he's gunning for me?"

Hugo sighs. "I think you pissed him off one too many times. I think he thought he was going to get rid of you today in that police station, and when he didn't, he got desperate."

"Has everyone gone home?"

Hugo shakes his head. "Most of the guys are still down by the pool, drinking. They're too riled up after the whole thing with Frankie."

"And Ryan?"

"I don't know. He's well-equipped there, sure, but if Tyler shows up with a group of guys..."

"Tyler doesn't have anyone anymore. Everyone in town is done with him. But you're right. We should go. Gather whoever's here. Tell them to load up. We'll go check it out." I glance back at the closed door behind me. "Someone needs to stay with Sloane."

"I'll get Ronny," he says. "He's not good under pressure anyway."

What game is Tyler playing?

"Julian!"

I push Hugo aside and rush down the hall, meeting Bram at the end of it.

"Explosion at the warehouse," he says.

"Fuck. Alright, let's go. Gather everyone. Tell Ronny to come back here."

I duck back into my room, sad to find Sloane sitting up in bed, covers pulled up around her. "What's going on?" she asks.

"I'm not sure. It looks like Tyler might have just hit the warehouse."

"Why?" She doesn't understand any more than I do. What does Tyler think he's going to find at the warehouse?

"My guess is that he's angry. He's making a fuss. Trying to scare us. But I don't know for certain," I say, bending down to pick up the clothes I left on the floor. "He could be waiting to strike again. We'll go in prepared. If this is a matter of outright attack, we're stronger than Tyler. Maybe we weren't a week ago, but now that he's an island..."

She crawls to the edge of the bed, her hair tousled and her eyes worried. "Are you sure?"

"Yes. This is what we wanted. To get him alone and make our move. I just didn't think he would make one first."

"I'll get dressed," she says, already pushing the blanket away.

I spin back to her, my pants halfway buckled and my shoes untied. "What the fuck are you talking about? You're not going anywhere."

She stands at the side of the bed in her lacy underwear. "What? You think I'm not going to go?"

"Of course you're not going to go. You stay here. You stay safe."

"But you taught me how to shoot for a reason," she says, coming around to watch me lace up my shoes.

"To protect yourself. Not to go into open battle." I stand and do up my shirt.

"There's no way you're leaving me here. What if—"

I take her face in my hands, stopping her words with my mouth. Her lips tremble against mine. "Stop this," I tell her. "Everything's going to be okay."

"But what if it's not okay? What if—"

"No matter what, we outnumber him and we have far more experience." I push a strand of her long blonde hair behind her ear. Even when she's all sniffly and teary, she's so beautiful. "We have to take care of this. We knew there was a chance it would come to this. I'm going to end it."

"Julian, I..." She looks like she wants to say something else, but I can't hear it. Not right now.

So instead, I kiss her once more, taste her soft, pink lips. "I'll be back," I assure her. "Ronny's at the door and Xander is down at the gate. Everyone else is coming with me. We'll be back."

She nods, and I leave without looking back.

I see the smoke, even against the dark sky. As we pull up to the warehouse, everyone's on high alert, searching for anyone they can find in the woods, on the road. An ambush, a barricade, any evidence that Tyler isn't working alone.

But there's nothing. Just quiet. We turn off the road, and Ryan meets us as the car comes to a stop. The warehouse is on fire. It crackles and pops as things inside continue to trigger explosions.

"Have you seen anyone?"

Ryan shakes his head. "Other than the bomb, it's been completely quiet. The cameras are still out."

He hands me the laptop he keeps in the hut with him. I have access to the cameras on my phone, but he can see more than I can: the alarms on the hut, on the warehouse, the fact that all of the locks are still engaged, even while it's on fire. I can see it from here, the padlock, surrounded by flames.

"They didn't try to get in," I say, more to myself than him. "No."

"What is this?" I turn and ask Bram. "What is he doing?" The men are still in their cars, waiting for orders.

"I don't know," Bram says. "None of this makes sense. Why blow up the warehouse? It was already mostly empty. He had to have known we were going to clean it out after the cops. Maybe he was trying to blow it before we had the chance. But for what, just to fuck up one car sale? The thing was going to go on the market in twenty-four hours anyway."

Nothing is adding up.

"There was nothing weird at the compound?" Ryan asks.

I hand him back the laptop. "No. Perfectly quiet. The guys scanned the grounds before we left. Checked for explosives, tripwires, shit like that. Nothing. Everything is locked up tight." I gesture at the warehouse. "Even that mess."

"You know Tyler isn't the brightest," Bram says. "Maybe it was just—" His words cut off and his eyes go wide. "Get down!" He launches himself at me.

After that, the world is just sounds. The sound of our shoes scrabbling in the dirt as we fall to the ground. The sound of our impact. The sound of us breathing.

"What is it?" I shout.

"Sniper," he says. "Laser sight, right on your forehead."

I lift my head and scan the dark woods around us. "They didn't shoot."

He shakes his head. "No, but he's here. He's clearly trying to scare us."

"He's going to do it like a coward," I say, sitting up with my back against the Beast. "From a distance." We wait for someone to come out, to shoot, to do something, but nothing happens. If it weren't for the fire, it would be a damn-near peaceful night.

In the dark, with the cameras out, there's no way we'll be able to find him before he finds us with a bullet.

"What the fuck is going on?" Ryan asks.

"He was clearly trying to get you here," Bram says. "But why, if he's not going to kill you?"

"Or he was trying to draw you out."

My eyes slam back to Ryan, back pressed to the security hut feet away from us. "What do you mean?"

He shrugs. "Maybe he was trying to get you away from the compound. It wasn't about you being here. It was about you not being there."

Fear knifes through me. I whip my phone out of my back pocket and open up the security system for the compound. As soon as I see that all the screens are black, I shoot to my feet.

"He's going for Sloane. Everyone back to the compound!"

SLOANE

I can't seem to fall back to sleep. All I can think about is what might be going on over at the warehouse. Julian seemed so confident that there was no way Tyler would be able to get him.

Retribution. It wasn't just the cops. That was Frankie's retribution. But we've turned everyone against Tyler, so he decided to take it upon himself.

But is it just him? What can he do alone? Even as the thought springs into my head, I hear voices down the hall. At first, I think they're coming from the foyer, but I know Ronny is the only one here, so it doesn't make any sense.

No, the voices are coming from outside.

A gunshot rings loud in the quiet, making me jump.

I get out of bed, grabbing the handgun off my nightstand, where I keep it when I'm asleep. I focus on breathing, keeping myself calm, like Julian taught me.

I slowly and quietly open the bedroom door and step out

into the hall. There are no voices inside that I can hear, no sounds outside either. It's like none of it was real, just echoes inside my own worried mind. I walk slowly down the hall, Winston following behind me. Ronny finds me immediately.

"What's going on?" I ask him.

"I'm not sure," he says. "Xander saw headlights on the road and then he went radio silent." He already has his gun in his hand. The rest of the house is empty, all of the men at the warehouse. Ronny jerks his chin back down the hallway. "Go back. You can hide in the boss's library."

Right. Julian's dad's library. No one would be able to find me.

"I'll come get you when it's safe."

Before I've even taken a step, something smashes into the door, cracking it around the frame. Ronny grabs my arm and shoves me towards the library.

"Go," he says.

But it doesn't matter. It's too late. Behind him, the door crashes open, the reinforced locks popping loudly as someone shoots them. It swings in.

I'm frozen. Maybe I could have made it if I had turned and run right then, but I don't. Instead, I watch as Tyler appears in the doorway, raises his gun, and shoots Ronny.

I scream just as Tyler says, "Hello, beautiful."

57

SLOANE

My eyes are on Ronny as I lift my gun and point it at Tyler. He steps toward me slowly, and I back away.

"What do you want?" I shout.

"I think I've made it pretty clear what I want, Sloane. But seeing as how what I want was just stolen from me, I think I'll take what *he* wants instead."

I scramble back, willing myself to shoot. But I can't. This is Tyler. I don't have it in me to shoot my ex-boyfriend.

He bares his teeth at me. I don't even recognize him anymore. "Fucking sluts are all the same. You don't care if a man has guns. You don't care if he hurts people. You don't care if they're bad men. You just want to fuck them if they have the biggest wallet and the biggest dick. Right?"

I squeeze the gun tighter in my grip. "Are you admitting that Julian has the biggest dick?"

He narrows his eyes. "Cute." He's slowly walking toward me. He has me almost in the dining room now.

"He treated me better when he wasn't trying to get in my pants than you ever did as my boyfriend."

He snorts. "You're talking about the man who locks you up."

I gesture toward the house with the barrel of the gun. "I'd rather be locked in his house than be free and on your arm."

He finally stops moving toward me. He holds my eye as he sticks his gun in the back of his chinos. "I didn't come here to get violent with you, Sloane. You're a reasonable person. I came here to negotiate."

"I don't negotiate with terrorists."

He shrugs. "Then I'm sure you won't mind if I share your little gangbang video with the dean."

My eyebrow wrinkles. "What, are you serious? That's all you've got? Go ahead. Show him. If the dean has a problem with a grown woman having consensual sex with whoever she pleases, that's his own fucking problem."

Not that the video would ever make it to the dean. Between Ronan and Claudia, I can make that video disappear before the dean knows it exists.

He laughs. I don't like the tone of it. "I didn't figure you'd come with me for your own sake, but I thought you might for theirs."

My eyes go to Ronny, his unmoving form, now laying in a puddle of blood. Out of the corner of my eye, I see Tyler offer me something, his hand out.

His phone.

I turn my head to find he's moved a little closer, close enough that I can see the phone's screen. It takes me a second to figure out what I'm looking at.

It's Julian, moving in the dark, a red dot against the side of his head.

"No!" I say, lunging forward to grab the phone from his hands as if Julian can somehow hear me. It's a video, and I can't even tell if it's live. On the screen, Bram tackles Julian to the ground and I feel a wave of relief, even as my pulse kicks up like a drumbeat. "What is this?" I demand.

"Motivation. You're going to come with me. I have a sniper in the trees at his little warehouse. They can't all hide from a threat they can't see. I can start picking them off, one at a time. You come with me, I let him live."

"I don't believe you."

"Are you willing to risk it?"

I look down at the screen again. The camera—and whoever is holding it—is moving through the woods, walking until they're on the other side of the warehouse, where they have a clear view of the guys crouched behind the Beast, trying to use it as a shield.

They think they're safe, but they're not. If I go with Tyler, he might just kill them anyway. But he might not. If I don't go with him, he absolutely will. While I'm still trying to figure out what to do, Tyler reaches forward and snatches the gun out of my hand. He shows it to me and then tucks it in his pants with the other one.

It doesn't even matter. I wasn't going to use it on him. I couldn't have even if I tried.

"Why are you doing this? You don't even want me, Tyler. You've made it very clear that I disgust you."

He smiles. "I'm going to prove to him that I can't be beaten. He tried to take everything from me, and he mostly succeeded. And now I'm going to take everything from him. I'm going to destroy his business and his home, and I'm going to take the thing he wants most."

"You're making a lot of assumptions about how important I am to him." I'm trying to somehow work my way out of this, but I'm not seeing a lot of options.

"Oh, I don't think so," he says, taking a step toward me. "You see, when I offered you up in that race, Julian thought he had me. He had no idea what you meant to me. It's true that I didn't want to lose you. I wanted you on my arm. I intended to have a nice future with you. But I didn't lose sleep over you being gone. It didn't destroy me."

He raises his arm and presses his gun to my forehead. It sends a shock through me, like electricity along my skin. I know he won't do it because then he wouldn't have any leverage. But maybe if he got angry enough, he would.

"I'm doing this because even though Julian was too stupid to know you meant nothing to me, I'm not too stupid to know what you mean to him. I intend to have everything I want. I'm going to enjoy making him watch while I have you, Sloane."

My stomach turns. "He'll kill you."

"He can certainly fucking try. The thing is, I have nothing to lose now. He and my father destroyed everything. The empire I was trying to build. If I take off with you, I win."

It's this that convinces me he's finally lost it. Everything that's happened to the two of us since we moved to this town has finally caused him to snap.

He looks down at his phone. "Hmm. Looks like your boyfriend's on the way back. You've got ten seconds, Sloane. I can have him shot before he gets in his car. Or you can get in mine."

My eyes fall to Ronny again. He's dead, I know it. I can't lose any more of them, especially not Julian.

"Okay, I'll go with you."

Like I've said the magic word, the front door opens and in walks Weston. My eyes meet his, and he winks at me. "Hey, Sloane."

"There's no one else here," I tell him, thinking maybe he's coming to scour the house and kill anyone left.

Tyler nods. He shoves me toward the door, and I stumble. He keeps me from falling, but then drags me out the door with a bruising grip on my wrist.

I glance back just before he pulls me out onto the front steps. I see Weston lift a can of gasoline that seemingly comes from nowhere, dousing the foyer. Dousing Ronny's body.

"No!" I scream, trying to fight Tyler's grip, but he's so much stronger than me. "No!" Tyler's arms go around me, and he lifts me up off the ground and carries me down the stairs. "Stop! Why! Why are you doing this?"

But it's too late.

As Tyler shoves me into the backseat of his car, the foyer goes up in flames. He slams the door shut, and I watch out the back window as fire swallows everything.

I cry as the house gets further and further away.

Julian's father's house. His home. The guys' home. My home. Gone.

58

"Oh God," Bram says, his eyes focused on something in the distance out the windshield. When my own eyes find it, my heart stops beating.

The compound is on fire.

I slam my foot down on the gas pedal, race down our street with shaking hands. When I turn into our driveway, I almost can't keep going. So much fire, so much smoke.

I throw the car into park and get out.

I don't even realize I'm screaming until I'm halfway up the stairs and Bram is putting his arms around me to keep me from running inside. "Sloane!" I scream, shoving Bram's arms off of me. "Sloane!"

She's still in there. I left her in there.

Bram fights me, grabbing onto my clothes and trying to hold me still. "She's not in there," he says, his voice barely registering.

My eyes are burning, my lungs burning, everything burning as I watch the flames rise.

"Julian." Bram takes my face in his hands, forces me to look down at him. "She's not in there," he shouts at me.

I look at his face, flickering orange in front of me. "How do you know?" I ask, shoving his hands away. "Where else would she be?"

"He took her."

We both whip around to look at Claudia. She's coming up the driveway with Xander propped against her, his arm over her shoulders, and Winston in her arms. Xander has his hand pressed to his side. I can see blood soaking through his shirt. Claudia's words pierce my skull like a drill.

"Where the hell were you?"

"I was in the garden. I didn't know what was happening until I saw the fire. Xander tried to warn Ronny, but he wasn't quick enough. Ronny is dead."

Beside me, Bram makes a choking sound. *Ronny is dead.*

"It was Tyler and one other guy," Claudia goes on. "They came, they set the house on fire, they left. I came around the front and saw the three of them taking off. I went in to get the cat and then walked down to get Xander. The whole thing happened in minutes, Julian."

Bram steps forward and puts his arms around Xander. "You need medical attention."

Xander, pale, shakes his head. "I'll be fine. Is Sarge on his way back?"

"Yes, but it doesn't matter. It's not like he has anywhere to treat you." Bram's eyes turn up to the burning house behind me. The heat is making me sweat.

"How long ago did they leave?" I ask.

Claudia considers, her hand moving against Winston's fur. "Maybe three minutes ago?'

I run back to the car. Three minutes. I can still catch them.

"Julian!" Bram calls after me.

"Stay with him," I shout back, climbing inside the Beast. "Get him to the hospital as soon as Sarge gets here."

"You don't even know where they're going!"

I ignore him and spin the Beast around in the driveway, already dialing Ronan as I go. When I pull back onto the road, I see the other guys' cars in the distance, their headlights hazy in the almost-morning light.

"That you, boss?" Ronan answers.

I fly by them and keep going. "I need you to locate Sloane. Tyler took off with her."

"What! Oh, shit!"

It seems they've just discovered the burning compound. I know that between all of them, they'll get everything sorted without me. "Ronan! Find her," I growl, trying to get his attention back on me.

"I don't have a tracker on her," he says, his voice distracted. "You took her phone, remember?"

"What about the security cameras on the highway? You're looking for a car with Tyler and a second man in the front seat. You probably won't even be able to see Sloane."

"Could take a moment. Hang on."

There's rustling on his end, and in the distance, I can hear the guys' voices as they wrangle the fire and Xander, deciding how to handle both problems.

When I come to the end of our private road, I have to know which direction they went. I have to know where to go. "Ronan!" I shout into the phone.

"They're headed south on Highway 10. Gas station on the corner of Latham Road picked them up on a security camera just before they got on."

I slam a left at the end of the street and speed toward the highway.

"Tell Bram to come as soon as Xander is at the hospital." I hang up and press down harder on the gas.

SLOANE

"Where are you taking me?" At first, I thought Tyler was taking me back to campus, back to the frat house to, I don't know, lock me in a closet or something. But he got on the highway instead, heading south.

"Well, we can't stay here, now can we?" he says, eyes meeting mine in the rearview mirror.

I sit with my arms crossed in the backseat. There's nothing I can do. Not yet, at least. Weston has a gun on me—my gun, to be exact. I hate seeing it in his hand, the gun that Julian left in that box for me.

"We're going back to California," Tyler says.

"What!" I lean forward between the seats and Weston uses the barrel of the gun to push me back down. "You can't take me back to California."

Tyler scoffs. "What did you think was going to happen, Sloane? That I was going to take you from him and then you were going back to classes, back to normal life?"

Sort of, yes, but I can see how that isn't an option.

"What's your plan then, Tyler? You're going to go back to your dad and tell him that this experiment of yours failed? What are you going to do, force me into marrying you so you can fool everyone into thinking you're something you're not?"

He laughs. "I don't want to marry you. You're not the perfect little housewife that I thought you would be. You're just a whore, like your mother."

I ignore the jab. It's so unoriginal. "Then, why?"

I watch the needle on the odometer climb up and up and up as his anger becomes more palpable. The highway is still silent in the early morning. "Because I know you won't be able to afford to make it back," he says. "You'll be stuck there with your whore mom in your fucking trailer. You're stupid if you think Julian is going to come for you all the way out there. He's not going to leave his turf for you."

He's not even going to try to keep me. He just wanted to take me from Julian and dump me somewhere like an unwanted litter of puppies. He's right. I can't afford a plane ticket. I don't have a car. I don't have any way to get back to Julian.

Is he right? Would Julian be unwilling to cross state lines just to get me back?

No. He's just saying things to piss me off, to make me feel like I'm alone when I'm not. Whatever exists between Julian and me now, it's permanent. Just as permanent for him as it is for me. Even if I end up back in Fresno, Julian will come for me. But it'll be a lot harder.

Back home, Tyler has different protections than he ever could have hoped to have in New Hampshire. His father, his father's business associates, the community that Tyler built when we were in school, it won't be as easy to unravel as it was here. Would I want Julian to come for me just to end up with a target on him?

"And what about you, Weston?" I ask.

He shrugs. "I've always wanted to go to California."

What he means is that New Hampshire is no longer an option for him. And why *would* it be? Without Tyler here, Weston also doesn't have protection. How long would it take for the cops to come for him after all of this shit hits the fan?

Weston looks so smug as he says this, and then slowly, his smirk disappears. His eyes go over my shoulder and widen. "What the fuck!" he says.

I spin around in my seat, and there, on the empty highway behind us, is the Beast.

"What the fuck?" Tyler echoes. "How did he get here so fast?"

I can't keep the smile off my face. "Turbocharger," I say to myself and feel the car speed up.

Tyler might think his cars are fast, but he doesn't have anything as fast as the Beast.

"What are we supposed to do now?" Weston asks.

In the second that his attention is not on me, but on Tyler instead, I reach forward, snatch the gun out of his hands, and lift my leg to kick him in the nose. I hear a satisfying crunch, and there's blood everywhere.

"Fuck!" Weston screams, covering his face.

Tyler swerves and one of our tires hits a patch of gravel. The car skids. He manages to keep it on the road, but we're going far slower than we were before. Julian has gained on us, made all the more obvious when his front bumper taps the back of our car.

I put the gun to Tyler's head. "Pull over," I tell him. "You know you've lost."

"And I know you can't pull that fucking trigger," he says. He swerves, knocking me off balance. I slam back into the backseat just in time for Julian to tap us again.

Before I can get back up, Weston has a hand wrapped in my hair. He yanks and I scream, finding his face between the seats and punching him in his probably broken noise.

He whimpers and lets go of me.

Maybe Tyler is right. Maybe I can't kill him. But I have no problem hurting him.

Pushing up between the seats, I press the gun against his thigh and shoot. Tyler screams, letting up off the gas. I grab the wheel, jerking it to the right, until we're in the grass beside the highway.

I reach over the console and pull up the parking brake just as we hit a tree.

We're going slow enough that the impact is minimal, but it still jars the three of us. While the men are groaning in the front seat, I try to open the back. Tyler has the fucking child locks on.

I still have the gun in my hand, but I bang on the window with the other, watching Julian get out of the Beast and rush toward us. He fumbles with the door handle, his eyes locked on mine. Just as it un-latches, Weston, slams into him.

The two men are in the grass, throwing punches, Weston on top of Julian.

My first thought is to spin around and point my gun at Tyler, knowing he still has a gun of his own, but he's not there. I lower my gun and look out the windshield. Tyler is limping down the highway.

"Fucking coward," I say to myself and shove my door open. I hop out onto the grass right as Weston lifts a knife that seemingly comes out of nowhere.

I shove my gun against his temple. "I won't shoot to protect myself, but if you don't get your fucking hands off of him, I will make sure they never find all the pieces of your fucking brain, Weston."

He complies immediately, dropping his knife into the grass before climbing off of Julian, who struggles to his feet beside me.

I want to throw myself at him, but we have this fucker to deal with, and I'm not taking this gun off of him for even a second.

"Give me the gun, baby," Julian says, covering my hand with his. "No blood on your hands."

I let him take it and without a second of hesitation, he shoots Weston in the head. His eyes move past me, searching. "Where's Tyler?"

"He took off."

Julian sighs and leans down to put his arms around me. I

latch on to him, happy to be safe in his arms. "I'm so sorry," I say, my voice breaking.

"For what?" he asks, taking my face in his hands. "It's not your fault Tyler did this."

"But Ronny." I grab onto his wrists, trying to steady myself.

He nods. "It's okay. That's not for you to apologize for."

The sound of tires crunching down the road makes it to us. We both turn to see a car come to a stop behind the Beast. Bram gets out of the driver's seat. Relief floods me at the sight of him.

But his face is pale as he shouts, "Get down!"

The warning doesn't come quick enough. A shot rings out loud from the direction of the trees beside us. The bullet misses, but just barely, hitting the side of Tyler's car right between Julian and me.

We spring apart on instinct, him going one way and me going the other. I land in the grass just in time to turn and see Tyler lift his gun again, no longer hiding in the trees. He's going for Julian, not me.

I rush at him, knocking him off balance. The gun flies into the air, going off in my ear before it lands in the grass. Julian still has mine.

Everything happens so quickly. I reach for the gun and see Julian out of the corner of my eye pointing his at Tyler just as a sharp pain lances through my side.

The world seems to spin as the pain makes me dizzy. I land on my knees on the side of the highway. I hear screaming off in the distance, or maybe it's right beside me.

I look down and see the handle of Weston's knife sticking out of my side. I've never known pain like this. Didn't know that things could hurt so much.

"Bram!" I hear Julian scream. "Get him!"

I think he means Tyler. Tyler, who must have made a run

for it again. Julian's arms are around me, and he holds me up against him.

"Baby," he says. "Baby, no. No, no, no." I can see his dark brown eyes in my vision, his hand there for some reason, red. I feel it on my chin. "Baby, don't go. Don't go."

He's doing something on his phone, screaming into it for an ambulance

I try to tell him he can't call an ambulance. He can't take me to a hospital. When they find this disaster area...

My voice doesn't come out.

59

JULIAN

"Your girlfriend is not going to be out of surgery for quite a while, so why don't you just explain to me why there was blood all over the side of the highway?"

Bram and I sit quietly in the uncomfortable hospital chairs. They've stuck us in an ICU waiting room. An old sitcom plays on the TV. The county sheriff sits across from us.

"I told you. Some psycho kidnapped my girlfriend, the one who's fighting for her life in surgery right now. They burned down my house and they took her."

"And the guy in that room down the hall, he was what, living with you?"

Xander. The ironic thing is the fact that they were hit in almost the exact same spot. The bullet went clean through him. The knife did a little more damage.

I don't say anything. Between me, Bram, and Xander, we gave them enough to keep them from arresting me when they saw Weston's dead body and all the blood on my hands. But they're not getting anything else until Graves gets here.

"There's a whole lot of bad shit going down in my county," the sheriff says. "This really has the mark of a gang war."

"Everything that went down was in self-defense or to protect my girl. I'm happy to give you a formal statement once my lawyer gets here."

As if I summoned him through sheer force of will, another cop approaches, hands grasping his utility belt. When he peers down at me, I know his face. Finally, one of the bad ones.

I smile up at him. "It's Keith, isn't it?"

The man, hardly older than myself, tips his head to one side. "Do I know you?'

"No, but I know you. I think you worked with an old associate of mine, Tyler Price."

He goes very still, but in that way that you go still because you're trying not to react, trying not to give anything away. "I don't know a Tyler Price," he finally says.

I nod. "Yeah, me neither." I hold his gaze, make myself very clear. He's on my side now because if he's not on my side, he's unemployed, maybe jailed.

Keith tips his head toward the sheriff. "Maybe we let this one lie for now. We got a call about a robbery out on the 10."

"Alright," the sheriff says, standing. He starts to walk away with the other officer, but turns back. "For what it's worth, I hope your girlfriend's okay. We'll be in touch."

Somehow, I doubt that. I'm sure by the time they get to their next job, Tyler's bitch will have convinced the sheriff this isn't worth looking into any further.

As soon as they're gone, I lean back in my seat and let out a shaky breath. "How much fucking longer?" I growl.

"Probably a while," Bram says. "Listen, the cops are still handling the crime scene and she's still out. Maybe we should deal with Tyler. We need to get it taken care of before people start poking around."

"All right. Have Ronan go through his phone, see if he told anybody he was heading back to California, especially his father. If his dad can corroborate that he was already headed home, it'll be a lot easier to make him disappear on the road."

"That's what I was thinking," Bram says, standing and putting on his coat.

"Where do the guys have him?"

"They took him out to your dad's old warehouse."

"Fuck. That's a trek."

"Last property still standing. I'll ask Sarge to come wait with her. He'll let us know when she's out."

"Okay. Tell the men I'm coming."

I thought maybe it would bring some kind of satisfaction, some kind of happiness to find Tyler strapped to a chair from his shoulders to his ankles.

Dad used to use this place before he died, but I didn't like the drive. I got the warehouse closer to the compound, but I never got around to selling this place. I had a hard time, since my father's name was on the deed.

"What are you going to do to me?" Tyler asks, his voice grizzled and hoarse.

"If this were any other day, Tyler, things might have gone differently. You know what's funny?" I step up to the chair, crouching in front of them. "She was really making me soft. If you had kept running, going all the way back to California, I probably would have left you alone. I wasn't about to go chasing a nobody, someone who wasn't a real threat. But that's not how it's going to go now."

I straighten, pull the knife out of my pocket. "I had to make it seem like you were never there," I tell him. I lift the knife, waving it, watching his eyes follow it like a cat with a rubber ball. "I replaced it with one Magnus had on him. Put your idiot's fingerprints all over it. This one..." Her blood is still on it, up to the hilt. "This one's for you."

Stepping forward, I take hold of his thigh, strapped to the chair.

"No, no, no, no, no!" Tyler screams before I dig into the wound with the knife. I push in deep as he screams, until I find the bullet Sloane put there with the tip. Tyler starts to cry, which is disappointing. I really thought he'd hold out longer than that.

"That's not even the worst of it," I say, twisting the blade so I can extract the bullet. Blood spews from the wound. Tyler has gone silent, his eyes glassy. I hold up the bullet for Bram, who takes it from me with a paper towel. He grimaces and sticks it in a bag.

"What are you doing with that?" Tyler asks, dazed.

"Just getting rid of evidence."

"What?" He's out of breath, sucking air in through his mouth.

"Must hurt. Probably not as bad as having your small intestine nicked by a blade, but..." I hold out my hand and Bram sets a pair of pliers into my open palm. "Sloane's really going to be sad that she didn't get a chance to sell the Audi. She worked hard for it."

"Sell the—" But he doesn't finish his sentence because I have my pliers in his mouth, yanking out one of his teeth. I hold up the pliers and Bram takes them from me as Tyler screams and screams.

It's amazing what happens when you've never felt pain before, when you've spent your whole life in comfort.

"That one was just for fun. And to throw them off the scent for a little bit."

"What are you going to do to me?" Tyler asks, his voice broken from the pain.

"First," I say, "I'm going to make sure you understand why I'm doing this. That you understand it's because you tried to take what's mine and when you couldn't have what's mine, you put her in the hospital. I'm doing this so you understand that there are consequences to your actions and that this is my town, plain and simple. Not that any of this really matters because you're going to be dead soon."

"Wait, wait," Tyler says. "I can get you money."

"No, you can't. You're not worth anything and neither is your father. He'll probably be happy to unload you. Dartmouth is expensive." I grab his jaw, making sure to put pressure on the hole where his tooth was. "You tried to kill Sloane. You almost killed Xander. You killed Ronny. There is no universe in which you get to walk out of here and go back to your father. There is no universe where you have anything to offer me but the sound of your screams. I'll see you in Hell, Tyler."

I step back and watch the men douse him in gasoline while he screams and begs for his life. My eyes find Claudia in the corner of the room. She's watching everything from the shadows, ready to see an end to all of it.

When they're done, Bram hands me a lighter. It's pink.

I raise an eyebrow at him.

"For her," he says.

"For her." I light the lighter, watch the flame for a moment, and toss it at Tyler.

60

JULIAN

"Boss." Ronan runs up to me, his cell phone in his hand. "Sarge just called. She's out of surgery."

I nod, leave behind the men who are sweeping up ashes from the center of the room. "Did you take care of the paperwork?" I ask him as we head back outside.

He nods. "If the ICU gives you any trouble, have them bring up the paperwork again. It says you're the next of kin. There's been a staff change since she went under, so it should be fine."

"Can you get a plane ticket to her mom?"

He stops walking. "You sure you want to do that? She might start asking questions."

I open the door of the Beast, slap one hand on the roof. "I'm sure. She needs her mother."

He nods. "Whatever you say."

"Thanks, Ronan."

He slaps me on the shoulder. "Go get your girl."

Even though it's a long drive back, Sloane is still asleep when I get to the ICU. They told me the surgery was complicated, that they had to remove part of her intestine, that the recovery—as long as she makes it through the next few nights —will be a long and painful one. Apparently, the risk of infection is high and her blood pressure took a hit during the procedure.

I hold her hand and watch the monitors. I don't know how to read them. I don't know what they're telling me, just that her heart is still beating. I trace the lines on the back of her hand. Her nails are still perfect. It feels like something that shouldn't be possible, but there's not a single chip. That money I shelled out for that manicure really paid off.

"You know, leaving was never an option, Sloane," I tell her, feeling her soft skin under my fingers. "It's still not an option. I wasn't holding you prisoner before, but maybe I am now. Because I can't be without you. I *won't* be without you. I don't know how you did it," I say, looking up at her face, her long blonde hair fanned out over the pillow.

"When I joined my father's business, I thought I knew exactly how I was going to spend the rest of my life. I was going to spend it the way he did. Alone, focused, the men above everything else, always. When my mother came to my father and gave him an ultimatum, her or the business, he didn't even hesitate. He chose this business over her. And she left both of us.

"She had to have known then, even though I was just a kid. She had to have been able to see it in my eyes that this is exactly where I was going to end up. That as long as I was my father's son, I was going to follow in his footsteps. I wasn't sure, at first, if I wanted it, but it just came so easily. It made sense in a lot of ways."

I run the back of my hand across her pale cheek. I hate how cold it is. It makes me want to pile blankets on top of her. "If you asked me to walk away, I would. No questions, no hesitation. I'd do whatever you told me to. I'd go anywhere you wanted to go. I—"

I press her limp hand to my forehead, close my eyes and breathe. "Fuck. I love you, Sloane. I'm so in love with you that I swear to fucking God, if you die in this hospital, I will die with you. You're mine. And you're not allowed to leave. I won't let you."

I set my head on the mattress next to her arm, hold her hand and focus on the soft, sweet smell of her skin as she sleeps.

SLOANE

"I'm so in love with you that I swear to fucking God, if you die in this hospital, I will die with you."

I hear Julian's voice far off, not really sure it's real. I keep telling myself to open my eyes. *Open your eyes, Sloane,* but it's like they have extra weight on them, like they're too heavy.

Sleep sucks me down again.

The next time I'm aware, I hear Bram's voice. I don't know how long it's been, only that Julian is still here, hand wrapped around mine.

They murmur in low tones, and I try to make out words, but my head feels like an anvil at the bottom of an ocean, so after a minute, I just give up, and the comforting sounds of my two favorite men lull me back to sleep.

The next time I wake, I don't know how, but I feel the passage of time. I still can't open my eyes, but I can see the sun shining through my lids. Julian must have opened the blinds.

Awareness springs into me, my mind alive even though my body is still. Julian isn't holding my hand, and I can hear my *mother's* voice.

"I just don't understand how this happened."

"I'm sure she would want to tell you the story, Ms. Moretti." Julian, somewhere far away.

"And I'm supposed to believe you didn't do this to her?" Her voice is loud with anger.

"Yes. You're supposed to believe that I didn't stab your daughter. I love her, and I intend on taking good care of her when she's out of here." Julian's voice is surprisingly calm.

"When she's out of here, she's coming home with me."

"I'm sorry, but that's not going to happen. Sloane belongs with me."

"She belongs with her family."

"We *are* her family, Ms. Moretti. I'm sorry to say it, but where have you been for the last year?"

There's a long silence, and my heart squeezes. For Julian, who's trying to protect me, and for my mother, who might not be cut out to be a parent but who did the best she could anyway.

When she speaks again, my mother's voice is quieter, all the anger gone. "I tried to call her a few weeks ago, but her phone was off. I thought maybe her boyfriend changed the number. He did things like that, making decisions for her, like where she was going to go to college and what she was going to wear and who she was going to be friends with."

There's a sniffle. Is she *crying?*

"I just don't want to see her go through that forever. And I don't even know who you are!"

"I'm the man who's in love with your daughter. And I'm not going to try to control her, and I'm never going to let anyone hurt her. I promise you, she's safe with me."

"She's in a hospital bed."

"And the person who put her there has paid for what he did."

There's a long silence before my mother says, "Why do I think you really mean that?"

"Because I do."

This time, when sleep comes for me, it rips me away. Because I don't want to go. I want to stay here with Julian and with my mom. I want to be awake. I want to tell Julian I love him. I want to live.

When I finally wake, coming up fully out of the abyss, it's with Julian's name already coming out of my mouth, like talking in my sleep, voice rough and hoarse.

"Julian?"

I can finally open my eyes. He's there. Right there beside me, just like I hoped he would be. His dark eyes meet mine and he shoots up off the chair, leaning over me and putting his hands to my cheeks.

"I'm right here, baby. I'm here."

It's only then that I register the pain. It must have been what finally pulled me to the surface. "It hurts."

"It hurts?" he asks, his voice tinged with panic. "It shouldn't hurt." He reaches over and hits a button on the wall. When nothing immediately happens, he hits it again and again.

"Julian." I try to calm him, but he's lost to me. Yes, it hurts, but not enough that he needs to cause a global outcry over it.

"I'll be back," he says and rushes into the hallway. I see him through the doorway flagging down a nurse and speaking calmly to her.

That is, until she responds with something other than the answer he wants.

Then his voice is loud enough for me to hear. "What, you think she's fucking lying? She said she's fucking hurting, so make it stop fucking hurting."

I sigh. "Julian," I say, trying to speak loud enough for him to hear, but he doesn't.

"Sir, I don't need you to use that language with me," the nurse says, even as she turns toward my room.

Julian walks through the doorway behind her with his hands up. "I'm sorry, I'm sorry, but she... she said she's hurting."

The nurse smiles kindly when she sees me, and I'm glad she's not going to punish me for Julian's bad behavior. "Well, look at you, Little Miss Blue Eyes. It's nice to have you back. Are you in pain?"

I nod as Julian stands at my other side, gently brushing the hair out of my face. "Yes. I'm sorry, I—"

"Don't apologize," she says as she administers more of whatever I'm hooked up to. Relief finds me quickly and I take a deep breath.

"Better?" Julian asks.

I nod.

The nurse makes a sound in the back of her throat and says, "What it must be like to have someone who cares that much." She pats me gently on the arm. "I'll have your doctor come by and check on you, make sure everything is as it should be."

As soon as she's gone, I turn to Julian. "How is everyone?"

He shakes his head. "You almost died and you're worried about everyone else."

"Everyone else almost died, too."

He knows I'm right. "Everyone is okay. Everyone except Ronny. Xander's one room over. Tyler shot him on the way into the compound. He's okay. His surgery was a little bit more simple than yours. He wasn't in nearly as much pain."

"Did you get Tyler? Is he gone?" The last thing I remember is Julian telling Bram to go after him.

Julian presses his forehead to mine. "Yeah, baby, he's gone. Your mom is downstairs. I hope that's okay."

"Of course, it's okay. Thank you for getting her here." Now that the pain is gone, I can feel myself starting to drift again, the wave of sleep threatening to pull me under. "You're not gonna leave, though, right?" I say, forcing the words back up through the haze.

"I'm not going anywhere, baby. I live right here next to you."

I nod, my eyes already closed. "Okay. Julian?"

"Yeah, baby?"

"I'm in love with you, too."

I think he says something, but my brain has lost all purchase, and I fall back to sleep.

$$61$$

SLOANE

"Maybe you should stay in the car," Julian tells me, and I angrily shove his hand out of the way.

"You can either help me out of this car, or I'll have Bram come over here and do it for you," I say, and just like he always does when I threaten to use Bram against him, Julian rolls his eyes.

He doesn't get to argue with me. I am, after all, the one who got stabbed, not him. He takes my hands, gently pulling me up out of the Beast. It hurts like hell, but I grit my teeth and try not to show it.

"You're not hiding that very well," Julian says, holding an arm out to me.

"I have to be able to move on my own at some point," I tell him, looping a hand through his elbow. It's been almost a month since everything went down with Tyler. I'm so frustrated that I still can't move like I'm used to because of the wound in my side.

We walk slowly up towards the slab where the compound

used to be. The guys have been coming in shifts to sift through the ashes, but it's taken a while to get the process started as there were so many other things that needed to be dealt with first: taking care of Xander and me, having Ronny's funeral, filing police reports, etc.

There's been a lot of paperwork over the last month. A lot of people died that night. Not just Frankie and Ronny, whose families were here—Frankie betrayed his and Ronny died for his. There was also Weston, who had a family here in Hanover and a big memorial service at the school.

And Liam, Krista's boyfriend, who was apparently the one in the trees that night at the warehouse. Ryan found him after everyone else left and took him out because that's what he was meant to do. He had no idea who he was, that we were trying to keep him out of the line of fire for Krista's sake. But he was the one who pointed a gun at Julian, so my sympathy is limited.

And, of course, there's Tyler. Tyler, who conveniently went missing. The Audi was taken apart, sold for parts. His father called me a few times. I answered at first, listened to him cry over the fact that his son was lost. But over time, I stopped answering. He'll move on, just like I did.

Although, we're the ones standing in a pile of ash. Have we really moved on at all?

I stand just inside where the front door used to be and look around at the men. They all look exhausted. They've been living in hotel rooms since the night of the fire. All except Xander, who stayed in the hospital with me for a little while. Julian stayed in the hospital, too. Right by my bed. But the rest of them have been bunking together at a hotel over by the university.

"Have a look around," Julian tells me, "but try not to touch too much. You don't want to get it in your lungs."

I nod and tuck my hands under my arms to show that I can be a good girl. He sends a smirk my way.

If I was in perfect health, it wouldn't be so hard to dodge all the debris, but every time I have to lift my leg more than three centimeters, I get a twinge in my side. It's slow going.

"Need help, cupcake?" Bram asks.

I rub my eyes. "No, I'm fine."

Everyone mostly keeps to themselves. Once in a while, someone will find something whole, a pair of dirty cuff links, a silver picture frame, someone's watch. When Ronan finds the chain Ronny always wore around his neck, I have to turn away so I don't gag.

"Here it is, boss," Magnus shouts from the other side of the slab. I look up and watch him shove a large piece of drywall off of a safe.

"Nice work," Julian says, squeezing Magnus on the shoulder. I don't know how much is in that safe, but hopefully it's enough to make up for the men's salaries, the work they're losing while we put all this stuff back together.

Luckily, the garage was separate from the house. Tyler and Weston didn't have the wherewithal to set it on fire as well. The investments are safe, at least for the most part. What was in the warehouse is gone, with the exception of what's in the safes.

Julian bends to open the safe and Hugo and Magnus take everything inside and shove it down into what looks like a pillowcase. Everything except something small that Julian takes out and puts in the pocket of his coat. I'm too far away to see what it is.

When the safe is empty, Julian walks with me through the part of the house that was Julian's room. The base of his lamp is still there. One of the handles from the drawer of his nightstand. And then I find the soot-covered bust of Winston Churchill.

"Oh, Julian," I say, bending down to it. It's too heavy for me to lift, now that I don't have abdominal muscles to use. Julian pushes my hands away and picks it up.

"Stop trying to do too much," he says, setting it aside.

"Your father's books." It's like I was hoping that by setting aside the bust I could open the door again, that the door could still exist and the books beyond it.

"The expensive ones were insured."

"It doesn't matter." I spin to face him. Getting a really good look at all the rubble hits me in the chest. "All of his stuff..."

"Stop it, Sloane. My father has been gone for years, and no amount of mementos and keeping his stuff around was going to bring him back. And besides, that wasn't my father's library anymore. It was yours."

I shake my head. "I'm just so sorry for everything."

He takes my face in his hands, tilts my head up. "Enough apologizing, okay? We got what we came here for. Finish up, because there's a Christmas Eve feast waiting for us at the diner."

I want to be buoyed by this, but it just feels sad.

I go through more of the rubble, but nothing is recognizable. I watch Julian as he speaks with Bram over by the Beast. He's safe. That's all I could have wanted.

We take the biggest table they have at the diner but it's still not big enough and they have to pull over an extra one for us.

Just like at home, Julian takes the seat at the head and I sit beside him with Bram across from me.

"So what do we do now?" I ask after we've all settled and

ordered drinks. The diner's quiet, seeing as how most people are at home with their families. I look around the table at all the worn-out faces of my new family. There's nowhere else I'd rather be on Christmas Eve.

"I'm glad you asked," Julian says. He glances around to get everyone's attention. "We have a few options here. We're going to put it to a vote." His eyes meet mine, like he's unsure. "Our first option is to re-build the company from the ground up again, just like we did after Dad died. We still have what was in the garage, what was left in the safes. We're just going to have to find the extra workspace, but the insurance money should be coming through soon."

"There's another option?" Bram asks.

"Yeah," Julian says. There's already a mug of black coffee in front of him. The waitress brought one for everyone the way she would ice water in summer. "We could split all the assets among all of us and go our separate ways."

"What!" All eyes land on me. Maybe I wasn't supposed to speak, but I don't care. "What are you talking about? Go our separate ways?"

"Sloane," Julian says, his voice firm. He spares me a glance, then turns back to everyone else at the table. "It's just an option. This is an opportunity to get out, to live a normal life like normal people."

"Just like that, huh?" Bram asks. He sounds about as happy about this as I am.

"Not just like anything."

I can tell Julian is starting to become exasperated with our questions. Maybe he thought this was going to be some golden offer. He doesn't even realize how much his men don't want to leave him, don't want to be part of something else.

"I never said it would be simple or easy. I'm just looking at this as an opportunity. Frankie wanted an out. He wanted to be part of a group where he could lead, but he didn't feel like he could leave. I don't want anyone else feeling that way. Maybe you want to move to the city somewhere and settle down and find a wife and have kids. Fine, no one blames you. If you want an exit ramp, it's here in front of you, but we need to be in agreement on how to move forward."

The table is silent. I'm not sure what he was expecting. Maybe for someone to speak out in favor of the idea, maybe for everyone to. Instead, all the men just look back at him, doe-eyed.

"Who wants to rebuild?" he says.

All the hands go up, including mine. I see the curl of a smile on his mouth. He didn't want to separate any more than we did.

"Alright," he says. "Once the insurance comes through, we do have a little bit of freedom. Anyone ready to venture outside of Hanover?"

"Where else would we go?" Magnus asks from the other side of the table.

Julian shrugs. "Anywhere."

EPILOGUE

SLOANE

"So how are you liking Buffalo?" my mom asks as we drive through Fresno.

"Yeah, it's nice," I tell her.

All the men agree that everything about the new place is better. The location, the jobs, the people, the new compound. It's smaller than the old place, which is probably for the best. There was so much space that wasn't being used. All the men moved to Buffalo with us, but Claudia stayed behind. Once she got the revenge she was looking for, she decided she wanted to stay behind in Hanover. Julian gave her a cut of the insurance money and agreed to let her move on. He said she was never really one of them, always on the outskirts.

"When is Julian coming by?" Mom asks.

"I'm not sure he's going to be able to on this trip. He has a big meeting this afternoon. It needs his full attention."

"Ah," she says, starstruck by the idea. "Very busy and important man."

I know what my mom thinks. I suspect she thinks I'm doing what she would do in my place. She thinks I'm with Julian just for his money. Even though she's spent plenty of time with him, seeing how gorgeous and kind and loving he is, she's still convinced that it's just about security.

I guess I can't really blame her, seeing as that was part of the reason I was with Tyler.

I pull into the driveway of the condo and turn off the car. "Here we are."

She looks out the windshield, her eyebrows furrowed. "Where are we?"

I hold out a key to her. "It's the one on the left."

She looks at the gold key, not taking it. "I don't understand."

"It's yours," I tell her.

Her smile disappears at that. "Oh, honey. Oh, no, no, no!"

"Yes, yes, yes!" I shove the key into her hand and get out of the car.

We walk up the path to the condo, and I watch her unlock it.

"It's not a huge place," I explain as she swings the door open. "But it has a lot of windows, which I thought was nice, and the bathrooms are updated. Two bedrooms upstairs and everything else downstairs." It's certainly enough for her.

I watch her take in the living room, watch her run her fingers along the counters in the kitchen. She looks out the windows in the living room, taking in the backyard, big enough for a small dog.

She spins around to face me. "Why did you do this?"

I'm surprised by the question—how it's almost accusatory. "You need a place to live. The trailer is falling apart."

"And if it is, it's my problem," she says. "You didn't need to do this."

"It's not that big a deal. It wasn't terribly expensive. I'll pay the rent as long as you can cover the utilities. Can you do that?"

She nods and turns away again.

"I only ask that you... stay safe."

She keeps her back to me, arms crossed. "Is this about my job?"

"I'm not passing any judgment. I'm just saying that I worry about you. Having strange men in your home, it's not safe. Maybe you could go the online route. Something a little less... vulnerable? I just worry," I say again.

She turns her face toward me. A wrinkle forms between her brows. She crosses her arms. "Did I raise you?" she asks. She pushes her long, blonde hair off her shoulder, the hair that looks so much like mine, proof that she did, in fact, raise me. "Who taught you how to be this way?"

"To be what way?" I ask, feeling defensive. I've never been good at putting a wall between us, even when I should.

"Like this." She gestures at me. "Kind and... positive."

That's...not what I was expecting. "Mom," I say, a lump forming in my throat, realizing this isn't an attack on me. It's an attack on herself.

"I was a terrible mother," she says.

"No." I take her by the shoulders, feel the leathery texture of her skin. She always did sunbathe a little too much. "You just did the best you could."

"I never protected you. When you were gone, I didn't worry about you like you worry about me. And maybe that's horrible to admit, but it's true."

"Well..." I let my hands drop. I want to tell her she had nothing to worry about, but that's far from the truth. Maybe I could have used a mom back home who was worried.

"I know things didn't end well with Tyler," she says, stepping away from me and into the small nook that serves as a dining room. "I don't know exactly what happened, but I know what your boyfriend told me. And Mr. Price, he's a big deal, or at least he was, and I know his company didn't do well either. I don't know what happened out there in New Hampshire, but you left with Tyler and came back with a very scary-looking man."

"Julian is a good man," I interrupt her.

She puts up her hands. "I'm not saying he isn't. I'm just saying I wish I had known what was happening. I wish I had known that you were on your own out there, ending a relationship with a man who put you in the hospital, even if I don't know how. Moving in with a man you barely knew. And then Tyler going missing—"

"Mom." Her eyes meet mine. Ocean blue. "Everything's okay. Yeah, things were bad there for a little while, but Julian got me through it. We got *each other* through it."

She nods. "Okay, well..." She looks around. "I don't think the couch from the trailer is going to look very good in here."

I smile. "I'll put a little extra in your account for some furniture. The master's pretty big, so you'll want a new bed anyway. I should probably get going. I'm supposed to meet Julian for dinner."

"Of course," she says, waving me off. I can see the far-away look in her eyes.

I can't fix everything with a new condo. Just like I couldn't fix it with the car I bought her, and I won't be able to fix it with new furniture, but at least she's a little safer. At least, I've done something.

JULIAN

Sloane is twenty-two minutes late for dinner. Not that I would expect any less.

When she finally shows, she meets me at our table, and I stand to greet her. It's immediately clear why she was late. She's wearing a new dress—a slinky black thing that makes me want to touch every inch of her—her nails are a different color, and her bangs are particularly poofy, which means she washed and blow-dried them.

"Sorry I'm late," she says as I bend and kiss both of her hands. "My hair was greasy and I had just enough time to get my nails done—"

"Everything's fine," I tell her, pulling her seat out for her.

Her eyes catch the window beside us, floor to ceiling, overlooking the ocean. She smiles. "This is beautiful."

Not nearly as beautiful as her. It's been two years and I still haven't quite figured out why the fuck this girl is with me. But I'm thankful for it.

"I hope your mom didn't mind me stealing you away."

"Of course not. I think she can only handle me in little pieces anyway. Plus, I don't think she would much like a place like this."

She seems to take in the room then, eyes traveling from empty table to empty table that she didn't notice before in her haste. I didn't buy out the whole restaurant, just this side of it. I just wanted to be alone with her like this for a little while before our trip is over. The candles, the city lights through the window.

"Why did you do all this?" she asks. "I know it's our last night in California, but we'll be back next month for Christmas."

"I just wanted to," I say, lacing my fingers with hers on the table top. "This job today, this contract, it's going to be a big one."

She says in the back of her throat, "Do we feel good about it?"

"I'll let you look over the paperwork when we get back to the hotel."

"I trust you," she says.

"And I don't make a deal without it going through you," I counter. "I've made that very clear."

I discovered quickly that Sloane is good at dealing with clients and that she loves it, loves buttering them up, smiling at them when they aren't expecting it, bringing them pies, which is a new development. Something about being sold guns by a sparkly princess always throws clients off.

I wanted to take her to the meeting today, but she wanted to take her mother to the new condo, so I let her sit it out.

She smiles. I know she enjoys it, being so needed, being important. Just like she enjoys going to Buffalo State more than she did Dartmouth.

After everything that happened, the idea of an Ivy League was no longer interesting to her. Now that she's no longer fighting for survival, she doesn't need an Ivy League on her resume. She still wants a degree, which is certainly fair, and her knowledge helps. No one else has a business degree. She's helping plug all the holes that we've struggled with since Dad died.

She fit right in, and I love her for it.

The waiter brings the bottle of champagne I ordered, and Sloane lights up. "The good stuff," she says, her smile wide. She loves champagne. She says it makes her horny, which I enjoy the benefits of.

I pop the cork and pour us each a glass.

Her smile dims a little. "Are we celebrating? We haven't

signed the contracts yet, and we haven't even acquired the car."

"It's not that," I say, pushing her glass toward her, watching with satisfaction as she takes a long drink. "We're celebrating something a little different." While she still has her head tipped back, I push the envelope and the ring box across the table.

She looks down and her mouth parts beautifully. "What is this?" she asks, setting down the champagne glass and reaching for the ring box first. I'm actually glad she decided to go get her nails done. She'll enjoy taking pictures of the ring with her new manicure.

"I think it's pretty clear what it is." I take a deep breath and let it out slowly. "I wasn't sure if I was ever going to get to give it to you." When her eyes jump up to mine, wide with alarm, I put up a hand to stop wherever her thoughts are about to take her. "Not because I don't want to marry you. I do. But because I wasn't sure we needed that."

She pops open the box and gasps. "Julian..."

I lean forward on my elbows and her eyes rove over my face, landing on my mouth. I love that she wants me as much as I want her. And boy, do I want her. Her eyes find mine again. "If you tried to leave me, I'd lock you up. I'd tie you up in the basement, baby. Lock you in my closet. Shackle you to my bed. There's no getting away from me now."

Her mouth tips up in a small smile. "I have a bullet with your name on it if you ever try to leave."

I reach down to adjust myself. Those words mixed with the heated look on her face, the way her cheeks are flushed, are making me regret not doing this at home. "We already have everything we want without a marriage certificate. You're mine, I'm yours. We live together, we have a family, we have a business. But..."

She bites her lip. "But?"

I sigh. "It's the most chauvinistic, caveman bullshit. But remember a couple months ago, when we stayed at that hotel in Toronto when the delivery got delayed? And the guy at the desk called you Mrs. Shaw?"

She giggles, just like I knew she would. "Yes, I remember. You liked it, huh?"

"I did, a lot. My dick really liked it."

She giggles again.

"So, I just thought, why not? That ring, it was my dad's mother's. It was in the safe in the old compound. The funny thing is, I put it in there when you moved in. I didn't want you to stumble on it at some point and snatch it." I laugh. "And now it's yours, if you want it."

I reach across the table and take the box, pulling the ring out. "We can have a big to-do or a little thing at home. Whatever you want, it's yours. What do you say?"

She narrows her eyes. "That there's no way I'm going to say yes until you actually ask me, Julian."

She knows me too well, knows how difficult it is for me to do this, even after we've been together for so long, how sometimes I still want to stuff all the emotions back down inside me for fear that she'll wake up someday and realize she's made a huge mistake.

"Sloane, will you marry me?"

All the breath rushes out of her, the amusement on her face melting into something sincere. "Yes, Julian. I'll marry you."

Before I can reach across the table to put the ring on her, she lifts the envelope. "So, then, what is this? Insurance on the ring?" She opens the envelope and pulls out the piece of paper folded up inside, her eyes alight with curiosity. But it fades as she looks at the picture on the print-out. "What is this?" she asks again.

"Our own place."

"What?" She sets the paper down on the table and smooths it out like that will help her read it better. "What about the compound?"

"The men will continue to live in it. A couple of the guys have been grumbling about there being too much work for the small crew. So, we're looking at hiring a few new people. With us gone, there will be more space if we decide to take on anyone. Maybe it will help if we get out of the way."

She's bent over the page. At first, I think she's examining the photo of the house. I don't realize she's crying until a tear hits the paper, leaving a dark stain.

"Hey." I tip her chin up. "If you want to stay in the compound—"

"It's not that," she says, swiping at the tears with trembling fingers. "I've just never had my own space before."

"What about the compound?

"It's different," she says, her voice thick. "We really only own a piece of it. And it's so...masculine. A house that I'll get to decorate. That I'll get to paint." She smiles down at the page, taking it in her delicate fingers. "I'll get to actually go in the kitchen without Xander swatting me away."

"Hey, if Xander's swatting—"

"Everything's fine," she cuts me off quickly. "Everything has always just felt like ours, the men and ours, but not *ours*, yours and mine. In a house of my own, I can have a garden and not have to clean used condoms out of it in the morning."

I'm a bit surprised by the dreamy look on her face. She's already there in her mind, our new home.

"I've been wanting to get a dog," she says. "Maybe two or three. Ones that will get along with Winston. I want to have bird feeders and antique furniture."

"You can have anything you want, baby."

"Anything?" she asks. I shouldn't be all that surprised that her eyes have turned molten. "Because we're in this big, empty room," she says, looking around, "and I'd love to thank you for such a lovely gift."

"Sloane..." I warn.

She sends me a devious grin. "The best part of having a house of our own? You can fuck me anywhere you want, anytime you want."

That's all it takes for me to go stiff. "You know the men wouldn't argue if we wanted to have sex anywhere we wanted now."

She shakes her head, runs her tongue along her upper lip. "Just me and you, Mr. Shaw." She leans back in her seat and runs her hand along her chest, above the dip of her neckline. My eyes follow her fingers. She hums in the back of her throat. "I guess I need a little appetizer, since I'm *so* hungry." She slips out of her chair, disappearing under the table, and I choke.

"Baby, the waiter."

I lift the edge of the white tablecloth and watch her crawl toward me on her hands and knees. "Guess you'll just have to be quiet," she whispers before reaching for my belt.

"Fuck," I breathe, letting the tablecloth fall and watching her fingers as she undoes my belt and then the button on my pants. She reaches in, pulling out my cock, hard in the palm of her hand.

I'm lost. Whatever objections I might have had at being caught by the waitstaff go out the window. It's always like this with Sloane. When she has me in her hand, I'm helpless. She can do whatever she wants with me.

I feel her hot tongue circle the head of me, and my hips buck. Sloane has given me head more times than I can count, perfect and delicious every time, but something about not being able to see her now makes it all that more incredible. I'm forced to close my eyes and imagine her mouth around me when she swallows me down the way she's so good at.

I'm clutching the tablecloth, but it's not enough. I feel like I'm going to fall out of my chair as she takes me to the back of her throat. Deciding that all hope of being inconspicuous is long gone, I reach under the tablecloth and fist her perfect hair in my hands.

She hums around me, and my eyes roll back in my head. She loves it when I'm rough with her during oral, and thank God for that because I don't think I could be gentle right now if I tried.

I yank her forward by the grip I have in her hair and hold her down for one second, two, three, and then let her go, listening in the quiet restaurant as she gasps for air.

"Again," she whispers, and I swear, my head almost pops off. Her wet heat surrounds me again, and just as her lips settle at the base of me, our waiter steps into the room.

I wouldn't be able to remove my cock from Sloane's throat if my life depended on it. I shake my head at the waiter, who takes one look at Sloane's empty chair and my hands beneath the table and turns and leaves again.

Sloane comes off me with a soft cough. Her throat is going to be sore tomorrow. Stubborn girl never knows when to stop.

I lift the tablecloth and look down at her, her hair wild and her lipstick smeared. She smiles that wicked smile of hers, knowing she's turned me to putty in her hands. Holding my eye, she leans forward and sucks one of my balls into her mouth. I suck in a breath through my teeth.

"Not gonna last," I tell her, and she looks up at me with dreamy eyes, pressing the hard length of me to her cheek.

"You gonna come down my throat?"

"Jesus, Sloane. Have mercy."

She giggles. "I'd prefer not to." And with that, she sucks

my cock back into her mouth. She gives me a few shallow strokes, using her hand on the rest of me, and then, eyes glued to mine, she takes me to the back of her throat, and I shoot off, almost passing out when she swallows around me one last time.

"Holy fuck," I say when my balls have stopped pulsing and she's sitting back on her heels, hands in her lap and a smile on her face like she's innocent.

I shove myself back into my pants and bend down to lift her off the floor, knocking the table as I get her up into my lap and sending champagne all over the table. I don't give a fuck. "Come here," I tell her, reaching for the diamond and pearl ring that's still sitting on the tabletop. Right there, both of us messy and disheveled, I slip the ring onto her finger.

It's perfect there, just like I knew it would be. I didn't have to measure her. I know the size of her hands, the way they fit through my fingers, the way they fit around my dick, the way they feel against my chest in the middle of the night.

"You're such a sap," she says.

"Only for you, princess."

She looks at the ring, and I swear, there's a sparkle in her eyes to match. "I love you, Julian."

I wrap my arms around her, take two handfuls of her ass through her dress. "I love you, too. Now get your ass in your seat so we can have dinner."

ABOUT THE AUTHOR

Sebby Randall is the alter ego of B. Randall, which is also an alter ego, but that's a story for another time. She lives in Dallas with her husband. In her free time, she likes to go biking, spends time working on jigsaw puzzles, and watches a lot of Formula 1.

ALSO BY SEBBY RANDALL

WRITING AS B. RANDALL

The Berserkr Gym Series

Come In With The Rain

Make It To Me

Take My Love

Find Me Here

Let Me Fall

Give Your Heart Away

One Last Auction

The Vegas Duet

A Man After Midnight

Late Night Talking

Braving the Waves

Love Is an Open Door

Love in Slow Motion

Anywhere But Here, Anyone But You

Serving Tegan

WRITING AS WINTER RANDALL

My Best Friend's Mate

The Vamp and I

Five Nights With The Fire Monster

www.ingramcontent.com/pod-product-compliance
Lightning Source LLC
Chambersburg PA
CBHW061038310726
48969CB00004B/1004